### *Autumn Bones*

"In Carey's capable hands, all this seems not just convincing, but enchantingly normal, thanks to the flawless backdrop, skillfully articulated plotting, and splendid characters. A fine addition to the series." — *Kirkus Reviews*

"Carey's gift of storytelling ensures that every scene is immersive and engaging as she slowly builds to a surprising climax that will have readers starving for the next installment in this wonderfully imaginative series." — *RT Book Reviews*

"[It's] supernatural chick lit, magical small-town slice-of-life drama . . . a lighthearted cozy mystery . . . offers promise for future volumes." — *Publishers Weekly*

"The series/characters have a vaguely Sookie Stackhouse type of vibe, including the small-town setting of Pemkowet, and if you like lighthearted urban fantasy peppered with great creatures, intriguing love interest(s), with an easy-to-read style, then I'd definitely recommend that you check out Jacqueline Carey's Agent of Hel series." — Paranormal Haven

"It's light, it's funny, yet has just enough of a touch of horror that you might feel the need to close the blinds against a darkening night." — Parnassus Reads

*continued . . .*

### *Dark Currents*

"Carey turns to contemporary fantasy, showing off her talent for building engaging, detailed settings that feel utterly natural despite their inherent strangeness. . . . Carey has set up a complex social ecosystem full of delightfully distinctive characters who warrant exploration in future volumes."
— *Publishers Weekly* (starred review)

"A terrific paranormal whodunit . . . action-packed."
— Genre Go Round Reviews

"Mythology, all forms of supernatural creatures, small-town life, mysticism, and magic all intertwine wonderfully in this rich, charming, and, yes, at times very dark urban fantasy. You'll fall in love with Daisy and her supporting cast, and you'll most definitely want to come back for more. Can't wait for the next one!" — My Bookish Ways

"I loved all the detail that went into *Dark Currents*. Jacqueline Carey paints such a vivid picture that it makes you feel as if a town like Pemkowet, with all its fantastic creatures, could actually exist. A mix of fantasy and urban fantasy, *Dark Currents* has a lot to offer, and I think if you're a fan of both genres, you should check it out."
— Paranormal Haven

"This is a very promising start for a new series. . . . The conflict between the otherworld and humanity feels real, and the resolution to the central mystery of the novel is utterly heartbreaking." — *RT Book Reviews*

**Roc Books by Jacqueline Carey**

*Dark Currents*
*Autumn Bones*

# Autumn Bones

## AGENT OF HEL

## JACQUELINE CAREY

**A ROC BOOK**

ROC
Published by the Penguin Group
Penguin Group (USA) LLC, 375 Hudson Street,
New York, New York 10014

USA | Canada | UK | Ireland | Australia | New Zealand | India | South Africa | China
penguin.com
A Penguin Random House Company

Published by Roc, an imprint of New American Library, a division of Penguin
Group (USA) LLC. Previously published in a Roc hardcover edition.

First Roc Mass Market Printing, October 2014

 REGISTERED TRADEMARK — MARCA REGISTRADA

ISBN 978-0-451-46521-4

Printed in the United States of America
10   9   8   7   6   5   4   3   2   1

# One

Labor Day weekend in Pemkowet started off with a bang. Or more accurately, a whole lot of banging.

I was sitting at a table down at Union Pier, listening to a band with my boyfriend, Sinclair—well, I'm not sure I can call him that yet. We've been dating for about three weeks and taking it slow.

Okay, maybe I'd better back this up.

My name is Daisy Johanssen, and I'm an agent of Hel. That's Hel, the Norse goddess of the dead, who relocated to Pemkowet during World War I and currently presides over a modest underworld located in a buried lumber town beneath the shifting sand dunes that make Pemkowet one of Michigan's premier resort destinations. Wild, untrammeled dunes, white sand beaches along the Lake Michigan shoreline, and a booming business in paranormal tourism.

Most of the time, things run fairly smoothly, but not always. That's where I come in. As Hel's liaison, it's my job to keep the peace between mundane authorities, such as the police, and the eldritch community. Things got ugly earlier this summer when a young man from a nearby college was found drowned in the river. Undines witnessed it, there were ghouls involved—long story short, it was a mess.

Anyway, the one good thing to come out of it was that Sinclair Palmer and I started dating.

So on Friday evening of the last big weekend of the summer, we were listening to music at Union Pier, a riverfront bar located in the shadow of the SS *Osikayas*, the old steamship permanently docked there.

Most people who know me can tell you I have a thing for music, though I have to admit that the Mamma Jammers wasn't a band I would have picked. As you might guess from the name, they were a jam band, which meant they played long, improvisational songs that went on for-freaking-*ever* while stoned-looking kids in retro T-shirts swayed and nodded.

But they were friends of Sinclair's from Kalamazoo and he'd gotten them this gig, so I was glad to be there. It was nice to feel Sinclair's thigh brush mine under the table, nice to feel like maybe I was a couple of dates away from using the b-word out loud, even if that wasn't entirely fair to him.

See, my life is . . . complicated.

It's not that there are other guys in it. Well, okay. There sort of are. Just not nice, normal human guys. Not that Sinclair's *entirely* normal. For one thing, he sees auras. For another . . . well, we're still in the getting-to-know-you phase, and I'm pretty sure there are some significant things I don't know, like why his parents split. Why his dad took Sinclair and emigrated from Kingston, Jamaica, to Kalamazoo, Michigan.

To be fair, my issues have kind of taken precedence. I guess that's natural. Normal or not, Sinclair's definitely human. Me, I'm only human on my mom's side. My father is Belphegor, lesser demon and occasional incubus. Mom didn't mean to invoke him—she was only a teenager at the time—but that's another story. My mom's one of the nicest people I know, and I inherited her white-blond Scandinavian hair, pert nose, and fair skin.

From my father, I inherited night-black eyes and a propensity to struggle with the Seven Deadly Sins, especially anger. Bad things happen when I lose my temper. Oh, and also my existence represents a chink in the Inviolate Wall that divides the mortal plane from the forces of the divine, and could potentially trigger Armageddon under the right circumstances, like if I claimed my demonic birthright. So far, I've managed to avoid the temptation. Fear of unleashing an apocalypse is a pretty good motivator.

So, yeah, my stuff's taken precedence, and we're taking it slowly. Not just emotionally, but physically, too. There's been a lot of kissing, a little above-the-waist action. Nothing lower. Which, yes, is frustrating. But I don't blame Sinclair for being careful about dating a hell-spawn, and there's one little detail I haven't shared with him yet.

At the end of the pier, the Mamma Jammers wrapped up another interminable jam. After applauding, Sinclair slung one arm around my shoulders and smiled at me. "So, what do you think? You gonna come back to the house tonight and hang out, spend some time with the guys?"

I smiled back at him. "Oh, I don't know. I don't want to get in the way of guy time."

"I wouldn't ask if I didn't mean it, darling." Sinclair delivered the line in the lilting Jamaican accent that charmed the tourists. He had his own business, Pemkowet Supernatural Tours, which had debuted this summer as an unqualified success. I'd played a large part in it by arranging for regular appearances by pretty, sparkly fairies. Sinclair gave my shoulders an affectionate squeeze. "Hey, dem's my bwais and you're my girl. Of course I want you to come over."

I'll admit it—that gave me a case of the warm fuzzies. Still, I leaned back so I could look him in the face. "Oh, yeah? What have you told them about me?"

He pursed his lips, which, by the way, were nice and full and highly kissable. Let me state for the record that Sinclair Palmer is a bona fide hottie. He falls into that elusive sweet spot between handsome and cute, with cocoa-brown skin, high, rounded cheekbones, an infectious smile, and Tour de France–worthy thighs. "Honestly? I thought I'd let them get to know you before I sprang it on them, Daisy," he said in a serious tone, dropping the accent. "Do you blame me?"

"Nooo . . ." I admitted. "Not really."

"So come over." He gave me another squeeze, his smile returning. "Ain't no big thing, girl! We'll put some steaks on the grill, drink a few beers." He paused. "Maybe you could spend the night?"

A jolt of desire ran through me, and beneath my short skirt, my tail twitched in an involuntary spasm.

Uh, yeah. That was the little something I hadn't mentioned to Sinclair yet. It has a tendency to freak guys out.

"You're sure about that?" I asked him.

Sinclair regarded me. "You think I'm ashamed of you?" He shook his head, his short dreadlocks rustling. "I'm not. We don't have to *do* anything, Daisy. Look, I'm not saying it's time to get it on. Not tonight, not with the Mamma Jammers crashing on my living room floor. That's not what this is about." His gaze was steady and unflinching. "I just want you to know I want you there. And I want them to know it, too."

My stomach did a somersault. "I, um . . . didn't pack a toothbrush."

He raised his eyebrows. "Pretty weak. Is that all you've got?"

"Well . . . yeah."

The Mamma Jammers launched into another song, which sounded pretty much exactly like every other song they'd played. This would be their last number, since Union Pier closed at sunset. On the far side of the river, the sun was sinking below the tree line, gilding the rippling water. After a day on the big lake, sailboats and other pleasure boats were easing upriver, making their way back to the marinas for the night. I watched a pair of tourists on Jet Skis play a complex game of tag, carving up the surface of the river, their vehicles tossing up rooster tails of water. Although I hated Jet Skis on principle, I had to admit it did look like fun.

"I'll make you pancakes in the morning," Sinclair murmured in my ear. "I make a mean pancake."

"Yeah?"

"Mm-hmm." He sounded amused. "And I'll even let you use my toothbrush, too."

It was at that exact freaking moment, when I was feeling good and happy and sexy and melty and excited and wanted and trepidatious and a bazillion other things, most of them nice, that my phone rang.

I fished it out of my bag. "Sorry, I've got to take this."

"Work?" Sinclair asked.

"Looks like it."

Technically, I'm a part-time file clerk at the Pemkowet Police Department, but as Hel's liaison, I assist with any issues that might involve members of the eldritch community. Cody Fairfax, aka Officer Down-low, and I had worked together earlier this summer investigating the Vanderhei kid's death. I thought we'd made a good team, but then, I was biased. I'd had a crush on Cody since I was in the fourth grade. Unfortunately for me, he wasn't interested in pursuing a relationship outside his species, and the fact that he had a tendency to turn furry and howl at the moon once a month was a fairly well-kept secret. Hence, the nickname.

"Hey." I rose and walked down the dock to get away from the Mamma Jammers' wall of sound, the phone pressed to my ear. "What's up? Is there a situation?"

"Hey, Daise. Yeah, maybe." Cody sounded uncertain, which wasn't like him. "Bart Mallick went to investigate a noise complaint at Rainbow's End twenty minutes ago. It should have been five minutes in and out, tops."

"So?" I didn't mean to be rude, but this seemed like straight-up cop stuff. It's not like Rainbow's End was some den of mischievous leprechauns. It was a gay nightclub. "Did he call for backup? Do you think something happened to him?"

"He's not responding to his radio."

I covered my free ear with my other hand. "Maybe he can't hear it."

"Yeah, maybe. Where are you, anyway? And why are you shouting?"

Oops. Hadn't realized I was shouting. "Union Pier." Lowering my voice, I walked a few more yards away from the din. "Where are you?"

"I'm in the parking lot at Rainbow's End," Cody said. "I

was passing, so I swung by to see if there was a problem. Bart's cruiser's here. Lights are on. But something's funky."

"Funky?" Okay, I was confused. "Like hinky? You think something's going on? Drugs?"

"I mean *funky*." Cody's voice dropped to a lower register. Not a deliberately sexy register, but a growly, furry, hackle-raising register. Which, in fact, was pretty damn sexy, just not on purpose. "Even from the parking lot, this place reeks of pheromones."

"Doesn't it always?" I asked.

"Not like this." Now he sounded more certain. "Look, call it a hunch. I didn't have to call you, but I think maybe there's something going on that should concern Hel's liaison. Whatever it is, I thought you might want to catch it in the act. So are you in or out?"

I sighed. "I'm in, I'm in! Give me ten minutes."

"I'll give you six." He hung up.

I walked back to the table where Sinclair was sitting, bobbing his head to the endless jam, looking cute and mellow and ... emotionally available. He glanced up at me with genuine concern. "Hey, girl. Everything okay?"

"Hope so," I said. "But I've got to go check something out. I don't think it will take long. Is your offer still good?"

"Definitely." He smiled his infectious smile. "You go take care of business and come on by."

"Okay." I found myself smiling in response. See? That's what an infectious smile does. There really ought to be a better, less disease-suggestive name for it. I leaned down to kiss him. "Later?"

Sinclair kissed me back. "*Most* definitely."

# Two

Approximately six minutes later, I pulled into the parking lot of Rainbow's End alongside Cody's patrol car.

From the outside, everything looked normal. The lot was already packed, which was a little unusual before sunset, but it was a holiday weekend. Bart Mallick's patrol car was sitting empty and abandoned before the entrance, bubble-gum lights flashing. The place was definitely jumping. I could hear the thumping bass of techno music so loud it seemed like the entire building was vibrating. Again, not unusual. Rainbow's End averaged five or six noise complaints over the course of any given summer.

Cody got out of the cruiser looking twitchy. Okay, that *was* unusual. "Hey, Pixy Stix." His nostrils flared. "Ready to go?"

Oh, gah. One time—*one time*—someone called me that, and Cody decided it was a permanent nickname. Serves me right for calling him Officer Down-low, I guess. "Hang on." I reached into the front seat to retrieve my belt and sheath. "Might as well go in prepared."

So, um . . . yeah. About that. I have a magic dagger. Hel

gave it to me herself with her left hand, the hand of death. When I'm not on her official business, I carry it in my leather messenger bag with the special inside sheath. Cody, who does leatherworking in his spare time, made it for me. He made the belt, too.

"So are you still dating the fake Jamaican?" Cody asked as I settled the belt around my waist and buckled it.

"He's not a fake Jamaican," I said, annoyed. "He was born there. He has dual citizenship, okay?"

"Defensive." He grinned, a hint of phosphorescent green glinting behind his topaz eyes. "You must like him."

"Jealous?" I retorted.

Cody shrugged. "His shtick just seems a little phony. I hear he gives his tours some big spiel about how his grandfather was a famous obeah man. That's what gives him his 'special connection' to the eldritch community."

I eyed him sidelong. "Did you just use air quotes?"

"Maybe."

I eased *dauda-dagr* out of my bag. It shimmered beneath the patrol car's lights and the bar's neon signs, runes etched along the blade flaring silver-blue. Its name means "death day," and it's capable of killing even the immortal undead. "So he tells people what they want to hear. Big deal. It's a business, Cody. Everyone does it." I shoved *dauda-dagr* into the sheath. "Ready when you are."

He nodded, his nostrils flaring again. "You really can't smell that?"

I sniffed the air. "No. What, pheromones? What does it smell like?"

"Sex."

Cody wasn't kidding.

I might not have wolf-keen olfactory senses, but the reek hit me like a ton of bricks the instant we walked through the door of Rainbow's End: a deep, rich, redolent funk of sex. And not shampooed, deodorized, minty-fresh-mouthwash-and-clean-sheets sex, but down-and-dirty, no-holds-barred nastiness.

It took a few seconds for my eyes to adjust to the dim

lighting inside the bar. As soon as they did, I saw the reason for the odor.

There was an orgy under way.

I couldn't make out *exactly* what was going on because it registered as a sea of sweat-glistening, writhing flesh, entangled limbs, and heaving parts. I'm not talking about a little hanky-panky on the dance floor. I'm talking about a full-blown orgy. The majority of Rainbow's End's clientele were gay men, but there were knots of women here and there, and what appeared to be a few indiscriminate free agents of either gender eager to avail themselves of whatever was closest at hand. Beneath the pounding bass beat making the speakers tremble, there was a symphony of moans and groans of pleasure, resonant and weirdly melodic, like some kind of universal mantra to sexuality.

"Holy *crap*!" I'm pretty sure the words came out of my mouth, although I could barely hear them beneath the techno music and the om-mani-fuckme-hum.

Cody tapped my shoulder and nodded toward the dance floor, which seemed to be the orgy's epicenter. His teeth were clenched so hard I could see the muscles along his jaw twitch. That should have warned me.

We got halfway there before the second wave hit us. Not the funk, but the *effect* of the pheromones.

Cody and I exchanged a glance. There was a hectic sheen in his eyes. I'm pretty sure there was in mine, too. He grabbed my shoulders and spun me around, shoving me against the edge of the bar.

My last conscious thought was, "Damn, I wish this had happened a month ago." And then there was no thinking, just a deep, primordial desire to copulate, to be a part of the whole wet, slippery, thrusting celebration. Cody's mouth covered mine, his urgent tongue pushing past my lips. His hands dropped to my hips, jerking me against him.

My tail shivered with pleasure. I wrapped my legs around his waist and slid my hands up his arms, lacing them behind his neck and pulling his head down. There was definitely too much fabric in the way, not to mention his utility belt.

Not good. I wanted bare skin. I wanted *more*. My finger-tips trailed over the bronze stubble of his cheeks, finding the collar of his dark blue uniform shirt. I yanked it open with strength that would have surprised me if I'd been ca-pable of rational thought, buttons flying. Cody reached be-tween us to unbuckle his utility belt, letting it fall before pulling me against him again.

Yeah, better; much better. I could feel his erection strain-ing beneath his trousers, pressed hard against my core. My hips thrust involuntarily as I ground against him. Cody was kissing me again, and I found myself moaning into his mouth. Om-mani-fuckme-*hum*, baby. He pushed up my tank top, hands gliding over my skin, fondling my breasts with an eager roughness that made me arch my back....

Against my waist, I felt a rill of pure cold so intense it jolted me into awareness. Cody made a strangled sound deep in my mouth, jerking away from me.

"Shit!" he said fervently. There was a scorched-looking patch of skin on his bare torso, faint wisps of frost rising from it.

*Dauda-dagr.* I dropped my hand to its hilt, the hilt of the dagger no one but one of Hel's agents could touch with impunity. Its coolness was bracing, further clearing my thoughts.

Cody, on the other hand, was beginning to look glassy-eyed again. He shook his head and started back toward me.

"Whoa! Down, boy." I drew *dauda-dagr* and held it be-tween us, surreptitiously tugging my tank top down over my exposed breasts. "Cody!" I shouted over the music. "Take my hand. Just be careful not to touch the dagger."

With a shudder, he reached for the dagger's hilt, wrap-ping his fingers around mine. The glaze lifted again. "Daise? What the hell's going on?"

"I wish I knew." My wits more or less functioning, I glanced around the bar.

Whatever was going on, it definitely centered around the dance floor, and around one guy in particular. Tall, well built, strongly etched features, a pointed tangle of beard, a grin plastered to his face, and . . . well endowed.

Like, really, really well endowed. His glistening, um, endowment jutted forth from his crotch, bobbing above the dance floor before an enthusiastic orgiast dropped to his knees before it, obscuring my view. There appeared to be a waiting line for the privilege. Staring at the grinning recipient, I felt the telltale tingle that identified him as a member of the eldritch community.

Cody leaned forward, his lips brushing my ear. "He's one of ours."

It was enough to set me abuzz with lust all over again. Clutching *dauda-dagr*'s hilt, I suppressed it. "Yeah, I know. But I don't know *what* he is or why this is happening. Do you?"

"No," he admitted. "Not a clue."

The kneeling orgiast backed away, a long strand of . . . Okay, never mind. Part of my brain said, "Eww!" Another part . . . didn't.

"Daisy." Cody's fingers tightened over mine. "We've got to put a stop to this. Any ideas?"

"One," I said. "But you won't like it. Any sign of Bart Mallick?"

"No." He looked around the bar. "Oh . . . shit. Yeah."

I followed his gaze. "Oops."

Longtime patrol officer and family man, married father of three teenaged kids, Bart Mallick was . . . You know what? It's not important. Suffice it to say that I doubt his wife would have approved.

Taking a deep breath, Cody let go long enough to retrieve his utility belt and buckle it feverishly around his waist before grasping my hand again. "Can you get him out of here?"

"I think so."

We edged our way through the orgy toward the dark corner where Bart Mallick was . . . doing what he was doing. With, let me add, a very willing partner.

"Bart. Officer Mallick?" I touched the tip of *dauda-dagr*'s blade to the nape of his neck. His spine straightened with an involuntary jolt. He turned his head, glazed eyes clearing slightly. "It's Daisy Johanssen and Cody Fairfax.

Can you hear me? I need you to pull up your pants, take my hand, and come with us, okay?"

He nodded.

With their hands atop mine and mine wrapped around the dagger's hilt, I managed to haul Cody and Bart stumbling over myriad writhing bodies into the parking lot, away from the immediacy of the driving, incessant beat and the pervasive, compelling funk.

Officer Mallick slumped against his patrol car looking dazed. "Oh, Jesus, *fuck* me. Fuck me sideways!"

"Bart!" Cody took him by the shoulders and gave him a shake. "Whatever happened in there? Not your fault. Right, Daisy?"

"Right," I agreed. Total lie. There are rules governing the eldritch world, and one of them is that desire, genuine desire, can't be compelled. Pleasure and infatuation, yes. But genuine desire? No. It's like true love. "Everyone okay? I have to make a call."

Cody eyed me suspiciously. "You're not calling—"

My finger hovered above my phone's screen. "Look, I told you that you wouldn't like it." I jerked my chin toward the door. "It would take all night to use *dauda-dagr* to escort everyone in there out here by ones and twos, and we still wouldn't have any way to contain patient zero in there, or the first notion of why this is happening. Do you have a better idea, Officer Down-low?"

He shook his head, and I hit the CALL button.

Although I hadn't talked to Stefan Ludovic in more than a month, he picked up immediately. "Daisy. What is it? Are you . . . all right?"

A wave of self-consciousness washed over me. Of course, Stefan would suspect. He was a ghoul, or as they call themselves, one of the Outcast, condemned for eternity to exist on the emotions of others. And because I'd given him permission to taste mine, he was attuned to them. He couldn't have missed that giant preternatural spike of pure lust.

"Um . . . yeah, I'm fine, but we've got a situation. Do you

have enough people you trust to defuse an orgy without losing control?"

Stefan didn't hesitate. "I'll be right there. You're a mile or so to the north?"

"Rainbow's End," I confirmed. "Parking lot."

"I'm on my way."

Not that long ago, ghouls and biker gangs were two things I'd go out of my way to avoid. That was before Stefan Ludovic came to town. He's done a lot to improve the image of the Outcasts, which, by the way, is the name of the biker gang—or motorcycle club, to use the polite terminology—to which most of the local ghouls belong, and related to but not entirely synonymous with being one of *the* Outcast. Okay, it's confusing.

Anyway, after taking over Pemkowet as his turf, one of the first things Stefan did was issue a ban on selling drugs, particularly crystal meth. Since that had been a big component in establishing a cycle of human dependency and misery that sustained a lot of ghouls, what he did was actually pretty huge. Of course, it touched off a rebellion that led to a great deal of unpleasantness, but again, long story short, Stefan came through.

So why had I been avoiding him since? One, he held out an offer so tempting it scared me, a promise that he could show me ways to experience the full intensity of my supersize emotions without risk.

Two, I'd seen him die. And not just die—die and *come back*. That's what happened with the Outcast. They're condemned to the mortal plane because neither heaven nor hell would have them.

It's complicated, and I don't pretend to understand it. Even Hel—that's Hel the goddess—admits it isn't her purview. Different cosmologies and all. But the fact is, I watched a gunshot, crippled Stefan Ludovic impale himself on his own sword so he could die and come back whole and intact, and I'm still a little freaked out by it.

Nonetheless, when Stefan and five other bikers roared into the parking lot, I was glad to see them.

"Daisy Johanssen." Stefan greeted me formally, removing his helmet. His ice-blue eyes caught the neon light. Did I mention that he was ridiculously good-looking? Consider it mentioned. He glanced toward the door of the nightclub, his pupils waxing large before shrinking to controlled pinpoints. "I think this no ordinary bacchanal. What passes within the nightclub?"

"I'm not sure," I admitted. "But it seems to center on a naked eldritch dude with a huge schlong."

Stefan frowned. "Could you identify him?" I shook my head. The eldritch always recognize one another, but we can't necessarily put a name with that recognition. "I'll have to see him for myself."

"No ravening, right?" Cody interrupted him. "We don't want to make the situation worse."

Stefan's gaze shifted to him. Without a word, he took in Cody's disheveled hair and ripped-open uniform shirt. "No. No ravening, Officer."

*Ravening* was what happened when a ghoul lost control. As far as I could tell, that never happened to Stefan.

"You vouch for your men?" Cody pressed.

Stefan hesitated. "Under ordinary circumstances, yes. But if you succumbed to the creature's spell, we are also vulnerable." His pupils waxed. "We do have ordinary mortal desires, too. How were you able to break free?"

"*Dauda-dagr*'s touch," I said, showing him the blade. "But don't ask me why."

"Ah." He nodded. "Death's touch offsets the drive toward life. Perhaps you and I should investigate alone, Daisy. If we can contain the source, my men can assist with the others."

His men stood silent behind him in the parking lot, pupils glittering. I recognized one of them, his loyal lieutenant Rafe. The others were either vaguely familiar or new to me, including a blond-haired boy who didn't look older than seventeen. But among the eldritch, looks could be deceiving. For all I knew, he was centuries older than me.

"Hel's liaison?" Stefan inquired courteously in his faint, unplaceable accent, inclining his head in my direction.

I took a deep breath, suddenly acutely aware that beneath the thin cotton of my tank top my nipples were still jutting and hard, and I could feel the thumping techno beat pulsing between my thighs. Nonetheless, I had a job to do.

"Okay," I said. "Let's do this."

# Three

Inside the bar, Stefan's hand squeezed mine atop the dagger's hilt as the funk hit us. Glancing at him, I saw his pupils zoom large, practically eclipsing his irises before dwindling to normal size.

No doubt. *Dauda-dagr*'s touch might mitigate the effect of the pheromones, but the waves of lust rolling off a hundred people making major sexy-time had to be pretty damn potent.

"You okay?" I asked him.

He nodded, his lips set in a hard line. "Where is he?"

I pointed with my free hand. "Dance floor."

We picked our way across the crowded, teeming bar, doing our best not to step on anyone. The vortex of activity still swirled around the dance floor, and yep, there was the naked, grinning man, hands on his pumping hips as he received tribute from another eager admirer. At the risk of being totally rude, a part of me really hoped we were just talking blow jobs here, because if we weren't, there could be some serious damage done.

"It's a satyr," Stefan murmured in my ear, his slightly too

long black hair brushing my cheek. I shivered involuntarily at the sensation. Okay, I know the music was loud, but hot men whispering in my ear was not helping fight the funk. "I thought it might be, but I haven't seen one in centuries."

"Great," I said. "What's he doing here?"

"I don't know," Stefan said. "But he's in rut."

As a Michigan girl, I knew what that meant. Did you know male deer in rut can be dangerous to human women? Well, they can.

"Okay," I said. "How do we get him *out* of rut?"

"I'm not sure." He sounded apologetic. "But I fear it's like ravening for us. There's nothing to do but let it run its course."

"Yeah, that's not an option." I gestured at the orgiastic sea. "This is *not* safe sex, Stefan. Can we use *dauda-dagr* to de-rut him?"

"No. But it may neutralize the effect long enough for us to establish control of this particular situation." Stefan shifted. I wondered if *his* control was wearing thin. "If I may make a suggestion, I recommend that you call your patroness for advice before we make any attempt on the satyr."

"Hel?" I asked. "She, uh, doesn't exactly communicate using modern technology."

He shook his head. "The lamia."

Oh, right. *Patroness* was the sort of old-world terminology Stefan favored. As far as I was concerned, Lurine Hollister was my friend. Well, and my former babysitter. But she'd made it clear to Stefan that she considered me under her protection, which was okay by me. And it made sense. With an origin reaching back to ancient Greece, Lurine probably had experience with satyrs.

There was no point in trying to make a call in the nightclub. Stefan and I beat a hasty retreat back to the parking lot.

"Well?" Cody gave me an inquiring look.

"He's a satyr," I informed him. "And he's in rut."

"How do we get him *out* of rut?"

"Good question." I sheathed my dagger and took out my phone. "Hopefully, I'm consulting an expert."

Just when I was starting to fear my call was going to voice mail, Lurine picked up. "Hey, cupcake. How are you?"

"I'm okay," I said. "Lurine, we've got a problem. We've got a satyr in rut here."

"Really?" Her voice took on a note of surprised delight. "How fun!"

"No, *not* fun! This isn't some woodland romp with horny nymphs, Lurine. He's set off an orgy over at Rainbow's End. A human orgy! We're talking public health hazard, massive PR nightmare, possible lawsuits!"

"Okay, okay," Lurine said mildly. "Keep your shirt on, baby girl. What do you want me to do? Take him off your hands?"

I tugged self-consciously at my tank top, which I had in fact not kept entirely on so far tonight. "What I want is to find a way to contain . . . wait, you can do that?"

"Do what?"

"Take him off our hands?"

"Sure." She sounded amused. "Why not? It's been ages. If that's what you want, give me a few minutes to freshen up and change my clothes, and I'll be right over."

"Um . . . yeah." Glancing toward the nightclub, I did the math in my head. Lurine's lakeshore mansion was only six or seven minutes away, but the freshening up could easily triple that amount of time. "Can't you come as you are?"

"Daisy." Now she sounded reproving. "I have an image to maintain."

This was true. Over the millennia, Lurine has maintained a long series of identities. Currently, the world knows her as a small-town-girl-makes-good B-movie starlet who married a very, very wealthy octogenarian and retired to her hometown after his prompt expiration.

I sighed. "Well, if you can hurry, I'd really, really appreciate it. Is there any way we can turn down the volume on his rutting effect before you get here? I thought I might try using *dauda-dagr*. It works on humans."

"Mmm." Definitely dubious. "No, I wouldn't recommend it unless you actually mean to kill him. You don't, do you?"

"No! I just want to make him stop."

"Well, then you should definitely avoid making contact or his urge could overpower yours, even with Hel's dagger. But it may still be useful as long as you don't touch the satyr. Try circumscribing him with salt and iron. That might hold him for a while. I'll be there as soon as I can." On the other end of the phone, Lurine blew a kiss before hanging up.

"Wait—" I made a face as the line went dead. "Okay, she's on her way. Anyone know how to circumscribe someone with salt and iron?"

"Yes, of course," Stefan said. "Do I understand that she's offered to take the satyr into her own custody?"

"Yeah, but not until she's freshened up, which could be a while. So what's the deal on this circumscribing?" In my own defense, let me say that it's not like being Hel's liaison came with a handbook. "And crap! Where am I going to get salt?"

"There should be salt somewhere in the bar supplies," Cody offered. "For rimming margarita glasses. Daise, are you saying Lurine's going to take that, um . . . guy in there home with her?"

"Uh-huh," I said. "I'm pretty sure that's what she meant."

He shuddered. "Brave woman."

Well, sort of. If I understood correctly that Lurine meant to take the satyr home and screw him senseless until the rut passed, I was pretty sure she meant to do it in her true form, which was more than a match for any supernatural penis.

"Wait," Bart Mallick said faintly, still slumped against his squad car. Oops. I'd forgotten about him. "Lurine *Hollister*?"

"Eldritch code of honor," I said to him. Lurine's nature was known to people she trusted, but it was far from common knowledge. The tabloids would have a field day if it got out. "You keep our secrets, we keep yours. Okay?"

He flushed and nodded.

"Stefan?" I said. "The circumscribing?"

"It is as it sounds, Daisy," Stefan said. "Pour a line of salt around the subject, and draw a second circle around him with the point of your dagger." He looked genuinely concerned. "Are you sure it's worth the risk if your patroness is on her way?"

"I'm sure." That was a lie, too. But this was my responsibility, and I couldn't bear the thought of standing around the parking lot doing nothing, waiting for someone else to save the day. With every minute that passed, the possibility of things taking an ugly turn in that nightclub increased.

Stefan inclined his head. "I will accompany you."

Cody's nostrils flared. "*I'll* go."

The patient, watching ghouls glanced from one to the other with interest. In certain circles in the eldritch community, there's nothing they like better than a standoff between a pair of alphas. Okay, make that most circles.

I drew *dauda-dagr*. "Thanks, guys, but this is going to be tricky. Either one of you would just get in the way. I have a better chance going it alone. Stefan, if it works, I'll call you with a go-ahead to bring in the troops. Okay?"

Reluctantly, they agreed, which I guess makes me the real alpha in this particular scenario.

Yippee.

Taking a deep breath, I headed back toward the nightclub. Third time's a charm, right?

"Daisy?" Stefan called. "If you can turn off the music, it may help." He gave me a faint, worried smile. "It turns out your parents were right about rock and roll."

Okay, so he was off by a couple of generations, and I wouldn't exactly classify a techno dance club mix as rock and roll, but I appreciated the advice. Giving him a quick thumbs-up with my free hand, I yanked open the door and plunged into the club.

In the five minutes I'd been outside, the funk had ripened further and the om-mani-fuckme-hum had reached a deeper register that vibrated in the very marrow of my bones. Even with *dauda-dagr* clutched tightly in my hand, I could feel the atmosphere's effect. Honestly, I'd never *stopped* feeling it, but I had a lot of experience with containing my emotions. When I was a little kid, my mom read a book about creative visualization and used the concept to make up techniques to help me deal with my frequent temper tantrums.

I tried to use one now to cope with the effect of the pheromones, imagining it as a brimming cup of desire, tipping it and spilling it away.

Yeah, that didn't work. The contents of that cup refused to spill.

I tried a different one, one my mom had invented especially for emotions too strong and stubborn to be dismissed. I put my funk-driven lust in a box and tied a bow around it, a pretty package to open later.

It worked.

Feeling clear and sharp, I headed for the bar, dodging writhing bodies and ducking under the pass-through at the service station.

"Whoops!" I tripped over someone. Well, a pair of female someones. One of them wore what looked to be a bartender's apron around her waist, and nothing else. "Excuse me," I said, tapping her on the shoulder. "Do you know where I can find the salt?"

She lifted her head from what she was doing, giving me a glazed look and reaching for me with one languid hand.

"Yeah, thanks, not right now." I plucked her hand from my leg and transferred it atop the hand I had wrapped around *dauda-dagr*'s hilt. "Are you a bartender? Is there salt back here?"

Her eyes cleared. "What the fuck?" She looked down at the figure beneath her. "Who is this? Do I even *know* her?"

"I have no idea," I said apologetically. "Do you have any salt?"

*"Salt?"*

"Yes!" I was getting impatient. "Look, I'm sorry, but I don't have time to explain! Do you have any salt?"

Looking bewildered, she pointed to a shelf. It took me a few seconds to identify the plastic tub of bright green lime-flavored margarita salt as the item I wanted. "Perfect." Grabbing it, I scooted away from the entangled pair. "Thanks."

There was no answer. Well, not a verbal one. The funk was back in effect.

On the far side of the dance floor, the DJ booth was empty. I managed to work my way around the edges of the floor and climb into the booth, where an imposing array of lights and switches confronted me. I'm pretty sure aircraft control panels are less complicated. Since I didn't have a clue, I hit anything and everything that looked like it might be a power switch until the bass-heavy dance mix went mercifully silent. Now it just sounded like the sound track to the world's most ambitious gay porn movie.

I went back into the fray. Getting to the satyr was going to be the hard part. There was a constant slow-motion swirl of activity around him, a dense concentration of men swapping places, partners, and positions as they waited their turn to kneel at the altar, as it were. Men of all shapes, sizes, and ages, ranging from burly bears with furry chests to waxed-chested gym rats with six-pack abs to drag queens with heavily smeared makeup. I pushed my way into the throng, squeezing past the vertical bodies and clambering over the horizontal ones until I was close to the epicenter.

"Bitch, please!" One of the buff gym rats disengaged to give me a look of glazed indignation. "No cutting in line."

Holding *dauda-dagr* in a reverse grip, I pressed the back of my hand against his forehead. "Police business. I need you to step back and clear this space, sir."

"Huh?" He blinked at me, the glaze only semi-clearing. Either the effect of the funk was stronger this close to the satyr or gym boy was under the influence of something else. Or both.

I touched *dauda-dagr*'s tip to his bare chest. "Step back."

With a pained hiss, he did. If that's what it took, fine. I stole a quick look at the satyr, who appeared oblivious to my intervention, happily grinning and thrusting away. Prying the lid off the plastic tub of lime-flavored salt, I made a circle around him and his current tribute-giver, tilting the tub to pour out a stream of salt with one hand and using *dauda-dagr* to clear space with the other.

Luckily, once the salt was poured it seemed to keep the

orgiasts at bay, and it clung firmly to the dance floor, which was slick with viscous fluid. Yeah, that's pretty much a straight-up "Ew!" I left a gap in front of the satyr and his partner and retraced my steps, using the point of the dagger to draw a line through the salt.

Sometimes it's better to act than think, and doing what it would take to close the circle was definitely one of those times. Holding *dauda-dagr* and the salt tub awkwardly in one hand, I wrapped my free arm around the waist of the guy kneeling before the satyr and executed a sort of half-assed hip throw on him.

It wasn't pretty, but it worked. I didn't spend four years in Mr. Rodriguez's Li'l Dragonz Tae Kwon Do classes for nothing.

The satyr looked down at me, his grin faltering briefly. It returned as he took a step in my direction, his erection glistening obscenely as it bobbed above me. As strange as it may sound, it was also weirdly hypnotic.

Tearing my gaze away, I used the last of the salt to close the circle, dragging the point of the dagger through the ridge of lurid green crystals to seal it.

Done.

The effect of the funk didn't vanish, but it began to dissipate. I could feel the level of sexual tension start to ratchet down. I scrambled to my feet and faced the satyr. Looking perplexed, he reached out one bare foot to test the salt line with his toe, then withdrew it to consider his next move.

I had a suspicion the circle wasn't going to hold him for long. I held up my left hand palm outward to show him the rune written there: Ansuz, the rune of the messenger, indicating that I was Hel's liaison between the worlds. Mortals couldn't see it, but the satyr could.

If it meant anything to him, I couldn't tell. So I showed him the dagger instead. He tilted his head from side to side, the sinews of his neck tightening visibly.

"Look," I said to him, "I don't want to hurt you. I just need you to stay put for a few minutes. Okay?"

The satyr reached out one toe.

"No!" I shifted into a defensive posture. "I need you to *stay*! Do you speak English? Do you understand?"

The satyr met my gaze. His eyes were dark and deep and wild. Moving with slow deliberation, he reached for his supersize erection, wrapped his fist around it, and began to pump.

Believe it or not, I'm pretty sure that meant "Yes."

# Four

As soon as the satyr consented to his containment, I called Stefan.

The head ghoul and his posse entered the nightclub with silent efficiency, spreading out to circle the perimeter just as the orgiasts were emerging from their collective stupor.

From a ghoulish perspective, it must have been a freaking smorgasbord of emotions: lust, chagrin, confusion, shock, outrage . . . I couldn't even begin to imagine. Okay, that's another lie. Actually, I could. It was just better if I didn't.

The ghouls' glittering eyes were half-closed in the dim light as they siphoned off a measure of every emotion, rendering the balance bearable.

As for the satyr, his eyes were half-lidded, too, and there was a faint smile on his lips as he stood in the ring of lime-green salt and continued to stroke himself with lazy pleasure. I'd always thought satyrs were sort of half goat, half man, but this guy was more or less human in form, the less being the tufted ears that poked out of his hair and the long, luxuriant horsehair tail that jutted out above his buttocks.

Beneath my skirt, my far more modest tail gave a sympathetic twitch. You had to give the guy credit for just putting it out there. Like, literally out there. In a way, I envied him. His urge to rut was tied to the natural world. Oh sure, giving in to it might touch off an inadvertent orgy, but at least it didn't threaten to blow a hole in the Inviolate Wall.

I guess there might be something ironic in the idea of a prime mover in the drive toward life ending up in a gay nightclub, but I suspect that the satyr was simply drawn toward the biggest locus of desire in town. I'd felt the effect of the funk, and although fertility and procreation might be by-products, that wasn't what it was about. Even in containment, the satyr radiated a joyful vitality, a vibrant celebration of sex for the sake of sex, for the sheer, unmitigated, nasty, down-and-dirty pleasure of it.

Which I had been very close to experiencing with Cody Fairfax.

Now that I was no longer in crisis mode, that particular fact struck home forcefully, along with a very vivid physical memory of the encounter. Damn. I could feel the bow I'd tied around my mental box of lust loosening.

"Daisy." Stefan appeared before me, his expression neutral. "If you wish, I can assist you."

"No." Wrapping my arms around myself, I shook my head. "I mean, thanks, I appreciate it. But I don't want you rummaging around in my mind right now."

Stefan inclined his head. "As you will." He hesitated. "Do you expect the lamia to arrive soon? I fear that neither the control of my men nor the patience of the satyr is limitless."

"She should be here any minute. And maybe you shouldn't hire teenaged boys," I added pointedly, glancing at the blond kid I'd spotted earlier. "Or induct them into your posse or whatever you call it."

"Ah." He followed my gaze. "You took notice of my new lieutenant. Cooper is more than two hundred years old," he continued conversationally. "He was hanged in the Irish Rebellion of 1798."

I swallowed hard. "Oh."

"Yes. On the scaffold, he dared God to send him to hell so that he might continue fighting."

"I take it God declined?" I said.

"No." Stefan arched one eyebrow. "The Lord accepted his offer. Hell declined to honor it. Since then, Cooper has been Outcast."

Okay, see what I mean about ghouls? It's just hard to get your head around the circumstances of their existence. And no, for the record, I had no idea why Stefan was numbered among the Outcast. Whatever he'd done to get himself cast out by heaven and hell alike, I hadn't the faintest idea.

Thankfully, I was spared the need for further speculation, not to mention the threat of ravening ghouls and a released satyr, by Lurine's arrival.

I'd assumed that for the sake of discretion, she would wait outside in her Town Car while we brought the satyr to her—although exactly how that was to be accomplished, I hadn't thought through.

Anyway, I was wrong. Lurine sauntered into the nightclub, pausing to survey the aftermath of the orgy and its shell-shocked participants. She'd pulled out all the stops, wearing a shiny black latex dress that clung to her curves, stretching and undulating with every movement. Tacky, yes, but so magnificently tacky that it wasn't. And it was offset by a classic chignon, oversize sunglasses, and crimson lipstick.

There was a collective indrawn breath as Lurine sashayed across the floor, followed by a murmur of speculation. As you might guess, Lurine Hollister was a huge icon in the gay community.

"Hey, cupcake," she greeted me absently, adjusting her sunglasses to peer over them at the satyr. "Ooh, he's quite the specimen, isn't he?"

I gestured feebly around the nightclub, indicating the audience. "Are you sure you want to do this? I mean, here?"

Lurine gave me an affectionate look. "Oh, don't worry, they'll think half of what they saw and did tonight was a hallucination. Including me." Her eyes widened slightly as she considered me. "You're all riled up, aren't you, baby girl?" She smiled. "Want to come home and watch?"

"No!"

She laughed.

Okay, see, here's the thing. I would trust Lurine with my life, but she *is* a predator, and seduction is her method. Well, one of her methods. For her, flirting is just a way of keeping her hunting instincts honed. Which I wouldn't mind, except I actually do find Lurine in her true form incredibly hot, which she knows. I like to think of my tastes as pretty conventional, but thanks to my infernal heritage, there's a perverse streak in there that crops up in unexpected ways.

"My lady Hollister," Stefan interjected, his voice tense, "it would be best for all involved if you do not dally here."

They exchanged glances. Fraught, fraught glances. Stefan's pupils zoomed and glittered. Lurine pursed her crimson lips. "Hmm, you're close to losing control, aren't you? That could be interesting."

He looked involuntarily in my direction; and yep, definitely close. His irises were an icy rim around his pupils and there was a faint sheen of sweat on his ghoul-pale brow. When I'd let Stefan drain my anger in an emergency situation, he'd been in perfect control and I'd felt a deep well of stillness within him. This was the flip side of the coin, a profound, avid, and complex hunger.

And it was directed at me and my beribboned-and-bowed box of desire.

"Or maybe not." All the teasing went out of Lurine's voice, giving way to protective pragmatism. "Let's get down to business. *You're* coming home with me," she said to the satyr. "Got it?"

A wide grin spread across the satyr's face. Placing his hands on his hips, he nodded enthusiastically, giving his pelvis a little thrust for emphasis. Kind of like he was offering up the world's most startling door prize. And now that I thought about it, he did look like some of the figures I'd seen cavorting on Greek pottery in my favorite teacher Mr. Leary's Myth & Lit class back in high school.

Another, more alarming thought struck me. "Ah . . . Lurine?" My fingers tightened on *dauda-dagr*'s hilt as I glanced around the club where the stunned orgiasts were just beginning to retrieve their scattered clothing. "What happens when the circle's broken? Is it going to start all over again?"

"No, honey," she said complacently. "Not as long as I keep a firm grip on him. Are you ready?"

The satyr nodded even more vigorously, his shaggy pointed beard bobbing.

With the expertise of an Indy 500 racecar driver maneuvering a gearshift, Lurine reached out to grasp his ginormous shaft with one hand, tugging him out of the salt circle. "All right, then. Let's get you home, Mr. Happy."

I held my breath, but Lurine was telling the truth. Nothing happened as she led the satyr out of the nightclub. He trotted happily behind her, his horse-tail switching with anticipation.

I followed them to the door. "Are you sure you're going to be okay?"

"Of course." Lurine shot me an amused look before settling her sunglasses into place with her free hand. "I can absorb a *lot* of vitality, cupcake. Just get those goddamn ghouls out of here before they start ravening. And stay out of trouble for a few days, will you?" She glanced down at her throbbing door prize. "I'm going to be busy."

"Deal," I said gratefully. "Thanks, Lurine."

She blew me a kiss. "Go home and take a cold shower."

I watched Lurine lead the satyr into the parking lot, where her unflappable driver stood waiting to open the door to the Town Car. They disappeared into its depths. I couldn't help but think about it, at least a little bit. Lurine would wait to get him home before she shifted, probably into the swimming pool, wrapping him in those shimmering, rainbow-hued serpent coils. . . .

"Daisy." Stefan's taut voice made me jump. "The situation appears to be under control. Your intervention was timely, and I do not sense that anyone here sustained great harm tonight. But I think it best we leave now."

Oh, right. I took one look at him and made a shooing gesture. "Go, go! And, Stefan . . . um, thanks. I appreciate it."

With an obvious effort, he gave me one of his courtly nods. "You did well, Hel's liaison. I thank you for your trust."

Stefan beckoned, and one by one, his ghouls trooped past me and out the door, clad in denim and leather. His two-hundred-year-old teenaged lieutenant, the one he'd called Cooper, was the last to pass. He gave me a broad wink with one glittering eye, tipping an imaginary hat in my direction with an engaging, crooked grin. He had a narrow face with a spray of freckles over the bridge of his nose.

Hell, I hadn't even known there was an Irish Rebellion of 1798.

For the next forty-five minutes or so, Cody and I dealt with the aftermath, Cody having sent a shell-shocked Bart Mallick back out on patrol, which may or may not have been a good idea.

An EMS vehicle sat in the parking lot. A few of the participants got themselves checked out for minor cuts and bruises, but as Stefan had said, no one seemed to have been seriously injured. Most were content to gather their clothes and slink into the darkness. No one was especially eager to give a statement, which was fine, since we weren't especially eager to take one. Under the circumstances, it wasn't like we were going to be charging anyone with public indecency. Obviously, Rainbow's End would be closing early this Friday.

Okay, so, crisis averted.

That left the unspoken.

After the last patron had departed, I glanced sidelong at Cody. "So . . . about what happened between us?"

A muscle in his jaw twitched. "Nothing happened, Daisy."

"About what *almost* happened?"

He lifted his head, phosphorescent green flashing behind his eyes. "What about it?"

I looked away. "Nothing. It's just . . . you know genuine desire can't be compelled, right?"

Cody was silent for a long moment. When he spoke, his voice was gentle. "Daisy, I never said I didn't find you attractive. But attraction's easy." He gestured toward the nightclub. "You saw what happened in there. Most of those people were strangers. And I have an obligation to my own clan, to my own people. You . . . you're not a potential mate. You know that. And I care about you too much to mislead you, okay?"

My eyes stung. Goddamn werewolves.

"Daise?"

My phone rang. I fished it out of the pocket of my skirt. It was Sinclair. I let the call go to voice mail and then listened to it. "Hey, girl!" He sounded affectionate, only a little worried. "Hope everything's okay. Stop by, all right?"

Cody may have wanted me, but he didn't *want* to want me. And that made all the difference in the world.

"The fake Jamaican?" he asked, a slight edge to his voice. Well, too bad.

"Ha-ha." I put my phone away. "Look, if we're done here, I have a date to get back to."

"After this?" Cody raised his brows. "Do you really think that's a good idea?"

No, of course it wasn't. I'd just been dowsed with satyrfunk and had a brief, intense make-out session with my lifelong crush, who was standing in the parking lot eyeing me skeptically, his uniform shirt half undone because I'd torn off buttons when I ripped it open. "I don't think it's any of your business," I said, walking past him. "I'll let the manager know we're leaving."

"Daisy!"

*"What?"* I turned around to glare at Cody.

"Just . . . be careful, okay?" He gave me a wry smile, resting his hands on his utility belt. "Because I know when I get off duty, I'm going to go home and kill something."

Sure, that's healthy. And yet the thought of Cody hunting in wolf form gave me a shiver. Go figure. "Duly noted."

Inside the nightclub, the staff were making a cursory effort to clean up. Now that the place was empty, you could see how trashed it was. There were spilled drinks, crushed cups, and broken glass everywhere, abandoned flip-flops, discarded boxers, briefs, and panties that no one had wanted to reclaim.

The manager, Terry Miller, was still in a state of shock. He nodded absently when I told him we were leaving. "I just don't understand what happened," he murmured. "What am I going to tell the owners?"

I patted his arm. "Tell them the truth. It wasn't your fault. There wasn't anything you could do about it."

He turned his stricken gaze to me. "But what *was* it?"

"A satyr in rut," I said patiently. I'd already explained it to him twice, but apparently Lurine was right. Most mundane humans' memories were sketchy about the events of the night. "Big naked guy?"

"Right." He sounded uncertain. "What if there are lawsuits? Are we liable?"

I shook my head. "I don't know, but I doubt it. You can't insure against eldritch influence, can you?"

"Nooo . . ."

See, that's the problem with paranormal tourism. Tourists flock to Pemkowet expecting sparkly fairies and frolicking naiads, or maybe the covert thrill of glimpsing a vampire or a ghoul, but the fact is it can be downright dangerous here. And there's no way to anticipate or control a wild card like a rutting satyr. Although I bet I was going to get an earful about it from Amanda Brooks at the Pemkowet Visitors Bureau anyway once the story—or at least the rumors about the story—got around.

I gave Terry the manager another pat on the arm. "Look, I've got to go. Good luck. Officer Fairfax and I will give Chief Bryant a full report. If the owners give you a hard time, have them call the chief."

"Okay." That seemed to make him feel a bit better.

I ducked into the ladies' room to wash up before I left, scrubbing my hands and face and basically as much bare skin as I could reach with soap and cold water. I felt a lot cleaner when I was done, but the effects of the funk lingered. In the mirror, my eyes looked dilated and fever-bright.

Outside, the parking lot was mostly empty. I got into my Honda Civic, knowing I should go home.

Go home, and take a cold shower like Lurine had told me. Pour myself a drink, feed the cat, curl up on the couch, and listen to someone like Billie Holiday singing plaintive songs of heartbreak, not down-and-dirty blues.

My phone buzzed. Glancing at it, I saw it was a text from Sinclair. WHERE U AT GIRL? :)

It was the smiley face that got me. I really, really didn't want to go home alone right now.

So I drove to Sinclair's.

# Five

Sinclair's place was a ramshackle house in the country-side just north of town, where he was doing some fixer-upper work in return for reduced rent. You couldn't miss it, since his renovated double-decker bus, painted bright yellow, red, and green with PEMKOWET SUPERNATURAL TOURS on the side, was parked in the driveway.

I pulled in beside the bus and sat for a moment, listening to the music spilling out of the house and wrestling with my conscience. That beribboned box of desire was straining at the seams, practically rattling. If I went in there, I wasn't going to be able to keep it contained.

And if I didn't?

I'd understood exactly what Cody meant when he said he was going to go home and kill something. It was that strong a drive, and it needed to be vented somehow. As far as the Seven Deadlies went, I was probably better off sticking with lust than letting it turn to envy or anger. So I went inside.

All four members of the Mamma Jammers were there, jamming, because apparently a three-hour-long jam session at Union Pier wasn't quite long enough. They'd set up their gear in Sinclair's living room.

Sinclair was messing around with them, banging on a cowbell with a pair of grill tongs. It was a warm night and he was shirtless and barefoot, wearing nothing but a pair of khaki cargo shorts that sat low on his hips.

*Ka-pow.* My mental image of the gift-wrapped box exploded. I felt the air pressure in the room change, lifting my hair with an electrostatic charge. Huh. That sort of thing usually only happened when I got angry. There was a long squall of feedback before a tube burst in one of the Mamma Jammers' vintage amplifiers with a brief shower of sparks.

In the silence that followed, everyone stared at me. Sinclair took a long breath and blinked a few times. "Daisy? Are you okay? Is everything . . . okay?"

"Yeah." Realizing I still wore *dauda-dagr* belted around my waist, I touched the hilt, taking strength from its bracing coolness. Okay. I could make myself walk away from this if I had to. "Is this a bad time? I can go."

"What? No, of course not. I invited you here."

I shifted restlessly from foot to foot. "Then can we talk alone for a minute?"

Sinclair gave the Mamma Jammers an uncertain look. "Are you crazy, man?" one of them said. "Go!"

Inside his bedroom, Sinclair closed the door behind us. I unbuckled my belt and let it fall to the floor with a heavy clunk. I didn't want him to get frostbitten.

"Daisy." He laid his hands on my shoulders. Unable to help myself, I traced a line on his bare torso with one finger, between his pecs down toward his navel. He caught my hand and removed it, although he laced his fingers through mine. "Whoa! Slow down, girl. Mind if I ask what happened out there to turn a night hanging with the boys into a booty call?"

"No." I shook my head. "Rutting satyr-funk. It set off an orgy. But it's okay. We defused it."

"So this is about some funky satyr?" he asked slowly. "Not you and me?"

"A little," I admitted.

"I'm not sure how I feel about that." Sinclair's face was unreadable in the dim light. "This isn't how I wanted it to go down between us."

"Yeah, me either," I said. "This was a mistake. I should go."

"Probably." There was a certain lack of conviction in his voice. "I guess."

Neither of us moved. "So . . . do you *want* me to go?" I asked him. "'Cause if you do, I think you're going to have to tell me. Like, in no uncertain terms."

"I'm thinking."

"Okay, well, before you make up your mind, there's one other little thing I haven't told you."

Sinclair raised his brows. "What?" I shifted his hand around to place it firmly on my butt, untucking my tail in the process and letting him feel it wriggle. His eyes widened and his body went rigid, but he didn't pull away from me. "What the fuck?"

I watched his face, trying to gauge the degree of freak-out. "Look, as tails go, it's pretty small. You should have seen the satyr's."

He gave me a blank look. "How is this something I never noticed?"

"I tuck."

"You tuck."

"Yeah." I laid my palm flat against his chest, feeling it rise and fall. His dark brown skin was warm, as though it retained the heat of the sun on the docks. Afraid of seeing rejection in his eyes, I lowered my gaze and kept it there, centered on the groove between his pecs. "Look, I really do like you. I like you a lot, Sinclair. I wouldn't be here if I didn't. As strange as it might sound, I wouldn't trust myself with someone I didn't care about right now. And I wanted to try the whole normal boyfriend/girlfriend thing. But the truth is, my father's an incubus, I'm a hell-spawn and Hel's agent, and this is Pemkowet. Normal's not really in my wheelhouse. There's always going to be an element of weird. Maybe a lot of weird. So—"

"Daisy." Sinclair interrupted me. Removing his hand from my ass, he reached for the pendant I wore.

It was a silver whistle in the shape of an acorn and it had been given to me by the Oak King, a member of genuine old-school eldritch pagan royalty, as a means to summon him at need. Sinclair had been there when it happened. Both of us had been touched by the wonder of it.

And then I'd been stupid enough to leave it at home in my jewelry box when the ghoul rebellion went down, which is why after that I'd had it strung on a chain of dwarf-mined silver so I could wear it around my neck.

Anyway.

"Remember?" Sinclair asked me.

I nodded. "Of course."

He smiled. "For a memory like that, I can handle a lot of weird." He slid one arm around my waist, pulling me closer. "So I guess what I'm saying is, what the hell. If this is what you want, let's do it."

It wasn't the time or the circumstances I would have chosen, and it shouldn't have been good, but in fact it *was* good. Even knowing what had almost happened with Cody that same night, even knowing that the Mamma Jammers were right outside the bedroom and that sooner or later I'd have to face the walk of shame past them. It was still good.

"Let me see it," Sinclair said after he'd undressed me, his voice low and husky with a mix of desire and trepidation. He sat on the edge of the bed, his knees spread. "Go on, Daisy. Show me."

Obediently, I stood between his knees and turned around. I felt him draw one finger down my spine, lingering at the base of my tailbone, at the root of my tail. I shivered.

"Is it sensitive?" he asked uncertainly.

"Yeah." I fought the urge to coil it around his fingers, pretty sure that would send him straight into freak-out territory. In all honesty, I don't think anyone had touched it since my mom when I was in diapers, and the fact that Sinclair was doing it now brought tears to my eyes. "Very."

"Huh."

I turned around to straddle his waist, lowering my head

to kiss him until both of us were breathless. "Let's not talk any more about my tail tonight." I reached for the zipper of his khaki shorts. "Okay?"

Sinclair gave me a lazy grin, lying back to grab my hips and pull me atop him, my hair spilling around his face. "Definitely."

Somewhere outside the bedroom door, the bass player for the Mamma Jammers struck up a *bom-chicka-wow-wow* groove. Apparently, that wasn't his amplifier I'd accidentally blown. I don't know if it was meant to be funny or thoughtful, but either way, it was effective.

So, yeah.

*Bom-chicka-wow-wow.*

Afterward, exhaustion hit me like a ton of bricks. My eyelids felt like they weighed a hundred pounds apiece, and the thought of trying to make polite conversation with Sinclair's friends made me want to hibernate.

"Is it okay if I just crash here?" I mumbled into the pillow. "For a little while anyway?"

"Yeah, of course." Sitting on the edge of the bed, Sinclair fished for his shorts. "I promised you pancakes, didn't I?" He stood. "I'm just going to go out and explain things to the guys."

I cracked open one eye to peer at him. "What are you going to tell them?"

He shrugged. "Guess I'll go with the truth."

"Oh."

I wanted to stay awake long enough to find out how *that* went, but all I remember is hearing a brief, low murmur of male voices before I was spiraling down into sleep, the memory of *bom-chicka-wow-wo*w sex with Sinclair blurring with the memory of kissing (and yes, okay, grinding on) Cody, the satyr's grin, and the shocking jolt of hunger in Stefan's gaze. Somewhere in the recesses of my mind, I heard a deep, resonant chuckle of pure demonic amusement and entertained the fleeting thought that if my father, Belphegor, was pleased, I definitely shouldn't have done what I did tonight.

Screw it. I'd feel guilty in the morning.

And if real life was like the movies, I would wake up in the morning to realize I'd blown things with a nice guy I actually liked by rushing into something neither of us was ready for, just like Kristy McNichol in *Little Darlings*. Which, in case you're not familiar with it, is an old movie where Kristy and Tatum O'Neal make a bet at summer camp about who's going to be the first to cash in her v-card, only they don't call it that because . . . well, it's an old movie. Like, an eighties movie before John Hughes made eighties movies a thing. When I was growing up, Mom used movies to teach me important life lessons, and she used the movies she knew best. Also, the movies that we could rent for free from the Pemkowet District Library, because we didn't have a lot of money.

Anyway, I should have felt awful and this should have been a disaster. In fact, I woke to early-morning sunlight and Sinclair sprawled in the bed next to me, one arm flung carelessly over me. And I felt pretty damn good.

I held still for a moment, listening for the echo of demonic laughter. Nope. Either I'd imagined it, or dear old Dad was amused by something more complicated than the fact that his half-human daughter had thrown caution to the winds and given in to licentious behavior. Which . . . wasn't entirely reassuring, but I'd take it.

"Hey." Sinclair roused himself sleepily. His head was on the pillow beside mine, and his dark eyes gazed into mine at close proximity. Like, so close I almost felt cross-eyed looking back at him. "You okay, Daisy?"

I wasn't used to this kind of intimacy. All of the sexual encounters I'd had had ultimately ended . . . well, awkwardly. This morning-after business was new to me.

"Yeah." I tried the sentiment on for size. It fit. "You?"

"Uh-huh."

My stomach rumbled.

Sinclair laughed. "Come on. Let's make some breakfast."

Okay, time to suck it up and take the walk of shame. It wasn't pleasant, but it wasn't the worst thing I'd endured in my life. I'd grown up in a small town where everyone knew my story, and I was used to curious stares. At least Sinclair's friends were polite and didn't make any jokes about what was obviously a total booty call or ask if I filed my horns down like Hellboy. I got that a lot back in high school when the first movie came out. I kept my tail tucked and did my best to make a good impression, memorizing their names and asking them questions about themselves.

They seemed to be good guys, laid-back and easygoing. Over a mountainous stack of pancakes—Sinclair hadn't lied, he made them from scratch with buttermilk, and they were probably the best pancakes I'd ever had—I learned that Roddy, the drummer, was also of Jamaican origin. His mother had a Caribbean restaurant and his uncle owned the custom auto shop where Sinclair's dad worked.

Under the guise of making small talk, I asked him why his family had left Jamaica, secretly hoping to gain some insight into Sinclair's situation.

"Poverty," he said simply. "Unless you have the right connections, there are no real job opportunities, no way to change your lot in life."

"Is that why your dad left?" I asked Sinclair.

"Dad knew Roddy's uncle Joseph." He set a platter of bacon on the table. "He knew there would be a good job here for him."

Huh. As an answer to a direct yes-or-no question went, that was sort of a nonanswer. "Why Kalamazoo?" I asked curiously, reaching for a piece of bacon. "I mean . . . why Michigan at all?"

As it transpired, apparently Kalamazoo, Michigan, has been host for many years to a world-class reggae festival, one of the largest in the United States. Hence, the long-standing connection to Jamaica from whence many of the festival's headliner acts have come. I felt a little silly for not knowing this about a city only an hour away.

"Damn, girl! You need to get out of Pemkowet more often," Ben, the bass player, teased.

"I guess," I said. "But there's no underworld there."

Oops. A little silence settled over the crowded table in the breakfast nook. "You mean . . . hell?" Roddy inquired cautiously.

I shook my head. "No, I mean an actual physical under-world that exists on the mundane plane, ruled by a deity of a non-apex faith."

"That's what allows an eldritch community to exist and thrive." Sinclair rescued me, sliding into the seat beside me. "Here in Pemkowet, they call it Little Niflheim. Right, Daisy?"

I nodded. Little Niflheim was where Hel held court, be-neath the shifting sand dunes that had buried the lumber town of Singapore—the very dunes said to be haunted by the ghost of Talman "Tall Man" Brannigan, the lumber baron responsible for the deforestation that caused the dunes to swallow Singapore. Tall Man Brannigan, who slaughtered almost his entire family in a fit of madness and despair.

It was a typical urban legend. No one I knew had ever seen the Tall Man's ghost, but everyone knew someone who knew someone whose cousin or brother claimed to have done so—and then died after the sighting. But Little Nifl-heim was real. I'd been there on a number of occasions.

"I've seen the world tree," Sinclair added, cutting into his pancakes and stabbing a forkful. "Yggdrasil II."

For the next half hour, he entertained the Mamma Jam-mers with the kind of patter he used to entertain the tour-ists, a blend of history, conjecture, and fact, all extolling the wonders of Pemkowet.

"Speaking of . . ." Sinclair glanced at the watch on his wrist. "It's almost showtime. I've got to get ready for the first tour of the day."

The Mamma Jammers packed their gear and beat an ef-ficient retreat, thanking him for the gig and the place to crash.

In the kitchen, I helped him do a quick washup of the breakfast dishes. My body still felt languid and relaxed, but my mind was buzzing. "Hey, Sinclair?"

He shot me a sidelong look. "Uh-huh?"

I scrubbed diligently, declining to meet his gaze. "How come you never talk about your mom?"

More silence.

I snuck a sideways peek of my own. Sinclair reached over to turn off the water faucet. "My mother is a very powerful woman, Daisy."

I remembered what Cody had told me. "Oh, yeah? Is she an obeah woman?"

"She's a judge." His voice was flat. I felt a powerful surge of white-girl guilt. Yeah, given the first opportunity, that's where I'd gone. Ooga-booga island voodoo. But then Sinclair's full lips compressed to a tight line. "And yeah, she's an obeah woman," he admitted. "A very, very powerful one. Dangerous, too. It's in our bloodline. If you really want to know, that's why my father left Jamaica. My mother worked some shady magic. In her legal dealings and her personal dealings, too. He had his doubts about her intentions. He felt he might have been compromised in their relationship and didn't want me further exposed to it. That's why we left. And that's pretty much the whole story. I don't like to talk about it because I don't like to think about it. Okay?"

I nodded. "Okay."

Sinclair leaned over to kiss me. "Cool." He glanced at his watch again. "Look, I really do have to run. Call me later?"

"You bet."

# Six

I finished the dishes and let myself out, locking the door behind me. It was a bright, sunny morning, and being alone in broad daylight in yesterday's clothes—which were probably tainted with satyr-funk—I felt more than a little slutty.

Which, I have to admit, wasn't entirely a bad feeling. Except maybe for that guilty thrill I felt when I thought about what had happened with Cody at the nightclub, not to mention the latent shock of discovering that Sinclair's mother was an obeah woman, whatever that meant.

So, yeah. It's complicated.

Heading for my Honda, I went over a mental checklist of Things to Do Today. What I really wanted to do, first and foremost, was call my best friend, Jen, and give her the 411 on everything that had just gone down. In a close second place, I wanted to do some research into exactly what an obeah man or an obeah woman was. I mean, obviously we were talking about some sort of magic worker, but beyond that, I was clueless. Not a lot of call to study up on Caribbean lore here in the Midwest. Casimir, aka the Fabulous

Casimir, might be able to help; he was the head witch in Pemkowet's local coven. Or my old teacher Mr. Leary, who knew more about eldritch history and folklore around the world than anyone I knew.

Of course, what I *had* to do first was head down to the station and fill out a report on the orgy for the Pemkowet X-Files. Checking my phone, I saw there were voice mails from Chief Bryant and, oh, gah, Amanda Brooks at the PVB.

Okay, those could wait. After all, I was reasonably certain that Lurine had the satyr situation under control. If all hell had broken loose again, Cody knew where to find me. Before I did anything, I was damn well going to go home, take a shower, and change my clothes.

I was reaching for the driver's-side door handle when something sharp stung the back of my neck. "Ow!" I brushed frantically at the spot, thinking a bee had stung me, but nothing was there. "What the hell?"

It stung me again.

"Goddammit!" Spinning around, I waved my arms in the air. "Seriously, what the . . . oh, crap."

Ten feet away, beside a scraggly juniper bush, a joe-pye weed fairy with green skin and clumps of pale purple hair piled atop her head hovered in the air. Her face was contorted with jealous rage, her translucent wings were a blur, and she was carrying some kind of sling-type weapon made of woven grass.

"Hey, Jojo." I held up both hands in a peaceful gesture. "Look, I was just leaving."

"Foul, sluttish hoyden!" she shrilled, whirling the sling and whipping another pebble at me. "Leave him be!"

I dodged. "I really don't—"

"Hell-spawned, urchin-snouted doxy!" She flung another, her tip-tilted eyes bright with tears and fury. "I hate you!"

Um, yeah. So ever since we struck our bargain with the Oak King to have the smallest and sparkliest of his subjects make regularly scheduled appearances along the tour route, it turns out the fairies kind of *like* Sinclair. This one in particular, whom we'd nicknamed Jojo, had a wicked crush on him. Usually Jojo confined herself to skulking around and spying on him, but apparently I'd crossed some sort of invisible line by spending the night with him.

"Look, I'm sorry!" I said in frustration. "I know how you feel. Really, I do. But he's just not that into you, okay?"

"Mewling, milk-livered strumpet!" Baring her sharp teeth, she wound up like a teeny-tiny major league pitcher to loose another pebble.

Yanking open the car door, I ducked inside the Honda. Pebbles rattled against the window as I stuck the key in the ignition and got the car started, throwing it into reverse and backing out of the driveway.

So much for the idea of Sinclair Palmer as a nice, normal human boyfriend. First I find out his absent mother's the gavel-wielding Jamaican equivalent of a voodoo queen and then I get attacked by a jealous fairy.

Oh, well.

I drove to downtown Pemkowet, circling the blocks until I found a parking spot, always a challenge during tourist season and especially on the last holiday weekend of the summer. My apartment was located on the second story of an old building alongside a public park in a prime location above Mrs. Browne's Olde World Bakery. Mogwai, the big calico tomcat I'd more or less adopted, was stalking chipmunks under the rhododendrons in the park and didn't deign to come when I called him. Upstairs, I filled his dish anyway. There was a torn screen on the back porch that served as a cat door so he could come or go as he pleased during the summer months. We'd renegotiate come winter.

I allowed myself the luxury of showering and changing before I listened to my voice mail. The chief's just said, "Daisy. Call me."

Amanda Brooks's message was considerably longer and delivered at a pitch of barely contained fury that rivaled Jojo the jealous fairy's. Apparently she'd already gotten wind of the incident. I held the phone a foot away from my ear, wincing as I listened, then called the chief. I had a feeling he'd gotten an earful from her, too.

I was right.

"So is there any way you could have prevented this?" he asked me without preamble.

"No, sir," I said. "I didn't even know it was a possibility. Amanda Brooks is on the warpath, isn't she?"

"Uh-huh. Now that you know, is there anything you can do to prevent it from happening again?"

"I'll find out."

"Good. I want you to meet with Amanda and do your best to smooth things over."

I made a face. "Yes, sir. As soon as I type up my report."

"Cody's already filed an official report," the chief said. "The X-Files version can wait. Call Amanda ASAP, Daisy. Understand?"

I sighed. "Yes, sir."

Truth be told, Amanda Brooks is very good at her job. Paranormal tourism? She *invented* that industry. Oh, there have always been tourists in Pemkowet—it's a pretty town, our beaches are lovely. It's been an artists' colony since the late 1800s, long before Hel established Little Niflheim, and there used to be a huge dance pavilion—I mean, like, *seriously* huge—that was a big draw before it burned down a couple of generations ago. I guess it's always been a quirky place, even before Hel's underworld made it a magnet for the eldritch.

And from what I understand, tourism actually declined in the second half of the twentieth century, after the big pavilion burned and Pemkowet was left with a reputation as an artsy place where weird shit happened. It wasn't until Amanda Brooks took over the PVB and had the brilliant idea of turning a negative into a positive that the industry took off. Come to Pemkowet, where weird shit happens!

Now, people do. They come expecting to find a real-life Midwestern version of Sunnydale or Bon Temps or Forks or whatever their paranormal poison of choice might be. So, yeah, Amanda Brooks is really good at her job; but she seems to have a hard time grasping the fact that there's an element of chaos at work here that can't be controlled. This isn't Disney World and the rides aren't inspected for safety. There are no OSHA standards in the eldritch community.

Also, okay, I'm a little biased. During high school, her daughter, Stacey, was the head of the local mean girls' clique and my own personal nemesis. I got suspended for a week thanks to her.

Still, duty beckoned, so I made the call. I was braced for the worst, but Amanda actually sounded a bit distracted.

"I've got to take a meeting," she said. "It won't be long. Can you be here in half an hour?"

"Sure." Ending the call, I quickly called Jen, only to get her voice mail. Damn. I sent her a text asking if she was free to meet for lunch, which left me with twenty-five minutes to kill and an urgent need for girl talk. I thought about calling my mom, but . . . yeah, no way. Mom's great, we have a great relationship, and I'm pretty honest with her about almost everything, but this was a bit too far outside the mother-daughter comfort zone.

Unfortunately, the only other person I could think of calling was Lurine, who I figured was still engaged in a mar-athon shag-fest with a horny satyr. On the other hand, I really did need to talk to her, since she was probably the best person to ask about preventing another satyr-funk in-cident.

Maybe they took breaks. I gave her a try, but no such luck. So I left a message asking her to call me when she had the chance, then spent the remaining twenty-four minutes tidying my apartment.

The Pemkowet Visitors Bureau, in a charming little shingle-sided building on the riverfront near the main en-trance into the town, is adorned with sleek, modern furni-ture, glossy magazines, and Stacey Brooks's haughty-faced presence behind the desk since her mother gave her a re-ceptionist's job there. She was usually yammering into the fancy Bluetooth earpiece of the office phone—why the hands-free option was so important I don't know, since it's not like she did anything but answer calls—but not today.

"Daisy." She greeted me in a snide tone. "My mother's meeting is running a little late. Have a seat."

"Thanks." Determined not to be baited, I sat.

"So I hear there was a big gay orgy out at Rainbow's End last night." Stacey arched her perfectly plucked ash-brown eyebrows at me. "I hear *you* were there."

"I was." I fished my Pemkowet Police Department ID out of my bag and showed it to her. "On official business."

"Oh, please!" She sniffed. "Everyone knows you're just a file clerk."

I shrugged.

Stacey let the silence stretch for a moment, but she wasn't the type to handle silence well. "So what was it?" she asked. "Kevin McTeague heard it was a bad batch of ec-stasy, but Jane Drummond heard it was witchcraft." Lower-ing her voice, she gave me a significant look. "Was it a succubus thing? A *gay* succubus thing? Is that why you were there, Daisy?"

Oh, for crying out loud. Despite my resolve, my temper stirred. "I'm not a succubus!"

She smirked at me. "Oh, so it's just a gay thing?"

Yeah, I know. In this day and age, that shouldn't be a via-ble taunt. Especially in a town that prides itself on welcoming diversity, especially coming from the freaking receptionist of the tourist bureau of said town. But there you have it. High school bully tactics never change. I shouldn't have let Stacey know she'd gotten to me with the succubus thing. Now she'd just keep pushing gay, gay, gay until I couldn't stand it and issued a denial I knew was (a) perfectly unnecessary, (b) be-neath me, and (c) exactly what Stacey wanted.

Or, I could go with a classic change of tactics. "You know, I really can't discuss the incident before I've had a chance to talk with your mother," I said to her. "So, are you seeing anyone these days?"

Bingo! Of course I knew she wasn't. It's a small town. Sta-cey's eyes narrowed. "Are you still seeing that bus driver?"

Nice try. I smiled. I'd actually met Sinclair for the first time in this very lobby and I knew damn well Stacey thought he was cute, too. "Yeah, I am. It's going really well. I mean, except for the gay orgies and all."

Her expression turned ominous. "Wait until he finds out what you—"

I interrupted her. "He knows."

At that moment, the door to Amanda Brooks's office was opened by a man with a briefcase showing himself out. My skin tingled with the telltale sign of eldritch presence and all thoughts of exchanging barbs with Stacey went clean out of my head. The man strode into the lobby, then stopped in his tracks and looked in my direction.

My tail twitched with alarm . . . and a sort of kindred recognition.

At a glance, he *looked* normal. Average height, early thirties, a decent build. Good-looking in a *GQ* sort of way, with a summer-weight suit that looked expensive and short, stylish light brown hair in a hundred-dollar haircut.

But his eyes were black, as black as mine. Ordinary mortals don't have truly black eyes. A brown so dark it looks black, yes. Not the kind of black where the only way you can differentiate between the iris and the pupil is that the iris doesn't admit light.

And there was a *smell*, like a whiff of sulfur . . . only not really a smell. More like a bad taste lingering in my mouth, like I'd eaten something rancid. Only that wasn't right either. It wasn't a sense I could put a name to.

Anyway, he was definitely a hell-spawn. And I suspected that, unlike me, he had claimed his birthright.

Now that was a scary thought.

I held my breath, half expecting to feel the Inviolate Wall tremble and threaten the architecture of existence.

But it didn't. The man inhaled briefly, his nostrils flaring, his black eyes curious. Even without seeing, I could tell his own tail was swishing back and forth beneath his well-tailored linen-blend trousers.

And then he left, striding out the door.

I let out my breath and eased my hand out of my messenger bag. I'd been reaching for *dauda-dagr* without realizing it.

Oblivious to it all, Stacey gazed after him in a reverie.

"See, *that's* the kind of guy I'm looking for," she murmured. "We need more like him in Pemkowet."

Yeah, right.

Ignoring her, I admitted myself into Amanda Brooks's office. She was seated at her desk, but her chair was swiveled to allow her to gaze at the river, and she didn't turn around when I took a seat opposite her.

"Ms. Brooks?" I cleared my throat. "Daisy Johanssen. You wanted to see me?"

"Oh . . . right. Yes, of course." Her reply sounded absentminded. She spun her chair around slowly. There was a vagueness to her usually keen features. "I'm sorry, Daisy. What was it again?"

My skin still felt prickly. "Ms. Brooks, who was that guy? What did he want?"

She blinked behind the lenses of chic glasses that probably cost more than I made in a month. "Who?"

I concentrated my gaze on her. "That guy! The one who just left."

"Mr. Dufreyne? Oh, he's a lawyer. He was just inquiring on behalf of a client about purchasing some lands that have been in the Cavannaugh family for generations." Her expression began to swim into focus. "As I'm sure you're aware, the Cavannaughs are one of the original founding families. It's my maiden name, of course."

"Of course," I echoed her. "Whatever he was asking, you didn't agree to it, did you?"

"No." Amanda Brooks frowned. "You know, the Cavannaughs were here before there was a Pemkowet. We trace our ancestry back to the lumber days of Singapore." She glanced toward the river, her expression veering back toward uncertainty. "I can't imagine why I'd even entertain the idea."

"Don't," I said bluntly. "I've got a bad feeling about that guy. Whatever he wants, don't give it to him."

Under ordinary circumstances, Amanda Brooks would have reacted with indignation if I'd dared to speak to her that way. Today, she simply cleared her throat. "Yes, well. As I said, I can't imagine why I would." Her gaze sharpened to its usual level of piercingness. "Now, about this orgy—"

Back on track, the infernal cobwebs cleared away, she delivered a scathing fifteen-minute diatribe on public health hazards, risks, liabilities, negative publicity, and my general irresponsibility in allowing such a thing to occur. I was relieved enough to see her back in form that I just sat and nodded in agreement, waiting for the tongue-lashing to end before explaining what had happened at Rainbow's End and promising to do my utmost to ensure that nothing like it ever happened again.

As soon as she was finished, I beat a quick retreat. In the lobby, Stacey gave me the traditional Pemkowet High mean girls farewell, flashing devil horns at me with her right hand. Since she wasn't on the phone, she stuck out her tongue, too.

Nice.

On the off chance that he ever asked her out, I debated telling her that the *GQ*-looking lawyer was a hell-spawn.

I decided against it.

# Seven

Having faced down the dragon in her den, I went to the
station to write up a report on the orgy. Since I was
there, the desk clerk, Patty Rogan, gave me a stack of
yesterday's reports to file.

I browsed through them first, looking for signs of eldritch involvement. That's how I had come by my unique
role in the department in the first place, which led to Hel's
invitation to serve as her liaison to mundane authorities.
Nothing jumped out at me in the first few reports—a minor
fender bender, an altercation outside a bar, a citation for
public urination—but the fourth one intrigued me. Some
irate tourists had come in to file a complaint about being
pickpocketed after playing a shell game that a pair of kids
was running on the dock.

"Did you take this one?" I asked Patty. "The shell game?"

"Yeah." She smiled. "I thought that one might interest
you. There are a couple of others like it."

I flipped through the paperwork and found them. In all
three instances, the complainant had won money at the

shell game, only to find nothing but dry, brittle leaves in his or her wallet afterward. "Anyone check it out?"

Patty nodded. "Oh, sure, but the kids running the game were long gone." She raised her eyebrows. "If they *were* kids in the first place."

"Right." Since I'd been going through the files, other members of the department had gotten more savvy about spotting eldritch signs. The dead leaves were a dead give-away. "Give me a call if you get another complaint."

"Will do."

I took a stroll down the dock anyway. No sign of the kids this morning, but I stopped by a few of the restaurants and bars along the river and asked the managers to call me if the kids returned. My phone buzzed with a reply from Jen, offering to meet me for lunch at Callahan's Café at twelve thirty. After sending a confirmation, I swung by the Sisters of Selene, Pemkowet's local occult store, to pick the Fabulous Casimir's brain.

Technically, I guess Casimir is a drag queen, although his cross-dressing has to do with the shamanic tradition, too. Either way, he cuts an imposing figure. He's over six feet tall without the wig, and the towering Marie Antoinette number he was sporting today put him closer to seven.

He caught my eye as I entered. I waited patiently while he finished ringing up a purchase and the store emptied for a moment.

"Hey, Miss Daisy." Casimir fussed with a display of charmed crystals that the last batch of tourists had disturbed. "Whatever went down at Rainbow's End last night, I hope you know none of my people were involved." He gave a little shiver. "From what I heard, that was no love spell."

"No, I know," I said. "It was a satyr."

"A *satyr*?"

"A satyr in rut," I clarified. "Any thoughts?"

Casimir's lips pursed. "I deal in magic, not mythological beasties."

"Okay," I said. "How about obeah? That's a kind of magic, right? Do you know anything about it?"

His long-fingered hands went still. "Not really, *dahling*, no. It's a little outside my geographic purview." Beneath heavy makeup and false eyelashes, his eyes were shrewd. "Mind if I ask *why*? Because I don't think that had anything to do with the shenanigans at the club last night."

I shrugged. Sinclair hadn't given me permission to discuss it, so it was best to honor the eldritch code.

"Never mind." Casimir tapped his carmine lips with one fingertip. "I can guess. Is it causing . . . problems?"

"No," I said honestly. "I'm just curious."

"Curiosity killed the cat, girl. There's a time and a place for gathering knowledge, and it ain't necessarily during the early days of a young romance. Romance is fragile, Miss Daisy." He shook his finger at me. "If you want my advice, don't go looking for trouble or you might just find it."

"I'm not!" I protested.

The door chimes rang as another group of tourists entered the store, and the Fabulous Casimir turned his fabulous attention toward them. Checking the time on my phone, I decided to pay a visit to Mr. Leary before lunch.

"Daisy!" Casimir called after me.

I paused in the doorway. "Yeah?"

"I didn't mean to put you off, honey." Beneath the mask of white makeup and strategically placed beauty marks, the expression on his face was serious. "If your young man finds himself in trouble, I'm sure we can figure out a way to help him."

I smiled. "Thanks, Cas. No one's in trouble. You're right— I'm just being nosy."

He made a shooing gesture. "Then go on—get out of here!"

I drove across the bridge from Pemkowet to East Pemkowet, a distinction that many find confusing for good reason, since the communities are intertwined. In terms of tourism, they're joined at the hip. In terms of governance, they are actually two separate entities, and there's a little bit of rivalry on the local level, too. I have fond memories of taking part in the annual Easties vs. Townies battle that goes down every Halloween night, complete with water balloons and eggs.

Once upon a time, East Pemkowet was a little more down-to-earth and homespun than its sister-city across the bridge, but in the past ten years, it had become a haven for upscale dining and boutique shopping. Driving down Main Street, I couldn't help but notice the improvements, which included some pretty ambitious street- and landscaping. Well, except for Boo Radley's house.

That's what we called it in high school, anyway. I don't know what it was called before *To Kill a Mockingbird* came out. It was the oldest house on Main Street, a rambling Tudor Revival with crumbling white stucco and dark exterior woodwork, the kind that looked like it was integral to the structure, not just a veneer.

According to local legend, Clancy Brannigan, the last living descendant of Talman Brannigan, owned the place. I'd never seen him, but the cashiers at Tafts Grocery claimed there was a standing order for a weekly delivery dating back decades. No one ever got to go inside the house, though. The bill was paid in advance by a check drawn from a business account and deliveries were left in the shuttered, decrepit wooden gazebo in the front yard. Generations of schoolkids had haunted the place, trying to catch a glimpse of our local Boo Radley, to no avail.

Anyway.

Mr. Leary's cottage was infinitely more pleasant, a charming little place with a wonderful garden. Late-blooming cosmos and zinnias provided a riot of color, and a line of tall sunflowers nodded alongside a weathered picket fence.

"Daisy Johanssen!" My former teacher hailed me from the screened porch, hoisting a glass as I came up the front path. "If it isn't my favorite teleological conundrum. Would you care for a glass of iced tea?"

I did a little bit of a double take; first, because I'd never known Mr. Leary to voluntarily partake of nonalcoholic beverages, and second, because he had company. As far as I knew, he was a lifelong bachelor, and I'd always found him to be fairly reclusive outside the classroom even before he retired. But no, there was a woman on the porch with him.

And then I did a triple take, because I knew her. Emma Sudbury. I'd, um, killed her sister.

It's a long story, but the upshot of it is that Emma Sudbury's sister, Mary, was a ghoul, cast out from heaven and hell for drowning her infant son and believing it was God's will. That happened back in the late 1950s. For the next fifty-some years, Emma took care of Mary, growing older and more desperate while Mary stayed ageless and batshit crazy. Right up until the end, at least. At the very end, after doing some pretty terrible things, she had a moment of lucidity and begged me to administer Hel's justice.

I swallowed hard, my right palm tingling at the memory of *dauda-dagr*'s hilt clutched hard against it, the shudder of Mary's final death.

"Come in, come in!" Mr. Leary held the door open for me. "Miss Daisy Johanssen, may I present Miss Emma Sudbury?"

"We've met," I said softly. "Nice to see you again, ma'am. You're looking well."

It was true. When I'd first encountered Emma Sudbury, she was haggard and unkempt, worn down by grief and terror. Now her white hair was rinsed and set, and she wore an attractive old-lady pantsuit.

But the shadow of sorrow was still there. It would never leave.

"Thank you, dear," she said with quiet dignity before turning to Mr. Leary. "Thank you, Michael. I've enjoyed our chat, but I should be going."

I watched him usher her out the door and down the front path, his head with its leonine mane of white hair bent solicitously over hers. The last time I'd seen her, Cody and I had delivered the news of her sister's death. I hadn't told her it had been by my own hand, only that her sister Mary was at peace with it. We hadn't volunteered details and she hadn't asked for them.

I wondered if she suspected she'd rather not know.

Mr. Leary returned to the porch, the expression on his saturnine face unreadable. "Please, have a seat. May I pour you a glass of tea?" He indicated a pitcher sweating on the table. "It's a blend of jasmine and lemongrass, with just a hint of ginger."

"Yes, thanks. It sounds wonderful." I accepted a glass. "How did you and Miss Sudbury meet?"

He took a sip of tea, swishing it delicately around in his mouth. "We met at the senior center. That infernal do-gooding busybody Sandra Sweddon persuaded me to attend a function there. I believe she's a friend of your mother's?"

I nodded.

"Well." Mr. Leary set down his glass. "As it happens, it wasn't as entirely dreadful as I'd imagined, and Emma has an interest in gardening, although of course she hasn't pursued it for many years. I like to think our chats have helped draw her out. Hers is a terribly sad story, you know."

"I know."

His gaze lingered on me. "I daresay you do. So!" His tone lightened. "How may I enlighten you today, Daisy?"

On the one hand, Mr. Leary was probably a good bet for some satyr lore; on the other hand, his knowledge was largely academic. If I got him on the topic, I'd most likely get an earful of Euripides or Sophocles, not practical information regarding satyrs' rutting cycles, which was what I really needed. And once Mr. Leary got the conversational bit between his teeth, it was hard to get him to change course. So I went ahead and asked him about what I *really* wanted to know.

I guess Sinclair's revelation bothered me a little more than I realized.

"Obeah," I said. Usually, all it took was one word. I waited for Mr. Leary to go into his familiar mnemonic trance, tilting his head back and closing his eyes before rattling off a string of facts, anecdotes, and conjecture mined from a lifetime of arcane research.

Instead, he frowned. "Alas, I fear obeah is far and away the most oblique and poorly documented of the Afro-Caribbean belief systems. But I have some excellent resource material on vodou or Santería if that might help."

I shook my head. "I don't think so. How come there isn't more on obeah?"

"Why," he said.

"Um . . . why what?"

"*Why* isn't there more information available on obeah," Mr. Leary said sternly. "Not *how come*."

Once a strict grammarian, always a strict grammarian. I winced. "Sorry. Why isn't there more information available?"

He crossed his legs. "For one thing, unlike other belief systems emanating from the African diaspora, obeah doesn't appear to have been syncretized with Christianity."

"Could you, um, elaborate?"

"Plantation owners in the Caribbean did their best to suppress any expression of faith rooted in the traditions of African slaves and their descendants," he said. "They feared, not without cause, that those they oppressed would find sufficient inspiration in such worship to entertain notions of rebellion. In some places, such as Haiti and Cuba, practitioners continued to worship in a covert manner. They simply established an association between their own existing deities, their loas and orishas and what have you, and Catholic saints. For example, Papa Legba in Haitian vodou, a probable descendant of the Yoruban Elegua, is the god of the crossroads. He's commonly associated with Saint Peter, who performs a similar function as a gatekeeper."

"So someone could appear to be praying to Saint Peter when in actuality they were praying to Papa Legba?" I asked.

"Precisely." Mr. Leary nodded. "Or Saint Lazarus, I believe . . . something to do with a cane and a dog. I'd be happy to look it up for you if you think it might be helpful— Oh, but you were asking about obeah."

"Right." I sipped my tea, which really was insanely refreshing. "Which wasn't syncretized. So that meant it was driven deeper undercover?"

"It's conjecture on my part," he said modestly. "It's also entirely possible that little is known simply because there's little to know, that rather than a complex, multifunctional belief system, obeah is merely an umbrella term for a particular accretion of superstition and folklore."

I give Mr. Leary a lot of credit for the fact that I have a not-totally-embarrassing vocabulary for a small-town hell-spawn with a high school education, but it took me a few seconds to tease the meaning out of that one. "Maybe." I had the sense that the Right Honorable Mrs. Sinclair's Mom was involved in something a bit bigger than an accretion. "But I wonder, does it *work*?"

"Does it work?" he echoed.

"Obeah magic." I swirled the tea in my glass, making the ice cubes rattle. "How can it? You know the saying: As below, so above. As far as I know, Jamaica doesn't have an underworld. So I don't see how it can have functioning magic."

"Ah." Mr. Leary laid one finger alongside his nose, à la Saint Nicholas in "'Twas the Night Before Christmas." "Forgive me for being trite, but there are more things in heaven and earth, Horatio, than are dreamt of in your philosophy. But that, my dear Daisy, is your bailiwick. I can tell you what history has or has not recorded of obeah. I cannot tell you if it *works*."

After finishing my iced tea, I thanked Mr. Leary and headed back to Pemkowet to meet Jen for lunch.

Callahan's Café is right downtown, but maybe because it's only a block and a half from the police station, it's always been more of a cop shop and local hangout than a tourist joint. It's plain and unpretentious, a diner rather than a bistro; the kind of place where you can always get a decent sloppy joe or tuna salad sandwich. My mom has her own business as a seamstress now, but she waitressed here for a lot of years when I was growing up, so it holds fond memories for me.

"Hey, Daise!" Jen, already seated in a booth, waved me over. I slid into the seat across from her. Her brown eyes were sparkling with curiosity. "What's the scoop? I'm dying! Were you out at Rainbow's End last night? What happened out there, anyway? The whole town's buzzing."

"Oh, yeah." I glanced around to make sure no one was in earshot, then leaned forward and lowered my voice. "I was there. And that's just the beginning."

I gave her the story. The *whole* story.

Jennifer Cassopolis and I have been best friends since high school, when her older sister, Bethany, took up with an insufferable vampire prat named Geoffrey Chancellor and I was the only person willing to go out to the House of Shadows with Jen to check on her. Eight years later, that situation's still unresolved, but at least we check in on Bethany often enough to know she's okay, or as okay as she can be under blood-thrall to a snotty vampire. Anyway, Jen and I are a good balance for each other. She grew up with a crappy home life: slutty older sister; abusive, alcoholic dad; battered mom; and a much younger brother she tries to protect.

Meanwhile, my mom's great. Growing up, we had a pretty good home life under the circumstances. Jen used to take refuge there a lot when she couldn't deal with her own situation. But then there's the Belphegor factor. Demon father is a pretty big trump card, especially since he totally took advantage of my mom's teenaged naïveté to knock her up when she accidentally summoned him with a Ouija board.

So, yeah, Jen and I balance each other pretty well. Since we've been friends, I've only kept one secret from her and that was my crush on Cody. Which, to be fair, I kept in part because he and the whole Fairfax clan are on the eldritch down-low. But it all came out earlier this summer, and the upshot of the matter is that I admitted my crush to Jen and outed Cody as a werewolf in the process. Which I should have done a lot earlier, since Jen's friendship is more important to me than the eldritch honor code, and I knew she'd keep Cody's secret.

So, okay.

What that all meant *now* was that the whole story included the part at the beginning where Cody and I were groping and making out like über-horny teenagers, as well as the evening's culmination in *bom-chicka-wow-wow* sex with Sinclair.

Jen stared at me. "Are you serious?"

"Uh-huh."

"Wow." She toyed with some leftover fries on her plate. We'd both ordered the daily special, Monte Cristo sandwiches. Yum. "You and Sinclair used a condom, I hope?"

"Yeah, of course!" Although I felt a little guilty thinking about all those orgiasts who hadn't.

"So what happens next, Daise?" Jen asked me. "I mean, how do you feel about it all today?"

"A little confused," I admitted. "Okay, a *lot* confused. I mean, I like Cody, and obviously he feels *something* for me. But it never would have happened if it hadn't been for the satyr. Cody's made it clear that he's looking for a mate and I'm the wrong species. I like Sinclair, too. I like him a lot. What happened with him was pretty awesome, too. And the whole idea of having an actual boyfriend . . . it's appealing, you know?"

"I know." She sounded sympathetic. "So . . . no temptation scenarios?"

"No." I shook my head. That was the term I'd coined for the times when my father, Belphegor, was able to whisper through the gaps in the Inviolate Wall, which was not exactly as inviolate as its name suggested, to promise me the wonders that would exist if only I claimed my birthright. "So maybe there are worse things in the world I could do than act like a normal, healthy twenty-four-year-old woman, right? Hey, that reminds me. Ever hear anything about a lawyer named Dufreyne?"

"No." Jen frowned. "Why?"

I told her about the guy in the PVB office.

"Huh." She propped her chin on one hand. "You know, now that you mention it, I have heard rumors about some out-of-town investor buying up lots around the river channel. You think this guy's representing him?"

"I bet."

Jen eyed me. "Sounds like he's got some kind of power of persuasion if he could actually get Amanda Brooks to consider it. She's always going on about the founding families and her heritage."

I thought so, too. And okay, my tail gave an envious little twitch. It kind of sucked to be a hell-spawn with no discernible benefits. But envy was one of the Seven Deadlies. I was already skating on thin ice with lust, and thanks to my mom's upbringing, I was committed to being one of the good guys, dammit.

"Yeah," I said. "But I talked her out of it—or at least I think I did." I made a devil-horns sign with my right hand. "Oh, and by the way? The hell-spawn lawyer dude? Stacey Brooks thinks he's hot."

Jen made a face. "She would. Did you warn her?"

I smiled. "Nope."

She laughed. "I wouldn't have, either."

# Eight

After getting off to a wild start, Labor Day weekend seemed to be settling into a more sedate pace, which was okay with me. Having had the chance to debrief with Jen, I felt more settled myself, no longer bursting at the seams with my news.

I called my mom to touch base, giving her an edited version of last night's events. Like everyone else in town, she was dying to know about the orgy.

"Oh, my goodness!" she exclaimed when I gave her the lowdown. "Well, that explains why Lurine isn't answering her phone today." She paused. "Are you sure she's all right?"

"Yeah." I smiled. "At last glance, I'd say she had the situation well in hand. Literally."

"Daisy!" Mom tried to sound scandalized, but I could tell she was laughing. "So no one was hurt? And you're okay?"

"I'm fine," I assured her. "No one was hurt."

I hoped it was true, anyway. Stefan had said he sensed no one had taken great harm from the experience. Which reminded me that in my capacity as Hel's liaison, I probably owed him a formal thank-you for his assistance last night.

If I thought about it for too long, I'd talk myself out of it, so instead I drove over to the Wheelhouse after I ended the call. Not that long ago—like, just earlier this summer—the Wheelhouse wasn't a place I'd have gone to alone. It's a biker bar and a ghoul hangout, and it's always had a dicey reputation.

But now it was Stefan Ludovic's headquarters, too.

Even so, I took *dauda-dagr* out of the hidden inner sheath in my messenger bag and belted it around my waist before I ventured into the Wheelhouse. The first time I'd walked into this bar, I'd been on an investigation with Cody and the atmosphere was markedly hostile. But that was before Stefan had successfully squashed a rebellion and consolidated his power over the Outcast in Pemkowet. It was also before I'd killed two ghouls: poor Emma Sudbury's deranged sister, Mary, and her . . . boyfriend, I guess, who I only ever knew as Ray D.

I hadn't been in here since.

It hadn't changed all that much. It was still a rough place where rough-looking guys in leather vests or jackets with Outcast motorcycle club colors gathered to shoot pool and drink beer, many of them with eyes that glittered a little too brightly in the dim light, watched by tired-looking mortal women who had histories of violence and hardship etched on their faces. But it *was* different. It felt different. Still dangerous, but somehow not quite as seedy, not quite as dissolute.

Huh.

"Hey, darlin'." The blond kid from last night peeled himself off the wall he'd been leaning against. He checked me out with an impudent look. If I hadn't known he was more than two hundred years old and had been hanged to death, it might have tickled me. "Here to see the big man himself, are you?"

"If he's free." I put out my hand. "Cooper, right?"

"Best you don't." He shoved his hands into the pockets of his jeans. He wore a chambray shirt with the sleeves cut off and his bare arms were thin and wiry. "Miss Daisy, right?"

"Right." I was having a hard time reconciling his age with his appearance. "So no leathers for you, huh?"

"Haven't passed the initiation yet." He looked me up and down again, pupils flaring briefly in his angelic blue eyes. "No disrespect, m'lady, but you're a wee mite to be carrying such a big dagger."

"Yeah, well." I laid my hand on *dauda-dagr*'s hilt. "You know what it can do, right?"

"Oh, I do!" Cooper flashed a grin that was at once charming and unnervingly fearless. "You're the angel of death in a feckin' ponytail. C'mon, I'll take you to see him."

I followed him to Stefan's office in the rear of the bar. Patrons moved out of the way with alacrity. Cooper may not have been initiated into the motorcycle club yet, but he'd obviously gained their respect. No one here showed any inclination to challenge Stefan's choice of lieutenant.

"Daisy." Stefan rose to greet me. He sounded surprised. "Is everything well? I thought the situation resolved."

"It is." The room seemed to get smaller as Cooper exited and closed the door behind him. Conscious of Stefan's gaze on me, I had a vivid and not entirely unwelcome memory of the hunger in it last night. Taking a deep breath, I suppressed it. "As Hel's liaison, I came to offer my official thanks for your assistance."

Stefan smiled.

It was a genuine smile, one that brought out the dimples he had no earthly right to possess. One that gave me a funny feeling in the pit of my stomach and made me wonder if that really was why I'd come here in the first place, and . . . oh, gah! What the hell was wrong with me, anyway?

"It was my pleasure, Hel's liaison," Stefan said. "I'm glad that you called upon me, and I hope you will not hesitate to do so again."

"I won't."

"Good." He sounded serious. "With practice, discipline, and will, the Outcast can become a force for order in this community, and learn to take sustenance in the process."

See, he had me right up until the bit about taking sustenance, which unfortunately reminded me that I'd let Stefan take sustenance from *me*, which meant he was attuned to my emotions, and . . . um, yeah. That outburst of lust I'd let loose last night that had blown one of the Mamma Jammers' amps? He'd probably sensed it. And maybe the *bom-chicka-wow-wow* that followed it.

My face got hot.

I don't know how Stefan followed my train of thought, but he did. Hell, it probably wasn't that hard. After all, he'd had centuries of practice. He smiled a little, but soberly, without dimples. "Your personal business is your own, Daisy," he said in a quiet voice. "It is as I have said. Your emotions are exceedingly powerful. If you desire my aid in expressing them without consequence, I will gladly give it to you. But the bond between us does not exist for the sake of prurience, and I am capable of deflecting my awareness at need."

Oh, my God, he totally knew. "Can it be broken?"

Stefan raised one eyebrow. "I assure you—"

"It's okay." I held up one hand—the left hand, letting him see the rune etched on my palm. "I believe you. But I have a right to know."

He hesitated. "Not that I'm aware of, no. Even if there were a way, I would be reluctant." He took a sharp breath, his pupils dilating in a rush. "Your position is not without its dangers, Daisy. It brings me a measure of comfort to know that if you are in distress, I will sense it."

The memory of Stefan coming to my rescue, sword in hand, rose in my mind. Unfortunately, it was accompanied by the memory of Stefan impaling himself on that same sword, dying, and being restored to wholeness.

"Did it leave a scar?" I asked him. He looked blankly at me. "The sword. The other month, when you . . ." I touched my chest with my fingertips.

"No." He shook his head. "No matter how many times we die, we remain as we were when we were first Outcast."

"Oh."

Stefan cleared his throat. "There is one method you may

employ to deflect your own emotions from my awareness, and indeed, the awareness of others among the Outcast. It is a temporary measure, and one that requires discipline and concentration, but I can teach it to you if you wish."

I thought about it. "Yeah. I'd like that."

I ended up staying for a while. As it turned out, Stefan's method was a lot like the creative visualization techniques my mom taught me when I was a kid, except instead of focusing on containing my emotions and getting rid of them—or wrapping them up to be dealt with later—it was about deflecting them. Stefan had me visualize a shield with an interior polished to mirror brightness and then hold it between us in my mind.

Sounds simple, right? Well, it wasn't.

For one thing, I'd never seen a shield in real life. All I had to work from was movies. God knows I'd seen enough of them, but still, it wasn't the same. Apparently, you had to be really precise about the details, and I kept waffling between one half-remembered vision—Perseus in *Clash of the Titans*, Captain America, Richard the Lionheart in various versions of *Robin Hood*—and another.

After an hour, Stefan gave up. "You've a good grasp of the concept, Daisy," he said to me. "You just need to articulate your vision."

"I know, I know." My head was aching with the effort. "I'll try looking online later. Or maybe the library has a good book on armor."

Again, there was a brief hesitation. "I may be able to procure something that would assist you. Allow me some time to . . . assess the matter."

That seemed a little unnecessarily cryptic, but then, that was par for the course among the eldritch. "Okay, thanks." My phone buzzed. Glancing down, I saw that it was a text from Sinclair, and also that it was later than I'd realized. "I should really be going."

"Of course." Stefan inclined his head to me. "Thank you for the courtesy of your visit. It is appreciated."

Cooper escorted me out of the bar, his hands shoved back into his pockets. Oddly enough, I felt safer in his pres-

ence than I did with any other ghoul except Stefan—and
maybe even than with Stefan, come to think of it, since
there was no risk of my being attracted to a skinny Irish kid
who looked six or seven years younger than me. But between the fact that he'd died daring God and the deference
with which the others treated him, I had a feeling he was
pretty badass in his own right, and given the care he was
taking not to touch me, I suspected he was rigorous about
enforcing Stefan's orders.

"How long have you known Stefan?" I asked him at the
door.

"Oh, a while." His narrow shoulders rose and fell in a
shrug. "Since the late eighteen hundreds, I reckon." He gave
me a challenging look. "He's a good one, you know. Most of
us aren't."

"Why is that?"

"Too easy to get bitter. It's hard to have a good relationship with the world when you're in it but not of it." Cooper's
mouth twisted. "It passes us by. Even a vamp can turn a
mate. All we can do is use 'em up and throw 'em away. Can't
even be with our own kind. *You* know how that goes."

I did. A romance between two ghouls, like the late Mary
and Ray, was doomed to set off a ravenous loop. "What
about other immortals?" I asked him.

He shot me an amused look. "Going to fix me up with a
nice dryad, are you? It's no good." He shook his head.
"They won't have us. Even if they did, it's human we were,
and it's human companionship we crave."

"I'm sorry." Without thinking, I put my hand on his arm.
Oops.

Cooper's pupils waxed alarmingly, sending a jolt of fear
through me. Licking his lips, he took a step backward, removed one hand from his pocket, and wagged a disapprov-
ing finger at me. "Don't go giving me a taste, Miss Daisy.
Not if you want you and me to be friends."

"Sorry!" I tried raising my imaginary shield. Nope, still
couldn't get it quite right. "I didn't mean to."

"I know." His pupils steadied anyway. "Go on, now. Mind
yourself."

Outside, the late-afternoon sun beating down on the parking lot intensified my headache. I got into the Honda, turned it on, and cranked up the air-conditioning before checking out Sinclair's text.

THINKING OF YOU! :)

It made me smile, but it also made me realize that I was no longer feeling settled. After an hour with Stefan Ludovic, I was feeling distinctly *un*settled. My poor aching head was roiling with shields and ghouls and gallows, satyrs and orgies and werewolves on the down-low, hell-spawn lawyers and sketchy land deals, island magic and African gods disguised as saints, shell games and pickpockets, pancakes and bacon and pissed-off fairies.

I called Sinclair.

"Hey, girl!" His voice sounded warm and cheerful. "Just getting ready for the last tour of the day." He lowered his voice. "Got any plans tonight?"

Okay, just hearing his voice made me feel more settled again. "No," I admitted. "But honestly, I don't feel great. I've got a killer headache."

There was a brief silence on the other end. "For real?" he asked. "Or are you freaking out on me, Daisy? Because you know, if anyone in this situation should be freaking out, it really should be me."

"*Are* you?"

Sinclair laughed. "Are you serious, sistah? Yeah, a little. But I still want to see you."

I smiled. "Me, too. But I really am beat. Is it okay if we take a step back today and start over where we left off tomorrow?"

"Regrets?" His tone was light, but there was a worried edge to it. "Or is it about what we talked about this morning?"

"No regrets," I said firmly. "And, um, I'd like to talk more about what we talked about this morning, but . . ." I remembered the Fabulous Casimir's warning. "But only if and when *you* feel like it. If you don't, you don't, and I'm good with that, too. Okay?"

"Hang on." In the background, I could hear the muffled

sound of Sinclair in his Jamaican accent directing a group of tourists to begin boarding the bus. I fidgeted with the air vents in the Honda. "Yeah, okay. You're sure?"

I nodded. "I'm sure. So, tomorrow?"

"Deal. But I want to take you out on the town," Sinclair warned me. "Dinner at a fancy restaurant, the whole nine yards. I want the full-on Labor Day weekend in Pemkowet experience."

I laughed. "Okay, but if you want the *real* Pemkowet experience, you've got to do the Bridge Walk with me on Monday morning."

"Seriously?"

"Seriously."

He sighed into the phone. "Okay, you've got it. So we're on for tomorrow night?"

My tail tingled, remembering his lingering touch at its base. I shifted in the driver's seat, wriggling a little. "Absolutely."

"Good. Look, I've got to go. Meet me for dinner at Lumière at seven o'clock tomorrow."

"Okay."

Sometimes it's good not to think too hard, especially after a day of thinking too hard. Putting the Honda in gear, I drove to the convenience store just down the road that still carried a certain brand of wine coolers. I think they may be the last store on earth to stock them, which they do for the sake of my mother, who may be the last person on earth to drink them. I bought a four-pack and drove out to Sedgewick Estate, the riverside mobile home community where I grew up. Mom still lives there. As of three years ago, she paid off the mortgage on her lot and so she owns her home outright now.

She's proud of that fact, as she ought to be. And I'm proud of her.

"Daisy baby!" My mom greeted me at the door of her double-wide with delight and a big hug. "I wasn't expecting to see you."

I hugged her back with one arm, holding up the four-pack of wine coolers with the other hand. "I'm sorry, I should have called. Is it okay? I brought libations."

"Libations!" Her blue eyes sparkled at me. "You must have visited Mr. Leary recently. Of course it's okay. Come in, come in. Let's go sit on the deck."

Mom's place was tidier than usual—she hadn't had a major commission since the Sweddon wedding last month—but there was still a hint of organized chaos about it. She rolled a rack of samples out of the way, and we trooped past it and out onto the deck, which overlooked a broad, marshy expanse of the river. We settled into a pair of Adirondack chairs that I remembered her salvaging and refinishing when I was in ninth grade, and cracked open a couple of wine coolers.

Despite having been the unwed teenaged mother of a hell-spawned half-breed, my mom's got a very calming presence. When Sinclair met her, he said she had a tranquil aura. It didn't surprise me. As we sat together in companionable silence, sipping our wine coolers and gazing at the river, I felt my headache dissipate.

"I would have thought you'd be out on the town tonight," Mom said after a while, stealing a glance at me.

I shook my head. "I needed a little escape. This is perfect, thanks."

She reached over to pat my hand. "Any time."

"Sinclair's taking me out to dinner tomorrow night," I admitted.

Mom gave a little sigh of relief. "Oh, good! I didn't want to pry. So things are still going well with the two of you?"

"Yeah, they are." I picked absently at the label on my bottle. "I mean, I *think* so. It's really too early to tell, right?"

She gave me a universal mom look, one of those looks mothers give their kids when they know there's something more going on. "Do you want me to read your cards?"

Okay, so that's not exactly a universal mom gambit, but she's got a knack with the cards. Which, by the way, aren't a traditional tarot deck. She taught herself to tell fortunes using a deck of *lotería* cards left over from a high school Spanish class, library books, and a system of symbolism that she invented on her own.

I kind of did, but at the same time, I kind of didn't. I already had enough going on in my head. "Not right now, thanks."

"Okay, honey." She used the universal mom tone for "I know there's something more going on and I've given you an opening to talk about it, but you're not ready yet. I'm here to listen when you are." It's pretty amazing how much moms can communicate by tone alone.

We went back to sitting in silence and watching the river together. I loved the way it was so vast and open here, sedge grass growing along the verges, and even a few poplars and one big willow tree where it was especially shallow. A slight breeze ruffled the surface of the water. There wasn't any hint of autumn in the air yet, but it was late enough in the summer that the evening sun hung lower on the horizon, slanted rays gilding the tops of the ripples. A flock of sand-hill cranes passed overhead, calling to one another in their wild, chuckling voices.

"Oh, Daisy!" Mom's voice was hushed. "Look, the willow's awake!"

Across the water, the great willow tree stirred, raising her graceful, trailing branches in salute, the dryad's delicate features emerging from the slender trunk. I held my breath as she swayed in the evening breeze. It was the first glimpse of magic I remembered from my childhood. Droplets of water fell from the leaves of her uplifted branches, sparkling in the sunlight.

And then the cranes passed into the horizon and the breeze died. The willow's branches sank back to droop gracefully into the water, the dryad's face vanishing once more beneath the bark.

I couldn't help but think of Cooper—not his remark about fixing him up with a nice dryad, but the bitterness in his voice when he said it was hard to have a good relationship with the world when you were in it but not of it.

And I thought that despite the fact that my life was far from perfect, I was very lucky to have it. Leaning over, I gave my mom a kiss on the cheek.

She smiled at me. "What's that for?"

I smiled back at her. "Just for being."

# Nine

Although I meant to make an early evening of it, I ended up staying at Mom's later than I had intended. We were on our second wine cooler when her neighbor Gus lumbered over to offer us a couple of the bratwursts he was grilling, which, by the way, I confirmed he hadn't made himself. Gus is an ogre, and while he hasn't eaten anyone in the last century, I have my suspicions regarding a few of the neighborhood cats and dogs over the years.

Anyway, the bratwursts were store-bought, so we invited Gus to join us on the deck, where he sat hunched to approximately the size and shape of a boulder-strewn hillock and gazed adoringly at my mom.

I think it's sweet that he has a crush on her, and aside from his latent appetite for human flesh, he seems to be a gentle soul.

Once the sun set, the mosquitoes began swarming. But by then it seemed a shame to go home *too* early, so Mom and I said good night to Gus and went inside to watch an episode of *Gilmore Girls*. Which, yes, I've seen half a dozen times, but if you're not familiar with it, it's about a single mom in a quirky little town raising a teenaged daughter she'd had out of wedlock when she was just a teenager herself, and it's cute and smart and funny, and since it originally aired when I was, like, twelve years old, it's always been our show. I bought Mom the first season on DVD with my first official paycheck.

Of course, one episode turned into two, then three, before I finally made it home to find an indignant Mogwai demanding that I refill his bowl.

"That's all there is," I told him, emptying the dregs of a bag of cat food. He flicked one notched ear in my direction. "Hey, it's not my fault if you struck out today and were forced to survive on kibble alone, mighty hunter."

Mogwai lifted his head from his dish long enough to give me a look of disdain.

"I'll go to the store in the morning," I promised.

Lying alone in bed, I let myself relive the memory of waking up this morning in Sinclair's bed with his arm over me, trying to decide how I felt about it. Short answer: I felt good.

So as I drifted off to sleep, I resolved that tomorrow I'd do something nice and distinctly girlfriend-like for him. Cookies. Yeah, cookies. He didn't know it yet, but I knew my way around the kitchen, too. I'd bake cookies for Sinclair.

It was a good idea, anyway.

The morning started out well enough. Since it was Sunday, I was technically off duty. I woke up in time to make a run to the grocery store, stocking up on cat food and baking supplies before the after-church hordes descended.

By noon, I had my wet and dry ingredients whisked, sifted, and separated and the late, great Katie Webster blasting some Swamp Boogie Queen blues on the stereo. My trusty electric hand mixer was plugged in and ready to go when my phone rang. It was a local number, but not one I'd programmed into the phone.

I lowered the volume on Katie. "Hello, you've reached Daisy Johanssen."

There was a lot of noise in the background on the other

end, too. "Hi? This is Mark Brennan at Bazooka Joe's. You asked me to call?"

My mind was a blank. "I did?"

"If those kids came back?"

Oh, crap. Right. I shifted my phone to a better angle. "The kids running the shell game? They're back?"

"Yeah, right here down on the dock," he said. "Got a pretty big crowd, too."

"Thanks," I said. "I appreciate it."

Okay, so the cookies would have to wait. On a hunch, I exchanged my cute but slippery-soled sandals for a pair of white Keds sneakers. If my suspicions were right, I might need speed and agility. For the sake of mobility, I would have preferred to wear *dauda-dagr* on my belt, but since I didn't want to spook the alleged kids, I went with the messenger bag instead, strapping it across my torso. Since I wasn't sure how well my face was known in the wider eldritch community yet, I added a pair of sunglasses.

Being an agent of Hel sometimes requires compromise. At least I looked enough like a tourist to pass.

Truth be told, I actually enjoy this part of my job. It's a game in a way; one that involves enough adrenaline to make it fun, but low enough stakes that I won't castigate myself if I lose a round. Although I do *like* to win. It's when things get serious, like they did earlier this summer, that it gets scary.

My apartment was a couple of blocks away from the docks. At a brisk walk, it only took me minutes to get there.

Sure enough, it appeared that a trio of kids was running a shell game. To the mundane eye, it was a charming affair. There was the hawker, who looked like a miniature version of a young Justin Bieber in an oversize baseball cap, sweeping bangs over his eyes, doing the whole "Ladies and gentlemen, step right up!" bit. And there was the operator, a solemn-looking towhead, kneeling on the dock over a piece of cardboard, his hands moving swiftly as he shuttled a dried pea among three empty walnut shells. Last was their bagman, a chubby-cheeked, freckled redhead holding twenty-dollar bills fanned like playing cards in one hand.

Norman-freaking-Rockwell would have been proud of these three.

I sidled through the crowd, ignoring a few protests. Blinking my eyes, I concentrated on seeing through the trio's glamour.

Hobgoblins, all three.

I have to say, it was obvious they were having great fun. Their feral nut-brown faces were contorted with gleeful malice, long, pointed noses drooping toward wide, grinning mouths filled with an erratic straggle of teeth. Sharp, bristly ears twitched with mirth and bright little hedgehog eyes gleamed with delight.

"You, sir, you look like a sharp-eyed gent!" the Bieber-goblin said encouragingly in a clear, piping voice, identifying a new mark. "Try your hand?"

A portly tourist in a polo shirt and Dockers cleared his throat. "I don't want to take advantage, son."

"Oh, it's all right, sir," the Bieber-goblin assured him. He laid one hand on the towhead's shoulder. "Nate here just needed to find his rhythm. He's got it now." He winked. "Right, Nate?"

The ostensible Nate returned his wink, hands moving more swiftly as he passed the pea from shell to shell. "Right you are, Tommy!"

Oh, gah! It worked, though. I watched the portly tourist pony up a twenty-dollar bill for his bet. The seemingly freckle-faced bagman made a big show of inserting the twenty into the array of bills he held fanned in his hand. The towheaded operator made a number of smooth passes with the pea and the walnut shells, just fast enough to be credible, just slow enough to be detectable. The portly mark was sharp-eyed enough to follow him. With a show of reluctance, the bagman plucked out two twenty-dollar bills and made good on the bet.

"Double or nothing, sir?" the Bieber-goblin asked.

And again, I had to admit, it was a pretty damn clever scam. It was a *reverse* shell game. The hobgoblins were paying out worthless fairy gold in exchange for cold, hard, mundane cash.

I almost hated to bust them.

Almost.

While the mark debated whether to go double or nothing, I pushed my way to the head of the crowd. Beneath my skirt, my tail swished back and forth in an involuntary stalking reflex. The Bieber-goblin's long nose twitched as he detected an eldritch presence in the gathered throng. His bright, beady eyes scanned the faces before him, pausing with uncertainty when he reached mine.

I held up my left hand palm outward, revealing Hel's rune. "Sorry, guys. You're busted."

"Scatter!" he shouted.

I lunged forward to grab him . . . and promptly went sprawling as someone clipped me hard behind the knees. Damn. Apparently, there was a fourth hobgoblin. I caught myself on my hands on the piece of cardboard they were using as a gaming table, which promptly slid out from under me, sending me to my belly. The air went out of my lungs with a *whoof* sound and my sunglasses clattered to the dock.

"Thanks!" The Bieber-goblin vaulted over me, stooping to snatch up my sunglasses with one gnarly, long-fingered hand. "I'll take these." Someone let out a startled shriek as he put them on his face. In the heat of the moment, he'd dropped his glamour. "Oops."

Spinning on the cardboard like an old-school break-dancer, I took him down with a leg sweep and pinned him to the dock. "Gotcha."

Behind me there was more shrieking and a loud, angry buzzing sound interspersed with oohs and ahs. I barely had time to wonder what the hell was going on before someone grabbed my ponytail and yanked it hard enough to make me yelp. The buzzing sound was right at my ear, vibrating the air like a hummingbird on steroids.

"Loose him, you churlish, ewe-necked trollop!" a voice shrilled. The Bieber-goblin squirmed out of my grip and broke into a run.

"Dammit, Jojo!" I scrambled to my feet. A dozen cameras went off as I confronted the hovering fairy. "I'm working!"

Jojo didn't even deign to reply, just gave an indignant sniff and winked out of sight.

"Aw, man!" one of the tourists complained, fiddling with his camera. "Why'd you have to scare her off, lady?"

My temper stirring, I gave him a look that shut him up, then scanned the area. Three of the four hobgoblins were nowhere to be seen. They couldn't vanish into thin air like fairies, but they were fast, and they could camouflage themselves as rocks or bushes in the blink of an eye. As long as they held still, it was hard to spot them.

Lucky for me, the bagman-goblin wasn't as speedy as the others; when the Bieber-goblin yelled scatter, he'd taken off down the dock, where there was nowhere to hide for a good hundred yards.

I raced after him, my Keds thudding against the wooden dock. Hearing my footsteps, the bagman-goblin turned on the jets. If I'd had a clear shot, I could have caught him, but there were tourists strolling along and that little bugger was agile. He scooted underneath a distinguished-looking Great Dane being walked on a leash and bounded over a baby stroller being pushed by a young couple.

I had to go around them, apologizing breathlessly. I *should* have caught up to the bagman-goblin in the park with the gazebo, but by the time I reached it, he'd gone to earth, hiding.

"Where are you, you little creep?" I looked around. "C'mon, I know you're here." A group of tourists gave me an odd look.

I ignored them. There was a hedge of boxwood around the base of the gazebo. And unless I was mistaken, that bit of shrubbery on the end was trembling. Squinting, I peered through the camouflage glamour to see the bagman-goblin trying very hard to hold perfectly still, his narrow chest heaving with exertion.

So lazy hobgoblins could get out of shape. Who knew? I tackled him before he could run again.

"Oof!" Lying on his back, he raised his hands in surrender. "Okay, okay! I give." He batted his beady, lashless eyes at me. "We were just having fun."

"I know." I plucked a crumpled wad of twenties from his clutches. "And I'm just doing my job."

"Spoilsport," the hobgoblin grumbled.

"Uh-huh." I sorted through the bills, separating the real ones from the fairy gold counterfeits.

"We'll give you half our take," he said in a wheedling voice.

"No can do." I dropped the false twenties on his chest, where they turned to dry, brittle oak leaves. "And I'd like my sunglasses back."

"Yeah?" The hobgoblin smirked. "Good luck with that."

I got off him and stood, patting my messenger bag. "You know, I could have drawn steel on you and I didn't."

A hint of fear crossed his face. "You wouldn't. Not for this."

"Don't push me," I said sternly. "You know you're not supposed to break mundane laws. Do you want me to report you to Hel?"

"Over a pair of cheap dollar-store sunglasses *I* didn't even take?" Now the hobgoblin sounded incredulous.

"No, you nitwit. For defrauding tourists. What's your name?" I asked him. He didn't answer. Reaching into my bag, I unsheathed a few inches of *dauda-dagr*, enough to let him see the hilt. "On pain of cold steel, what's your name?"

Although they've developed a higher tolerance in the last few centuries, most of the fey retain an aversion to iron and its alloys. They can be around it, but they can't bear its touch. "Tuggle," the hobgoblin said sullenly. "Name's Tuggle. You really going to tell her?"

There was no way in, well, hell, that I was going to bother the Norse goddess of the dead by reporting on a relatively harmless hobgoblin scam—and Hel has her own ways of keeping tabs on what's going on aboveground in the mundane world—but Tuggle didn't know that. I thought about forcing him to rat out his accomplices and decided against it. I was here to keep order, not make enemies. "We'll see," I said to him, easing *dauda-dagr* back into its hidden sheath. "Tell the others to consider this a warning. And I really would like those sunglasses back."

Tuggle shrugged. "I'll see what I can do."

"Thanks, Tuggle." I gave him a hand up, which he accepted. "No hard feelings?"

He shrugged again. "Eh."

"Hey, lady!" a concerned voice behind me called. "You okay?"

I turned around. "Fine. Why?"

It was a teenaged kid, maybe sixteen or seventeen, out wandering the town with his girlfriend. They were doing that thing where they had their arms wrapped around each other's waists and their hands in each other's back pockets. All the cool couples in high school used to stroll the halls that way. Of course, Jen and I had made fun of them, but secretly I was always a little envious of them. I'm pretty sure Jen was, too.

"It's just that you've been talking to that bush for a while," the kid said in an apologetic tone.

His girlfriend blinked. "Wait a minute. What bush?"

Apparently, Tuggle the hobgoblin was skilled at maintaining a glamour and had a knack for timing a getaway. Glancing behind me, I saw he'd made his escape, probably shifting back to his freckle-faced-kid guise when no one was looking.

Oh, well. At least I'd made my point.

"Welcome to Pemkowet," I said to the teenagers. "Where weird shit happens."

# Ten

I backtracked along the dock to see about refunding the actual money to the hobgoblins' marks, but the crowd had already dispersed. Unless the marks had checked their wallets, they probably didn't realize they'd been ripped off yet.

So I swung by the police station to log my time and fill out a report for the X-Files, leaving the money I'd retrieved in the desk clerk's keeping in case anyone came to claim it. At the risk of courting avarice, I hoped no one did. What can I say? Working irregular hours on a part-time basis, I was always short of cash. I'd collected two hundred and forty dollars from Tuggle, and if no one claimed it in three months, it was mine.

Upon returning to my apartment, I found my sunglasses placed neatly on the doorstep in the alley, each lens cracked into a perfect spiderweb. That's what you get for messing around with hobgoblins; and I'd taken it *easy* on them.

"Ha-ha," I said aloud to thin air. "Very funny." It got me more peculiar glances from a trio of middle-aged ladies passing by, their arms laden with shopping bags, but the rhododendrons lining the park rustled, sounding distinctly like a snicker.

Upstairs, I discovered that Mogwai had gotten up onto the kitchen counter. Based on the mess and the sticky paw-prints, he'd explored the bowl of wet ingredients before knocking the bowl of dry ingredients onto the kitchen floor and dashing in a panic out his escape hatch on the screened porch.

At least the chocolate chips were safe. I sighed, dumped the ingredients, and cleaned up the mess.

By the time I finished, the urge to bake was a distant memory. I spent the remainder of the afternoon with my battered old laptop, looking at images of shields online and practicing the visualization Stefan had tried to teach me. It probably didn't help that I took a break every ten minutes to trek into the kitchen for a handful of chocolate chips. And okay, yes, I also searched for information on obeah. There really wasn't a lot out there, at least not a lot that looked credible. I jotted down a couple of obscure out-of-print book titles I came across, resolving to pursue it later.

I gave up in time to freshen my makeup, change my clothes—a black linen sheath dress, my classic fallback—and meet Sinclair at Lumière at seven o'clock.

Since it was only a few blocks away, I walked. Sinclair was waiting for me on the sidewalk outside the restaurant, his touring bicycle chained to the wrought-iron fence that hemmed the patio.

Oh, crap. I was a *terrible* girlfriend. Sinclair's place was a couple miles north on the rural highway and he didn't have a car, just the tour bus and the bike, which he used for trans-portation when he wasn't working. Hence, those Tour de France–worthy thighs I mentioned earlier.

He smiled at me. "Hey, girl! There you are."

"I'm so sorry!" I said in dismay. "I should have picked you up—"

"Daisy—"

"I just wasn't thinking! You should have reminded—"

"Daisy!" Sinclair raised his voice. I shut up. He held out

a single red rose. "This is a date. A romantic date. No way I was going to let you drive. Okay?"

"Okay." I accepted the rose, hiding my face in it to conceal the fact that I was blushing a little. No one had ever given me a rose before. I peeked over it at Sinclair. He was wearing a fitted black T-shirt that showed off his torso, neatly creased khakis, and a pair of huarache sandals. Upscale casual. It looked good on him. "You look nice," I said. "Did you bike down here wearing that?"

"Nah." He grinned. "Spare clothes are in the saddlebag. I changed in the bathroom. You look great, too." He crooked his arm. "Ready, sistah?"

Although I don't have anything to compare it to, I'm pretty sure that as potentially awkward post-hookup dates go, this one was close to perfect. The hostess seated us on the patio near the gently splashing fountain. It was an intimate space, and the surrounding buildings blocked the light of the lowering sun, giving us a jump on candlelit ambience. The music of Édith Piaf was piped in at the exact right level to enhance the French bistro atmosphere without overpowering it.

From the first time we'd met, small talk had come easily to Sinclair and me. There was an affinity between us. Maybe it had something to do with the fact that we were both only children raised by single parents coming from adverse supernatural circumstances, although it's not like I'd known *that* until just the other day. Anyway, I was glad to find that the easy connection was still there, that the new level of physical intimacy between us just took it to a different, more charged level. We held hands atop the table and played footsy under it. We pored over the wine list and pooled our limited knowledge of French wines. We talked about favorite movies, an inexhaustible topic, over salad and bread. We exchanged stories about our respective days over salmon almondine (me) and coquilles St. Jacques (Sinclair), debating his prospects for running a scaled-back tour in the coming fall and winter months, the antics of vengeful hobgoblins, the depths of Jojo the joe-pye weed fairy's crush, and exactly who the hell St. Jacques was and what the hell he had to do with scallops.

I thought about asking Sinclair back to my place, which I hadn't done yet. This whole boyfriend–romantic date thing was awfully seductive. Based on the steady heat in his eyes, he was thinking about it, too.

But . . . yeah. There was a pretty big elephant on the patio with us. And every time I tried not to think about it, I did.

"It's killing you, isn't it?" Sinclair asked me over dessert. "Not asking about it."

I winced. "Is it that obvious?"

"Not really, no." He leaned back in his chair, cocking his head. "But I know you *just* well enough to be able to tell."

"Do you blame me?" I met his gaze.

"No." Sinclair gave me a rueful look. "I truly don't."

I looked down at the table, my spoon toying with the ramekin of chocolate mousse we were sharing. I know, you'd think I'd had enough of chocolate today, but you'd be wrong. "I guess it's just that I've been really up-front with you." I kept my voice low. "You, not so much."

"Look, Daisy." Reaching across the table, he took my hands in his, spoon handle and all. "For a long time I didn't have a choice in the matter. My father sent me back to my mother one month out of every summer. It was part of their . . . agreement. When I turned eighteen, I got to decide for myself. I haven't been back to the island since, even though . . ." He fell silent a moment. "Well, I haven't. I put it behind me."

"Things don't always stay where we put them," I said softly.

"No, I know." Sinclair squeezed my hands, his gaze earnest. "But can we leave it there for just this weekend? Let's enjoy tonight and tomorrow. Things in town are going to slow down after this, and we've got all fall and winter to talk about it."

My stomach did a flip-flop. He made it sound like he was in this for the long haul, which both delighted and, yeah, terrified me. "Promise?"

"Yeah." His strong thumbs rubbed the backs of my hands. "I promise."

"Okay." I took a deep breath. "Did you happen to pack a toothbrush along with a change of clothes?"

"Maybe." Sinclair smiled. "Does that question mean what I think it does?"

I glanced out toward the darkening street. "Well, I'd hate to think of you biking down the highway at night."

"Oh, I've got good lights on my bike," he said with a straight face. "Don't go to any worry on that account, girl."

"Fine." I withdrew my hands from his and folded them on the table. "Would you like to come over to my apartment?"

He grinned. "Love to."

After finishing dessert and paying the tab, we strolled slowly back to the apartment, Sinclair walking his bike alongside me. There were a lot of people out, and most of them smiled at us. Maybe a few of them recognized Sinclair from his tour, but mostly it seemed like they were smiling because we looked like a young, happy, attractive couple having a fun night out on the town. And okay, maybe we were too old to do the hands-in-each-other's-back-pockets thing, but I have to admit, for the first time in my life, I got what it felt like to be one of the cool couples.

Sinclair was right, I decided. It would be stupid not to enjoy the moment for what it was.

It felt strange to have him in my apartment, but a good kind of strange. The place was modestly furnished and decorated, but throughout my childhood my mom and I had gotten good at salvaging and rehabbing stuff from thrift stores, yard sales, and, yes, even Dumpsters, and I thought it looked pretty decent. After checking in vain for Mogwai, I gave Sinclair the tour—living room, kitchen, screened porch, bedroom, and bath—then left him to poke around while I found a bud vase for my rose and poured us each a few inches of single-malt scotch, my one mature indulgence.

In the living room, Sinclair was examining my music collection, the neat array of CDs I'd never gotten around to digitizing. "Thanks," he said absently when I handed him a glass. "So you really *do* like the blues, huh?"

I'd told him that on our first date. "Why would I make that up?"

"Yeah, well . . ." He looked amused and a little apologetic. "Chalk it up to shit white girls say to impress a brother. Which is funny, because I know fuck-all about the blues. But you've got quite a collection."

"Yeah." I took a sip of scotch. "It belonged to a guy my mom dated for a while. A jazz bass player. He left it to me."

"He took off?"

"No." I shook my head. "He was killed in a car accident. It's okay," I added, forestalling his sympathy. "I mean, it's not okay, but it was twelve years ago. He was a good guy. It turns out the blues calm me down, especially the female vocalists. He helped me figure it out."

"Must have been a good guy to recognize this would mean so much to a kid," Sinclair mused. "Play me something? One of your favorites?"

Feeling self-conscious, I fussed over my choice. Of course, now that he'd mentioned it, my immediate impulse was to pick something out of the pop culture mainstream, something like Ma Rainey's "Deep Moaning Blues," that would establish my blues credentials. But I didn't want to be that girl, and if Sinclair really knew fuck-all about the blues, there was no point, so I went with something obvious instead.

Strings swelled in a simple, familiar arrangement, paving the way for Etta James's effortlessly powerful vocals as she sang with impassioned tenderness about how her lonely days were over now that her love had come at last.

Okay, I really hadn't thought about the implications of the lyrics. Way to go, Daise.

"Ah . . . don't read too much into it," I said hurriedly. "It's a classic, that's all. You know, she just passed away a couple of years ago. Etta James, that is."

"Daisy." Sinclair set down his glass on a bookshelf. "It's okay. It's just a song."

Out of habit, I tucked my tail between my legs, clamping it tight as his hands curved around my waist and pulled me close to him, just like I'd done at every high school dance

I'd attended, at every nightclub I'd ever danced in. And it may seem like a small, silly thing, but it was a moment of pure bliss to realize I didn't have to.

I unfurled my tail and slid my arms around Sinclair's neck, gazing up at him as we swayed slowly together. He lowered his head to kiss me, tasting of scotch tinged with a faint hint of chocolate, while Etta sang in the background.

Hands down, most romantic evening *ever*. Way better than a funky satyr booty call. Although that had had its merits, too. Just thinking about it, I felt my temperature rise a few degrees. But this time I wasn't going to be the one to make the first move. I'd wait for Sinclair to do it.

I didn't have to wait long.

The song ended, and Sinclair tilted his head toward the bedroom with an inquiring look. "Shall we adjourn?"

I smiled up at him. "Love to."

# Eleven

"**W**hat the *holy hell*?"

"What?" Jolted awake, I sat upright, looking frantically for my phone, or *dauda-dagr*, or . . . I don't know what. "What?"

"This . . . thing!" Sinclair was lying flat on his back beside me with Mogwai perched high on his chest, paws neatly tucked, purring contentedly as he gazed down at Sinclair with slitted eyes.

I laughed out loud. "I told you I had a cat!"

"That's a *cat*?" He took a sharp breath, Mogwai rising obliviously with his chest. "More like a duppy."

"A what?"

"Nothing." He let out his breath in a sigh. "S'okay. Is he your familiar or something?"

I lifted Mogwai off Sinclair's chest and set him on the bed between us. It was true that he was a pretty big cat, eighteen pounds and none of it fat, and according to the vet, male calicoes were a genetic rarity. Other than that, he seemed pretty normal. "Something, I guess. He likes you."

"Good thing." He eyed Mogwai, then reached out to

give him a tentative scratch under the chin. "You startled me, bwai! Give me a chance to get to know you, eh?"

Glancing toward my bedroom window, I saw sunlight. All right, I had a sexy naked guy in my bed, but it was Labor Day in Pemkowet and I had an agenda. "Okay, here's the plan. I'm going to make coffee, then run down to Mrs. Browne's for a couple of cinnamon rolls. If you want to shower before we do the Bridge Walk, now's your chance."

Sinclair stretched, slow and leisurely, giving me a significant look. "Bet I've got a couple of hours before my first tour. You *sure* about this Bridge Walk?"

Um . . . no?

"Yes," I said sternly. "You said you wanted the full-on experience, and this is a proud local tradition." I poked him. "You're not backing out on me, are you?"

He gave a good-natured laugh. "Nah."

"Good."

Forty minutes later, we were on our way, clean and fed and caffeinated. I'd offered to drive, but Sinclair wanted to bike home to pick up the tour bus, so after some debate I wound up riding perched on his bike seat while he stood on the pedals—which, I have to say, afforded me a nice view of his butt.

Okay, so the annual Labor Day Pemkowet Bridge Walk is sort of an elaborate joke. It was inspired by the annual Labor Day Mackinac Bridge Walk, which has been going on for, like, more than fifty years, and isn't a joke. A little background for non-Michiganders: The Mackinac Bridge spans the straits between the upper and lower peninsulas—peninsulae? Mr. Leary would know—and at about five miles long, it's one of the longest suspension bridges in the world. Thousands of people do the Bridge Walk every year. It takes a couple of hours to make it across, after which you receive a certificate.

The bridge between Pemkowet and East Pemkowet is exactly zero point one nine miles long, and it takes about five minutes to walk it . . . after which you receive a certificate and an invitation to a pancake breakfast at the Masonic Lodge.

See, the thing is, it's not just the eldritch community that makes Pemkowet a place where weird shit happens. It's the people, the mundane people, too.

For example, we have a town crier. You know, the guy who shows up in a long wig and a frock coat, ringing a bell and doing the whole "Hear ye, hear ye!" thing. It's not a paid or elected position or anything. There's just a guy who does it.

And yep, there was the town crier, surrounded by a bunch of other people in period attire. Except for some prominent tattoos, they looked like they'd walked out of the nearest Renaissance faire. There were ladies from the Red Hat Society, people walking dogs, people pushing kids in strollers, people towing kids in little red wagons.

Sinclair was laughing. "This is crazy!"

I smiled. "Yeah, I know."

Oh, and there was Stacey Brooks taking publicity photos for the PVB. I smiled even wider and gave her an obnoxious little finger wave, watching her scowl in reply and fight the urge to flash devil horns at me in public.

We lined up behind the wooden barricade, milling and chatting. Glancing over at the squad car that blocked the west end of the bridge, I saw Bart Mallick was on duty. Since I hadn't been one of his favorite people before the whole Rainbow's End incident, I didn't bother to greet him, but I ran into my mom's friend Sandra Sweddon, there with her daughter Terri, who was now Terri Dalton, and made a point of introducing Sinclair to them.

At nine o'clock, the town crier issued a proclamation announcing the start of the annual Pemkowet Bridge Walk. Everyone streamed around or over the barricade. About twenty yards in there was a guy holding a sign reading THE FAINT OF HEART SHOULD TURN BACK NOW!

"You know this is absurd, right?" Sinclair asked, walking his bike beside me.

"Uh-huh. Aren't you glad you didn't miss it?"

"Yeah," he admitted.

At the halfway point, just under one tenth of a mile, the Pemkowet Historical Society had set up a refreshment station with Dixie cups of Gatorade. I took one for tradition's sake, even though I think the stuff's vile.

"Hey." Sinclair downed his Gatorade and tossed the cup in the trash. He patted the handlebars of his bike. "Hop up. I'll ride you the rest of the way."

I gave him a dubious look. "You sure about that?"

Straddling his bike, he balanced on the pedals, making it stand upright and motionless, then went a few inches forward and backward before returning to perfect stillness. "Sure. C'mon, hop up."

"Oh, fine."

Yes, it was totally showing off, but you know what? It was fun. Sinclair rode as slowly as possible to keep pace with the walkers, weaving only a little with the added weight of me on the handlebars. The sun was shining and a slight breeze ruffled the surface of the river. It was a holiday and it felt like it.

"Did you really like that Etta James song I played for you?" I asked Sinclair over my shoulder.

"Yeah, I did."

"We should go to the Bide-a-Wee Tavern tonight," I said. "They have live jazz and blues, and there's always a big bash for the end of the season. It's mostly locals, too, since a lot of summer people and tourists leave this afternoon."

"Sounds great." The bike wobbled slightly. "Oops."

"You're sure?" I glanced back at him again. "I mean, we didn't have plans or anything."

"Hey, I made you sit through the Mamma Jammers. It's only fair," he said, then laughed at the expression on my face. "I'm kidding! It sounds like fun."

"Okay. Call me when you get home, and I'll pick you up."

"Deal."

We made it across the bridge. I hopped down from the handlebars, and Sinclair and I received our official certificates, Xeroxed copies of a form signed by the mayors of both Pemkowet and East Pemkowet.

"I'll cherish it forever," Sinclair teased me, stuffing his in the saddlebags of his bike. "Maybe I'll start a scrapbook."

"You do that." I was distracted by the sight of Cody Fairfax standing beside a squad car at the east end of the bridge, where a line of vehicles was waiting for the barricade to be lifted. The sunlight brought out goldish glints in his bronze hair. My stomach tightened a bit. Cody didn't usually work day shifts, but Chief Bryant liked to schedule an additional officer on duty during the holidays and Cody tried to pick up an extra shift around the full moon to compensate for lost time.

He was talking to a young woman in an impeccably tailored off-white linen business-casual suit, a short jacket nipped in at the waist, a hint of flare to the pant legs. Hey, as my mother's daughter, I notice these things. Under the jacket she wore a silk camisole in a vivid hue of yellow that contrasted perfectly with her rich cocoa-brown skin—it was one of those colors I could never wear without looking jaundiced.

She had short, almost shorn hair that clung to her skull, and high, rounded cheekbones. She looked familiar, and I'm embarrassed to say that for one fleeting moment as I tried to place her, I thought she looked like a contestant I remembered from one of the earlier seasons of *America's Next Top Model*.

Annnd . . . then I realized that Sinclair had gone stockstill beside me, and the reason she looked familiar is that she looked a hell of a freaking lot like *him*.

As though he'd called her name, she glanced over at him. Something intangible passed between them, and then her face broke into a wide, bright smile. "Sinny!"

*Sinny?*

"Emmy," he murmured half under his breath, and I realized that although we'd spent the past night and day playing boyfriend and girlfriend, I definitely didn't know him well enough to read his reaction. That was pretty well confirmed when he walked away from me and toward her without another word.

Not knowing what else to do, I hung back.

Cody ambled over, a studiedly neutral look on his face. "Looks like your boyfriend's sister's in town."

Sister, huh? "Looks like it," I agreed.

"Must be a surprise visit," Cody said. "She was asking directions to the tour bus pickup stop."

"What a nice surprise." Damned if I was going to give anything away to Officer Down-low. If he didn't want to be a part of my personal life, he didn't have the right to pry into it.

Unfortunately, Cody and I had put in a lot of hours working closely together on the Vanderhei case earlier this summer, and he *did* know me well enough to read my reaction. His amber eyes narrowed. "You didn't even know he had a sister, did you?"

At that moment, Sinclair beckoned me over, sparing me the necessity of a response. "Daisy, I'd like you to meet my sister." Talk about neutral—the tone of his voice was the epitome of neutral. It was neutral raised to the nth power of neutrality. "Daisy Johanssen, Emmeline Palmer."

"His *twin* sister," Emmeline corrected him with a smile before greeting me with an airy European double-cheek kiss that I was totally unprepared for. "Hullo, Daisy. Lovely to meet you."

I'm not sure what threw me for the biggest loop—the cheek kisses, the twin sister revelation, or the fact that Emmeline appeared to have a British accent overlaying her musical Caribbean lilt. Maybe it was that faint tingle of otherness I got from her, suggesting that both of the Right Honorable Mama Palmer's babies had a touch of an eldritch gift. Or maybe it was the fact that she looked like she'd just stepped out of the pages of *Vogue*, while I was wearing an old floral-print sundress that suddenly made me feel all of sixteen years old, which is about what I'd been acting.

Or maybe it was that Sinclair *hadn't bothered to freaking mention that he* had *a twin sister, who was standing right in front of me*!

Those were the thoughts that went flashing through my head while I stood blinking like an idiot, finally managing to stammer out, "Nice to meet you, too."

Emmeline gave me a sympathetic just-between-us-girls wink before turning to Sinclair. "Right, so I'll go find that coffee shop and meet you at the tour bus in a few." She glanced back toward the line of parked cars. "Looks like we're about to get going. Daisy, I'll see you later?"

"Um . . . sure?"

Sinclair and I got out of the way as Cody pushed the barricade aside and traffic began to move across the bridge. All I could do was stare blankly at him.

"Look." He raised both his hands, palms outward. "Daisy, I'm sorry. I had no idea."

"You had no idea *you had a twin sister*?"

"No idea she was coming." He sounded tired.

My tail began lashing back and forth in agitation. "Oh, and where exactly did Emmy pop in from, Sinny dear? Did she drive up from Kalamazoo? Because I don't recall you mentioning a sister. And it sounded a lot like jolly old England, which I don't recall you mentioning, either. Is that something else you put behind you? Or maybe putting on accents is a thing with the Palmer clan. Pip-pip, cheerio—"

"Kingston!" Raising his voice, Sinclair cut me off. "She flew in from Kingston, all right?" He ran one hand over his dreadlocks. "And the accent's not phony. I grew up in Kalamazoo. Emmy grew up in boarding schools overseas." He gave me a faint, wry smile. "She took her law degree at the University of Oxford a year ago."

"Oh." My tail went still.

"Just . . ." Sinclair sighed. "Look, I meant what I said last night. I just really wasn't expecting this." Reaching out, he took my hands. "It's complicated. I'll explain it when I can, but right now I'm not even sure why Emmeline's here." His dark eyes were clear and steady. "Can I count on you to have my back?"

I softened, my temper subsiding. "Yeah, okay. Fine."

"Thanks, Daisy." He gave me a quick kiss before glancing at his watch. "I've got to run. I'll give you a call later, okay?"

"Okay."

Leaning against the guardrail at the entrance into town, I watched Sinclair pedal with swift determination along the shoulder of the highway. Cody pulled the squad car up before me and leaned over toward the passenger door. "Can I give you a lift, Daise?"

I scowled at him. "No."

"You sure?" he asked mildly. "I'm headed back to the station."

"Oh, fine."

We rode in silence, but it was a comfortable silence. Funny how that works when you've spent a lot of time together.

Cody parked in one of the station's reserved spaces. He gave me a sidelong glance, a reflective film of green shimmering behind his amber eyes. "Just so you know, I'm not sure about that guy. There's something sketchy about him. And I *will* kick his ass seven ways till Sunday if he hurts you."

I nodded. "Duly noted. But Sinclair's a good guy, Cody. Sometimes people hurt each other anyway. If it happens, it won't be on purpose."

His lip curled, baring his eyeteeth. Yep, definitely getting close to the full moon. "Doesn't matter."

"Yeah," I said to Cody, who had hurt me without meaning to. "It does." I got out of the squad car. "Thanks for the ride."

# Twelve

Jojo the joe-pye weed fairy was lying in wait for me outside my apartment, bursting out of the rhododendrons in a cloud of sparkling pollen, slingshot at the ready.

"Jesus!" Startled, I jumped and threw up my hands in a defensive pose. "Are you trying to give me a heart attack?"

"I saw what passed atop the bridge. What new slattern ventures onto the stage?" Her tiny face was set in a fierce expression. "Speak, you ruttish, whey-faced scullion!" A handful of tourists passing through the park exclaimed with delight. I'm pretty sure they'd missed Jojo's actual commentary.

"Oh, for God's sake!" I glared back at her. "She's his sister, you, you . . . dew-swilling nitwit."

Jojo paused, hovering. "I knew not he had a sister."

"Yeah, neither did I." Out of the corner of my eye, I caught sight of Mogwai stalking toward her under the rhodos. Damned if I was going to warn her. "And I don't know what she's up to. If you want to find out, I suggest you go spy on *her*."

Something in my face must have given the game away a split second before Mogwai pounced, because Jojo glanced sideways, then shot two feet higher in a blur of translucent wings and fairy dust. Showing a mouthful of needle-sharp teeth, she hissed at him. Not the slightest bit fazed, Mogwai hissed right back at her.

Now the tourists looked uneasy. "Mouth closed, Jojo," I reminded her.

The fairy shut her mouth with a tiny but audible snap before winking out of sight. Good riddance.

Upstairs, I showered Mogwai with praise and opened a can of tuna as a special treat, then went to stare disconsolately into my closet. You'd think a seamstress's daughter would have a stellar wardrobe, but the truth is that I went through a bit of a rebellious stage in my teens—I know, surprise, right?—followed by a conscientious phase where I wouldn't let my mom waste time and effort on me that could be spent on paying clients. As a result, other than a few simple classics like the dress I'd worn last night, my wardrobe could really use an update.

In light of the arrival of Sinclair's stylish sister, maybe it was time to take Mom up on her offer. At least I could afford to pay for materials now. Probably.

I was still contemplating the idea when my phone rang.

"Hey, cupcake!" Lurine greeted me, sounding languid and pleased with herself. "Sorry it took me so long to get back to you."

"No problem." I shifted the phone under my ear. "You warned me. Is everything okay?"

"Oh, sure. What's up?"

After the scene at Rainbow's End, I needed a little more concrete assurance. "So he . . . I mean, the satyr . . . isn't in rut anymore?"

"Nico? No, he's fine for now. It's run its course."

So the satyr had a name. Who knew? "Good, that's great. I was hoping you might have some advice on making sure it never happens again."

"Well, of course it's going to happen again," Lurine said mildly. "He's a satyr. You can't fight nature, honey."

"Um . . . yeah. I mean the part where it sets off an orgy," I said. "A human, public-health-hazard-type orgy."

"Oh, right." There was the sound of a champagne cork popping in the background. "Are you okay, Daisy? You sound a little distracted."

"I'm fine. Do you have any suggestions?"

"Mmm." Lurine wasn't buying my dismissal. "You're not working today, are you?"

"No," I admitted. "Not unless I get called in on a case."

"Well, then, here's a suggestion for you. Why don't you put on your bikini and get your cute little behind over here? It's a perfect day to lay out by the pool and discuss orgy prevention. Oh, and stop on your way and pick up some peach nectar, will you?" Lurine added. "Tell Edgerton I feel like Bellinis."

She hung up before I could answer, which annoyed me for a second or two before I realized that I really couldn't imagine a better way to spend this particular day.

Lurine lived in a mansion on the lakeshore. The property came with lakefront access, but it was situated inland, nestled in the woods for maximum privacy. It was big and ostentatious and new, and a very far cry from the mobile home in Sedgewick Estate where Lurine Hollister née Clemmons had been my neighbor and babysitter when I was growing up.

Honestly, I can't say the fabulously wealthy B-movie starlet and infamous widow Lurine Hollister was any happier or more content than simple, small-town bombshell Lurine Clemmons had been, or vice versa. They were just masks to her, and I don't know that she preferred one to the other.

She probably had more *fun* being the notorious Lurine Hollister, but it was as Lurine Clemmons that she'd forged a genuine friendship with my mom and me, and over the course of this summer I'd come to realize that it meant a great deal to her, because it didn't happen often to an immortal monster like her.

All credit goes to my mom on that score. Apparently raising a hell-spawn baby gives you a special knack for caring about monsters. Oh, and to put it up front, Lurine has made generous offers of financial support to both of us.

Mom's always been adamant about refusing, and I don't want to undermine her decision on this.

At any rate, Lurine's butler buzzed me through the gated drive and greeted me at the door. "Ms. Hollister is expecting you."

"Great." I handed him the jar of peach nectar I'd purchased on my way. "She said she wants Bellinis."

He inclined his head. "Of course."

Lurine was lolling in a lounge chair beside the pool in a gold lamé bikini and sunglasses, looking every inch the Hollywood movie starlet. "Hey, sweetie!" Reaching over, she patted the lounge chair nearest her. "Grab a towel and come soak up some sunshine."

Realizing that she wasn't alone, I hesitated. Nico the satyr was diligently wielding a long-handled pool skimmer, clad in a pair of loose-fitting board shorts with a sizable hole cut out to accommodate his flowing horse's tail.

"What?" Lurine followed my gaze. "Oh, it's fine. Don't worry, he'll behave himself now. Won't you, Nicodemus?"

The satyr gave her a surprisingly sweet smile. "Yes, *kyria*."

I have to admit I still felt a bit self-conscious stripping down to my bathing suit with the memory of Nico's ginormous schlong bobbing in the air—not to mention my own response, along with everyone else's, to his funky satyr pheromones—but true to his word, he ignored me, concentrating on his task. I took a neatly folded towel from the cupboard beneath a pergola that looked like something from the set of a Pottery Barn photo shoot and went to join Lurine, who lifted a mostly empty champagne bottle from an ice bucket beside her and regarded it with a critical eye.

"Nico!" she called. "Go see if Mr. Edgerton's got the Bellinis ready, will you?"

"Yes, *kyria*." Setting down the pool skimmer, the satyr trotted toward the French doors, his tail swishing amicably.

"So . . . you're keeping him?" I asked Lurine. That didn't sound right, but I wasn't sure how else to phrase it.

"Oh, for a while. He doesn't know anyone else in the area."

"How did he end up here?"

Lurine shrugged. "Most places with a functioning under-world tend to be pretty metropolitan these days. Cities built atop the ruins of cities. He heard that Pemkowet's a better fit for pastoral types and decided to check it out."

"Nice timing," I said sardonically. "Jesus, I didn't even think he could *talk* the other night."

"Oh, he couldn't," she said without irony. "Satyrs in rut revert to a preverbal state. But don't worry, it only happens every twelve years."

"Really?"

"Immortals live long lives, cupcake. And it's not like sa-tyrs are impotent between their cycles." Her lips curved in a smile. "They're just not hyper-potent."

The satyr returned, balancing a tray with two champagne glasses filled with sparkling wine and peach nectar. After delivering them, he went back to skimming the pool. I sipped my Bellini thoughtfully, watching him. "So I don't have to worry about Nico going into rut for another twelve years?"

"Right."

"But I need to be prepared for it," I said. "I mean, assum-ing he stays and Hel doesn't fire me for not knowing what the, um, hell I'm doing half the time. Which means I need to keep track of his cycle." I glanced over at Lurine. "Do you think he's staying? Does he like it here?"

"Well, he's not thrilled that I made him put on shorts," she said. "But that was just for your sake."

"Thanks," I said. "I appreciate it. But that's not what I meant."

"I know." Lurine gave me an amused look. "Yes, he likes it here. I don't know if he's staying. But if I were you, I'd err on the side of caution and assume so. And I'd assume there may be others that will follow."

I thought about that, and about the warning I'd given Tuggle the hobgoblin, and the myriad other instances where members of the eldritch community had violated mundane laws. Sure, there were reports in the X-Files, but that wasn't exactly what I needed. "You know what I should do?" I said, thinking aloud. "I should create a central database with information on the entire eldritch population of Pemkowet, or at least as much as I can gather." Lurine sipped her Bellini without comment and I began to second-guess myself. "You don't think it's a good idea?"

"No." She took off her sunglasses. "I do, actually. It's just a measure of how quickly the world is changing, and how much it has changed in the past century." She smiled again, but it was a wistful smile. "I've been the subject of myths, legends, and poems. I've never been an entry in a database."

"I didn't mean *you*!" I said quickly.

Lurine cocked her head at me, and I fell silent. Of course it would have to contain an entry on Lurine, and Cody, too, and all the rest of his clan, including his two rambunctious nephews. Stefan and all his ghouls. And Mrs. Browne from the bakery, and Gus the ogre, and any other members of the eldritch community I considered friends. Me, too, for that matter.

"Maybe it's a bad idea," I said.

"No," Lurine said quietly. "It's not. It's an idea of its time, that's all. It would help you do the job Hel appointed you to. And that's important, Daisy. All of this . . ." She made a gesture that somehow included not only the mansion and the surrounding trees, the satyr skimming the pool, and Lake Michigan in the distance, but all of Pemkowet. "It's a lot more fragile than it looks."

"I know," I murmured. Things had gotten ugly with the Vanderhei case earlier this summer, reminding me just how delicate a balance existed between the eldritch and the mundane, and how the latter far, far outnumbered the former.

"So!" Lurine tilted her champagne glass and drained the remainder of her Bellini. "Problem solved. No more unplanned rutting satyr orgies. Henceforth, they will be anticipated, and appropriate safety precautions will be taken to protect the mundanes." A mischievous sparkle returned to her blue eyes. "Now I'm going for a swim, and you're going to tell me what's *really* bothering you."

I made a noncommittal noise. Ignoring me, Lurine rose and stripped off her bikini before diving into the pool.

The shift into her true form was spectacular and instantaneous. It would probably look incredibly cool in slow-motion photography, but in real time it flowed so swiftly that the naked eye couldn't quite follow it. Lurine's human figure cleaved the water and before the ripples could begin to spread, the lamia's undulating coils filled the pool, shimmering blue and green in the sunlit water, crimson spots scintillating. She swam the length of the pool and back underwater, diving below and above the serpentine coils of her own lower half in a complex, intertwining ballet.

If you're thinking it would be one of the most beautiful, surreal, and terrifying sights ever, you'd pretty much be right.

Lurine surfaced at the far end of the pool, water streaming over her bare shoulders. Her tail snaked out with nonchalant grace to snag an inflatable lounge chair and drag it into the pool. Nico the satyr watched with obvious approval, the front of his board shorts stirring visibly. "Hmm." She eyed him. "Nicodemus, why don't you get us fresh Bellinis and go prune some trees."

"Yes, *kyria*." He sounded downcast, but he went.

"Now—" Slinging her arms along the edge of the pool, Lurine flicked her tail toward me, lightning-quick. I barely had time to yelp in surprise before her slick, muscular coils wrapped around my waist, plucking me from my poolside lounge chair and depositing me unceremoniously atop its floating equivalent, where I floundered in an effort to get my balance. At least it gave me the chance to conceal the disconcerting effect Lurine's stunt had on me—not that she didn't know anyway. "What's on your mind, baby girl?"

Two months ago, I'd poured out a tale of woe regarding my crush on Cody and his possible interest in my best friend, Jen. Now, feeling more than a little silly, I updated Lurine on the latest regarding Sinclair.

"A secret twin sister!" she said with relish when I finished. "That's straight out of a soap opera."

I smiled reluctantly. "I know. So what do you think?"

Lurine reclined against the wall of the pool, her coils stirring absently, creating eddies. My floating chaise rocked atop them. "You like him?"

I nodded. "I like him. Hell, Mogwai likes him."

"You could pick a worse judge of character than your cat," she said in a pragmatic voice. "Cut the young man a little slack, Daisy. You're only just getting to know each other. People are allowed to have secrets."

"Secret *twins*?"

"Well, it does happen all the time in soap operas." Lurine poked my floatie with the tip of her tail, sending me drifting a bit. "The thing is, cupcake, Sinclair might have told you all about his sister tomorrow. But you'll never know, because he never got the chance, which is why I think you should cut him some slack."

"What about the whole obeah thing?" I asked.

She shook her head. "Not my area of expertise."

"Does it even work? I mean, how can it?" I was thinking aloud again. "There's no underworld in Jamaica, is there?"

"Oh, that." A loop of iridescent coil rose to halt my drift. "Islands have their own rules, especially if they're blood-soaked."

"Ew."

Lurine shrugged. "Where there's blood and death in abundance, there's necromancy. And islands are circumscribed by salt water. It concentrates the effect."

"Well, technically all land is circumscribed by salt water, isn't it?" I said. "I mean, oceans cover something like seventy percent of the earth's surface, right?"

"Aren't you the smarty-pants!" A submerged segment of Lurine's tail gave the underside of my floatie an affectionate bump. "It has to do with scale, Daisy. I'm sure there's some sort of formula," she added idly. "Gallons of blood spilled per acre. The gods only know, there was blood and death aplenty throughout the entire West Indies during the centuries when the slave trade was flourishing."

I shivered in the bright sunlight. "Okay. Enough said."

"You asked," Lurine reminded me in a mild tone.

"I did," I agreed.

Pushing away from the edge, she sank beneath the water to swim the length of the pool and back again. Ensconced in my floating chaise, I rode out the surging waves generated by Lurine's passage, gazing at the green treetops silhouetted against the bright blue sky and thinking about the terrible fragility of life.

# Thirteen

Somewhat to my surprise, Sinclair wanted to keep our date to go to the Bide-a-Wee Tavern that night. The only difference was that his sister would be joining us.

"You're sure?" I asked him on the phone.

"Positive," he assured me. "Emmy's looking forward to it. It will give you the chance to get to know each other."

"Does she . . . know about me?" There's really no delicate way to ask, oh, by the way, does your until-recently-secret twin sister know you're dating a hell-spawn?

There was a pause. "Emmy's like me," he said. "She sees auras. I didn't want to lie to her. We actually had a good talk today."

According to Sinclair, most people's auras were just little shimmers flickering around the edges of their bodies, while mine was a five-alarm fire shot through with veins of gold. If my memory was correct, Emmeline hadn't shown any sign of surprise at it.

Interesting.

"Daisy?" Sinclair asked. "Are we okay?"

"Yeah, of course," I said. "I wouldn't want you to lie to

her, either. And I guess she had to find out sooner or later. Did she freak?"

"She's curious," he admitted. "I wouldn't say freaked. But, um, it wouldn't hurt for you to keep a lid on—"

"Yeah, yeah." I cut him off. "I'll try to make a good first impression. Not like I did with the Mamma Jammers. No funky satyr booty calls, I promise."

He gave a deep, rich chuckle that made my spine tingle and my tail twitch. "Just between you and me? I kind of liked the funky satyr booty call."

I smiled. "Pick you up at seven?"

"Why don't we pick you up?" Sinclair suggested. "Emmy's got a rental."

As it transpired, not only did Emmy have a rental car—Emmy had a brand-spanking-new rental convertible that was much, much nicer than my poor ten-year-old Honda Civic. At seven o'clock sharp, she and Sinclair pulled into the alley between my apartment building and the park to pick me up. Oh, and it was also a stick shift, which she drove with reckless aplomb.

I sat in the backseat, my blond hair whipping wildly around my head in the backwash of wind.

"Are you quite all right, Daisy?" Emmeline's eyes met mine in the rearview mirror, concern in her gaze. Her close-cropped hair was unaffected. "Shall I put the top up?"

I rummaged in my bag for an elastic band and dragged my hair back into a ruthless ponytail. "Not on my account."

Sinclair inhaled deeply. "It still smells like summer."

I poked him in the back of the head. His short dreads were tight yet supple, stirring in the wind. Once a week, he treated them with an organic product containing essential oils, and I always knew because it smelled a lot like fresh rosemary. "I think that's your salon treatment you're smelling."

Reaching behind himself, he swatted at my hand. "Natty Dread got to look fine for his ladies, darling."

Out of the corner of my eye, I watched Emmeline give us both an indulgent smile in the mirror before downshifting. Something about her and her presence here in Pemkowet put me on edge. But since I couldn't put my finger on it, I resolved to keep my promise and do my best to make a good first impression.

The Bide-a-Wee Tavern is located out in the sticks, a couple miles southeast of town along the rural highway. Frankly, it's not the venue I would have chosen if I were trying to make a good impression on a first-time visitor to Pemkowet, or at least not a poised visitor oozing style and sophistication. It's not a dive, but it's pretty rustic: basic American bar food on the menu, well-worn carpeting and dented wood paneling that were probably installed in the 1970s.

Don't get me wrong—I love the place. I love the sameness of it, and the fact that it hasn't changed since I was a kid drinking Shirley Temples with my mom while her boyfriend Trey played bass guitar in the house band, eyes half closed and a beatific smile on his face. Just the memory filled me with tenderness.

That was what I'd wanted to share with Sinclair. But with Emmeline there, I couldn't help but see it through her eyes, too.

It looked dingy and a little sad. As I'd promised, the place was full, but the clientele was older and overwhelmingly white. The latter's sort of unavoidable since Pemkowet's mundane population is fairly racially homogenous, but . . . let's just say that there were a lot of frumpy middle-aged Midwestern ladies in their finest appliquéd sweatshirts.

"It's early," I murmured to Sinclair. "We could probably still get into Lumière."

Sinclair glanced uncertainly at his sister.

"I think it's brilliant," Emmeline said in a firm voice, her British accent emerging in a clipped and authoritative manner. "Very authentic." She turned to the hostess. "Table for three?"

So we stayed.

At first it was awkward, but eventually, music and food and beer greased the conversational skids. In between numbers, I asked Emmeline questions about herself, about her education at boarding schools and at Oxford. She responded with engaging tales laced with self-deprecating humor, asking me about myself in turn—about growing up in Pemkowet, about how I'd helped Sinclair secure the regularly scheduled appearances by pretty, sparkly fairies that helped popularize his tours.

Here's what we didn't talk about: Jamaica, obeah, Sinclair and Emmeline's mother, and the fact that I was a hellspawn.

That was okay with me. If she wanted to avoid talking about the various elephants in the room, I wasn't going to bring them up. Sinclair definitely didn't seem inclined to do so, and I was taking my cue from him.

"Fascinating," Emmeline murmured when I'd finished telling the story of our bargain with the Oak King. "I must say, I thoroughly enjoyed riding along on Sinny's tours today. Well done."

"Oh, the tour is entirely Sinclair's doing," I said honestly. "It was all his idea. I just helped facilitate it."

She gave me an open, friendly smile. "Well, you're obviously very good at your job."

"Thanks." I smiled back at her and found myself relaxing. "I appreciate it. Half the time, I'm making it up as I go along."

Emmeline laughed. "I'm sure that's not true."

The band wrapped up a Louis Armstrong number and paused to confer among themselves and talk to the staff. From what I could gather, they were trying to convince the woman tending bar to sing a number. Sinclair rapped his knuckles on the table. "Excuse me, ladies, but I've got to use the restroom. Back in a minute."

As he left the table, the bartender acceded to demand and left her station to take the microphone. Her face was lined and weathered before its time, she was a hard-worn fiftysomething in faded jeans, a shapeless T-shirt, and a service apron, but I'd heard her sing before. Reaching for his mute, the trumpet player launched into the unmistakable opening bars of "Stormy Weather."

"She's good," I said to Emmeline. "I know, you wouldn't think it to look at her. But if you like the blues at all—"

All the warmth had fled from her expression. "I want you to stop seeing my brother."

I blinked at her. "Excuse me?"

"You heard me." Her eyes were as cold and hard as obsidian. "Look at this place. He doesn't belong here."

My tail twitched. Onstage, the bartender held the microphone in both hands and sang in a low, raspy, crooning voice that she didn't know why there was no sun up in the sky. A lot of amateurs emulate whatever singer made the song famous, but not her. She didn't try to sound like Lena or Etta or Billie; she made it her own. I let the music wash over me, trying to regain my composure and racking my brain to figure out what I'd said or done to offend Sinclair's sister. "I'm sorry, I don't understand. Is this a . . . a cultural issue?"

"Are you asking me if this is about race?" Emmeline's upper lip curled. "You're damned right it is. The *human* race."

She didn't add, "of which you're not a member." She didn't need to. It was implicit. All that pleasant conversation throughout dinner had been an act. Okay, now my temper was beginning to simmer. I took a slow, deep breath, visualized a pot, and clamped a lid on it. "You knew about that before you came here, didn't you?"

"Of course I knew!" Emmeline said sharply. "Did you think it wouldn't get back to our mother as soon as someone in the community found out?" I looked blankly at her. "The *Jamaican* community."

Belatedly, I remembered that one of the Mamma Jammers was also an immigrant—Roddy, the drummer, whose uncle owned the garage where Sinclair's dad worked. He must have told someone who told someone who got on the horn to the Right Honorable Mama Palmer to tell her that her estranged son was dating a hell-spawn, whereupon Judge Palmer dispatched dear Emmy to straighten things out.

"Oh, right," I said. "Frankly, no, it didn't occur to me. Sinclair hardly ever talks about his mother. And until this morning, I didn't know *you* existed."

As verbal slaps go, that was a pretty good one. Emmeline's head jerked backward, her eyes widening.

"Look, I'm sorry." Backing off, I went for a conciliatory tone. "Obviously, there are some serious family dynamics going on here that I know nothing about. But Sinclair's a grown man. He makes his own choices. Also obviously, I can't do anything about my father, but I'm a good person, or at least I try to be. That's how *my* mother raised me." I lowered my voice. "Does my aura say otherwise?"

Her face was impassive. "Not yet."

"I have *no* intention of claiming my birthright!" That would probably have sounded more convincing if the words hadn't come out in sort of a hiss.

Emmeline raised her eyebrows. "Not yet."

I glanced around to check on Sinclair's whereabouts. He'd gotten sidetracked on his way back to the table, shaking hands with an older couple I didn't recognize. Summer people, I'd bet. They'd probably taken the grandkids on the tour at some point, probably packed up the rest of the family and sent them home to their wealthy Chicago suburb earlier today. "Is that really what this is all about?"

"No." She leaned across the table, a cowry shell strung on a gold chain dangling from her throat. "This is about a great many things, none of which I expect you to understand. The path of obeah is a path of balance, a path between light and dark. *You* are one step too far into the darkness."

I opened my mouth to deny it.

"Wait!" Emmeline held up one hand. "This is about Sinny. This is about *my brother*. And I am telling you, he doesn't belong here." Her voice was low and fierce. "Look at him. Look!" She jerked her chin in his direction. Sinclair was posing with the couple, his arms slung amiably around their necks while an obliging member of the waitstaff took a photo. "I rode on that bus today," she said in a contemptuous tone. "I watched him play the part of a fool for the benefit of dull-witted American tourists, japing like a mountebank."

"He *likes* his job!" I protested. "Hell, he invented that job! And look, he's making people happy. What's wrong with that?"

She shot me a withering glance. "My brother is meant to be a young lion of Judah, not a neutered American house cat. He belongs at home with his own people."

"Again," I said, "may I point out that your brother is a grown-ass man who makes his own choices?"

Emmeline ignored me. "I want you to stop seeing him," she repeated in a clipped Anglo-Caribbean accent. "You wield influence here, no matter how ignorantly or clumsily. I want you to use it. Bid the fairies and whatnot to cease their appearances. Give my brother a reason to come home where he belongs. It's long past time."

"Are you serious?" I stared at her in disbelief. "Why in the freaking hell would I do that?"

She didn't answer, but I felt a palpable sense of menace rolling off her. As the legendary blues musician Muddy Waters would say, Emmeline Palmer definitely had her mojo working. A trickle of ice water ran the length of my spine.

"Are you *threatening* me?" In the moment, I was too incredulous to be angry. "Seriously?"

She glanced across the restaurant at Sinclair, who was making his way toward us. "Let's just say I'll give you a month to think about it, shall we?" Her gaze returned to me, hard and implacable. "You've got a charming little town here. It doesn't need my brother and neither do you."

Her ultimatum was delivered as Sinclair reached the table, which gave me only a split second to decide whether to respond in public and make a scene or suck it up and deal with it later. I chose option number two, getting to my feet so fast it startled Sinclair.

"Daisy? You okay?" he asked.

"Yeah, fine. I, um, spilled beer on my skirt." I pushed past him. "Just going to rinse it out."

I got halfway to the bathroom before a tidal wave of fury hit me, leaving me shaking with the effort to control it. I turned the cold water tap on full blast, leaning over the sink and splashing my face.

*You've got a nice little town here. Be a shame if something happened to it.*

Jesus! Seriously? I mean *seriously*? I was Hel's own

agent in Pemkowet. Emmeline had insulted me to my face, then demanded that I help her drive Sinclair out of town. That took a hell of a lot of nerve. Or stupidity.

But what exactly could I do about it? She hadn't made an explicit threat. She hadn't broken any mundane laws and she wasn't in violation of Hel's rule of order. At least not yet, anyway.

What I could do was talk to Sinclair, which I fully intended to do. But not here, not now. What I *wanted* to do was vent my fury. Give it full rein, let it bring the roof crashing down on our heads if that's what it took. The old pipes in the bathroom began to creak alarmingly and the sink began to rattle.

Uh-oh.

I took a deep, trembling breath and stared at the water pouring out of the tap, swirling down the drain, willing it to carry my anger away with it. When I thought I had myself under control, I glanced up into the mirror—

—into a sea of flames.

Double uh-oh.

That meant my temper had weakened the Inviolate Wall enough for my father to reach out to me from the infernal plane. Belphegor's face swam in the fiery sea, black eyes boring into mine, sharp, curving horns jutting from his temples.

*Daughter.* His voice echoed inside my skull, deep and amused and, weirdly, almost affectionate. *You have but to ask.*

"No." I gripped the edges of the sink, shaking my head. "No! Go away!"

The bathroom door opened. "Are you okay, honey?" a woman's concerned voice asked. Her hand patted me soothingly on the back. "Had a little too much to drink?"

With an effort, I let go of the sink and straightened. It was one of the frumpy ladies in the appliquéd sweatshirts. Hers was green with sunflowers on it, and she had kind eyes.

"I'm fine," I said gratefully, stealing a peek at the mirror. It was just a mirror again, showing me nothing but my reflection. "Thank you. I just—"

My sentence trailed off into nothing, because I wasn't sure what to say. I just . . . what? Needed a minute to collect myself because my boyfriend's secret twin sister had threatened me with obeah? Because I had accidentally invoked the specter of my father, the minor demon and occasional incubus Belphegor?

Fortunately, it didn't seem to matter to the nice lady in the sunflower sweatshirt. "As long as you're okay."

I turned off the tap. "Thank you. I appreciate it."

"Don't mention it." She gave me another pat and a warm, weary smile. "We've all got to take care of one another, honey."

Her kindness gave me the strength I needed to wrestle the last fraying tendrils of my temper under control and venture back out into the bar to face the prospect of making polite conversation with my boyfriend and his twin sister, who I wished had stayed a secret but who was apparently my new nemesis.

Stormy weather, indeed.

# Fourteen

Somehow I got through the evening.

The music helped. Ironically, it also helped that Emmeline was so adept at being two-faced, falling back on the easy, self-deprecating charm that had lured me into complacency in the first place.

Sinclair wasn't fooled, at least not by me. He knew I was on edge. When I first returned to the table, he gave me an inquiring furrowed-brow look. I replied with a barely perceptible headshake that meant I didn't want to talk about it now.

So we didn't.

We listened to the rest of the set, and when the band took a break, Emmeline asked if we'd mind making it an early night since it had been a long travel day for her. I don't think I've ever cleared out of a bar faster in my life. I was in such a hurry I almost forgot to leave a tip for the band in the fishbowl atop the piano. I hustled out the door into the parking lot—and then stopped abruptly.

A solitary figure was awaiting us under the lone flood-light that illuminated the lot, leaning against the pole, hands shoved in the pockets of his jeans. There was a motorcycle alongside him, a pared-down vintage model that looked like a prop from an old World War II movie. The light spilling from above highlighted his fair hair and the unnatural pallor of his narrow face and his skinny bare arms.

"Cooper," I said aloud.

"Evenin', m'lady." He freed one hand to tip an imaginary hat to me. "Everything all right?"

I should have realized that Stefan would sense the barrage of fury I'd very nearly unleashed. "Everything's fine. Did Stefan send you?"

"He did." Cooper levered himself away from the pole. "The big man himself. Said he felt a surge in the Force or somewhat and sent me to have a look. I had a peep through the window." He sauntered closer, hands back in his pockets. "Looked amiable enough to me, didn't it? A few chums having a pint. So I reckoned I'd wait out here."

Sinclair stepped forward to block him. "Daisy, do you know this guy?"

"Yeah." I put one hand on Sinclair's shoulder. "He's okay."

Cooper sniffed. "Faint praise, Miss Daisy!" Rocking back on his heels, he studied Sinclair. "This your bloke?"

"That," I said, "would be none of your business."

"Touchy touchy!" He gave me a crooked sideways grin. Neon light from the bar signs glittered in his pupils, which waxed as he turned his attention to Emmeline, and just as swiftly contracted to pinpoints. "Hello! What do we have here?"

"Emmeline Palmer." She extended one hand to him, cool as a cucumber. "Pleased to make your acquaintance. Mr. Cooper, is it?"

Cooper kept his hands in his pockets. "You're wearing a ward, aren't you, darling? Quite a powerful one. Don't think I fancy a taste of it," he added thoughtfully. "Afraid of the local hobgoblins and bugaboos, are we?"

"I'm a lawyer, Mr. Cooper." Emmeline gave a faint shrug. Light glinted on the polished leopard-spotted surface of the cowry shell and gold chain strung around her neck. "We like to be prepared."

He eyed her. "Right."

I glanced at Sinclair. He looked like he'd had as much covert tension and subterfuge as he could stand and was ready to blow. "Cooper! Will you thank Stefan for me and tell him everything's fine?"

"I will," he said. "He said to tell you to be in touch. He's got somewhat that might help out with your little project." With that, Cooper sauntered back toward his bike, straddled it, kicked it to life, and roared out of the parking lot.

Sinclair turned to me. "You want to tell me what the hell that was all about?"

I really, really didn't. Not here and now, not in front of dear Emmy, who was glancing back and forth between us with interest, waiting to see how this was going to play out. I, um, hadn't exactly been forthcoming yet about my bond with Stefan Ludovic. "It's nothing. Like Cooper said, he was just checking things out." I gave Sinclair my best puppy-dog eyes, pleading silently with him to let it go.

"All right." He sounded reluctant, but he agreed. "Let's get out of here."

Emmeline slid obligingly behind the wheel of her rental convertible. "What a peculiar young man," she remarked, pulling onto the rural highway. "Is he even old enough for a driver's license?"

"Cooper?" I met her gaze in the rearview mirror. "Yeah, you could say so. He's more than two hundred years old. He was hanged to death in the Irish Rebellion of 1798."

Funny how those kind of details stay with you.

Her eyelids flickered slightly. "I see."

"He's not a duppy, Emmy," Sinclair said. "He's a ghoul."

*Duppy.* It seemed like I'd heard that word before. I wanted to ask what a duppy was, but I kept my mouth shut on the question for now. It was worth noting that Emmeline hadn't been able to recognize a ghoul on sight. That, I thought, was why she'd offered to shake Cooper's hand; she was trying to get a read on him. It was also worth noting that she'd done it without the slightest trace of fear, and Cooper had been wary enough to refuse.

Okay, duly noted. Dear Emmy was packing some serious mojo and should not be underestimated.

By the time they dropped me off at my apartment, my head was aching with the effort of containing my various emotions. It was about half an hour later, around ten thirty or so, that Sinclair called. I'd thought he might. I was sitting on my screened porch listening to Billie Holiday, a few candles lit, a glass of scotch in my hand and Mogwai on my lap, kneading and purring. I was as calm as I was going to get.

"So what's up, Daisy?" Sinclair asked without preamble. "What's going on?"

"Is your sister there?"

"No," he said. "I offered, but she's staying at a B and B downtown. Why? What did she say to you?" He hesitated. "Does it have anything to do with that rat-faced little ghoul checking up on you?"

I stroked Mogwai's calico fur. "Do you know why she's here?"

"Yeah." Sinclair let out a sigh. "To try to talk me into coming home. Home to Jamaica. At least during the off season. But you know . . ." There was a faint wistful note in his voice. "I think she misses me, too."

"You must miss her," I said.

"We've spent most of our lives missing each other, Daise," he said. "But we're on different paths."

According to his sister, the path of obeah was a path of balance, a path between light and dark. That was one of those things that sounded good on paper, all profound and mystical, until you started wondering exactly what the hell it meant, what the real-world ramifications were for mundane and eldritch alike.

And I didn't know. I had no idea. All I knew was that Emmeline was on it and Sinclair wasn't, but she and their powerful mother thought he should be.

"Daisy?"

"Yeah." I shifted Mogwai's bulk into a more comfortable position. "Look . . . I don't want to get in the middle of this."

"What did she say to you?" Sinclair repeated.

I gazed out into the night, listening to the sounds of Pemkowet. It was quieter than it had been in months. It would get even quieter in the months to come. "Do you ever regret not following the same path as your sister?"

"*No.*" His reply was prompt and sure. "Daisy . . . listen, it's a long story. It's part of the conversation I promised you. But the short answer is no. A definitive no." He paused. "Are you going to answer my question?"

I scratched Mogwai under his chin. He lifted it to allow me access, curling his lip with pleasure to reveal a sharp eyetooth. "Emmeline asked me to stop seeing you. To call off the fairies, use my influence in the eldritch community. To give you a reason not to stay here. To go home."

There was a short, shocked silence. "She *what*?"

"Yeah."

Sinclair laughed. "Oh, hell, no! Emmy, Emmy! I know she only just met you, but what in the world made her think *you* of all people would agree to it?"

See, here's where it got tricky. Vague, creeping menace does not a coherent threat make. And I might be entirely in the right here, but I was also the outsider in this equation. Families, even dysfunctional families—hell, maybe *especially* dysfunctional families—tend to turn on outsiders who slander another member of the clan. I'd seen enough of it with the Cassopolis family to know that. Jen could bitch about her abusive father, her passive mother, and her blood-slut sister, Bethany, all day long, but heaven help anyone else who did the same. That right was reserved for family.

So I temporized. "Oh, I think she thought I'd be swayed by her formidable nature. She *is* pretty formidable, isn't she?"

"Mmm." He made a noncommittal sound. "What about the ghoul?"

"I don't know," I said. "What's a duppy?"

Again, Sinclair hesitated. "It's . . . sort of like a ghost, only not a ghost. A spirit. A duppy's what happens when someone dies and their earthly soul gets loose instead of going where it belongs."

"Okay."

"Sometimes they look like animals," he said. "But mostly like dead people. Daisy, did my sister threaten to set a duppy on you?"

"Um . . . no?" At least I didn't think so.

"Good." He sounded relieved. "Look, let me talk to Emmy. She's headstrong and she's used to getting her own way. But if I ever do go back to the island, it will be on *my* terms, because *I* decided it, not because my sister decided it was time. I'll tell her to leave you out of this, okay?"

"Okay," I agreed. "But as long as she's here, I'm staying out of the way."

"Fair enough."

After a few more innocuous comments, we said good night and ended the call. I sat on the porch for a while longer, petting Mogwai and thinking about the conversation while the candles guttered into wax pools. On a Daisy-and-Sinclair basis, I felt good about it. I'd taken Lurine's advice and cut him some slack. Other than dodging the whole ghoul issue, I thought I'd handled it pretty damn well from the standpoint of a supportive girlfriend, especially considering that the whole secret-twin-sister thing had just been sprung on me this morning.

As Hel's liaison, I wasn't so sure. Emmeline Palmer hadn't just threatened me. She'd threatened my *town*. My territory, my turf, my responsibility.

I hoped that it was all just posturing, that dear Emmy would back down when Sinclair confronted her.

But if she didn't . . .

"Bring it on, bitch," I said aloud.

Okay, so I wasn't entirely sure what *it* was or what I'd do about it if she did, but it felt good to say it.

# Fifteen

I awoke with a splitting headache, an excruciating toothache, and blurred vision. And I panicked.

Here's the thing: I don't get sick. Ever. Oh, I've had
headaches due to stress or fatigue, like the other night, and
I found out the hard way that I can get hangovers, but I've
never been *sick*. Never had the flu, the chicken pox, not
even the common cold. Toothaches? I'd never even had a
cavity. My mom's theory is that it's because my average
body temperature runs higher than a normal human's,
around a hundred and five degrees. She thinks it kills the
germs and bacteria. Maybe it's even true, although I've
never known a doctor to sign on to her theory.

So anyway, yeah, I freaked. First at the pain, which
seemed to be simultaneously radiating from a molar on the
right side of my jaw and pounding like a spike into my sinus
cavity; second at the blurred vision.

That was the one that really got me. I pried myself gingerly out of bed, trying to hold my head as still as possible.
In the bathroom, I splashed cold water on my face and into
my eyes, blinking furiously and willing my vision to clear.

No luck.

*Oh, crap.*

The small corner of my brain that wasn't panicking went into damage-control mode. I didn't know if I was having a stroke or an aneurysm or what, but I knew I needed help. And clothing. Hell if I was going to the emergency room in nothing but a tank top. I fumbled my way to the laundry hamper and pulled out yesterday's clothes.

Okay, that would work. Sidling along the edge of my bed, I felt atop my nightstand until I found my phone, the shape of it familiar and comforting in my hand.

The problem was that I couldn't make out the icons on the screen. And when I finally got to the keypad, through dint of trial and error, I couldn't make out the numbers to call 911. Every time I tried to focus, they shifted and blurred. I kept pushing numbers I didn't mean to, squinting in an agonized effort, unable to get to that magic combination. It was like a bad dream.

At some point I realized two things. One was that whatever the hell was happening to me, it wasn't getting any worse. Oh, it was bad. My jaw was throbbing, my head was pounding, and I couldn't see for shit, but I probably wasn't dying.

The other was the first inkling of suspicion that whatever the hell was happening to me might not be medical in nature.

If you're thinking I should have suspected that from the get-go, I'm not arguing. But it's really, really hard to think straight when your skull feels like it's being split open with a railroad spike and you can't see.

And . . . I wasn't sure what to do with that suspicion.

So instead I hoped like hell it was a medical issue and went through the whole trial-and-error bit to pull up my contacts on my phone. Elusive letters and numbers skittered across my vision, but if I concentrated like crazy, I could make out the contacts with photos assigned to them. Since I was kind of lax about that, there were only two, my mom and Jen. And while, on the one hand, I really wanted my mommy right about now, I also didn't want to freak her out, so I jabbed at the screen until Jen's contact came up.

"Hey, Daise." She answered on the second ring. "What's going on?" I was so relieved to hear her voice, I had to choke back an involuntary sob. "Daisy?" Jen's voice sharpened. "What's up?"

"Not sure," I whispered. "Either I'm having an aneurysm or I've been hexed."

"Are you serious? Jesus! Did you call 911?"

"No." I closed my eyes. Blocking out the light helped a very little bit. "Can't see to dial."

"Okay, hang on. I'm coming to take you to the ER."

"Wait, wait!" Now that my panic was ratcheting down a notch, the prospect of massive medical costs alarmed me. As a part-time employee, I didn't have health insurance, which had never worried me that much because I never got sick. And I'd never had to explain the quirks of my hell-spawn physiognomy to unfamiliar doctors. They'd probably want to hospitalize me for my temperature alone. "I just … it really might be a hex, Jen. Or a migraine! What if it's a migraine?"

"What if it's *not*?" she asked with acerbity. "And by the way, why do you think it might be a hex?"

"Long story." I cupped my right hand over my pulsating jaw. "I've got a toothache, too."

"A *toothache*?"

"I know, I know! But seriously, it feels like someone's trying to chisel it in half."

"Okay, listen." Jen's tone was pragmatic. "It doesn't sound like you're dying. More like maybe you have an impacted wisdom tooth or something. Maybe you're having a severe reaction because you never freakin' get sick. Let me call Doc Howard and see if he can take a look at you, okay?"

"Okay."

"Call you back in a sec. Oh, and, Daise? If he can't, I *am* taking you to the ER," she warned me.

"Okay," I repeated.

Within three minutes, Jen called me back to say Doc

Howard would see me and she was on her way to pick me up. Within ten minutes, her ancient LeBaron convertible pulled into the alley. I grabbed my messenger bag, put on my hobgoblin-cracked sunglasses, and fumbled my way down the stairs, my head swimming with pain. Even with the sunglasses, the sunlight hit me like a ton of bricks. Closing my eyes again, I began feeling my way around the Le-Baron to the passenger side.

"Jesus!" Jen got out of the car and steered me by the elbow. "You look like crap, Daise. Are you sure you don't want to go to the ER?"

"Yeah." I slid into the cracked vinyl seat. "I'm sure."

"Are you aware that your sunglasses are broken?"

"Uh-huh." I leaned my head against the headrest.

She put the car in gear. "Just checking. Now what the hell's up with this hex business?"

I got the gist of the story out on the drive to the doctor's office. Jen listened in disbelief, saving her commentary until after my appointment. I'd known Doc Howard since I was barely out of diapers. Even though I never got sick, Mom took me to the town doctor for all my regularly scheduled checkups. He took my temperature—which he pronounced Daisy-normal at a hundred and five—and blood pressure, listened to my heart, peered into my ears and eyes and throat with the bright-light scope thingy; or at least he did his best. It hurt so much I had a hard time keeping my eyes open during that part.

Bottom line, there was no sign of anything physically wrong with me, not even an impacted wisdom tooth.

Damn.

A part of me had been hoping for an impacted wisdom tooth.

"Daisy?" Doc Howard's concerned face floated blurrily in my vision. "I'm going to write you a prescription for migraine medication and recommend that you make an appointment with your dentist as soon as possible just to be sure about that tooth. Okay?"

"Yeah."

He scribbled on a prescription pad. "But if the headache

and blurred vision continue for more than seventy-two hours, call me and I'll refer you to Appeldoorn Community Hospital for a CT scan."

I took the slip of paper. "Okay."

"Have a lollipop," Doc Howard said sympathetically, holding out a jar I remembered from my childhood. "It might help bring up your blood sugar level. Just be sure to eat something healthy when you get home."

I tried to smile, but it hurt to move the muscles of my face. "Thanks, Doc."

Then it was back out into the skull-shattering sunlight. Swear to God, I had no idea pain could be this fucking *painful*. My head felt like it was swollen to twice its normal size and misshapen, ballooning around the jackhammering agony in my jaw.

*Bring it on, bitch.*

I had a feeling it had been brung.

"So what's it going to be?" Jen asked me. "Are we going to the drugstore to get your prescription filled or are we going to go kick some obeah woman ass?"

If I could have laughed, I would have. "Drugstore. Right now, I couldn't kick Stacey Brooks's ass."

Back in downtown Pemkowet, Jen double-parked outside the drugstore and came back with a vial of Imitrex, a bottle of water, and a pair of the darkest cheap sunglasses she could find. "Here." She popped the lid on the vial and shook out a tablet, handing it to me. "The pharmacist said to take one now, and another in two hours if the migraine persists."

"Thanks." I cracked open the bottle of water to wash down the pill.

"What happens if this doesn't work, Daise?" There was a worried note in her voice. "What are you going to do?"

"I don't know yet." I switched my hobgoblin-cracked sunglasses for the new ones. "I need to lie down in a dark room and think about it."

"Okay."

Jen drove me home and insisted on staying with me while we waited to see if the meds kicked in. She went around the apartment and closed all the shades while I lay on the futon with my eyes closed and held a plastic bag full of ice against my jaw.

"Do you need me to call in to work for you?" she asked softly when the room was as dim as it was going to get.

"Not yet," I murmured. "I'm not scheduled to go in until this afternoon. What about you? I don't mean to keep you."

"It's okay, I didn't have anything today but end-of-season cleanup on a couple of places that were just vacated." Jen worked for the Cassopolis family business, cleaning houses and rental properties. "What about Sinclair? I mean, if this *is* obeah, he ought to know what to do about it, right? It's his fucking sister that hexed you."

"Probably." It was easier to think while lying prone. "No, don't call him. Not yet. I need to figure this out on my own."

"Oh, yeah? How's that working out for you so far?"

"Ha-ha. If I call Sinclair, he'll confront dear Emmy," I said. "And I don't want her thinking I needed her brother's help to beat this."

"Even if you do?" Jen sounded skeptical. "No offense, Daise, but isn't pride one of the Seven Deadlies you're supposed to worry about?"

"Yeah," I said. "But it's not just pride. It's about status, too. That's a big deal in the eldritch community. I need to show Emmeline Palmer she can't sail into Pemkowet and fuck with Hel's liaison without consequences, which means I need to fix this before Sinclair hears about it."

"How?"

"Good question."

Now that I was past the panicking stage, my wits were working again. Slowly and painfully, but they were working. Option one: I could try to strong-arm Emmeline into unhexing me. Well, not me personally, not in this condition, but I could call on allies. The fact that Emmeline was wearing some kind of protective ward strong enough to make a two-hundred-year-old ghoul wary was an issue, but I was pretty sure that it wouldn't dissuade oh, say, Lurine. No matter what mojo dear Emmy was packing, I doubted it was a match for an eldritch being with fond memories of the

Bronze Age and the physical capability of crushing her to death one vertebra at the time. Or maybe Gus the ogre. He could always threaten to bash her over the head and eat her.

Of course, that also meant getting someone else to fight my battle. Which wasn't entirely unappealing—delegating wisely is an important skill and dear Emmy ought to know that there was more to Pemkowet's eldritch community than sparkly fairies and one brother-dating hell-spawn.

On the other hand, there was option two: I could get myself unhexed without the assistance of either of the Palmer Wonder Twins. It would require the Fabulous Casimir's aid, but again, he was a legitimate ally.

Somewhere in a dark part of my mind, my father's voice whispered to me that there was a third option, an option that was always an option. I could claim my birthright, and all the powers it included.

*You have but to ask. . . .*

I sighed, pushing the thought away. Okay, so it probably wasn't a great idea to involve Lurine or Gus unless I was actually willing to let Emmeline come to grievous bodily harm, which I wasn't. Or at least I was cognizant of the fact that to do so would be inappropriate in my role as Hel's liaison.

So, decision made.

"Hey, Jen," I said. "Let's go see Casimir."

"Are you sure?" She checked her phone. "It's only been about half an hour since you took the meds."

"I'm sure. If they're going to work, then they'll work. But I don't want to waste time waiting if they're not."

She shrugged. "Let's go."

Luckily for me, the Sisters of Selene was only a block and a half away. I still had to hold on to Jen's arm the whole way, wincing at the sunlight behind my dark glasses as she steered me around the lingering tourists and reemergent locals on the sidewalks.

"Hey, Miss Dais—" Casimir began greeting me as we entered the shop. "Holy Hecate! Girl, you look like seven miles of bad road."

I wished he'd lower his voice. "I feel like it. Cas, I need a favor. I've been hexed. Can you undo it?"

Casimir came out from behind the counter to lock the front door and turn the OPEN sign to CLOSED. "I don't know, sugar, but I'll do my best. Tell me all about it."

I filled him in on the details to the best of my ability. He let out a long, low whistle when I finished.

"Damn! Bitch has balls." There was a hint of admiration in his voice. "Did she get her hands on something personal of yours? Hair, nail clippings?"

"No," I said. "I don't think so."

"Are you sure?" he pressed. "Maybe a few strands of hair caught in your boyfriend's hairbrush? Pillow? Towel?"

"I don't know," I admitted. "Maybe. I did borrow his toothbrush. But I don't know how she'd know *that*."

"Neither do I," Casimir said. "But I told you before, I don't know a lot about obeah."

"So you're saying this bitch hexed Daisy with a fucking *toothbrush*?" Jen asked in disbelief.

"I'm saying it's possible, Miss Jenny-bird," Casimir said to her. "If you can take a DNA sample from a cheek swab, you can build a spell around a toothbrush."

All of this standing upright and talking was setting off fresh waves of agony in my pounding skull. "So can you undo it?"

"Well, we'll see, won't we?" He beckoned, or at least the two overlapping blurred figures of Casimir made a gesture that I interpreted as beckoning. "Come into my altar room, Miss Daisy. Ritual participants only," he added apologetically to Jen. "But there are some back issues of *Vogue* and *Occult Monthly* under the counter."

She nodded. "Thanks."

Casimir led me through the door at the rear of the shop into his altar room. From what I could make out, it was a lot more clean and spare than I would have expected, given his relative flamboyance.

"Step over the circle." He guided me unobtrusively. "Good girl. Now, just make yourself comfortable on the kneeling pad while I get everything ready."

Getting everything ready turned out to be a pretty complicated business involving numerous invocations, the donning of a tasseled and knotted scarlet cord around the waist, the lighting of candles and incense, the consecration of water with salt, the blessing of various instruments including an athamé knife and a sharpened quill feather, and the grinding of special ink in a mortar.

If I hadn't been in excruciating pain, it would have been fascinating. I'd never actually seen the Fabulous Casimir—or anyone, fabulous or otherwise—perform a ritual like this before. Under the circumstances, I pretty much just knelt quietly in front of the altar with my eyes closed and let it all wash over me, clutching my messenger bag and concentrating on remaining upright.

"Okay, Daisy." Casimir knelt opposite me. "I need you to hold still while I draw the seal."

"No problem."

He dipped the quill in the magic ink and began tracing a design onto my forehead. "This is a seal of protection. If it works, you'll be protected for as long as the image lasts, about as long as a henna tattoo."

Great, so I was going to look like a freak with a henna tattoo on my forehead.

The tip of the quill scratched against my skin. "You'll still need to find the charm and dismantle it to be safe."

"What charm?" I did my best to ask without moving my head.

"Whatever she used to fix the spell," Casimir said patiently. "Hair, toothbrush, whatever. It could even be a photo of you."

"Like a voodoo doll?"

"It's the same general idea." He dipped the quill again. "Sympathetic magic, basically. You know, in your line of work, you really should invest in a high-quality amulet," he added. "Or ideally, a permanent tattoo."

"On my *forehead*?" I said in alarm.

"Hold still," he reprimanded me, which I thought was a bit unfair under the circumstances. Kind of like when the dental hygienist asks you a question, then sticks an instrument in your mouth. "No, it doesn't have to be on your fore-head, Miss Daisy. Protection spells work a lot better if you employ them *before* you're the victim of a magical attack."

I squinted at his blurred face. "Cooper said she had a ward. A powerful one. Is that like a protection spell?"

"Mm-hmm." Having drawn what felt like a couple of circles and a series of straight lines, Casimir began drawing smaller, squigglier bits. "Who's Cooper?"

"A ghoul," I said. "He wouldn't touch her."

"Really." Casimir's hand went still. "That *would* be a powerful ward," he mused, more to himself than me.

"I think it was a cowry shell."

He resumed his squiggly drawing. "Cowry shells have a long, rich history of occult association."

Too much talking. The pain in my head protested by rising to a fresh crescendo. I squeezed my eyes shut, taking refuge in the darkness. I couldn't let myself rest there, though. "Cas?"

"Hmm?"

"Would a powerful ward protect dear Emmy from a physical ass-kicking?"

"Not in the slightest," he assured me.

"Good."

"All right, my dear." There were bustling sounds as Casimir fussed with his implements. "I'm going to invoke the spell. Try to keep your eyes open."

I cracked my eyelids and peered at his vague double image as he took up the black-handled athamé blade.

"Bound be all powers of adversity from the north, south, east, and west," Casimir chanted, touching the blade lightly around me. "Bound be all ill-wishers and those who practice violence against the bearer of my seal! Bound and sealed by my hand and name shall be all who to seek to harm Daisy Johanssen." He pressed the tip of the athamé against the center of the seal etched onto my brow. "By my will, so mote it be!"

Light flared around me.

For a brief, blessed instant, the pain simply vanished. It went away as though it had never been, and I could have wept with gratitude for the absence I'd taken for granted all of my healthy life. My vision cleared. The Fabulous Casimir's face sprang into sharp focus. He was wearing a bouffant wig today, looking like a 1950s housewife. I could see the pores of his skin beneath a thick layer of makeup, his shrewd, concerned eyes studying me behind the long false lashes he wore.

And then the seal on my forehead contracted with a sizzling sound, drawing my skin tight. I doubled over in agony as the pain came thudding back—the spike between my eyes, the jackhammer in my jaw.

Through blurred eyes, I saw bits of dried ink sift to the floor like rusty snowflakes.

"Well," Casimir said, "*that* didn't work."

# Sixteen

The bad news was that the Fabulous Casimir's failure meant that Emmeline Palmer's power exceeded his by a considerable degree.

The good news was that Cas was pissed off about it. "Let me talk to the coven," he said to me. "We'll schedule a ritual with the full circle. There's no way she's a match for *all* of us."

I nodded gingerly. "Okay."

"We can do this, Daisy," he promised me. "Don't start looking for alternatives, you understand?"

"You mean my father?" I asked.

He shuddered. "Hell, yes, I mean your father, girl."

I wasn't looking. As always, I kept a tight lid on that thought. But as always, it was there. And I had to admit as I walked blindly home, clinging to the arm of an uncharacteristically quiet Jen, doing my best to support the pain-filled balloon that was my head, my tail lashing with impotent fury, that I was really fucking tired of being so goddamn powerless in a position of responsibility.

Powers of persuasion and seduction would come in really handy right about now. So would a splendid set of bat-veined wings and a fiery whip, just because.

Oh, the possibilities!

But there was that whole business about cracking the Inviolate Wall.

As much as I wanted to face down dear Emmy on my own terms, it certainly wasn't worth unleashing Armageddon. And, too, in the back of my mind was the well-dressed hell-spawn lawyer I'd seen in the PVB office the other day, attempting to work some kind of wiles on Amanda Brooks.

He'd *smelled* bad. Rancid.

I didn't know what that was all about, what the lawyer was up to, and why his presence and his apparent acceptance of his birthright didn't threaten the Inviolate Wall, but I knew I didn't want that stink on me.

As if on cue, Jojo the joe-pye weed fairy popped up from her lurking place amid the rhododendrons alongside the alley by my apartment. "Stupid reeking slattern!" she screeched at me in a brain-drilling octave that didn't exist on any human scale, not even Mariah Carey's. "It's in your bag!"

Jen's arm tightened under my grip. "What the *fuck*?"

"Seriously, Jojo?" My head hurt so badly, I wanted to lie down and cry. "Not now, okay?"

Hovering several feet above the ground on agitated wings, Jojo swore up and down and sideways in what I suspected was a variety of languages. "It's in your *bag*! The charm is in your bag, dullard!"

I blinked. "What?"

Jojo let out another piercing shriek and tugged at her purple hair. "I can't touch it, you fool! There's cold steel and iron in there!"

"Um, Daise?" Jen said. "I think the fairy's trying to tell you that Emmy's charm is in your bag."

Jojo bared a mouthful of teeny-tiny shark teeth. "The dark-haired one is not such a lackwit as you."

"Gee, thanks," Jen said.

I had no idea why Jojo would switch from plaguing me to helping me, but right now I couldn't care less. Kneeling on the sidewalk, I eased *dauda-dagr* out of its hidden sheath and dumped the rest of the bag's contents unceremoniously onto the concrete. I sorted through them by feel. Wallet, phone, keys, comb, hair scrunchies, a packet of tissues, lipstick—okay, I may be a hell-spawn, but I'm still a girl—a tangled set of earbuds, receipts, the lollipop that Doc Howard gave me . . . and there, buried in the heap, a small leather sack tied shut with a cord. I picked it up and gave it a cautious squeeze. It held something hard and lumpy, something soft and yielding, and something sharp and poky.

"Is this it?" I asked Jojo.

A few pedestrians were rounding the corner toward the park. With a huff, Jojo cast a glamour over herself, her appearance shifting to that of a five- or six-year-old girl. "What else would it be, you beetle-brained churl? Open it!"

Now that I actually had the thing in hand, I hesitated, squinting at Jojo's blurry child-face. "Why should I trust you? Why would you help me?"

"You bade me spy upon her," she said impatiently. "The sister. *She* wants to take him away from here. At least you don't."

Aha. So dear Emmy had managed to piss off Sinclair's lovelorn fairy. Good enough for me. I began picking at the cord tied around the sack.

"Here." Jen held out her hand. "Give it to me. You can't even see straight."

"Does it matter who opens it?" I asked Jojo.

The fairy shook her head. "No. But I can't touch it." She shuddered. "Iron. I loathe iron."

It took a few minutes for Jen to get the cord untied, and she had to use her teeth. Jojo rummaged for a tissue in the pile of junk from my bag, spreading it on the sidewalk. Jen opened the leather sack and poured the contents out carefully onto the tissue, and . . . ah, *bliss*.

Once again the pain vanished; the agonizing spike drilling into my forehead, the throbbing in my tooth. The blurriness and double vision went away and the world returned to clarity, bright and crisp and beautiful.

This time it stayed that way. I held still and took a few

cautious breaths before examining the sack's contents, which appeared to be one discolored human molar, a crude iron nail, and a pile of dirt.

Jojo peered over my shoulder. "A coffin nail and grave-yard dirt, like as not."

"What about the tooth?"

She looked at me as though I were an idiot. "'Tis a tooth."

"Gross," Jen commented.

I poked at the objects. "She must have put it in my bag when I went to the restroom last night. But I don't see any hair or anything of mine."

"Maybe she brushed the tooth with the toothbrush you borrowed at Sinclair's place," Jen said.

Gah. "Maybe."

Jojo heaved an impatient sigh. "You had the charm on your person, lackwit, or at least near it under your own roof. The sorceress had no need to bind it to you further. Your warlock made a careless assumption based on his own knowledge of the craft. He condemned his effort to failure when he allowed the charm within his own altar circle."

"You know what they say," Jen said. "'Assume' makes an ass out of 'u' and 'me.'"

"That's a clever turn of phrase," the fairy said approvingly to her. To me, she said, "*You* should be grateful that I recognize the reek of iron and magic."

"I am." I'm not sure how sincere I sounded, but I meant it. "I owe you a favor, Jojo. A big one."

Her eyes widened. "Truly? Then I beseech—"

"I'm *not* breaking things off with Sinclair," I said. "That's not on the table. But if there's anything I can do in my capacity as Hel's liaison, ask."

"Oh." Jojo looked disappointed; and I have to say that her crush on Sinclair was even more disconcerting with the little girl glamour over her.

I concentrated on seeing through it. In her true form, Jojo exuded a miniature green-skinned pubescent sexuality that was disconcerting enough, but it was better than the toddlers-and-tiaras vibe. "Look, I'll put it in my ledger, okay?" By ledger, I meant the database I planned to create. "You can claim it anytime."

That appeared to mollify her. "Very well."

"So is this thing . . . defused now?" Jen asked, indicating the leather sack and its former contents. "It's not going to reactivate again, is it?"

"The charm is broken," Jojo assured her. "The sorceress would have to cast the spell anew."

"Good to know." I began returning items to my messenger bag, starting with *dauda-dagr*, then glanced up at the throaty sound of a motorcycle chugging down the street.

Oh, duh. Given the surge of panic I'd experienced when I woke up, the only surprise was that I hadn't had a concerned ghoul on my doorstep within the hour.

Stefan Ludovic pulled into the alley astride a gleaming black motorcycle. Well, parts of it gleamed, while others were a matte black that seemed to swallow the light. I happened to know that it was a Vincent Black Shadow, one of only seventeen hundred in existence; I knew this not because I knew anything about motorcycles but because Cody told me so when we spotted it in the garage of a suspect who couldn't possibly have legitimately afforded it.

Apparently, it now belonged to Stefan. I hadn't noticed that the other night at Rainbow's End.

He lowered the kickstand and cut the engine. He wasn't wearing a helmet, just a pair of wraparound sunglasses that should have looked tacky, yet somehow didn't. In the daylight, the pallor of his skin was vivid. Not undead pallor like a vampire, just sort of otherworldly. His slightly too long black hair brushed the collar of the leather vest he wore over a plain, skintight black T-shirt. I couldn't figure out how the hell Stefan made that look elegant, but he did.

"Holy shit," Jen breathed fervently beside me. "That's the hot ghoul you told me about, isn't it?"

"Outcast," I whispered. "That's what they call themselves."

Stefan took off his sunglasses, revealing those pale eyes, a shade of blue seldom seen outside the interior of a glacier.

His pupils were contracted and steady as he met my gaze. "Hel's liaison."

"You know," I said to him, "you don't have to come running or send Cooper to check on me every time I have a little emotional blip."

"A . . . *blip*." The word sounded funny in his mouth. He looked down at the contents of my bag and Emmy's charm strewn across the sidewalk, then back at me, arching one evocative eyebrow.

"It's okay," I said. "I handled it. By the way, this is my friend Jen. Jennifer Cassopolis, Stefan Ludovic. And . . ." I looked around for Jojo, but she'd made herself scarce. "Um, never mind."

Stefan dismounted from his bike in one fluid motion, took Jen's hand before she could react, and bowed slightly. "It is a pleasure, Miss Cassopolis."

Jen gave me an uncertain look. With a sister in thrall to a vampire, she tended to be wary of predatory eldritch species, although a bit less so since learning that Cody was a werewolf. It makes a difference when you've known someone since high school.

"It's okay," I said to her. "Stefan's got centuries of self-discipline under his belt."

She relaxed. "Nice to meet you."

Releasing her hand, Stefan nodded at the items on the sidewalk. "This is the work of the sorceress Cooper encountered last night, I take it?"

"Yep."

He met my gaze again and this time his pupils did the wax-and-wane thing. "This is a grave breach of protocol, Daisy Johanssen. For an outsider to enter a community such as ours and give insult to a vested agent of the resident deity is tantamount to a challenge."

"Yeah, I figured." I prodded the pile of dirt with my toe. "Don't worry. I plan on confronting her."

Stefan inclined his head. "I remain in your debt. My services and my forces are at your disposal."

"Thanks," I said. "But I'd like to try to handle this discreetly."

He smiled at me, those unexpected dimples forming in the creases of his smile. "I can be discreet."

I flushed and cleared my throat. "Um . . . yeah, no doubt. But it's complicated. She's, um, actually kind of my boyfriend's sister."

"Or more accurately, her kind-of boyfriend's actual sister," Jen added, not entirely helpfully. I shot her a quick glare. She responded with a "What?" face.

"As you wish, Hel's liaison." Thank God, Stefan chose to ignore our silent but not exactly subtle interplay. "The decision is yours, of course. When it's convenient, there's another matter I would discuss with you."

"Oh, right." Belatedly, I remembered that Cooper had mentioned it last night. "Sorry, I've been distracted."

"For obvious reasons," he acknowledged. "Call me when you're less distracted."

Sometimes the whole cryptic eldritch thing could be a bit much. "Can't you just tell me now?"

One corner of his mouth lifted. "It's not something I can tell you, Daisy. It's something I wish to show you. I believe it will help in the work we undertook together."

Oh. "Okay. Will do."

He inclined his head again. "Until then."

Jen and I watched him return to his Vincent Black Shadow, straddling it with easy grace before putting his wraparound sunglasses back on, kick-starting the motorcycle, and chugging away.

"Damn," Jen said. "Just . . . *damn*! You weren't kidding."

"Nope," I said. "I was not."

She punched me in the arm. "I think he's into you. So what's this work you're doing together? What's his story anyway? I thought ghouls—excuse me, Outcast—were all gross redneck bikers that fed on the pathetic emotional dregs of skanky meth-heads."

"Ow!" I rubbed my arm. "I don't know. He hasn't told me his story yet. But he doesn't allow drugs on his turf. And he told me once that ghouls in America tend to come from areas where . . . I can't remember exactly, but something about a conjunction of extreme ignorance and extreme faith. I think it's different for some of the old ones from back in ye olden times."

"Huh."

"He said he could teach me to deflect my emotions," I said. "That's what we were working on."

"*I* think he's into you," Jen repeated. "Did you even bother to ask him what his story was?"

"Yeah, I did," I admitted. "It was, um, a little too soon in our acquaintance. That's a big question, you know?"

"I guess. So, Mr. Ludovic," she intoned, "tell me, exactly what *did* you do to get kicked out of heaven and hell?"

"Something like that," I agreed.

"I wonder, though," she mused.

I wondered, too. But right now I had more pressing matters to deal with. Stooping, I finished gathering the scattered contents of my messenger bag. I wrapped up the graveyard dirt, coffin nail, and tooth in the tissue and stuffed it gingerly back into the leather sack, ready to dump it back out at the first twinge of pain. I wouldn't even have bothered if the nail wasn't already poking holes in the tissue. But it seemed that Jojo had spoken the truth, and the charm was well and truly broken.

"So what happens now, Daise?" Jen asked me.

I took a deep breath, slinging my bag over my shoulder. "First, I need to tell Casimir that he can call off the coven. Second, I need to talk to Sinclair before I confront Emmy. I can't leave him out of this. He needs to decide where he stands."

"Do you want me to go with you?" Jen offered. "Because I'll be there if you do."

"I know." I gave her a quick hug. "You're the best. This, I think I can handle. But I couldn't have gotten through this morning without you. Don't tell anyone how badly I freaked out, okay?"

She returned my hug, then did the lock-the-lips-and-throw-away-the-key gesture. "I'll take it to the grave, Hel's liaison."

It was the first time Jen had ever called me by my title, and I have to admit it felt a little weird. Not bad, just . . . weird.

"Thanks," I said. "Consider yourself the first member of my own personal Scooby Gang."

Like most everyone else our age in Pemkowet, Jen and I had grown up watching *Buffy the Vampire Slayer*. "That would be a lot cooler if I wasn't totally the Xander." She smiled wryly. "No skills to offer but loyalty and a smart mouth."

"Yeah, and life would be a lot easier if I had Slayer super strength," I said. "But we make do with what we've got."

"True," Jen agreed. "And it could be worse. We could be stuck with Stacey Brooks as our unlikely mean girl ally Cordelia."

I shuddered. "Perish the thought."

# Seventeen

As soon as Jen left, I hustled back to the Sisters of Selene to update Casimir. Beneath his heavy makeup, he flushed with anger. He squeezed his eyes tightly shut for the space of a few breaths, his long, crimson-lacquered nails digging into the counter.

"Daisy, I am *so* sorry," he said when he'd collected himself. "I jumped to a conclusion when I should have taken the time to do the research."

"It's okay," I said. "I lost my temper and it made me careless. I should never have left my bag unattended, not with *dauda-dagr* in it. And you warned me that you didn't know a lot about obeah."

"That's no excuse." His face was grim beneath his bouffant wig. "But it may mean she's not as powerful as we thought. I'll tell you, the law of threefold return's going to bite her in the ass, and I wouldn't mind helping it along. Shall I start working on a counterspell, darling? Something nice and vengeful?"

"What?" I blinked. "No! Jesus, Cas! You're the one who's always warning me not to be tempted by the dark side—

which, by the way, just makes me think about it when I wasn't. Anyway, I need to handle this myself."

Pursing his lips, he considered me. "I suppose you do. All right, hold on a moment." He went over to unlock a glass display case and rummage inside it, coming up with a small silver medallion etched with a Star of David inside concentric circles and various squiggly markings, along with a loop so it could be worn as a pendant. "Here. This is your basic Seal of Solomon. It's the same seal I used in the working earlier. It should give you a measure of protection from hostile spells."

"I'm a little short on cash," I admitted. I was always short on cash.

Casimir reached for my hand and plunked the medallion into it. "Don't worry, it's not the most expensive amulet I carry, honey. And they're more effective when they're given as a gift. Take it with my blessing and wear it in good health."

"Okay, okay!" I undid the clasp on my necklace and threaded the Seal of Solomon onto the chain. When I was done, it nestled beside the Oak King's talisman, clinking companionably against it in my cleavage. "Thanks. I'll, um, record the favor in my ledger."

He eyed me. "You keep a ledger?"

"I do." I stated it with a tone of authority, or at least I tried to. "In the interest of maintaining Hel's order, of course."

"Good for you." It must have worked, because there was a note of respect in the Fabulous Casimir's voice.

I really needed to get started on that database. Too bad I knew nothing about creating databases. For now, I'd just have to settle for making mental notes, because I had more pressing matters to attend to.

After leaving Casimir's shop, I went back to my apartment to take a quick shower and change my clothes. Since there was no point in trying to compete with Emmeline Palmer on the basis of style, I went practical instead, with a working wardrobe of jeans and a black scoop-neck T-shirt. Pants weren't as comfortable as skirts since they confined my poor tail, but I'd found that people tended to take me more seriously in them.

Last, I buckled on my dagger belt. People took me a *lot* more seriously with *dauda-dagr* on my hip, too. Well, at least people who had some inkling that it was an ancient and magical weapon that put fear into the immortal undead. Otherwise, they just thought it was some weird survivalist goth chick fetish.

I gave Sinclair a call. If possible, I wanted to talk to him alone and in person before confronting Emmy.

"Hey, Daisy." He answered on the third ring, sounding curious. "What's up? I thought you were lying low."

"Things have changed," I said. "Where are you? Can we talk?"

"Yeah, I guess." Now his tone was a bit cautious. "I'm doing some work on the house. I was going to meet Emmy for lunch in an hour."

"Perfect. I'll be there in five." I ended the call before he could reply. And okay, maybe that was abrupt, but I was angry. Not my usual reactionary loss of temper, but a slow, controlled burn. I'd cut Sinclair slack, I'd forgiven him for being considerably less than forthcoming, I'd offered to stay out of the way while he worked things out with his sister. And I'd woken up hexed for my trouble.

I drove over to his rental, parking beside the tour bus. He greeted me at the door. He'd been stripping some seriously ugly wallpaper in the living room, and there were shreds of it clinging to his skin and stuck in his dreads. Under different circumstances, I would have found it adorable.

"You okay?" he asked me, taking stock of my attire.

"Not exactly." I walked past him into the living room, turning to face him when he followed. "You see, I woke up this morning with a splitting headache." I fished in the pocket of my jeans and brought out the leather sack, holding it out to him. "Then I found this in my messenger bag."

Something in Sinclair's expression shifted. He took it from me without comment, loosening the cord and examining the contents.

"You know what it is, right?" I asked.

"Yeah." His voice was flat. "You might call it a conjure bag or a gris-gris here in the States. In the Caribbean, we call it a wanga bag. Daisy, I'm so sorry. I swear, I had no idea. I would *never* have let Emmy do that to you."

"I know," I said. "But she did. And the thing is, I'm not just some girl you're dating, Sinclair, hell-spawn or otherwise. I'm the agent of Hel's authority in Pemkowet. I was willing to let a vague threat slide, at least for a while. Not this." I shook my head. "I can't. In attacking me directly, your sister challenged Hel's order."

He swallowed. "I don't think she meant to, Daise. I don't think she knew what she was doing."

I raised my eyebrows. "Oh?"

"Here in Pemkowet," he clarified. "It's different on the island. Look—you know what, never mind. We can talk about it later. What happens now?"

I laid my hand on *dauda-dagr*'s hilt. "What happens now is that Hel's liaison needs to tell Emmeline Palmer to leave town."

"And if she doesn't?" Sinclair asked.

I hesitated. "It gets ugly. Which for your sake, for our sake, I don't want. Which is why I'm here."

"You want my help in convincing her to leave?" he asked. I nodded. Sinclair held the wanga bag balanced in the palm of one hand, contemplating it. Various emotions I couldn't read passed behind his dark eyes. "All right," he said at length, closing his fingers around the leather sack. "Let's go see my sister."

We rode in silence back to downtown Pemkowet. Emmeline was staying at the Idlewild Inn, which was the most expensive B&B in town. I'd never even set foot in the place before, but it was pretty much what I would have guessed from the outside, all English cottagey, comfortable and tasteful, with framed nature prints on the walls and over-stuffed floral cushions on the furniture in the lobby. The hostess's smile faltered at the sight of us, me in a T-shirt and jeans with *dauda-dagr* on my hip and Sinclair with bits of wallpaper clinging to him—he hadn't taken the time to tidy—but she directed us to a charming little interior courtyard where dear Emmy was sitting on a bench in the sun-light, reading a book and enjoying a cup of tea.

It made for a pretty picture. She glanced up at our approach, her face brightening briefly at the sight of her brother. "Sinny! You're early—"

And then she saw me, and her expression changed. It was like a thundercloud had blotted out the sun.

Without a word, Sinclair tossed the wanga bag at her feet.

"Ah." Leaning over, Emmeline picked up the leather sack. "I see."

A fountain in the center of the courtyard burbled cheerily. I held up my rune-marked left hand. "Emmeline Palmer, as the agent of the goddess Hel's authority in Pemkowet, I'm ordering you to leave town."

Her gaze was stony. "I don't take orders from you."

I met it without flinching. "Maybe not outside the sphere of Hel's influence, but within this ten-mile radius, you do."

Emmeline cocked her head slightly. "And if I don't? Do tell. You'll make me wish I had, right?"

"Emmy." There was a raw note in Sinclair's voice. "Don't do this. You crossed a line. Don't make this more difficult than it has to be."

"Very well." She set her book on the bench, placing the wanga bag atop it, crossed her legs, and took a sip of tea, replacing the cup carefully in the saucer on the end table. "I'll make it as easy as can be. Sinclair, come with me. We'll be out of town by sundown and on the next plane home."

Aha. So that was where this was leading.

He shook his head. "No."

She stared at him, and although she *looked* elegant and perfectly relaxed, lovely as a model posing for a photo shoot, I felt that same tangible sense of menace rolling off her like fog rolling over the lake when a cold front comes through. "It's where you belong, Sinclair. It's your *home*."

"No, it's *not*." If Sinclair felt menaced, it didn't show. In fact, his expression had turned as flinty as his sister's. "I made my choice a long time ago, Emmy. Why the hell can't you respect it?"

"Because we *need* you!" Emmeline came off the bench

as fast as a rattler striking, eyes blazing with sudden passion. I found my hand on *dauda-dagr*'s hilt and the blade half drawn without thinking, but she wasn't paying any attention to me. I might as well have not existed. "Dear God, Sinclair, do you not know why a country that ought to be a fucking paradise on earth is paralyzed by endless poverty? Do you need a history lesson?"

"No," he murmured. Well, that made one of us.

"Debt and desperation," she said grimly, ignoring him. "The International Monetary Fund's been imposing impossible conditions on Jamaica since before you or I was born, Sinny. Brutal austerity measures. Tearing down trade barriers that protected our fragile commerce. Do you know local farmers still can't compete with the price of imported produce? And they bloody well destroyed the dairy industry importing powdered milk when we were still children. Powdered milk! Have you forgotten?"

"I remember," he said quietly.

Emmeline jabbed a finger at him. "*That's* the battle our mother's been fighting her whole life!"

"Oh, really?" Sinclair shot back. "Funny how nothing ever changes, except that Letitia Palmer gets richer and more powerful every year, while anyone who dares oppose her ends up broken."

"It *will* change," his sister said emphatically. "She's spent a lifetime positioning herself for it. She's running for a seat in Parliament next year."

"And I'm sure she'll get it," he said. "The same way she's gotten almost everything she's set her will to."

"She needs you, Sinny," Emmeline said. "Your country needs you. *I* need you. I miss you. It's where you belong. It's what you were born to do. It's in your blood. It's your birthright. You can help us finally, finally make a difference. Just come home."

Hell, I was halfway convinced. She was good. But Sinclair looked away and shook his head again. A few scraps of wallpaper floated to the paving stones. "Maybe God draws straight using crooked lines, but I don't believe people do. At least not our mother."

"You never gave it a fair—"

"She put a *love spell* on our father, Emmy!" he shouted at her. "He hated everything she stood for! He never wanted anything to do with her!"

Ohh-kay. I was definitely in the thick of some serious family issues now. Ordinarily, I would have beat a discreet retreat, but I'd instigated this confrontation and my authority was still on the line.

"It's a path of balance," Emmeline said defiantly. "You know that! You've got to take the dark with the light. But you know what you can't do? Turn your back on it. And that's what you imagine you've done."

"Yeah, I did," he said. "By choice, when I became a man."

Now she shook her head. "It will find you, Sinclair. How do you think you ended up here?" She pointed at me. "With *that*?"

"Hey!" I protested.

His shoulders tensed. "Leave Daisy out of it. You've done enough to her already."

Dear Emmy laughed. "Oh, that little charm?" she said in a dismissive tone. "That was nothing. Just a friendly warning that I mean business."

Some warning. My tail twitched in the confines of my jeans. "I think we've gotten a little off track here," I said to her, my hand resting casually on *dauda-dagr*'s hilt. "This is *my* friendly warning that I mean business. You have twenty-four hours to leave Pemkowet voluntarily. If you don't, I'll have you escorted outside the boundaries of Hel's territory."

She gave me a long, appraising glance.

I returned it steadily. Along with being seriously pissed in a slow, simmering way, I was feeling pretty confident about my backup after Stefan's visit. If Emmeline wanted a showdown, I was ready for it. But she zigged when I was expecting her to zag.

"You know, you really should have agreed to work with me on this, Daisy. It would have been ever so much more civilized," she said, gathering her things. "Very well, I'll go.

But I'll be back. Sinny, this isn't over. You have a month to think about it."

His face was stoic. "I don't need a month. My answer is no."

"I won't ask nicely the next time," Emmeline warned him. "Whatever happens, it will be on *your* head."

"Nice," I said. "Classic abusive logic. Oh, and by the way? You're not welcome to return."

She ignored me. "Deep down, there's a part of you that wants it, Sinclair," she said softly. "I know you miss me. And you know that the two of us together could be more than twice as powerful as either of us alone."

Sinclair folded his arms. "That's what this is really all about for you, isn't it? Go home, Emmy."

Reaching up, she patted his cheek with her free hand. "Think about it."

# Eighteen

That afternoon, I called in sick to work—hell, after the morning I'd had, I figured I was entitled—and Sinclair and I had The Talk. By this time, I'd already pieced together most of the details, but it was good to get the whole story.

In a nutshell, his mother was a brilliant, ferociously ambitious lawyer, now judge, and obeah woman descended from a long line of obeah men and women, and had used her gifts throughout her life to obtain whatever she wanted, including Sinclair and Emmeline's father, who was a good-looking, hardworking, God-fearing man who had wanted nothing to do with obeah or those who worked it. When the twins were three years old, by sheer happenstance their father discovered the love charm that had bewitched him.

And no, I did not interrupt Sinclair's story to inform him that while infatuation could be compelled, genuine desire couldn't.

Anyway, it was at that point that his father fled the island of Jamaica, taking his son with him.

"Why did he leave Emmy behind?" I asked him. We

were on the dilapidated, butt-sprung plaid couch in Sinclair's living room, where he was lying with his head in my lap, eyes closed.

"He tried to take her," he murmured. "She didn't want to go. She screamed bloody fucking murder. So in the end he left her with the neighbor."

I stroked his temples. "Do you remember it?"

"I remember Emmy screaming," he said.

In the years that followed, the divorce and the terms of custody were settled. From the time he was a young boy, Sinclair spent one month out of every summer on the island, being trained in the tradition of obeah until he was old enough to choose otherwise.

"Why did you walk away from it?" I asked him. "I'm not arguing the decision by any means—I'm just curious."

He opened his eyes. "I saw what it did to my father, Daise. All my life, he's never been quite . . . whole. And my mother . . . you know, for all her power, I don't think she's a happy woman."

"What about your sister?" I asked. "What was that business about the two of you being twice as powerful together?"

Sinclair was silent a moment. "It's true, but it's not that simple. You know what she said about obeah being a path of balance?" I nodded. "Well, I'm drawn to the light. Emmy's drawn to the dark. Together, we're capable of finding balance in far greater extremes."

"Sounds kind of ominous," I said.

"It's dangerous," he said soberly. "Especially for her. That's another reason I left. What's the point in studying healing magic, blessings, and luck charms if it drives the person closest to you deeper into darkness?"

Okay, not exactly a question I could readily answer. "You know what's odd?" I said instead. "Emmy mentioned the whole balance thing to me last night, only she said that your dating me was one step too far into the darkness."

"Did she?" Sinclair smiled wryly. "I think what she really meant is that it's one step too far out of reach. This has been going on for a while, Daisy. But before, Emmy and my

mother could tell themselves that I'd be drawn back into
the fold eventually. It was when I came to Pemkowet that
they began to worry that I'd found something that suited
me better. Dating a, um, member of the eldritch community
was the final straw."

I was dubious. "I don't know how much she said to you,
but Emmy didn't think much of your life here." If I recalled
correctly, the terms "neutered American house cat" and
"japing like a mountebank" had been used, but I wasn't
about to mention that either.

"Oh, I'm sure she was horrified," he said. "All the more
so for knowing I *like* being the guy who drives the tour bus,
who brings a spark of magic and joy into the lives of people
she doesn't think deserve it."

"Sounds about right." Gazing down at Sinclair's face, I
sighed. "Dammit, you were supposed to be the normal guy!
The nice, uncomplicated guy with the great smile and killer
thighs, the guy I could talk to about movies and go out to
dinner with and hold hands and feel like a normal human
girl for once in my life."

"Sorry." He paused. "As opposed to who?"

"Oh, no one in particular." It was a total lie, because of
course I immediately flashed on the images of both Cody
Fairfax and Stefan Ludovic, my long-standing childhood
crush and the centuries-old Outcast who made me feel
quivery inside. "It's just . . . this was supposed to be simple."

"Life isn't, Daisy," Sinclair murmured.

"Tell me about it." I laid one hand on his chest, feeling
his heart beat steadily beneath my palm. When all was said
and done, there was something soothing in the contact.
"Your sister's coming back, isn't she?"

"Uh-huh."

"What happens when she does?" I asked him. "Because
I can order her to leave again, and I'm pretty sure I can
enforce it, but I can't stop her from coming."

Sinclair met my gaze. "I'll tell her no."

"And?" I prompted him.

He took a deep breath. "My guess? She'll try to set a
duppy on me, one that will haunt me until I say yes."

"Okay," I said slowly, thinking. "So that's what we need to plan for, right? Protecting you from a . . . a duppy."

"Right." Sinclair nodded. "And in a way, I think Emmy's right, Daisy. I've been running from something I *can't* run from. I need to take a measure of responsibility for my own protection. I know some, but not nearly enough. I left the practice too soon. Maybe your local coven can help?"

"Absolutely," I said. "I'm sure Casimir would be delighted. He's already got a grudge against your sister. Can you, um, do that? Just switch from one tradition to another?"

"I don't know," he admitted. "Probably not entirely. But there should be enough overlap that I can continue to learn from them."

"Good."

An awkward silence descended between us. Where did that phrase come from? I wonder. *Silence descended.* Descended from where exactly? Was it hovering over us like the alien spaceship in *Independence Day*? Maybe it wasn't really silence so much as it was the smothering weight of something unsaid, words we'd kept at bay, kept in the air, by talking about other things.

"So." Sinclair broke the silence and broached the unspoken topic. "Where does this leave us?"

"Us." Stalling, I echoed him. "As in you and me?"

"Mm-hmm."

"Honestly?" I shook my head. "I don't know, I really don't. Yesterday morning, I was coming from what was probably the most perfect and romantic night of my life, riding across the bridge on your handlebars and feeling on top of the world, and then . . . boom."

"Yeah," he said. "I get that."

I withdrew my hand from his chest. "You should have told me."

He levered himself upright on the couch. "Daisy, I swear, if I'd had any idea Emmeline was going to show up here, I would have told you sooner. I thought we had all the time in the world."

"I know." I blew out my breath. "But we didn't and we

don't. We have one month to figure out how to keep your evil twin sister from setting a duppy on you. By the way, is that four weeks or a calendar month? Because it would be helpful—"

"Emmy's not evil." Sinclair cut me off, then backtracked, trying to lighten the mood. "Sorry. Look, did you ever see *Legend*? Vintage Tom Cruise? Ridley Scott film? Without darkness, there can be no light, right?"

"Of course I saw *Legend*!" I shouted at him, my temper flaring unexpectedly. I'd kept it on a tight rein for too long. "And I don't need any lectures about light and darkness! What do you think *I* struggle with every day? And let me tell you, evil or not, your sister isn't making it any easier!"

The air pressure in the living room intensified at my abrupt emotional shift. Dangling scraps of half-stripped wallpaper shivered.

"Daisy, I know," Sinclair said in a low voice, calm and soothing. "Look, it's one of the things I *like* about you. You may have been conceived in darkness, but you're always struggling toward the light. I admire that. A lot."

My anger dissipated. "Thanks," I muttered. "Credit my mom."

"I do," he said. "Are you kidding, girl? I envy you your mother. I wish I had one like her."

"Okay," I said. "Let's just . . . I need time to process this, all right? It's a lot to spring on a person, Sinclair."

"Fair enough," he said.

And that was how we left matters. We talked a bit longer about pragmatic issues like meeting with the Fabulous Casimir to discuss studies in the magical arts, and the fact that Sinclair was really going to need a car to get around before winter and probably a part-time job to supplement his income in the off season, and maybe should consider taking in a roommate to help with the rent even though it was cheap on account of the work he was doing to improve the place, and whether the deadline for dear Emmy's ultimatum meant four weeks from today or the same date in October, because I really did want to be prepared. Sinclair guessed it was the latter, but he wasn't sure.

When I left, Sinclair walked me to the door and kissed me good-bye, his lips lingering briefly on mine. It was one of those indeterminate kisses that could mean anything or nothing depending on what I wanted to make of it, and I wasn't sure how I felt about it.

I wasn't sure how I felt about a lot of things.

Which did not include the pebble that stung my ear as I walked toward my Honda. That just plain hurt.

"Dammit, Jojo!" Clapping my hand to my ear, I whirled around, looking for her. "I thought we had a truce!"

She darted out from behind the slender trunk of a ginkgo tree, sling in hand. "Who said aught about a truce, you whey-faced scullion?"

I winced. "I assumed it."

A look of disdain flitted across the fairy's face. "You know what they say, lackwit. 'Assume' makes an ass of 'u' and 'me.' Although in this instance," she added judiciously, "I'll allow it's merely you."

"Okay, look." I held up both hands, spreading my fingers in a universal gesture of peace. "*I'm* calling a truce. Can we talk for a minute? It's about Sinclair's sister."

Jojo lowered her sling and tilted her head, regarding me. The afternoon sunlight angled into her cat-slitted eyes, turning them an eerie and luminous hue of lavender. "I am listening."

"She's leaving," I said. "But she'll be back in a month's time. And you're right—she wants to take Sinclair away. I want to stop her. And I want to know the minute she crosses the threshold into Hel's territory. Can you help keep a look-out for her?"

The fairy sniffed. "I cannot be in all places at once."

Funny, because it certainly seemed that way to me. The laws of physics appeared to be mutable when it came to the fey. "I thought maybe your brethren and, um, sistren could help." Was *sistren* a word? I hoped so. Mr. Leary would know.

"I will ask," Jojo said grudgingly. "None among us wishes him to leave. Will there be a favor recorded in your ledger?"

"Yeah," I said. "A big one for whoever finds her first."

Her minuscule features took on a calculating look.

"Might the favor take the form of forgiveness for a past, present, or future transgression?"

Oh, gah. I should have known better than to get myself into the position of bargaining with a fairy. That usually didn't go well for mortals. "Transgression?" I hedged. "You mean like pelting Hel's liaison with pebbles?"

Jojo's luminous eyes narrowed, her translucent wings buzzing with agitation. "That is a personal matter between you and me, strumpet!"

I dropped my right hand to *dauda-dagr*'s hilt. "Okay, you know what? As much as you'd like to believe it, it's really not. So here's the deal. I'm willing to consider forgiveness for minor transgressions, Jojo. Nothing major. Nothing that results in the harm of a human, especially a tourist-type human. And no changelings," I added sternly. "Under no circumstances will the stealing of a child and the making of a changeling be forgiven. Understood?"

The joe-pye weed fairy gave a reluctant nod. "It is understood, and I will carry word to the others to enlist their aid." She bared her needle-sharp teeth in a grimace. "We do not like an outsider threatening one of our own."

I nodded in solidarity. "Neither do I."

With our bargain struck, I made my escape, ducking into the Honda before Jojo could decide the truce was off.

I drove around aimlessly for a while. I had a lot of thinking to do, but I wasn't ready to be alone with my thoughts yet. Which I realize doesn't make a lot of sense, since technically I was alone in my car, but being alone in public spaces isn't the same as being alone in the solitude of your own home. And it was nice being able to get around town without all the tourist traffic. I tooled across the bridge, feeling a pang at the memory of how happy and carefree I'd been at yesterday morning's Bridge Walk.

Just past the bridge, the SS *Osikayas* loomed over the river, white and green, its yellow smokestack jutting cheerfully into the sky. At the end of the dock, Union Pier, where I'd listened to the Mamma Jammers with Sinclair, was already closed for the season.

I turned into East Pemkowet and idled along Main

Street with its boutiques and bistros and art galleries, with the crumbling, ivy-choked Tudor of Boo Radley's house smack-dab in the middle. I thought about the rumors of Clancy Brannigan lurking inside, scuttling along the breezeway in the dark of night to retrieve the groceries delivered to his shuttered gazebo, and wondered how or why anyone would live that way. Supposedly, he'd once led a normal life as some kind of famous inventor or engineer, but no one had actually seen him for decades.

To be fair, it probably wasn't easy being the sole living descendant of the town's infamous lumber baron and axe murderer. At least he didn't have to worry about his heritage causing a breach in the Inviolate Wall, just the urban legend about Talman "Tall Man" Brannigan's ghost roaming the dunes.

Contemplating axe murderers made me realize I hadn't eaten all day and was ravenous—hey, the stomach has its own logic, which will not be denied—so I drove over to the Tastee Treat and got a cheeseburger and a chocolate milk shake to go, because if ever there was a day that cried out for the solace of fast food, it was this one.

I took my guilty spoils to the beach, which was another off-season luxury since there was no longer a charge for admission, and ate sitting perched on the hood of my car, gazing at Lake Michigan. Although it was sunny and seventy-five degrees and still felt like summer, everything looked different. There were only scattered handfuls of sunbathers and kids frolicking in the water, and more people strolling the shore, quite a few of them walking dogs, which is what locals do when the tourists go home. Which, incidentally, is illegal, but the police department doesn't bother to enforce it unless someone complains.

There was one young couple with a little dog messing around at the water's edge. It was one of those energetic, bouncy little dogs, a fox terrier or a Jack Russell, dashing back and forth before the breaking waves and barking like mad while his owners played in the shallows, the guy chasing the girl and catching her around the waist, threatening to dunk her while she shrieked with laughter.

I watched their antics while I finished my milk shake, slurping up the dregs. I tossed my trash in a nearby garbage can, got in my car, and drove back to my apartment.

Although Mogwai had made himself scarce during the whole hexing incident this morning, he was back and demanding to be fed. Some helpful familiar he was. I filled his bowl with kibble, put Koko Taylor on the stereo, and curled up on the futon in my living room.

It had been a long day, a day that started with me waking up thinking I was dying of an aneurysm. It had been a long forty-eight hours containing some of the biggest highs and lows of my life.

Sinclair's question echoed in my thoughts. *So where does this leave us?*

Good question.

*I'm a-mixed up,* Koko Taylor sang in the background, an unabashedly fierce growl in her voice. *Mixed up about you.*

"Me, too, Koko," I said aloud. Just a little mixed up, and I didn't know what to do. That sounded about right.

I liked Sinclair. I liked him a lot. I liked spending time with him and I was attracted to him. The whole thing about being threatened and hexed by his secret twin sister was an issue, but that wasn't his fault. Okay, I felt a strong sense of betrayal that he hadn't been upfront with me about such a major aspect of his life, but I could forgive him for it sooner or later. We were still getting to know each other. I hadn't been one hundred percent truthful with him, either. I hadn't told him about my feelings for Cody, or whatever the hell it was I had going on with Stefan.

But if I was honest with myself, totally, completely honest, what I felt for Sinclair didn't compare. There was none of that deep yearning or searing emotional intensity that both compelled and frightened me.

What there was instead was something else I craved, something I'd missed out on throughout the course of my life: a sense of togetherness and desire, fun and belonging, all the sweetness of being young and infatuated and oblivious to the rest of the world. I wanted to know what it was like to be the teenagers in the park with their hands in each other's back pockets or the couple at the beach romping in the water while their stupid little dog barked his head off. I wanted the satisfaction of riding on Sinclair's handlebars while Stacey Brooks stared in envy.

Like I'd said, I wanted to feel like a normal human girl for once in my life.

But I wasn't. And this probably wasn't the best time to pretend I was.

*Dauda-dagr*'s hilt was poking into my side. I unbuckled my belt and slid the dagger from its sheath, holding it up with the blade at eye level. The hilt felt preternaturally cold and bracing against my palm. The reflection of my eyes gazed back at me in the bright rune-marked steel, black on black and inhuman.

Maybe if Sinclair was completely honest with himself, deep down, it wasn't the yearning for brightness in me that drew him, but the inherent promise of darkness. Maybe without knowing it he was seeking balance for his absent twin, his missing dark half.

Or maybe not. He hadn't fought for our relationship. Hell, he hadn't even put up much of an argument.

In the end, it didn't matter which was true. I made my decision.

Then I cried for a while.

# Nineteen

Since I had to work at eight, I showed up on Sinclair's doorstep at seven thirty the next morning.

He answered the door bleary-eyed and blinking, his dreads looking frowsy. However, he was also wearing nothing but a pair of plaid boxer shorts, which was almost enough to make me change my mind. "Daisy?"

"Okay, here's the thing," I said without preamble. "When I say I want us to stay friends, which I'm about to do, I don't just mean I want us to be civil to each other. I mean I want to stay *friends*. I want to be able to call you because I heard a good joke or I had a lousy day, and I want you to feel the same way. I want to get to know you better. I want to eat popcorn and make fun of bad movies with you. I want you in my Scooby Gang."

"Your *what*?" Sinclair stared at me in bewilderment. "Wait, hang on. Are you breaking up with me?"

"Well, since we never actually defined our relationship, I don't know if you can call it breaking up, but ... yeah." I winced. "Sorry. I've never done this before, and I kind of suck at it, don't I?"

"Yeah." He rubbed his eyes with the heels of his hands. "And I'm half asleep. Is it because of my sister?"

"Yes and no," I said. "Ultimately, no."

Dropping his hands, Sinclair regarded me. "And yet you're doing exactly what Emmy told you to do."

"No." I shook my head. "Sinclair, listen. If Emmy hadn't blown things up, I think we could have had a lot of fun together, and I wish we'd had that chance. But you're not just some nice, uncomplicated guy with a great smile. And I'm . . . me. In the long run, I don't think we're the right kind of complicated for each other. Do you?"

"No," he admitted after a long moment. "But I was happy to give the short run a try, Daisy."

"Yeah, me, too," I said ruefully. "But after yesterday, I think right now we can do each other a lot more good as friends. Are you okay with that?"

"Do I have a choice?" Sinclair asked.

I shook my head. "Not really."

"All right." Sinclair gave me a reluctant smile. "If I'm going to face down my sister, I need all the friends I can get. But if you ever need to make another funky satyr booty call, girl, I'm your man."

A sense of relief and gratitude suffused me. "You're the first person I'd call," I assured him.

We parted with a hug. There was regret in it, but there was genuine affection, too; and it occurred to me as I drove downtown to the police station that in a perverse way, Emmeline might have done us an unwitting favor. After taking a long, hard look at my own feelings, I doubted that any budding romance with Sinclair could have withstood the double-barreled assault of his sister's surprise visit and her return to either collect on the ultimatum she'd issued or deliver on her threat.

But friendship? Hell, yeah. It was a lot easier to forgive a friend in trouble than it was a sort-of-boyfriend who'd been less than honest. I had experience with standing up for my friends.

And all dear Emmy's prank with the charm had done in the end was warn me not to underestimate her.

Next time I wouldn't.

It actually felt good to settle into a familiar routine at the station, reviewing the stack of incident reports that had accumulated over the holiday weekend. Nothing suspicious of an eldritch nature caught my eye, which meant Tuggle and his hobgoblin buddies had the last hurrah of the high season with their shell game.

Well, except for Emmeline Palmer. A part of me—the part that was embarrassed by the fact that I hadn't exactly handled the encounter with aplomb—wanted to avoid documenting the incident. But it was my responsibility, and it was time I started acting more professional about it, so I wrote up a full report for the X-Files.

Chief Bryant came in just as I was finishing. After exchanging a few words with Patty Rogan at the front desk, he caught my eye. "Daisy. I'd like a word with you in my office when you're done."

A little knot of apprehension formed in the pit of my belly. "Be there in a few, sir."

He nodded and went past me into his office, closing the door. I shot Patty an "Am-I-in-trouble?" look. She shrugged. Patty and I had a decent working relationship, but not a great one. I knew there were times she thought the chief was guilty of favoritism toward me. And the fact is, it was probably true. I'd known Chief Bryant since I was little. When my mom waitressed at Callahan's Café, sometimes during a day shift she'd park me in an empty booth with a coloring book. The chief used to come in for coffee, and occasionally to cheat on his diet. That's when he first took a sort of paternal interest in Mom and me, which ultimately led to my part-time job here in the department.

Since that time, I'd never been less than a hundred percent straight with Chief Bryant. Well, at least until I called in sick yesterday, which is probably why I was feeling apprehensive. As a rule, I tried to avoid lying. It's not one of the Seven Deadlies—why, I don't know, since dishonesty seems a lot more like a sin than oh, say, sloth—but when it comes to temptation I like to err on the side of caution.

I drafted the last couple of lines of my report and printed a copy before knocking on the chief's door.

"Door's open." He gestured to the chair in front of his desk as I entered. "Have a seat, Daisy."

I sat.

Chief Bryant leaned back in his chair and studied me. He was a big man with sleepy, hooded eyes that always reminded me of the old actor Robert Mitchum. A lot of people missed the intelligence in those eyes and the fact that there was solid muscle under the extra pounds he carried. "You called in sick yesterday."

"Yes, sir."

"You're never sick," he said. "Never known you to have a sick day in your life. Your mother used to brag about it."

"I had a situation." I slid the report across his desk. He put on a pair of reading glasses and skimmed it, then folded the glasses and put them down.

"Palmer," he said. "That's that young fellow you've been seeing? Runs the bus tour?" I nodded, although I wasn't fooled. Chief Bryant knew exactly who Sinclair was. He prodded the report with one thick finger. "Sounds like his sister put quite the whammy on you," he observed. "You feeling okay today?"

"Much better, thanks."

He looked at the report again. "So this obeah woman . . . what is that? Is that like a voodoo priestess?"

"A little bit," I said. "Not exactly."

He fixed me with his deceptively sleepy gaze. "Do you think she's coming back to finish what she started?"

"Yeah," I said. "Unfortunately, I do."

The chief shifted in his chair. "It's a tricky business, Daisy. As long as she hasn't violated any actual laws, I don't know how I can help you."

"I know," I said. "It's okay, I'm not asking for help. This one's my responsibility, sir."

"You've got a plan?" he asked.

I temporized. "I've got a start. I'll ask Casimir and the local coven to work on it. If we can figure out how to protect Sinclair so she can't cast a spell or set a duppy on him, I think we'll be okay. She took me by surprise this time. The next time, I'll be ready."

He blinked. "What the hell's a duppy?"

"It's a kind of ghost."

Chief Bryant processed that for a moment. "All right. If there's anything I *can* do, you let me know."

"Just back me up if I need to have her escorted out of town," I said.

"Will do." He nodded. "We can always write her up for loitering or disturbing the peace. You want me to assign Fairfax to work with you on this? The two of you did a good job together on the Vanderhei case."

My heart leaped a bit, then subsided. "Cody's, um, on his time off, isn't he?"

"Mm-hmm."

"Emmeline Palmer said she'd be back in a month," I said. "I don't know if that's four weeks or by the calendar, but . . ." I didn't finish the thought out loud. Although I was positive that the chief knew about Cody, it wasn't something he'd ever overtly acknowledged in no uncertain terms.

"Cutting it close either way," Chief Bryant said in a neutral tone. "A lunar month is twenty-nine and a half days."

Okay, those were pretty certain terms. "Right."

He sighed. "All right, then. Fairfax is out. But if you need backup, let me know."

"Will do."

With that, the chief dismissed me. I went back to the front office and finished filing the reports I'd reviewed, then clocked out for the day.

I swung by the Sisters of Selene to talk to Casimir about setting up a meeting with Sinclair. He offered to contact the coven and promised to call me when they agreed on a time and place.

Just to be on the safe side, I stopped in at the Idlewild to make sure that Emmeline Palmer had checked out. The hostess wasn't too pleased to see me—I guess I didn't make as good an impression as Emmy—but when I showed her my police ID, she confirmed that Sinclair's sister had left late yesterday afternoon.

With that done, my time was my own. I went back to my apartment and spent an hour researching database software online before giving up in despair. I needed something more sophisticated than I could afford—like the police reporting software we used at the station but something I could customize for my own purposes. That is, if I had the faintest idea how to do such a thing, which I didn't.

I knew someone who did, though. Or at least I'd gone to high school with him. I tried the phone book, but there was no listing.

I called Jen. "Hey, do you have any idea how to get in touch with Lee Hastings?"

There was a pause on the other end before she asked in an incredulous voice, *"Skeletor?"*

"Yeah," I said. "I heard he moved back to town a while ago."

"Why do you want to get in touch with Skeletor?" she asked.

"I need a computer geek," I said. "And he sort of had a crush on me."

"Good luck," Jen said. "He skipped college and went straight into the gaming industry. I heard he made a shit-load of money out in Seattle before he moved back. Now he gets paid big bucks as a consultant. Basically, he's Alan Cumming in *Romy and Michele's High School Reunion*, only without the part where he came back better-looking."

"So you're saying I can't get him to do my homework just by promising to be nice to him anymore?"

"Is that how you got a B in computer science?" she asked. "I always wondered. You know, come to think of it, you were actually pretty decent to him. Let me call my mom. She keeps in touch with Mrs. Hastings."

"Thanks."

Fifteen minutes later Jen called me back. "Okay, this is going to sound weird, because it is. He doesn't give out his info, but you can try contacting him on his Facebook alias page. If he feels like it, he'll accept your friend request."

"What's an alias page?" I asked her.

"It's this persona he's created. Dan Stanton. Apparently it's a minor character in one of his games."

"Ohh-kay."

"Told you it was weird," she said. "Hey, how are you feeling today? How did it go with the evil twin sister?"

I hesitated. "I'm fine. And it went . . . okay for the moment. She left, but she's coming back. She gave Sinclair an ultimatum. Leave town or else."

"Damn!"

"Yeah." I lowered my voice. "We're working on it. But I broke things off with Sinclair this morning."

"I'm sorry, Daise." Jen's sympathy was genuine. "Because of his sister? Or because he didn't tell you about her?"

"Not really," I said. "I mean, yeah, I guess that set it off. But I realized we're better off being friends right now."

"Did it have anything to do with the infamous hot ghoul I met yesterday?" she asked shrewdly. "Or lingering feelings for a certain officer of the law?"

"Maybe a little," I admitted. "I realized I wasn't being entirely fair to Sinclair. But I think he and I are okay, honestly."

"Good," she said. "I like him."

Inspiration struck me. "You know, Sinclair's got a spare bedroom. He talked about taking a roommate to help with the rent now that business is slowing down. And you've been talking about moving out of your folks' place for ages."

"Um. . . . yeah." Jen didn't sound thrilled "Let's table that idea until the evil twin's out of the picture, okay?"

"Fair enough."

After we ended our call, I went back online and logged on to Facebook. I didn't use it often—I never got in the habit because my mom and I couldn't afford Internet access or expensive phone plans when I was growing up—but I had an account. Also, I had free wireless in my apartment courtesy of Mrs. Browne's Olde World Bakery downstairs.

A search for Dan Stanton returned two results. One was

some shirtless guy in Sydney, Australia. The profile picture for the other was a video game avatar of a soldier in battle fatigues. Betting on the latter, I sent a friend request. I would have added a personal message, but the option was disabled. All I could do was hope that Lee Hastings, aka Dan Stanton, aka Skeletor, remembered me kindly as someone who'd never called him that last one.

Well, at least not to his face. After all, it *was* high school.

Checking the time, I saw it wasn't yet three o'clock. Until I heard from Casimir or Lee, there wasn't much I could do on either Operation Contain Dear Emmy or Operation Database, which meant I had no excuse not to respond to Stefan Ludovic's request to contact him when I was ready.

So I called him, trying to ignore the fluttery feeling in my belly. Partly because it made me feel guilty and partly because the whole thing weirded me out. Hot or not, I still had the image of Stefan impaling himself on his own sword stuck in my memory.

"Daisy." Stefan picked up on the third ring. "Good afternoon. Are you well?"

"I'm fine, thanks," I said. "But then, you'd be the first to know if I wasn't, wouldn't you?" I was still a little pissed about the bond between us being established without my knowledge or consent, too. "Anyway, you asked me to call?"

"Yes," he said. "As I said, I have something I would like to show you. I think it will be of aid in the exercise we attempted the other day."

"Okay," I said. "Is this a good time for you? If it is, I can swing by the Wheelhouse."

"Your timing is excellent," he said. "But I think perhaps this would be better done in privacy. Would you care to meet me at my quarters?"

The flutters intensified. "Your . . . quarters?"

"My condominium," Stefan clarified, then paused. "Forgive me. I did not mean to make you uncomfortable. Would you prefer to meet at the Wheelhouse? Or somewhere else? I can retrieve the item I wished to show you."

Thinking about it, it probably made more sense to minimize my exposure to the emotion-starved Outcast throng.

And after what we'd been through together earlier in the summer, I did trust Stefan.

Mostly.

"No," I said. "You're right. What's your address?"

He told me.

I jotted it down on a piece of scrap paper. "I'll be there in ten minutes," I said before I could change my mind, and hung up.

# Twenty

Stefan met me in the allotted space in the discreet parking garage of his fancy condominium complex overlooking the river. I parked my run-down Honda next to his gleaming black motorcycle, giving it a pat on the dashboard in case it was feeling inadequate.

"Daisy." Stefan gave me one of his nods, indicating the staircase. "This way."

I followed him to his unit on the second floor. It wasn't large, but it was swanky, with high ceilings, polished wood floors, and a huge picture window overlooking the river. Late-afternoon sunlight streamed through the window, filling the place with light.

Curious, I looked around. The furnishings were sleek and modern and austere. There wasn't much that reflected the owner's personality, unless you counted the one wall hung with an array of weapons on display, including the longsword on which the aforementioned impaling had been done.

Which I guess you pretty much had to count.

"Jesus," I said. "You're like the Highlander, aren't you?"

There was one piece, a painted kite-shaped shield, displayed separately on a pedestal in its own little Plexiglas case. Glancing at Stefan for permission, I went to take a closer look. I thought medieval shields were all about heraldry—rampant lions and roses and chevrons and bar sinisters and such. But this was more like an actual painting on a coppery-gold background, depicting a woman in a flowing brocade gown and elaborate headgear presenting some kind of gift to a bareheaded knight kneeling in full armor. Although it was old and obviously damaged, the pigments were surprisingly rich.

Stefan was silent while I examined it, but I could feel him watching me. When I looked back at him, his pupils were dilated.

"It is a family heirloom," he said quietly. "A parade shield intended only for ceremony. It commemorates my father receiving a token of thanks from the queen of Bohemia in gratitude for his valor in helping her husband, King Charles, escape with his life at the Battle of Crécy."

"Oh." The syllable emerged in a feeble squeak. I searched my memory for anything in my high school history classes about a Battle of Crécy and came up blank.

"It was in 1346," Stefan said. "Part of what is now referred to as the Hundred Years' War."

Okay, at least that rang a distant bell. "Um . . . wasn't that between England and France?"

"Yes." He accorded me a faint smile. "Two powerful countries that called upon their allies to fight alongside them in their wars."

I didn't know what to say and I really, really didn't want to say something stupid. This was the most Stefan had ever shared with me, and whatever complicated emotions I felt for him, I didn't want to ruin the moment with my unfortunately stereotypical American ignorance of history and geography. So I studied the features of the dark-haired knight kneeling on the shield instead. Although they were blurred, you could see the resemblance. "What was your father's name?"

"Jakob," Stefan said, a world of centuries-old sorrow in his tone. "Jakob Ludovic, Count of Žatlovy."

I turned back to him. "I'm sorry."

The bond between us tightened, the air seeming to shiver. Stefan's pupils were immense and full of swimming darkness and pain. I could feel a part of my innermost self spilling into them—

With an effort, Stefan closed his eyes and took an abrupt step backward. The bond loosened. When he opened his eyes, his pupils were small and steady. "Thank you," he said. "It was a long time ago."

Yeah, like more than six hundred years. I cleared my throat. "It's an amazing artifact. I can't believe it's in such good shape."

"Yes," he said. "The piece is museum quality. I should donate it, but . . ." He shrugged. "It is my only keepsake."

I glanced involuntarily at the weaponry on display on the wall.

Stefan followed my gaze. "Mere tools," he said. "Implements of battle with little or no sentimental value." His tone changed, becoming more businesslike. "But speaking of shields, that is precisely what I wish to show you, Daisy. Or more accurately, to give you." He beckoned. "Come."

I trailed after him as he went to retrieve an item wrapped in dark blue velvet cloth from a sideboard. With one of his formal little half bows, Stefan presented it to me.

I removed the cloth to reveal a round steel shield. Other than a hand grip welded onto the concave back, it was plain and unadorned. It was both smaller and heavier than I would have imagined, and polished to a mirror-bright shine inside and out. "You got me a shield?"

"You were having difficulty visualizing one," he said. "I thought this might help."

"Where do you buy a *shield*?" I asked. "And it's so . . . petite! Did you have to have it custom made?"

He smiled deeply enough for his dimples to emerge. "I have an acquaintance in the historical replica industry. This is actually their standard base model buckler, but I had it specially burnished."

Flexing the fingers of my left hand, I curved them around the grip and hoisted the shield aloft.

It felt good.

I gazed at my distorted reflection in the concave surface facing me, then lowered the shield. "Okay. And, um, thank you. Shall we try it again?"

In the center of the living room, Stefan took a stance opposite me, his back to the window. "Yes."

When we'd done this before, Stefan hadn't menaced me in earnest. This time, he did. With the sun in my eyes, I couldn't see the warning shift of his pupils, but I felt the inexorable tide of his hunger pulling at me.

Without thinking, I swung the shield up between us. Brilliant sunlight splintered off the highly polished surface, sending a thousand scintillating points of light dancing around the room. And just like that, something clicked inside me. I kindled the same mirror-bright blaze in my thoughts, holding it between us, a barrier that reflected Stefan's hunger back at him while it reflected my own emotions and feelings back into me.

"Ha!" Stefan broke into a grin. "That's it! Perfect! You did it, Daisy!"

Blinking against the brightness, I held the shield—the real one and the one in my head—in place. "What happens now?"

"Now?" His grin turned fierce. "Now we practice."

If you think holding a single image blazing in your mind sounds like easy work, think again. Despite my breakthrough, it was hard. Stefan worked me ruthlessly. And just when I thought I was becoming adept, he made me put down the physical shield, forcing me to conjure the mental image without it.

By the time he called a halt, I was exhausted and elated. I could do it. I could conjure a shield capable of holding a six-hundred-year-old ghoul—oops, Outcast—at bay. And for the first time since I'd begun to serve as an agent of Hel, my frustration at my own relative powerlessness abated.

I could *do* something. Something magical.

"Thank you," I said again to Stefan, this time with the sincerity and gratitude he deserved. "This is amazing, truly. How did you know?"

"It was a hunch." Returning from the kitchen with two glasses of water, he handed one to me. "But I have some experience with these matters."

I took a long drink of water. "Teaching people to protect themselves from you?"

A shadow crossed his face. "Yes."

Okay, probably not the time to get too personal with that line of questioning. I sat on his leather couch. "Can anyone learn to do it?"

"No." Taking a seat in an adjacent chair, Stefan shook his head. "There is a quality one must possess in abundance. The ancient Greeks called it *pneuma*, the breath of life."

"How can you tell when someone's got lots of pneuma?" I asked.

"One learns to sense such things," he said. "Especially when one is Outcast." He sipped his water and smiled a little. "In your case, the fact that your emotions are actually capable of effecting change on your physical environment was a good indicator that you were brimming with it."

Huh. And here I'd thought my volatile temper wasn't good for anything. "What else does it work on other than the Outcast?" I asked him. "Could I stop Emmeline Palmer from putting a hex on me?"

"No," Stefan said with regret. "It is ineffective against spellcasting. But if you are diligent in your practice, you can defend yourself from all manner of compulsion, such as vampiric hypnosis and demonic persuasion."

"Ooh!"

He pointed a stern finger at me. "*If* you are diligent, Daisy. It is like any skill. It must be honed until it is second nature to you, until the act of raising and maintaining a shield requires no more effort than breathing."

"Duly noted." I shifted and began to curl my legs beneath me, then changed my mind when I saw a look of polite dismay flit over Stefan's face. Right. No shoes on the fancy leather couch. "Stefan . . . if this energy, this pneuma, can be used to raise a defensive shield, can it be used as an offensive weapon, too?"

Stefan didn't answer right away. His pupils contracted in

his pale blue eyes, giving him that eerie, sightless look. "Against some opponents, yes," he said at length, sounding reluctant. "But to do so is dangerous, exposing you to far greater vulnerability. Promise me that you will not attempt it."

"What if—"

His pupils zoomed. "If the time comes when I deem you ready, we will speak further of this. Until then, promise me."

"Okay, okay!" I raised my hands in surrender. Well, one hand and my water glass. "I promise."

"Thank you."

I considered Stefan for a while. "Why are you doing this?" I asked him eventually. "Helping me?"

"Why would I not?" he replied. "You are Hel's liaison, and there is a debt of honor between us."

I wasn't entirely sold. After all, he was the six-hundred-year-old son of a Bohemian count, and I was a twenty-four-year-old American hell-spawn who grew up in a mobile home. Of course, Lurine had a couple of millennia on him, and then there was the matter of Hel herself, but . . . somehow this was different. They weren't human. Stefan was, or at least he had been.

"And I like you, Daisy," Stefan added unexpectedly, summoning one of those surprisingly charming smiles. "Is that so difficult to believe?"

"A little," I admitted. "Do you mean you like me, or you *like me* like me?"

He raised one eyebrow. "Are you asking if I harbor romantic feelings toward you?"

"Do you?" I countered.

"How would you feel about it if I did?" Although his gaze was steady, the hint of a smile continued to play over his lips. I couldn't tell if he was teasing or flirting.

"Honestly? I'm not sure. And this isn't the best time for me to figure it out. But you probably knew that, too." I set my water glass on a polished marble coaster. "Look, I really should be going. Thank you again."

Stefan rose gracefully. "You are welcome. Take the buckler with you. It will help you focus as you begin to practice. Just take care not to become dependent on it."

"I will."

As he escorted me to the door, the painted shield in its Plexiglas case caught my eye again. This time I noticed that the case was carefully positioned to avoid direct sunlight, and I suspected it was climate controlled, too.

*My only keepsake,* he'd said. I snuck a look at Stefan's face, wondering if I dared risk a question. Judging by his expression, yes, but not a probing one. "Will you tell me its story one day?"

"Perhaps." Inclining his head, Stefan opened the door for me. "We will see."

I guessed that would have to do.

# Twenty-one

The next morning, I logged on to Facebook to find that Dan Stanton had approved my friend request. I felt awkward sending a message to an alias—what if this Dan Stanton turned out to be another shirtless Australian guy instead of Lee Hastings?—but I went ahead and composed a note saying I was hoping he was Lee and that he might be able to give me some advice on a computer project.

After calling in to the station to confirm there wasn't any new filing for me, I spent half an hour practicing shield drill.

Okay, twenty minutes. It was harder to maintain focus without an actual opponent.

I checked Facebook again to see if Dan Stanton had replied to my message. He hadn't, but a few minutes after I'd logged in, a chat bubble with his name on it popped up.

*U there Daisy?*

This might sound weird, but I'm not a fan of all things instant and chatty. It always feels like there's too much pressure to reply immediately. But then, I was the one asking the favor, so I didn't have a lot of choice.

*Yes. Lee, is that you?*

There was a short lag, then a reply. *If you want to talk, meet me at the glug-a-slug in fifteen minutes.*

On that cryptic note, Dan Stanton went offline. Well, not that cryptic. Back in high school "glug-a-slug" was what we called the Sit'n Sip, Pemkowet's only twenty-four-hour diner, located about half a mile from the interstate highway exit. It was where teenagers went to eat hash browns, drink coffee, and sober up after clandestine keg parties. But Lee wasn't the kind of kid who got invited to a lot of parties. He was the kind of smart, aloof, unpopular kid who wouldn't deign to use the in-crowd's pet slang terms, and I couldn't imagine he would have changed that much, which meant that the fact that he was using one of them now was weird and cryptic.

Then again, I'd contacted him through an alias, so I don't know why I would have expected anything else.

About ten minutes later, I walked into the Sit'n Sip. Lee Hastings was lounging in a booth in the far corner, long legs stretched out, the rest of him slouched intently over a computer tablet. Although I hadn't seen him in a good six years, I recognized his tall, bony figure immediately, even wrapped in a full-length black leather duster despite the lingering summer warmth.

"Hey, hon!" a cheerful waitress called to me. "Sit anywhere you like."

"Thanks," I said. "I'm meeting someone."

Lee lifted his head. He was wearing a khaki-colored Seattle Mariners baseball cap, which I thought was an odd choice with a black leather duster. Heck, maybe he had changed. Or maybe that was hip in Seattle. "Daisy."

"Hi, Lee." I slid into the seat opposite him. "It's good to see you."

He touched something on the tablet, making the screen go blank. "Is it?"

"Sure."

Beneath the shadow of his baseball cap's brim, his face was as gaunt as ever, dark eyes glimmering in bruised-looking hollows. Hence the nickname Skeletor. He'd grown one of those narrow beards that looked like a strip of Velcro glued to his chin and there were steel hoops in his earlobes. Okay, that was new and unexpected. "What do you want?"

"I need to create a database—" I began.

A look of disgust crossed his face. "Oh, for God's sake! A database? Do you know what I get paid for consulting on a project? This isn't high school, Daisy. I'm not going to teach you how to use Excel just because you promise to sit next to me in the cafeteria."

Lowering my voice, I plowed on. "A database documenting the eldritch population in Pemkowet."

"Are you—" Lee paused. "Say that again?"

I repeated myself.

"Why?"

The waitress came over with the coffeepot. I turned my mug upright for a fill and ordered a Danish. "Because it will help me do my job," I said in an even tone once she was out of earshot. "Did you hear about the orgy out at Rainbow's End?" Lee gave a brief nod. "Turns out it was set off by a satyr in rut."

"Satyrs go into rut?" He sounded bemused.

"Yeah." I blew on my coffee. "Every twelve years. And if I'd had a database to keep track of this one, I could have prevented the orgy."

Lee studied me. "So it's true?"

I took a tentative sip of my coffee, scalding my tongue, and grimaced. "What?"

"I heard a rumor that you were supposed to be some sort of diplomatic liaison to Little Niflheim," he said. "But I didn't believe it."

I looked around for the waitress, hoping to catch her eye and ask for a glass of ice water. "Why not?"

"With your temper?" Lee grinned. "Unless you've changed a lot in the last six years, you're the least diplomatic person I've ever known. Didn't you get suspended for threatening to cut Stacey Brooks's hair off in her sleep?"

"No," I said. "That was Jen Cassopolis. *I* got suspended because the pipes in the girls' locker room burst when I lost my temper because Stacey Brooks called my mother a Satan-worshipping whore. Anyway, yes and no. I'm an agent of Hel, and it's my job to serve as the liaison between her rule of order and the mundane authorities. No one ever said I had to be diplomatic about it, just effective."

"So you've actually been there?" Lee asked. "To Little Niflheim? You've actually *met* her?"

"Yes."

He took a deep breath. "Tell me about this database."

Between bites of my Danish, I filled him in on what I had in mind. I'm not sure if I was using the correct terminology, but I wanted to be able to sort and search the data by different criteria: proper names, type of eldritch, capabilities, date, location, transgressions, favors. And I wanted it synced with a calendar that would keep track of things like the full moon and satyrs' twelve-year rutting cycles.

Lee listened impassively. "Okay," he said when I'd finished. "That's doable. It might even be mildly interesting. What's your budget?"

I winced. "Yeah, about that . . ."

"I figured." He leaned back in the booth, stroking the landing-strip of beard clinging to his chin. I wanted to tell him it looked ridiculous, but I didn't think he'd thank me for the favor. "All right." He glanced around to make sure no one was listening. "I'll do it. But I want in."

"In?" I echoed. "In on what?" I mean, he might be able to sell it in other places with eldritch populations, but that was a niche market, to say the least.

"In," Lee repeated. "I want *in*, Daisy. To Little Niflheim." I stared at him. "Look." He leaned forward. "I create fantasy worlds, okay? That's what I do. Whether it's a first-person shooter set in Afghanistan or a *World of Warcraft* knockoff doesn't matter. It's a fantasy. But meanwhile, there's an actual mythological underworld with an actual fucking *goddess* right under my fucking feet!" He bared his teeth in a fierce smile that made him look more skull-like than ever. "I want to see it. I want in."

I stalled for time. "I see."

"Can you do that?" Lee slouched back against the booth,

his eyes intent in their deep sockets. "Because I'll give you everything you want for one glimpse of Hel."

Ironic phrasing, that.

"Okay," I said slowly, thinking. "We'll try it." It occurred to me that I really should get Hel's permission before moving forward with the project anyway. "But I can't make any promises. And even if it works out, I don't guarantee you'll enjoy the experience."

"I don't care if I enjoy it," Lee said. "I just want to *have* it."

I shrugged. "Fair enough. I live in the rear apartment over Mrs. Browne's bakery. Come by just before sunset tonight."

He activated his tablet, fingers skittering over the screen. "The sun sets at eight thirteen. I'll be there at ten after."

"See you then." I tossed a five on the table to cover the cost of my coffee and Danish, plus tip. Say what you will of the Sit'n Sip, but the prices are reasonable. "Is there a number where I can call you if something comes up?"

Lee glanced up at me. "You can reach me the same way you did before."

"Okay," I said. "Is there, um, any reason you're acting so squirrelly about your contact info?"

He gave me another Skeletor smile. "Corporate espionage. I don't want my enemies to know how or where to find me."

"Ohh-kay." I was getting the impression Lee was a bit paranoid. "Call me crazy, but isn't communicating by Facebook pretty much the least private, least secure method you could choose?"

"Absolutely," he said. "Which is why no one would ever think to look for me there."

I guess he had a point.

I left the Sit'n Sip and drove back to my apartment. By the time I got home, I had a voice mail from the Fabulous Casimir saying that the coven had agreed to convene at seven o'clock Saturday night. He rattled off his home address and told me to bring Sinclair there for a meet and greet.

I called Sinclair and found myself irrationally disappointed to get his voice mail in turn, but I relayed Casimir's message and asked him to give me a call to confirm.

Okay, so that was done.

Meanwhile, propped against the futon in my living room, the buckler that Stefan had given me offered a silent, shining reprimand for my lack of diligence. I checked the time and took another shot at it.

Nope, still not as good without an actual opponent. This time I lasted all of five minutes—hey, time passes a lot more slowly than you might think when all you're doing is holding an image in your mind—before abandoning my effort.

Acting on an impulse I didn't care to analyze, I tried calling Stefan to see if he might be available to help me train. After all, he seemed to be invested in the process. And, okay, let's be honest; despite the bad timing, the possibility that Stefan Ludovic might actually have feelings for me was intriguing.

No luck—just more voice mail.

I hoisted the shield again and spent a few more minutes angling it here and there to create bright points of reflected sunlight for Mogwai to chase across the floor. "Here's the thing, Mog," I informed him. "I want to get good at this, I really do. And I know I need to practice. I just think I need . . . incentive."

Finally copping to the fact that he was never, ever going to catch any of the dancing sunbeams, Mogwai shot me a look of betrayal, turned his back, and sat down to indulge in a vigorous bout of indignant grooming.

"It's no good because it's not real, right?" I said to him. "There's no satisfaction. You know what I mean?"

Licking one outstretched haunch, my cat didn't deign to acknowledge my comment.

For a moment, I entertained the thought of calling Cody to enlist his aid, but I wasn't sure about the protocol of disturbing a werewolf around the time of a full moon, and truth be told, a werewolf wasn't the kind of menace I needed.

I thought about calling Lurine, too, but . . . see, here's the thing. I don't know *exactly* what Lurine's capabilities are, other than the ability to shape-shift into a glorious and terrible monster. I mean, I have a pretty good idea that it involves sucking the essential life force out of the occasional ordinary human being to sustain her immortal existence, which may or may not be what she did to her late and relatively unlamented octogenarian husband, millionaire California real-estate tycoon Sanford Hollister, but I don't know for sure.

And I don't want to. After all, it didn't happen in Pemkowet, so it's not my concern. Call it a cop-out. I don't care.

But I was still restless and fidgety and spoiling for some kind of fight, enough so that I found myself grabbing my car keys and heading out the door with *dauda-dagr* on my hip and Stefan's buckler in hand.

If I wanted an opponent, I knew where to find one.

Okay, so I felt a *little* silly walking into the Wheelhouse carrying a shiny round shield in addition to my magic dagger, and it didn't help when Cooper set down a pool cue and came over to greet me with a broad grin.

"Well, if it isn't Joan of feckin' Arc," he said, giving me the once-over. "If you're looking for the big man, he's not here. He's off meeting with some fellow at that fancy microbrewery down the road."

"Maybe you could help me," I said.

Cooper's pupils dilated, glittering in his angelic blue eyes. "What did you have in mind?"

Yep, that helped. I raised my shield—my mental shield—holding it blazing between us in my thoughts. "I guess you could say I'm looking for a sparring partner."

There was an abrupt shift in the atmosphere in the bar. Since the rebellion earlier this summer, Stefan had solidified his position as the undisputed leader of the Outcast in Hel's territory and those under his command had been careful not to treat me and my super-size emotions as a potential all-you-can-eat buffet. Well, that and the fact that I'd dispatched two of their number to a final and lasting death.

This was different. There was a new measure of respect

in the eyes that gleamed out at me from the depths of the
bar, and a measure of speculation, too. They recognized a
challenge when they saw one. Or sensed one, I guess. Anyway, if I wanted a fight, there were half a dozen ghouls
ready to give me one.

And . . . that was a bit much for my fledgling skills. My
mental shield faltered and vanished.

"Jesus, Mary, and Joseph!" Cooper angled himself to
block me from view of the others. "You're a piece of work."

I hoisted the buckler and rekindled my mental shield in
the same motion. "Are you going to help me out or not?"

He glanced around. "Yeah, all right. Let's go out back."

I followed Cooper outside and around to the rear of the
building, where there was an area of hard-packed dirt
adorned with cigarette butts.

"So that's what himself's been up to with you?" Cooper
asked casually, shoving his hands in the pockets of his jeans
and rocking back and forth on the balls of his feet. He wore
a pair of lace-up construction boots that looked too big for
his scrawny frame. I still had a hard time wrapping my head
around the fact that teenaged-looking Cooper was never
going to grow into his feet. "Seems you're a good student."

I kept my shield in place. "It's a lot like the visualization
exercises I've done since I was a kid. Only harder."

His expression was unreadable. "So you really want me
to unleash the beast? I'll warn you, I don't have the kind of
control the big man does."

I was apprehensive, but I was curious, too. "Is that what
you call it? The beast?"

Cooper's pupils waxed. "It's what *I* call it. The beast, the
black beast that rides my soul." He gave me a grim smile.
"Do you know why we're cursed with our beasts, pretty
Daisy?"

"Honestly?" I said. "No, I don't. I didn't think anyone
truly understood it."

"Ah, well, if you're being technical, no." Cooper shrugged.
"How we exist and why, whether there's some purpose to it
or it's a mere accident of fate. But the beast . . . I understand
the beast."

I lowered my shield a fraction. "Tell me."

"Because we were forged in death at the pinnacle of our existence." Cooper looked past me into the distance. "Half saint, half sinner, facing death in a howling storm of rage or fury, despair or defiance, passion or hatred. We died filled with a blaze of terror and hope, not knowing if we were going to meet God or the Devil himself, and we woke to find ourselves cast back into the mortal world, lying in the stink of our own shit. But you know what? We want that moment back. We *crave* it. We ache to go back to that one terrible, horrible, glorious moment. And we can't. We're trapped. Outcast. And the eternal hunger rides us like a beast, claws gouging us like spurs." His gaze returned to me, clear-eyed and steady. "So we fill the void with whatever we can."

"Oh." The word came out in a whisper. I had a feeling I wouldn't have a problem with thinking of Cooper as a teenager after this.

"Now you know what you're asking for," he said to me. "Do you still want it?"

"I need to learn." I held his gaze. "Are you still willing to help me?"

"I am."

I flexed my left hand around the buckler's grip, holding its image in my thoughts. "Let's do this."

Cooper turned his beast loose and came at me hard. A ghoul's attack is a difficult thing to describe because it's not like anything else you've experienced. That void, that hunger, exerts a profound tidal pull on everything inside you, everything you feel, trying to suck out your innermost emotions and devour them, leaving emptiness in their wake.

And I understood immediately what he meant about not having Stefan's control. When I'd sparred with Stefan, he'd kept his beast on a short leash. His attack was tight and focused. Cooper's was all over the place, swarming me.

It was like trying to fight some kind of tentacled, soul-sucking fog. I battered frantically at it with my mental shield, left and right, high and low. Cooper circled me, forcing me to turn with him.

"Draw your dagger, you eejit!" he shouted at me. "If this was a real fight, you'd need it!"

Duh. It hadn't occurred to me. I wrapped my hand around *dauda-dagr*'s hilt and pulled it from its sheath.

Cooper took a few wary steps backward. "Right," he said. "Now put down the shield. You need to be able do this without it."

Without breaking eye contact, I tossed the buckler aside. It clattered on the packed dirt. My mental shield continued to blaze steadily and with *dauda-dagr* in my right hand, I felt balanced in a way I hadn't before.

"All right." Cooper grinned, his dilated pupils shining. "Let's dance."

I don't know how long we sparred, but it felt like a good long while and by the end of it, I was wrung out, even more exhausted than I had been after my bout with Stefan—in part because I didn't have that initial I-can-do-this rush of elation to sustain me and in part because Cooper had pushed me harder.

He took a moment to collect himself when I called for a stop, then excused himself and ducked into the bar through the rear entrance. I sheathed *dauda-dagr* and waited uncertainly until he returned a few minutes later, his pupils normal and a pair of cold Budweisers in his hands.

"Sorry about that." Cooper handed me a beer. "Needed a little something to take the edge off."

Somehow, I didn't think he meant the beer. I was pretty sure he meant one of the mortal barflies and hangers-on inside the Wheelhouse. "That's . . . okay."

He eyed me as he took a pull on his beer. "Makes you a mite squeamish, does it?"

"A mite," I admitted. "My first experience with, um, an Outcast's appetite wasn't a good one."

Cooper looked surprised. "Himself?"

I shook my head. "No, not Stefan. It was a guy named Al. He's gone—Stefan banished him. But he . . . tasted me against my will, and it sent him ravening." The memory of it still made me feel dirty.

"Ah, well. It's different when you're willing," he said, taking another swig of beer. "But then, you know that, don't you?"

"Yeah." I'd given Stefan permission to drain my anger when I was on the verge of losing my considerable temper and causing an ungodly scene at a funeral. The fact that it had felt as good and shockingly intimate as it had was almost as unnerving as being coerced against my will. "I do."

Cooper changed the subject. "You did well today. You've got the knack for this."

"Thanks," I said. "I appreciate your help." I took a sip of beer. "Would you be willing to do it again?"

He considered me. "Yeah, I would. You know, I thought my little speech would scare you off. But I reckon you're tougher than you look."

"It was quite a speech," I said.

"I hope so," Cooper said in a flat, dispassionate voice. "Because I meant every sodding word of it."

# Twenty-two

After leaving the Wheelhouse, I swung by Sedgewick Estate to visit my mom. I'd call it a whim, but the truth was, after everything that had happened in the past few days, I was in need of some maternal sympathy.

As it turned out, I was totally in luck. Mom was just putting a pan of lasagna in the oven, and there was plenty of time to fill her in on my latest trials and tribulations—although I didn't tell her the part about Emmy's charm sending me to Doc Howard's office—get some quality Mom-style commiseration regarding my breakup with Sinclair, eat a home-cooked meal, and still get back to my place well before sunset.

In the bedroom of my apartment, I went into my narrow closet to retrieve the iron casket I'd stashed on the top shelf, then fetched the key from its hiding place in the jewelry box on my dresser.

The casket wasn't much bigger than a jewelry box, but it was heavy as hell, ancient and battered and inscribed with intricate Norse knotwork designs. Hel had given it to me the first time she'd summoned me into her presence and offered me the position of serving as her liaison to mundane authorities.

I took it into the living room to unlock it and examine its contents. Everything was in order: the little copper bowl, the packet of scaly pine bark from Yggdrasil II wrapped in soft wool, the box of wooden kitchen matches I'd added.

Whether or not it would work, I couldn't say for sure. In the few years that I'd served Hel, I'd never had occasion to attempt to contact Little Niflheim. It had always been the other way around.

Truth be told, I was curious.

Lee Hastings appeared on my doorstep at exactly ten minutes after eight, looking like death warmed over and wrapped in a black leather duster. I bet he was one of those guys you could set your watch by.

"I'm here," he announced, proclaiming the obvious in a magisterial tone. "Shall we go?"

"Hold on, cowboy." I tucked the iron casket under my arm. "You don't just waltz into Little Niflheim uninvited. Besides, I don't have a dune buggy."

Lee frowned. "A dune buggy?"

"Jeep, four-wheel drive, all-terrain vehicle, whatever. I don't have one, and it's not a route I'd risk if I did. How else did you think we were going to get there?" I asked him. I might have been the only citizen in living memory to visit Pemkowet's underworld, but everyone knew where it was, more or less. Yggdrasil II is the entrance, and it's tough to miss a pine tree the size of a skyscraper jutting out of the sands that swallowed the old lumber town.

"I don't know," Lee admitted. "I imagined something less . . . prosaic."

"Well, let's see if we can get an invite," I said.

He followed me back downstairs and into the park across from the alley, gathering the folds of his duster around him to sit opposite me on the grass. There was a hint of afterglow along the western horizon, but dusk was falling and there was a slight chill in the air warning that autumn was coming.

I set the iron casket between us and opened it, taking out the copper bowl and nestling it in the grass.

"What is that?" Lee asked.

"It's a bowl," I informed him, unwrapping the woolen packet and extracting a scaly chip of pine bark. There were seven of them, each about the size of my hand and densely inscribed with lines of runic script. Hel hadn't given me any criteria for using them to contact her or any assurances that she would replace them if and when I'd used the last. I hesitated, second-guessing my decision.

"I can *see* it's a bowl," Lee said with irritation. He pointed at the pine bark. "What does it say?"

"I have no idea." I wondered what Hel would do if she determined I'd wasted her time to satisfy the whim of a geeky gaming genius. Then again, my rationale was a valid one. If Hel disapproved of the idea of a database documenting the entire eldritch population, I'd better find out now. I'd already made a few promises regarding the significance of my as-yet-nonexistent ledger. It was probably best to stick with my initial decision.

"You don't read futhark?" Lee asked in disbelief.

I scowled at him. "No, I don't read futhark. What's futhark?"

"Uh, it's only the runic alphabet." Clearly, he thought I was an idiot. "See here in the center?" He pointed again. "*H-E-L*. It's written horizontally and vertically. Probably some kind of summoning locus."

"Great," I said. "What does the rest of it say?"

He pursed his lips. "I can't tell. I'm afraid I don't actually speak Old Norse."

"Neither do I," I said. "Except for a few words here and there that I've picked up along the way. So that sort of invalidates the purpose of learning to read futhark, doesn't it?"

Lee couldn't bring himself to agree. "Knowledge is never wasted."

"Maybe not," I said. "But it can on occasion be somewhat superfluous." I watched a flicker of surprise cross

Lee's gaunt face and silently thanked Mr. Leary for drilling vocabulary words into me back in the day. "Look, do you want to sit there and tell me how to do my job, or do you want me to actually *do* it?"

He took a deep breath. "I'm sorry. I just want to know."

"Know what?"

"Everything." Lee tilted his head a little and smiled wryly. It was the first truly candid expression I'd seen on his face and it transformed him, bringing out an unexpected charm; less Skeletor, more mid-1990s heroin-chic male model. Well, except for the ill-advised facial hair, baseball cap, and goth duster. "Go ahead, Daisy. I'll shut up."

"Okay." I held the inscribed chip of bark harvested from Yggdrasil II itself in my left hand, struck a wooden match with my right, and touched the flame to the dry bark.

It caught quickly, kindling to a bright, dancing glow in the dim twilight of the park. I watched the flames lick at the runes neither Lee nor I could read, darkening and consuming them. The occasional spark snapped and a thin stream of aromatic, piney smoke trickled upward into the evening sky. When the flames got close to my fingertips, I dropped the bark chip into the copper bowl. It struck the bottom of the bowl with a faint ringing sound. In the trees above us, a trio of blue jays took flight in a raucous burst of chatter.

I smiled.

"What is it?" Lee asked, watching me.

I pointed after the birds. "They're Hel's harbingers."

*"Blue jays?"* he scoffed.

"Odin had ravens," I said as though I'd known it forever. Actually, I'd just learned it a month ago. "Blue jays are in the same family."

"Odin's ravens were named Hugin and Munin," Lee mused, tracking the flight of the blue jays. "Thought and memory. I'll be damned." He looked back at me. "What happens now?"

I stirred the ashes in the bowl with the burned-out matchstick, making sure there were no live embers left. "Now we wait and see. And, um, take this stuff back to my apartment and put it away," I added. "I forgot, I need to put on some warmer clothes. It's always cold in Little Niflheim."

We returned to my apartment and sat in awkward silence, Lee slouching on my futon.

"So . . . um . . . have you been in touch with any of your old friends since you've been back?" I asked, trying to remember the names of the two guys he'd hung out with in high school. Together, they'd been a sort of nerdy Three Musketeers. "Steve Geddes, or Ben, um . . . ?"

"Lewis," Lee said shortly. "Ben Lewis. He's in Afghanistan."

"He is?" I blinked. "In the *army*?"

"Well, he's not there on his honeymoon."

"You don't have to get sarcastic," I said. "I'm just surprised I didn't know."

Lee shrugged. "I don't know why you would."

"It's a small town," I reminded him. "So I guess that means you're still in touch with him?"

"Yeah." His voice softened. "The character Dan Stanton in my first-person shooter was named after a buddy of his. Kind of a tribute. Ben's the one who suggested it, even told me to use it as an alias. Said his buddy would have thought it was hilarious."

"This is a buddy who . . . didn't make it?" I asked. Lee nodded. I thought about that for a minute. Ben Lewis had been a short, stocky little guy in high school. Everyone called him the Hobbit. It was hard to imagine him in a war zone. "I'm sorry."

"You didn't know."

"How about Steve?" I couldn't remember anything about Steve other than his name, which was sort of ironic; he'd been the kind of kid who made so little impression, he didn't even have a nickname.

"He's fine. He's in New York."

"Doing what?" I asked.

"Set design." Lee regarded the toes of his Converse sneakers. "It was his major at NYU."

"Huh. Good for him." It felt strange to realize that two people I'd grown up with, however little I'd actually known them, had left Pemkowet to make such diverse lives for themselves elsewhere. Three, if you counted Lee. I wondered what had prompted him to return.

Before I could ask, Mikill and his dune buggy pulled into the alley beside my apartment, waiting patiently while Lee and I came down to meet him.

"Daisy Johanssen," Mikill greeted me in a booming voice, raising his left hand. A spear-headed rune glimmered on his palm, indicating that he was one of Hel's guards. "Your request for an audience has been granted." Rivulets of meltwater dripped from the icicles in his hair and beard. Mikill was a frost giant, eight feet tall with pale blue frost-rimmed skin and eyes the color of dirty slush.

Well, unless you happened to be mortal and of mundane birth. Then he just looked like a huge, hairy guy who was sweating profusely.

"Who the hell is *that*?" Lee asked, the words emerging in a squeak.

"Hi, Mikill." I raised my left hand in reply, displaying my own rune. "He's our escort," I said to Lee. "He's a frost giant."

Lee glared at me. Whatever goodwill had been emerging between us evaporated. "Oh, very funny. Ha-ha, you got me."

"Look, I realize he doesn't appear ... Mikill, can you drop your glamour for a minute?" I asked.

The frost giant shook his ponderous head, sending droplets of water flying. "It is of Hel's doing, Daisy Johanssen, that her servants might move freely aboveground at need. If it is your wish that the mortal accompany you, he will see clearly in Niflheim."

I shrugged. "You're just going to have to trust me on this one, Lee."

Lee backed away. "No. Oh, hell, no! What were you going to do?" he asked grimly. "Drop me off in the middle of the dunes at night and let me walk home? Hell, don't tell me! Is there someone else in on it? Maybe you've got some other big hairy guy out there pretending to be the Tall Man's ghost?"

"Lee—"

"I'm not falling for it, Daisy! I put up with enough shit like that in high school—"

"Lee!" I raised my voice and dropped my hand to *daudadagr*'s hilt. Amazingly, he actually shut up. "Look, I know you've got high school damage, okay? Everyone does. You've made it very clear that you're not the dorky nerd in high-waisted floods your mom bought for you anymore. You went away and made a ton of money and came back.... Why the hell *did* you come back, anyway?"

"My mom's not well," he said in a quieter tone. "Someone had to look after her."

"Okay, well, I'm sorry to hear it. But I'm not the same person I was, either," I said. "I'm not asking you to help me pass computer science. I get that you think this project is beneath you, but it's important to me, and I'm not pulling some stupid prank just because you've been kind of a dick about it."

Lee stared at Mikill and his dune buggy and swallowed hard, his Adam's apple bobbing. "If you drop me in the dunes, I swear to God, I'll never forgive you."

I felt bad.

It was easy enough to say everyone had high school damage, but the truth was, hell-spawn or not, I'd gotten off light compared to Lee and his friends. No one had ever held me upside down in the bathroom, dunked my head into the toilet, and given me a swirly. It had happened to Lee, though, probably more than once. And I didn't doubt that the shadow of that humiliation lingered.

"No one's dropping anyone in the dunes, Lee," I said to him, making my voice gentle. "I promise. Just don't fall out. Because unlike the Tall Man's ghost, Garm is real."

"The hellhound?"

"Uh-huh." I wedged myself into the narrow storage space behind the buggy's two seats, wishing I'd thought about the logistics earlier. "You'll find a loaf of bread on the floor at your feet. That's the offering to Garm. Lee, you're in charge of throwing it to him. Mikill"—I took a death grip on the roll bar—"drive carefully."

As soon as Lee climbed gingerly into the front seat and buckled his seat belt, Mikill gunned the engine and headed out of town.

A mile north on the highway, he turned into Pemkowet Dune Rides, passing the stable where the fancy dune schooners were sitting idle for the night and roaring into the path beyond it.

I'd made this trip before, but it didn't get any less frightening. Quite the opposite, considering I was squished into a cramped space without a seat belt and holding on to the roll bar for dear life.

And once we departed from the graded paths and set course for the massive, looming figure of Yggdrasil II, jouncing over the sand, it got worse. I narrowed my eyes against the stinging mist of ice pellets streaming from Mikill's hair, searching the darkness in the vain hope of catching a glimpse of Garm before he spotted us.

No such luck. As we entered the sand basin from which Yggdrasil II emerged, somewhere off to the left, an ear-shattering howl split the darkness.

"The hound is nigh," Mikill announced.

"Lee!" I shouted. "He's coming! Get the bread ready!"

In the passenger seat, Lee struggled, the folds of his capacious leather duster caught on something. "I'm stuck!"

Directly in front of us, Garm bounded into the headlights, yellow eyes reflecting the beams. He was approximately twice the size of the dune buggy and his slavering maw was big enough to chomp me in half in a single bite.

"Lee!"

"Why the hell is he attacking us?" he said in a high, panicked voice. "Isn't he on our side?"

"The hound is doing its duty," Mikill said, swerving violently. The hellhound snapped as we veered around him, jaws closing with a click that sounded like the world's biggest bear trap. "Throw the offering *now*, mortal!"

Lee yanked at his trapped coat. "But aren't we past—"

A fast, heavy tread padded behind us, and then a vast figure darkened the emerging stars overhead as Garm leaped over the dune buggy, landing with a thud and turning to face us, growling low in his throat and wrinkling his muzzle to show his teeth.

"Oh, for God's sake!" Letting go of the roll bar with one hand, I leaned over to snatch the loaf of bread from Lee's hand. Garm's ears pricked up. He wagged his tail hopefully, strings of drool dangling from either side of his jaws. "Here you go, boy!" I threw the loaf as hard as I could. "Go get it!"

The hellhound bounded after his treat. In the front seat, Lee turned to give me an incredulous look.

"What?" I said to him. "You want to visit Little Niflheim, you bring a loaf of bread for Garm."

"Um . . . why bread?" he asked in a faint voice.

"Because that's the way it is," I replied firmly. I'd asked the exact same questions on my first visit and gotten the exact same highly unsatisfying response. Somehow it felt better being on the other side of the equation.

Mikill gunned the buggy's engine again. "Be sure to keep your limbs inside the vehicle during the descent."

Lee looked around the basin. "Descent? Descend where?"

I pointed at Yggdrasil II. "There."

The fact that a gap large enough to admit a small vehicle looked like a mere crack in the mammoth trunk gives you an idea of the scale of the tree. Lee let out a terrified sound as we hurtled toward it, then slumped in deflated relief as we passed through the opening and began spiraling down the path carved into the walls of the hollow interior. The temperature dropped as we descended, an icy mist rising from the depths below us. Mikill stopped dripping, his hair and beard freezing.

Down, down, down we went, emerging beneath the immense canopy of roots that the three Norns tended with tireless care, drawing water from the wellspring and pouring it over Yggdrasil II's roots. One of them smiled at me, her eyes as colorless as mist in her grandmotherly face. I smiled back at her. She'd given me a piece of soothsaying earlier this summer that had saved a lot of lives.

"Are those . . . ?" Lee asked in a hushed whisper.

"The Norns," I said.

Turning his head, he looked at Mikill hunched over the steering wheel. "And he's . . . blue."

"I told you," I said. "He's a frost giant."

Little Niflheim really is little. There's nothing left of the buried city of Singapore but a single road and a handful of buildings, including the abandoned sawmill where Hel holds court. Or at least that's what it looks like, insofar as it's possible to see in the darkness and mist. I suspected that here, as elsewhere in the eldritch community, the laws of physics didn't necessarily apply.

*Duegars*, the ancient Norse dwarves whose magic had excavated Little Niflheim and kept the whole thing from collapsing, came out to observe our passage, silent and watchful, looking as knotty and hardened as though they'd been carved from Yggdrasil II's roots.

"What do they want?" Lee whispered to me.

I shrugged. "I don't know. I've never heard one speak. Maybe if you learn Old Norse, you can ask them."

In the driver's seat, Mikill made a muffled sound that might actually have been a chuckle before halting in front of the sawmill. "Come, Daisy Johanssen," he said to me. "You are expected."

"Hey, wait!" Lee clambered out of the dune buggy. "What about me?"

Mikill fixed him with an implacable slush-colored stare. "You are not expected."

"Daisy—"

I spread my hands. "Look, I told you I couldn't promise you anything. I'll ask, but don't hold your breath. She's a *goddess*, Lee. She's not some imaginary character made of bits and bytes and pixels."

"Okay." He swallowed hard, then glanced around at the misty darkness, the watching eyes of the silent *duegars*. "Right. Of course. Do what you can, and I'll . . . I'll just wait here with the car."

"Fine."

With that settled, Mikill escorted me into the sawmill.

Being in the presence of a living deity is another experience that's hard to describe. There's just so much . . . well, *presence*. It's awesome in the oldest sense of the word. It makes the very air feel different, charged and intense. It makes your skin prickle and raises the hair on the back of your neck. Whether you're a worshipper or not, you *will* tremble. And you will kneel and bow your head, whether you intended to or not.

Don't get me wrong—as Hel's liaison I was more than prepared to offer her honor and respect. I'm just saying it would have happened regardless.

"Rise, Daisy Johanssen," the goddess bade me, her voice tolling like a bell.

I rose.

Seated on a throne wrought from the immense saw blades that the *duegars* had salvaged and brilliantly repurposed, Hel regarded me. "So, my young liaison. What compels you to seek an audience?"

With an effort, I made myself return her gaze evenly, which wasn't an easy feat. On her right side, Hel resembled some Renaissance painter's idea of a goddess, fair-skinned, beautiful, and luminous, with boundless depths of compassion and wisdom shining forth in her gaze. That part was easy. The left side ... the left side was another matter, burned and blackened and withered, her sunken left eye glowing like a baleful red ember in its hollow socket. It was hard to meet that eye.

"There's something I'd like to do, my lady," I said to her. "But I felt I should ask your permission."

Her right eye closed, the right half of her face lovely and gracious in repose. Her left eye continued to blaze at me. "Tell me."

I outlined my idea for a database, floundering as I tried to couch it in terms that would be comprehensible to someone whose idea of modern innovation was the Gutenberg printing press. Aboveground, there were plenty of members of the eldritch community who have embraced technology. It was different in the underworld. Well, except for Mikill's dune buggy.

"Enough." Hel opened her right eye and raised her graceful, elegant right hand to stop me. "Although the means may be unfamiliar, the notion is not. Humankind has catalogued the world since first they began scratching marks in the soil. Even so, we have never abetted them in this task." She closed both eyes and fell silent a moment before opening them again. "Although I have misgivings, your idea has merit. I grant you permission to execute it."

I let out a breath I hadn't known I was holding. "Thank you, my lady."

Her right eye closed again. Oops, not out of the woods yet. "And this mortal you have brought into my demesne?"

"I would need his help to accomplish the task," I said. "You might say he's the only scribe in town."

Hel said nothing, which I took to be her equivalent of raising her eyebrows and saying, "And . . . ?"

Despite the cold, a trickle of sweat ran down my back beneath the old down coat I'd donned for the occasion. "He promised to give me everything I want for one glimpse of you."

The shadowy frost giant attendants behind Hel's throne murmured at the audacity of Lee's request. The goddess turned her head this way and that, revealing one perfect and one devastated profile in turn as she silenced them with a look. "I will consider it, Daisy Johanssen. Tell me, what else passes above?"

A blue jay roosting in the rafters gave a rather self-satisfied squawk, leading me to suspect it had observed me stumbling along the streets of Pemkowet the other day, half-blind, pain-dazed, and clinging to Jen's arm. I shot it a covert glare as I reported on events of the past month, including Emmeline's attempt to hex me and her threat to return.

But I managed to keep it on a professional level and Hel heard me out impassively. She was a goddess; she didn't care about petty issues—she cared about results. "Well enough, my young liaison," she said when I finished. "See that you continue to uphold my order."

"Yes, my lady."

Hel glanced upward. A pair of jays fluttered down to perch on the back of her throne, peering at me with bright, beady eyes. "There have been reports of a . . . person of interest . . . inquiring about purchasing large tracts of land in Pemkowet."

"A person of . . . oh." The sweat trickling down my back turned icy and my tail twitched uneasily. I remembered the lawyer I'd seen leaving the PVB. Hel was being polite. "You mean a hell-spawn like me."

"No." Closing her ember eye, her fair right side regarded me with gentle compassion. "Quite unlike you, Daisy Johanssen."

My throat tightened with an unexpected surge of gratitude. "Thank you, my lady," I murmured. "Have your, um, harbingers told you more? Is there something you'd like me to do about this?"

"No. I do not know." Hel was silent for a long moment, her expression undecipherable. "It troubles me. Learn what you may."

I inclined my head. "Of course."

"Now!" Her voice rose, making the rafters tremble. Her ember eye sprang open, blazing in the ruined left side of her face. "Send in this mortal who thinks to bargain for the sight of me!"

# Twenty-three

I have to admit, I took pleasure in witnessing Lee's initial encounter with the Norse goddess of the dead.

Maybe it would have been different if he hadn't been such a jerk to me, but he had. And yeah, I felt bad about the rough time he'd had in high school, and the fact that his mom was sick, but . . .

What can I say? It was satisfying. Right up to the point where it turned scary.

Mikill escorted him into the sawmill. Hel sat silent on her throne, the right side of her face stern, the left side terrifying.

Swathed in his voluminous leather duster, Lee looked like a gaunt scarecrow with a penchant for goth attire and baseball caps. His knees began to tremble so hard I could almost hear his bones knocking together; at least until he dropped to said knees on the floor of the old sawmill, bowing his head in Hel's presence.

"I'm sorry," he whispered. "I didn't mean to give offense."

Hel drummed the fingers of her left hand, black and withered as charred bones, on the arm of her throne. "Rise."

He stood unsteadily.

"You thought to barter for entrance to my demesne," the goddess said. "Now you are here." She raised her left hand, clawlike fingers cupping the empty air. "I could stop your heart. I could kill you with a thought, mortal."

Her left hand, the hand of death—the hand with which she'd given me *dauda-dagr*—squeezed.

Lee gasped and staggered, clutching his chest.

And okay, yes, at that point I started to worry. "My lady!" I said in alarm. "I brought him here. If there was offense given, it was mine."

It was true, but probably not the smartest thing I could have said. The baleful red gaze of Hel's ember eye shifted onto me, her clawed left hand twisting slightly. "And will you answer for his trespass as well, my young liaison?"

It felt like those withered fingers grasped the heart within my chest, squeezing, squeezing. I drew a choking breath, my heart struggling to beat within the confines of that iron grip.

I had no one but myself to blame, and it made me angry. I should have known better than to bring Lee here without asking permission. But at least now there was something I could do with my anger. I couldn't kindle a shield between us, not with the might of Hel's blazing left eye on me. Instead, I kindled one *inside* me, envisioning it shielding my vulnerable heart from her immortal grasp, giving it a scant space in which to beat. "Forgive me for my transgression, my lady," I wheezed. "I beg you to show us mercy."

Hel considered her response for what felt like an eternity. I held my inward shield in place to the best of my ability, my heart thudding painfully against it. I didn't think I could keep it up for much longer. Lee's face was dangerously pale and it looked like his eyes were beginning to bulge in their deep sockets.

At last Hel opened the hand of death, releasing us both. "Tell me, mortal," she said to Lee. "Was it worth it?"

"Yes," Lee breathed, lifting his head. The blood returned to his face. He gazed at Hel with awe. "If I die now, it was worth it."

I coughed, took a deep breath, and let the remnants of my inward shield go. Unless I was imagining it, Hel's gaze flicked toward me, and there was something in it that resembled amusement, insofar as a vast and ageless deity with disturbingly bifurcated features was capable of looking amused.

It was pretty quick. I probably imagined it. Then again, receiving a rapturous tribute from a mortal whose heart you'd very nearly stopped seemed like the sort of thing that might appeal to your sense of humor if you were a goddess of the dead.

"That is well." She lowered her left hand. "Now go forth and fulfill your bargain. Daisy Johanssen, I accept your apology. You have my leave to take the mortal and depart."

I bowed in acknowledgment and gratitude. "Thank you, my lady."

Doing his best impression of a newborn colt, Lee exited the sawmill on wobbly legs, his face flushed with ecstasy. "I didn't expect it to be so . . . so, so, so . . ." At a loss for words, he folded his lanky frame into the dune buggy's passenger seat. "So . . ."

Cramming myself into the storage space, I reached over to pat his shoulder. "Yeah. I know."

He laid one hand over mine. "Thanks. Sorry I doubted you."

Mikill drove us back to my apartment without comment, dropping us off in the alley. I thanked him for the ride. In response, he gave me a grave look. "Do not think to strike such a bargain again, Daisy Johanssen. Hel extended great tolerance to you on this occasion. She will not do so a second time."

"Duly noted," I said, chastised. If that was great tolerance, I definitely didn't want to find out what Hel's intolerance felt like.

Mikill nodded and drove away, his dripping beard wagging in the wind.

"I'm really sorry." Lee grimaced. "I didn't mean to get you in trouble."

I shrugged. "You didn't know. I should have." I rubbed my chest, which felt sort of bruised inside. "Look, I'm just asking because I know how intense that was. Do you want to come up for a drink before you go?"

"Oh, my God." He let out a sigh of gratitude. "More than words can say."

Upstairs in my apartment, I poured Lee a scotch and let him talk and talk and talk, rehashing and reliving the experience, examining it from every angle. As it turned out, words could say a lot. It was okay, though. I understood.

Eventually the conversation came around to mundane territory. I asked Lee about his experience in Seattle. Apparently, he'd been headhunted while he was still in high school and was considered a total wunderkind and a rock star in the gaming industry. And I asked him about his widowed mother, who was suffering from severe rheumatoid arthritis.

"I remember her," I said. "She used to chaperone field trips when we were in grade school."

"Uh-huh." Lee contemplated his glass. "She was the chaperone no one wanted to get stuck with."

I hadn't planned on mentioning that part, since I'd never actually gotten stuck with her. "Oh?"

He glanced at me. "Maybe you never had the pleasure. Mom never wanted the devil child in her group."

Well, that explained that particular streak of luck. "I see."

"Look, I love my mother, but she's not a particularly nice person. Do you really have a tail, Daisy?" Lee asked me, apropos of nothing other than whatever unfathomable chain of association was playing out in his thoughts.

I set down my drink. "I'll tell if you will. Which one's ironic, Lee? The leather duster or the baseball cap?"

"The baseball cap," he said. "Obviously."

I shook my head. "Wrong."

Lee laughed. It was a good sound, free and unfettered. "Are you calling me a poseur?"

I smiled at him. "Hey, if the duster fits . . ."

"I get it." He finished his drink and levered himself out

of the chair. "Daisy . . . thanks. I promise, I'll build you a kickass database."

I stood, too. "Good. Because I basically told Hel you were the only guy for the job."

He looked a bit pale, his Adam's apple bobbing in his throat as he swallowed. "Right. Let me give you my phone number. I'll call you in a few days when I've got something for you to look at."

I raised my eyebrows. "Are you sure about that? Trusting me with your actual phone number?"

"Yeah." He gave me a sheepish look. "I'm sure."

Once Lee had gone, I curled up on the futon, Mogwai purring in my lap. All in all, I thought that could have gone worse. Hel wasn't thrilled by the prospect, but she'd granted her permission. Okay, she'd given a very convincing demonstration of her ability to kill with a thought, but ultimately, she'd forgiven me for bringing an uninvited mortal to Little Niflheim. If Lee came through, and I was pretty sure he would, it could make doing my job a lot easier. The idea that there was an official ledger in which favors and transgressions would be recorded seemed to carry weight in the eldritch community, sort of like the way administrators used the idea of a permanent record in high school to keep us in line.

Yeah, it definitely could have gone worse.

Over the course of the following day, I jotted down notes on promises or threats I'd made since I'd conceived the notion of a ledger—notes like "Tuggle the hobgoblin + 3 unnamed associates, one warning for cheating tourists w/ a shell game," and "Jojo (nickname) the joe-pye weed fairy, one big favor owed for identifying a hex-charm created by Emmeline Palmer," as well as important save-the-date notices like "Labor Day Weekend 2024: Satyr Nicodemus goes into rut. MUST BE CONTAINED."

Feeling inspired, I talked to Chief Bryant about letting me borrow the hard copies of the Pemkowet X-Files. Those files had a lot of good data in them.

The chief agreed readily, shrugging his heavy shoulders. "Why not? Those reports don't exist as part of the official record. It's always been your brainchild, Daisy. Not that I don't see the merit in it," he added. "But no reason you shouldn't utilize them."

"Thanks, sir," I said.

He nodded. "Anything else?"

"Actually, yes." I hadn't forgotten about Hel's charge. "Have you heard anything about this lawyer who's been talking to people in town about selling off big tracts of undeveloped land?"

Chief Bryant frowned. "Ducheyne? Dufreyne?"

I nodded. "Something like that."

He leaned back, folding his arms behind his head, his desk chair creaking. "I've heard a few things. I heard this lawyer fellow talked Bob Ballister into selling a plot along the channel he bought back in the seventies and clung to like a limpet ever since. Bob was planning to build and retire there if a road ever went through." His shrewd, sleepy gaze slewed in my direction. "Though that doesn't seem likely at this point."

"A road, you mean?" I asked.

"Mm-hmm." He nodded. "Unless a *big* developer was involved."

"How big?"

"Big."

I thought about it. A plague of McMansions along the lakeshore notwithstanding, Pemkowet wasn't about big development. We had zoning laws in place to preserve the character of the place. Hell, we were the only small town in the Midwest that had managed to keep McDonald's at bay. "Any idea who's behind this Dufreyne?"

The chief shook his head. "Nope. Why?"

"Hel's expressed concern."

"Huh." His gaze sharpened. "I wonder what would concern a goddess, exactly?"

"I don't know," I said. "But I'll tell you one thing—that lawyer's not human. He's, um, a hell-spawn."

"Like you?"

"No." I couldn't blame him for saying it when I'd said the same thing myself. "I think he might have some kind of power of persuasion. I think he's claimed his, um, demonic birthright."

Chief Bryant glanced upward involuntarily, as though the Inviolate Wall were a visible sphere around us. "Isn't that supposed to be capable of unleashing you-know-what?"

"Yeah," I said. "At least that's what I was always told. I don't know. There's something weird about the whole thing."

"You're right." He unfolded his arms. "I don't know why I hadn't noticed it myself. I'll poke around and let you know what I find out."

"Thanks," I said. "And if you hear Dufreyne's been talking to anyone else, tell me. I know he was talking to Amanda Brooks about the Cavannaugh property."

"Are you kidding?" The chief snorted. "That property's been in her family forever. She wouldn't sell in a million years. The Cavannaughs are one of the founding families, don't you know? They've been here since before the sand swallowed Singapore. Hell, if the legends are true, it was a Cavannaugh that took down Talman Brannigan in the middle of his rampage. I'm surprised Amanda didn't refuse to take her husband's name when she got married."

"She was thinking about it. Selling, I mean," I clarified. I had no idea what Amanda Brooks thought about taking her husband's name.

He blinked. "You're sure?"

I nodded. "Yeah, I'm pretty sure. I came in just as he was leaving. She looked . . . unfocused. When I asked about it, she said she couldn't imagine why she even entertained the idea. I told her not to trust the guy, that I had a bad feeling about him."

"And she listened to you?"

"She seemed to." I shrugged. "It seemed to clear away the cobwebs, anyway."

"But you don't have powers of persuasion, right?" Chief Bryant asked. "No offense, Daisy. I just mean . . ." His voice trailed off, sounding embarrassed.

"It's okay." I smiled wryly. "No, no powers of persuasion,

sir. Don't worry, I haven't claimed my birthright. To be honest, I don't know why it worked. Maybe Dufreyne's ability is more like a power of suggestion. Maybe it takes time to work, and I just happened to be there at the right moment to nip it in the bud. Maybe two hell-spawns cancel each other out no matter what. I don't know."

The chief's face softened into an expression of paternal worry. "That can't be easy, being an enigma to yourself half the time."

Damn. Again with the unexpected surge of gratitude. My eyes stung a little. "Thank you," I murmured. "It's not."

"All right." He planted his hands on the desk with a meaty thud. "I'll put the word out. Anyone talking to Dufreyne should talk to you. Anything else? Where are we with this obeah woman situation?"

I cleared my throat. "On it, sir. The local coven is meeting with Sinclair this Saturday evening to discuss strategy."

"Good." He paused. "I have to admit, I don't actually know who's in this coven. Do you?"

"Other than the Fabulous Casimir? No," I said. "Not for sure. But I look forward to finding out."

# Twenty-four

L ate on Saturday afternoon, I got a call from Cody.

"Hey there, Pixy Stix." Even over the phone, his voice had a hint of a low rumble that would have made me feel tingly if I weren't so annoyed by the nickname. "Are you busy tonight?"

"Yeah," I said. "I have an appointment at seven. Why?"

"I have to pay a visit to Twilight Manor," he said. "I thought it might be a good idea to have Hel's liaison riding shotgun."

"What's up?"

"We've got a sixteen-year-old girl who went to a poetry slam at the coffee shop and never came home last night." All traces of humor vanished from his voice. "Witnesses say she left with someone who sounds a lot like Bethany Cassopolis."

"Shit." That was Jen's blood-slut sister. "Are you serious?"

"Unfortunately, yeah. I checked with the Cassopolises and they haven't heard from her since she went back to her vamp boyfriend," Cody said. "I stopped out at the manor, but it's locked up tight during daylight hours. Their minions won't even answer the door and they've got a state-of-the-art security system. Can you reschedule?"

"Not really. But sunset's not until a little after eight. Can I call you when my meeting's over?"

He hesitated. "I'll give you until eight thirty. If I don't hear from you, I'll go it alone."

I didn't like that idea. "I'll make sure I'm out by then."

"Good. Call me." He hung up.

Of course, I immediately called Jen to see if she knew anything. She didn't have any idea why Bethany would be picking up stray teens at the coffee shop, but she had the lowdown on the missing girl already—Heather Simkus, moody, isolated loner, alleged to be a serious cutter.

In other words, perfect vampire fodder.

I hadn't planned on attending the coven's meeting in agent-of-Hel working attire, but this put a different spin on the evening. When the time came, I opted for jeans instead of a nice skirt, and buckled *dauda-dagr* around my waist. For good measure, I hauled out a motorcycle jacket I bought at Goodwill, one of my all-time best thrift store finds. And yeah, okay, it's black leather, but it's not a duster. I don't care how cool it looked in *Blade* or *The Matrix*, no one in their right mind would choose to fight in a duster. There's just too much damn material. My jacket, on the other hand, is fitted and has a high collar that makes it perfect for calling on vampires. After my last visit to the House of Shadows, I'd take any extra ounce of protection I could get.

A bit before seven, I drove out to Sinclair's place to pick him up.

It was the first time we'd seen each other since the breakup, and there was a moment of awkwardness on the doorstep while we both tried to figure out if we were supposed to hug or play it cool.

Then Sinclair broke into a broad grin. "Damn, sistah! You look like you're ready to kick ass and take numbers. You expecting trouble?"

I smiled back at him. "No, something else has come up. I have to leave by quarter after eight or so."

He slung a friendly arm over my shoulders, giving me a squeeze. "Then let's roll."

The Fabulous Casimir lived in a charming Arts-and-Crafts-style bungalow in East Pemkowet, nestled under pine trees on a bluff with a distant view of the river. Casimir met us at the door in a brocade dressing gown and matching gold satin head scarf tied in an elaborate bow at the nape of his neck.

"You must be Sinclair Palmer," he said, extending one manicured hand. "*Enchanté*, my dear. A pleasure to finally meet you. We all appreciate the business your little tour brings into town."

"Thank you." Sinclair shook his hand. "I appreciate your meeting with me."

"Of course." Casimir glanced in my direction. "Thanks for bringing Sinclair, Daisy. I'm sure one of our members can give him a ride home."

I blinked at him. "Excuse me?"

Casimir pursed his lips. "Oh, this is awkward. I'm sorry, Daisy. But coven business is a private matter."

"Yeah, I don't think so." My right hand dropped to *dauda-dagr*'s hilt. Funny how the gesture had become instinctual in such a short time. "Not this time. I don't mean to pull rank, but I'm Hel's liaison, Cas. We're talking about a supernatural threat in Pemkowet. That makes it my business."

We had a polite staredown. For a moment I thought Casimir was going to call my bluff—and it was a bluff, since I didn't really have any options if he refused to admit me—but he relented.

"You have a point," he said. "Do I have your oath that you'll treat everything you see or hear as confidential?"

"As long as it doesn't interfere with my duty to Hel, yes," I said. "Fair enough?"

"It will have to do." He gestured. "Come in."

The living room looked more like I imagined the Fabulous Casimir's place would be than the sparsely appointed altar room at his shop. It was filled with cluttered elegance. Paintings with gilded frames hung in rows three-deep on the walls, knickknacks on every surface, old-fashioned stuffed furniture with scrolling wood trim, an Oriental carpet on the floor. And seated around the perimeter of the room, the other six members of Pemkowet's coven.

The only two people I'd more or less expected to see here were Mark and Sheila Reston, who owned the tattoo parlor across from the Sisters of Selene, because ... well. If you've got matching tattoos of the Wiccan rede—which, by the way, is "An it harm none, do what ye will"—around your neck, that's pretty much a dead giveaway.

The others ... not so much.

There was Kim McKinney, who graduated a year ahead of me and worked at the deli counter at Tafts Grocery. I didn't know her well, but I definitely didn't see that coming.

There was nice Mrs. Meyers from the historical society, her expression placid, her lap full of yarn, and her knitting needles clicking away industriously.

There was taciturn Warren Rogers, who owned a nursery and a landscaping business and had done some work out at my mom's place a couple of years ago in exchange for her making his plus-size daughter, Naomi, a kickass prom dress that flattered her curves to hell and gone.

And there—holy *crap*—was my mom's friend Sandra Sweddon, recently referred to by my former teacher Mr. Leary as "that infernal do-gooding busybody."

Okay, maybe I should have known that one. After all, I did know she collected crystals. But frankly, I hadn't even suspected it.

Casimir bustled around, pouring tea and making introductions. "Wonderful," he said once acquaintances were made or in my case, renewed in a very different context. "If everyone's ready, I'll give a quick invocation and then we'll begin."

A murmur of assent ran around the room.

Fetching a long-handled lighter from a drawer, Casimir lit the first of two candles on the coffee table, a silver pillar. "Hail, fair Lady, queen of night, enfold us in your grace," he said, and then lit the second, a gold pillar. "Hail, great Lord, ruler of day, protect us in this place." He set the lighter down. "So mote it be."

"So mote it be," the others echoed.

Now that I wasn't suffering from an excruciating hex-induced migraine, I could feel a faint charge in the air after Casimir's invocation—nothing like the vastness of Hel's presence, but a change. Interesting.

"We invoke the Lady and Lord in their archetypal forms," Casimir said to Sinclair. "Of course, everyone is welcome to address whatever particular facet of the deity speaks to them. Are you dedicated?"

I didn't understand the question, but Sinclair gave a brief nod. "You might say so. I was raised to honor Yemaya."

Also interesting. I made a mental note of the name.

"Wonderful," Casimir said again. "All right! Everyone, please help yourselves to the lovely cheese tray Kim was kind enough to bring for the occasion. Mr. Palmer, tell us about yourself and your situation."

Snacking on cheese and crackers, I sat and listened while Sinclair related his story. At the coven's prodding, he went into more detail about his own youthful studies in obeah, which involved using his ability to see auras to diagnose ailments in individuals and gradually acquiring the herb lore to prescribe cures.

"And you didn't think that was worth pursuing?" Warren Rogers asked in a neutral tone. He was a guy who knew a thing or two about herbs. "The healer's path?"

"Not at the cost." Sinclair met his gaze squarely. "The further I went down that path, the further my sister went down the other."

The other members of the coven nodded in understanding. I guess this whole path of balance thing was a cornerstone of most occult practices.

With a few assists from me, Sinclair finished up with a description of Emmeline's visit and her ultimatum, followed by a short discourse on the nature of duppies, during which the coven attempted to determine whether obeah's concept of an earthly soul that was somehow distinct from a heavenly soul corresponded to the notion of an etheric body that was distinct from the physical and spiritual bodies.

Okay, I tuned out for a while during that part. But at least the cheese was good.

At around twenty to eight, Casimir deftly turned the conversation to ways of protecting Sinclair from his sister's threat.

"Obviously, we should start with a ritual cleansing," Kim McKinney said. "I'd be happy to oversee it."

I'd just bet she would. I suppressed an irrational surge of jealousy.

"Have you done any work with crystals and visualization?" Sandra Sweddon asked Sinclair. "White light? Chakras?" He shook his head. "That's okay, honey. We'll work on it."

"How do you feel about ink?" Mark Reston stretched out his arms to reveal a pair of large and intricate seals tattooed on his muscular forearms. "Sheila and I have a portfolio of sigils we designed ourselves. Some of them are for protection. You're welcome to stop by the shop and see if any of them speak to you."

"I'll knit you a prayer shawl, dear," Mrs. Meyers said in her kind voice. "There's a blessing in every stitch." She caught sight of Sinclair's expression and chuckled. "Don't worry, it's more of a scarf than an actual shawl."

Warren Rogers scratched his chin. "Sounds like you've got a bit of herb lore, then. You any good with plants?"

"Not bad," Sinclair said. I wondered if that had anything to do with the elemental nature fairies' fondness for him.

The landscaper gave him a shrewd look. "I could use a new assistant. Lost a couple of college kids to the fall semester, and I hear your tour's only running on the weekends during the off season. You interested?"

"Point of clarification." Casimir raised one finger before Sinclair could answer. "Are you talking about a job or an apprenticeship, Warren?"

He shrugged. "Depends on Mr. Palmer here. I could use a good worker either way. Don't know that I've got a handle on this obeah business, but his studies sound close enough to my journey on the right-hand path. If he's willing to dedicate himself to *our* craft, I'm willing to mentor him."

Casimir turned to Sinclair. "Well? Are you?"

Sinclair frowned in thought. "What happens if I say no?"

"If you're asking if we'll withhold our assistance in the matter at hand, the answer's no." The Fabulous Casimir steepled his fingers. "We'll do everything in our power to protect you. But to be perfectly honest, it will be more effective if you're on your way to becoming an initiate. And if you're asking if we'd like to have you, the answer is yes."

Glancing around the room, Sinclair studied the members of the coven one by one—reading their auras, I assumed.

After a moment he nodded. "I'm in."

# Twenty-five

For another half hour, the coven discussed the specifics of implementing their various plans of occult protection. I listened and made mental notes on the individual members and their different areas of expertise, figuring it was all good input for my thus-far-hypothetical database.

Hey, I'd promised to keep confidentiality, but I hadn't promised not to make a record of what I learned. It might be useful someday.

At quarter after eight, I excused myself. "Cas, I've got to leave. Sorry, but duty calls. You said someone could give Sinclair a ride home?"

"I'll do it," Kim McKinney volunteered, smiling sidelong at Sinclair. "No problem."

He smiled back at her. "Thanks, sistah."

The Fabulous Casimir spread his fingers. "Et voilà."

It's not like I had any right to complain. I was the one who'd broken up with Sinclair, and I was the one to arrange this meeting. Now that he was back on the market, I couldn't blame Kim for flirting with him.

Still, it gave me an inward pang.

Of course, that was offset by the fact that I was meeting with my childhood crush and sometime partner in police business, Officer Down-low himself. Too bad we were headed out to Twilight Manor to locate a missing kid. Not exactly a fun date.

I called Cody from Casimir's driveway. He picked up on the first ring. "Hey, Pixy Stix. Ready?"

"Yep."

Unless I imagined it, there was a faint sigh of relief on Cody's end. No matter what he'd said, no one in their right mind wanted to enter the House of Shadows without backup. I know, I'd done it. "Meet me at the gas station on the corner of Sixty-fourth Street," he said. "I'll pick you up. If you're coming as Hel's liaison, I think it's best if we present a united front."

"See you in five," I said, and ended the call.

One thing about living in a small town: It's easy to estimate travel time. Five minutes later, I pulled alongside the squad car in the parking lot of Pineview Gas & Convenience.

Leaning over, Cody opened the passenger-side door for me. "So what was this important appointment you couldn't reschedule?"

I slid into the seat. "None of your business."

"I heard you broke up with the fake Jamaican," he said. "I heard he's not so fake, and his baggage is a problem."

I gave Cody a sharp look. "Did the chief talk to you?"

"He worries." Cody gave me a scowl in return. "I just wish the timing was better, Daise. Whatever's going down with this sister of Sinclair's, I wish it wasn't happening around the full moon."

"Yeah?" I buckled my seat belt. "Me, too. But right now, we've got a missing kid to worry about, right?"

"Right."

The House of Shadows was located on a huge piece of property out in the countryside, not far from the lakeshore. Depending on how far the actual boundaries of Little Niflheim extend, it might be situated atop the underworld itself. It was purchased in the 1940s by the mistress of the manor, the beautiful, wealthy, and undead Lady Eris, who promptly moved her brood of a dozen or so vampires into the place. I'm not sure what their number is today, although it hasn't grown as much as one might think. Vampires form blood-bonds with their chosen mortals, but they're very picky about who they actually turn. Bethany Cassopolis's undead paramour had been stringing her along for eight years.

For the record, I'd done some research into breaking the blood-bond. So far, the only method I'd found other than killing the vampire in question was a massive blood transfusion, which wasn't exactly a procedure that could be done on an unwilling subject.

Anyway, the House of Shadows was awake for the night, blackout curtains drawn, lights ablaze. I checked the zipper on the collar of my motorcycle jacket as Cody pounded the door-knocker.

"Yes?" The blond vampire who opened the door a crack sounded annoyed. Maybe it was because he'd been stuck on reception duty for years.

"Pemkowet PD." Cody held up his badge. "We're looking for a sixteen-year-old girl who's gone missing. I have reason to believe she may be on the premises."

Over Cody's shoulder, I saw the vampire's eyes narrow. Without thinking, I kindled the merest spark of a shield, holding it in my thoughts. "I assure you, Officer, there are no minors here."

"I'd like to have a look." Cody's voice sounded casual, but there was tension in the line of his back.

"Do you have a warrant?" the vampire inquired, curling his lip to reveal the tips of his fangs.

"Even better." I stepped out from behind Cody so the doorkeeper could see me, raising my left hand to display Hel's rune. "He's got me."

Maybe it was because I was bolder with Cody at my side and a psychic shield at the ready, or maybe it was because the word was out that I'd used *dauda-dagr* to dispatch two ghouls since last I'd been here, but the doorkeeper backed down a lot more quickly this time. "Wait here," he said with resigned disdain, ushering us into the foyer. "I'll announce you to her ladyship."

We waited.

The sound of classical music drifted in fits and starts down the majestic stairway that led to the grand ballroom on the third floor. It sounded like a string quartet rehearsing rather than a party in full swing, which is what I'd encountered the last time I'd been here. Periodically the music would stop, and we could hear someone issuing arcane instructions that hovered on the verge of audibility.

The doorkeeper returned. "Lady Eris will receive you in her sitting room," he announced. "She is *not* pleased by the early hour of your visit." He flashed another hint of fang tip. "You recall what passed the last time you displeased her, Hel's liaison?"

"I remember." Not as much had happened as he thought, actually, but I'd let Lady Eris save face in front of her minions in exchange for a temporary no-hunting decree. "But it was just after sunset that time, too."

The vampire heaved a sigh, a disconcerting sound in someone who breathes only in order to speak. "When the nights are short, we make the most of them. As they begin to lengthen, we enjoy a more leisurely pace."

"Some of us daywalkers don't have that luxury," Cody said in one of his more laconic tones.

The vampire glanced at him, his eyes narrowing again. At a guess, he'd identified Cody as eldritch, but hadn't placed him yet. "Follow me."

We followed him up the staircase to the second-floor landing, turning off down a hallway lit by sconces with fluted lamps of mauve glass. It made Cody's healthy complexion—and probably mine—look sickly, but it created a pleasing effect on the bloodless alabaster pallor of our guide. I wondered how any non-Caucasian vampires in the House of Shadows felt about Lady Eris's choice in lighting.

Our guide halted before the door of the master bedroom, knocking on it once. "Hel's liaison," he intoned. "And some cop."

Huh. Maybe he wasn't quite so ye olde world as he acted.

The door was opened from within. Lady Eris—which, no, I don't believe for a moment is her real name—was seated on an ornate padded stool being groomed for the night's revels. She wore a deep crimson satin dressing gown trimmed with black lace that, frankly, reminded me a lot of what the Fabulous Casimir was wearing tonight. One attendant was brushing out her long, jet-black hair while another knelt with one of her ladyship's elegant white feet in her lap, assiduously applying toenail polish.

"Daisy Johanssen," she said in flat acknowledgment. At least she wasn't pretending not to remember my name.

"Hi," I said.

Her ebony-dark gaze shifted to Cody, one eyebrow arching. "And Officer . . . ?"

Cody's nostrils flared. "Fairfax."

"Fairfax," she echoed him, smiling a little. "How very interesting! A lycanthrope on the local police force?"

Apparently she didn't have any problem identifying him, but if she was trying to use a touch of hypnotic vampire seduction on him, it wasn't working. Maybe werewolves were immune to it. Ignoring her question, Cody showed his badge again. "We have reason to believe there's a minor on the premises."

Lady Eris's eyelids flickered ever so slightly. "I'm sure that's not the case. My people are under strict orders."

"People make mistakes, my lady," I said.

Her gaze shifted back to me, and this time I felt its weight. "Last time, you came seeking a favor and I granted it freely, Hel's liaison," she said in a silken voice filled with playful menace. "What will you give me for this one?"

Oh, gah! That shouldn't be effective, but it was. I could feel my skin getting warmer, my blood rising. Clearing my throat, I let my mental shield grow from a tiny spark to the size of a mirror in a makeup compact and held it between us, trying to play my cards close to my chest. Lady Eris gave me the eyebrow arch anyway. "The courtesy of your response was noted in Niflheim, my lady," I said to her. Total lie, but I needed to put my own spin on it. "However, I am tasked by Hel herself to mediate between eldritch and mundane authorities, and this matter pertains directly to the House of Shadows."

I thought that was pretty damn diplomatic of me, not to mention well phrased, but the mistress of the manor was unamused. "In other words, this is not a request."

Inclining my head a few degrees, I kept my mouth shut.

"No," Cody said bluntly. "It's not."

Lady Eris came off her stool with blinding speed to slap him across the face with an open hand, her nails raking his cheek. Her attendants scattered out of the way. Cody's head snapped sideways, his face distorting in a snarl, his mouth suddenly full of too many teeth, hands clenching into fists. Hairy, hairy fists. She stood imperiously before him, unmoving, unbreathing. "Mind your manners, wolf. This is *my* territory."

He growled at her in response, blood trickling down his cheek.

"Whoa!" I found my voice. "Whoa, whoa, whoa, people! Let's not go all *Underworld* here." No one was listening to me. "Cody!" I thumped him on the back. He glanced at me with a low growl, his face still distorted and his eyes glowing with green phosphorescence. "Hey! You're in uniform."

I'm not sure what made me choose those words, but they worked. His features shifted back into human form. "I could arrest you for assaulting an officer," he said in a hard voice. "You're not above the law."

"You could try." Unimpressed, Lady Eris sat back down on her ornate stool. She raised her hand to taste Cody's blood on her fingernails with the tip of her tongue, then made a face. I guess werewolf blood wasn't yummy. She gestured to an attendant, who scrambled to bring her a bowl of water in which to dabble her fingers. "Is that what you really want?"

"No, my lady." I got the words out before Cody could respond, elbowing him in the ribs for good measure. "Just the chance to look for the child."

Lady Eris and I did the locked-gazes thing. What can I say? It was big in the eldritch community. I kept my expression neutral and my miniature shield shining between us.

"Naturally, I have no desire to be in violation of Hel's order," she said at length, snapping her fingers at her attendants. One hurried to arrange her hair in a loose chignon, while the other eased a pair of open-toed mules onto her feet, careful not to smudge the fresh nail polish. "Come! Let us review the latest acolytes."

Once acceptably attired, she swept out of the room before us, down the mauve-lit hallway and up the grand staircase to the ballroom on the third floor, where her early arrival—not to mention Cody's and my presence—provoked consternation.

"My lady!" A tall vampire with a supercilious face protested. "The spectacle isn't ready yet!"

I knew that face. Geoffrey Chancellor, the insufferable prat who was blood-bonded to Jen's sister.

"Oh, my lady! It's *so* important to get the lighting just right!" added a young mortal woman from above, tears in her voice.

And that would be Bethany Cassopolis, whom I did not expect to find up on a scaffold, arranging lighting. From what I could tell, they were in the midst of staging a scene from a play. On a low dais there were three, maybe four, people dressed in Renaissance-looking robes and frozen in poses around a platter with what appeared to be a bearded man's severed head on it. Hence my confusion regarding the actual number of people on the dais.

Cody took a step forward. "What the *fuck*?"

"It's a tableau vivant," Lady Eris said irritably. "Caravaggio's *Salome with the Head of John the Baptist*, tonight's surprise spectacle, which you've now ruined. Well?"

I studied the tableau. Unlike the members of the string quartet in the corner, sitting bloodless and motionless with their instruments at the ready, the participants were mortal. Now that I looked closely, I could see that the severed-head effect was accomplished using a black curtain affixed to the rim of the platter. Phew.

All of them held their poses resolutely, but the young woman playing Salome, draped in a red robe and ostensibly holding the platter, was trembling.

"Heather Simkus?" I said to her. She didn't respond, keeping her face averted. "Heather?"

"Goddammit!" Bethany Cassopolis came storming down from the scaffold, a lighting canister in one hand. "What the hell are *you* doing here?"

Ignoring her, I eased the folds of Salome's robes off her nearest arm, revealing dozens of lines of cutting marks, some of them old scars fading to pink, others still red and angry. Aside from trembling, she didn't budge.

"Leave her be!" Bethany grabbed my shoulder and yanked me away with surprising strength. "She's mine!"

"Excuse me?" I said, steadying my faltering shield.

"Not like *that*, duh!" she retorted.

Geoffrey the insufferable prat glided over, stopping a few feet away when Cody angled toward him. "With her ladyship's blessing, I gave Bethany permission to recruit an acolyte," he said, looking down his nose at me. "I assure you, she came most willingly."

On the dais, Salome—or Heather, I should say—gave the tiniest of nods. She had a pretty face in that sort of soft, unformed way some teenaged girls do. At the moment, there were silent tears trickling down it.

"It doesn't matter," I said. "She's a minor. She's sixteen."

"Do you think I didn't ask?" Bethany glared at me. I had to say, she actually looked better than she had in years; less strung out, more pissed off. Maybe recruiting acolytes agreed with her. "She's eighteen."

I glanced at Heather. Her trembling had turned to shaking. "She didn't show you ID, did she?"

"Miss Simkus, you can't stay here," Cody said in a gentle voice. "We've come to take you home."

At that, she abandoned her pose with a gulping sob, turning to Bethany. "You promised! Don't let them take me! I don't want to go!"

Bethany looked uncertainly at Geoffrey.

Geoffrey looked uncertainly at Lady Eris.

Lady Eris smiled. "I don't suppose you happen to have proof of the girl's age with you, Officer?" she asked Cody. "A birth certificate, perhaps?"

He stared at her. "You've got to be kidding."

"Not at all," she said in a complacent tone. "The mantle of my protection has been extended to the young lady. I take these matters very seriously."

I was pretty sure she was just yanking our chain because we'd ruined the evening's entertainment, but the musicians in the corner laid down their instruments and rose to add their pale and silently menacing numbers to the assembled vampires. On the dais, the remaining members of the tableau broke character, straightening to watch the events unfold with glazed, haunted eyes, and in the case of John the Baptist, a curtain-draped platter around his neck like a collar.

"Hel takes her rule of order very seriously, too, my lady," I murmured to Lady Eris. "She has banished others for defying it."

She looked at me out of the corner of her eye, tapping one mule-shod foot. "If you return with a valid birth certificate, I will relinquish the girl in accordance with Hel's rule and mundane authority," she said eventually. "But since the issue is in question, if you desire immediate satisfaction . . ." The living and the dead hung on her words, awaiting her decree. She smiled again, this time showing a hint of fang, her dark eyes sparkling with glee. "I declare myself neutral in the matter and proclaim this an individual dispute."

A murmur ran around the ballroom, where the number of vampires appeared to have multiplied as they emerged from their chambers to observe the confrontation. Someone did a polite golf clap.

"What does that mean?" Cody asked.

"It means Geoffrey and I have the right to stop you from taking her!" Bethany said defiantly, positioning herself in front of the dais. "Right, honey?"

Although he didn't look quite as committed to the battle, he joined her. "Right."

Cody and I exchanged a glance. Obviously, the smart thing to do would be to go get a copy of Heather Simkus's birth certificate and return. If we were lucky, her parents had it in a handy file at home and we'd be back within half an hour. If we were less lucky, they kept it in a safety-deposit box and we'd have to wait until the banks opened tomorrow. And if we were downright unlucky, it might be lost or in storage someplace where it would take days to retrieve it or to request and obtain a new copy, during which time God knows what might happen to Heather at the House of Shadows. She'd probably end up blood-bonded.

And then there was the ever-present matter of face. If we accepted Lady Eris's ultimatum and backed down from a fight, we'd lose face.

"What does Hel's liaison say about her ladyship's ruling, Daisy?" Cody asked me, his eyes glinting green. There were streaks of blood drying on his cheek and despite his police uniform he was looking distinctly . . . wolfish. "Is it fair?"

"Yeah," I said reluctantly. "I mean, she's splitting hairs, but it's fair. And, Cody, if you accept her—"

What I was going to say was that if he accepted Lady Eris's terms, according to Hel's rule of order he would be acting under eldritch auspices and not mundane law, which meant there would be no charging anyone with assault, but I never got the chance. Cody strode up to the dais, pushing his way between Bethany and Geoffrey the prat.

"I'm sorry," he said, extending his hand to Heather. "But it's time to go home, sweetheart. Your parents are worried sick."

Everything that happened after that was sort of a blur. It started to take place in slow motion, watching Bethany raise her canister in preparation to bash Cody across the back of his head with it. And then it was like the tape sped up, and I found myself struggling with Bethany for control of the canister with no recollection of how I'd gotten there while Cody and the prat rolled on the ground, grappling in a chaotic mess of fangs, unnaturally pallid skin, and police uniform.

"Fuck you, devil girl!" Bethany spat at me. "Why can't you just let me be for once in my life?"

"You know what?" I hooked her leg with mine, unbalancing her. "This really, really isn't about you."

Utilizing the skills I'd learned in Mr. Rodriguez's Li'l

Dragonz Tae Kwon Do classes years ago, I took Bethany down hard, the back of her skull thudding loudly against the ballroom's polished hardwood floor. She didn't exactly go limp, but she looked dazed. I scrambled to my feet.

On the plus side, Cody had managed to keep himself from shifting, which was good, since a wide-eyed young Heather Simkus was watching the whole thing unfold. On the downside, it meant Geoffrey the prat had the upper hand. Two large white hands, in fact, wrapped around Cody's throat. I wouldn't say Cody's face was purple, but it was definitely headed in that direction. Knowing Cody, I was afraid he'd rather be strangled to death than concede.

The weight of *dauda-dagr* was solid and reassuring on my hip. In that moment, I could have drawn it and knifed Geoffrey Chancellor in the back, putting an end to his undead existence; and if I understood Lady Eris's decree correctly, I'd actually be within my rights. I suspected that possibility had slipped her mind in her delight at the idea of pitting us against each other.

I have to admit, I considered it, not least because it would free Bethany whether she wanted it or not. But in the end, I wasn't a stone-cold killer, and no matter how much I disliked Geoffrey the prat, he hadn't sent Bethany out to recruit a minor. It wasn't his fault the girl had lied, and it wasn't his fault Lady Eris had decided to amuse herself. What he'd done wasn't a killing offense.

Not today, anyway.

Meanwhile, Cody was looking purpler by the second, and Bethany was on her hands and knees, trying to shake off her dizziness. Taking a page from her playbook, I hoisted the canister and whacked Geoffrey across the back of the head as hard as I could.

He made a weird, breathless, huffing sound, his hands loosening long enough for Cody to draw in a ragged gasp of air, get his legs underneath him, and thrust Geoffrey away with inhuman strength. A werewolf in human shape might not be vampire-strong, but he was strong.

This time I didn't hesitate. I dropped the canister, drew *dauda-dagr*, and pounced on the prat, straddling his chest and shoving the dagger's tip under his chin, pressing almost hard enough to draw blood. His body twitched reflexively, his neck stretching in an effort to avoid contact with the dagger. Vampires don't fear cold iron in general, but *dauda-dagr* is another matter.

I pushed a little harder. "Do you concede?"

Geoffrey fixed his gaze on me, working up a good dose of hypnotic allure. "The girl *wants* to be here, Hel's liaison. Why must you be so cruel?"

Oops, I'd all but dropped my mental shield. I let it blaze briefly, then dwindle to a compact size again. "Just doing my job."

Beneath me, his body tensed slightly, telegraphing his intent. Behind me, I heard Cody's rasping voice tell Bethany, "Don't even think about it."

"Yeah, I wouldn't either if I were you," I said to Geoffrey. "I mean, I know you're like ten times stronger and faster than me, and you could probably throw me across the room without breaking a sweat—which you probably don't do anyway, right? Sweat?—but the thing is, what if my hand slips when you do?" I eased the tip of *dauda-dagr* from beneath his chin and let it trail up his face, laying the flat of the blade against his skin and setting the keen edge against his supercilious nose. "What do you think happens when a dagger capable of killing the immortal undead wounds undead flesh?" I mused. "You know, it's an interesting question. I have to admit, I don't actually know for sure. But I'm betting the wound never heals. What do you think?"

What Geoffrey the prat thought was that it was better to lose face than his nose. "I concede," he grated.

I glanced up at Lady Eris. "Does that settle the matter, my lady?"

She inclined her head. "It does."

Sheathing *dauda-dagr*, I unstraddled Geoffrey and got to my feet. Somewhat to my surprise, there were several polite golf claps.

Vampires. Go figure.

# Twenty-six

Prat or not, Geoffrey Chancellor was right about one thing. Young Heather Simkus did *not* want to leave the House of Shadows.

Bethany led her away in tears to change out of her Salome robes and back into street attire. Cody and I stood around waiting uncomfortably until they returned ten minutes later, Heather still weeping.

She made one last plea to Lady Eris. "Do I *have* to go, my lady?"

"I'm afraid so, dear." The mistress of the manor touched the girl's cheek with surprising tenderness, a gesture belied by the fact that she licked her tears from her fingertips. Mortal sorrow, tastier than werewolf blood. "But you have the makings of a fine acolyte, and you may return to take your place among us when you're of age." She shifted her gaze, now markedly cooler, to me. "I trust tonight's outcome is satisfactory, Hel's liaison?"

That wasn't exactly the word I would have chosen, but at least we'd gotten what we came for.

Still . . .

"You played a dangerous game for your own amusement, my lady," I said in a low voice. "If it had gone the other way, I'd be trying to convince the chief of police not to return at sunrise with a search warrant and a battering ram."

Lady Eris lifted her chin and narrowed her eyes. "That would be *very* ill-advised for all concerned."

"I know." Whatever the outcome, I suspected it would result in a bloodbath that would shatter the tenuous peace Hel's order maintained between eldritch and mundane communities. "I'm just saying."

"Very well. If you're done 'just saying,' you have my leave to depart," her ladyship said pointedly.

"Come on, Daisy." Cody took me by the elbow, steering me toward the grand staircase, his other hand resting on Heather Simkus's shoulder. "Let's go. We've got anxious parents waiting."

On the second-floor landing, Heather pulled away from him to cast one last, longing glance toward the top of the staircase, where Bethany and Geoffrey were standing to watch her departure. He had his arm wrapped around her waist, and there were what appeared to be genuine looks of remorse and regret on their faces. I couldn't tell if the vibe was sexual or parental or cultish, or a combination of the three.

One thing was for sure—it was creepy.

Outside, Heather slumped morosely in the backseat of the police cruiser while Cody radioed in to report that she'd been found.

"Look," I said softly to her, "I know high school sucks. But it gets better."

"Easy for you to say," she murmured. "You were probably a cheerleader."

Beside me, Cody overhead the comment and snorted into the radio handset. "Um, yeah, not so much," I said to Heather. "I just mean . . . I know you thought that's what you wanted, but it's a very, very dangerous choice. Vampires in real life aren't like the ones in the movies. They weren't going to be playing baseball in a thunderstorm."

She gave me an anguished look. "You don't understand

*anything*. I know what it was like! I was there! With people who care about art and music, *real* art and *real* music, and history and poetry, and ... and languages, languages like Greek and Latin, and everything everyone I know thinks is *stupid* ..."

There was more, but it dissolved in a fresh onslaught of tears.

Huh. I'd never thought of Twilight Manor as a cultural mecca for disenfranchised young intellectuals.

"Heather." Cody's voice was deep and soothing. "There's a steep price for belonging to that community."

She sniffled. "I know! Jesus, duh! It's worth it!"

He shook his head. "You're too young to make that decision. The law says so, and I agree. But if it's really where you want to be, you've got to start thinking about time differently. How long until you turn eighteen? Two years?" He snapped his fingers. "That's nothing to an immortal."

Although I was dubious about the merits of Cody's advice, at least it calmed her down. We headed back toward downtown Pemkowet and by the time we pulled into the driveway of the Simkus residence, Heather seemed resigned to her fate.

I half expected to find something dark and abusive in the Simkus household, or at least a level of neglect that would explain Heather's profound sense of alienation, but her parents appeared to be perfectly normal, lovely people worried out of their minds by their daughter's disappearance. They greeted her with hugs and profound relief and offered profuse thanks to Cody and me. Watching their faces turn pale as Cody explained where we'd found their daughter, I felt bad for them.

After we dropped the girl off, Cody drove me back to Pineview Gas & Convenience to pick up my car. We were both silent for most of the drive, thinking about the night's events.

"Two years is a long time in a kid's life," Cody offered, turning into the parking lot. "A lot can happen."

"Yeah, well, I'm not sure it helped to tell her to think about time differently," I said.

He shrugged. "Maybe, maybe not. Maybe it will get her to think differently about immortality." He parked the cruiser beside my Honda. "Forever's a long time, too. A long time to fill with chamber music concerts and tableau whatsits."

"Vivants," I said automatically. "Did you get the sense there was anything hinky going on with the family?"

Cody shook his head. "You?"

"No." I unbuckled my seat belt but didn't make a move for the door handle. "I think she's just . . . a teenager, you know? A smart, lonely teenager."

"Yeah." He sighed, rubbing the scratches Lady Eris's nails had left on his cheek. I'd been afraid they might fester, but they were already beginning to knit. "Beth Cassopolis was only eighteen when she moved out there, wasn't she? I remember, because she didn't graduate with the rest of my class."

"Yeah, but—" I was going to say that Bethany wasn't a smart, lonely teenager. She'd had a slutty reputation long before she'd become a blood-slut. But the truth was, I hadn't known her then. I didn't really know her now except as Jen's troubled older sister. Maybe she had been smart and lonely. Maybe she'd been a wannabe theater geek who couldn't get taken seriously because everyone in school knew she'd given her first blow job when she was fourteen. Of course, that didn't excuse the fact that she'd tried to brain Cody with a light fixture tonight, not to mention abducting a minor. "Never mind. Are you okay?"

He tested his throat, clearing it. "More or less. You?"

"I'm fine."

"You were pretty tough in there tonight, Pixy Stix." Cody gave me an appraising look. "I hope you meant what you said to Lady Elvira, because if anything like this happens again, I'm not playing by her rules."

"I know," I said. "I meant it."

"Good." He nodded. "I'm glad you're on our side."

My pent tail twitched uncomfortably. "I'm not on anyone's side, Cody. I'm just trying to keep the peace."

"Okay."

"Okay," I echoed.

He gave me a little sidelong grin, one of his wolfish ones. Light from the convenience store windows glinted on his bronze stubble. "Anyway, it was a pretty good fight, don't you think?"

I smiled back at him. "Yeah, it was."

Leaning across me, Cody reached to open the door of the cruiser. "Look, I'm still on patrol. Take care, partner."

I got out. "You, too."

So that was that. I stood in the parking lot watching the taillights of Cody's squad car vanish down the highway, feeling a little alone, a little melancholy. Also, a little hungry, since my dinner had been cheese and crackers at the Fabulous Casimir's house. I went into the convenience store to buy a frozen pizza, then home to my apartment, where I baked and ate said pizza, sitting on the futon and watching reruns of *Iron Chef America* with Mogwai winding around my ankles and purring.

I thought about Sinclair, wondering if he felt he'd found a path he could follow in Casimir's coven. And I thought about Cody, wondering if there would come a time in his life when his own nature put him on the wrong side of the law and what he would choose if that ever happened.

Letting my thoughts roam, I thought about Stefan Ludovic with his father's fourteenth-century parade shield on display in his twenty-first-century condominium, wondering what untold stories lay behind his oblique facade. I thought about Cooper and the fierce passion of the unexpected diatribe he'd unleashed on me.

And I thought about Heather Simkus with her soft, pretty sixteen-year-old face and a lattice of self-inflicted scars on her arms, wondering what she felt was so wrong with her life that the House of Shadows looked like a haven of belonging.

I thought about Bethany, too.

When I was done thinking about them, I turned off the TV, put away the leftover pizza, poured myself a few inches of scotch, settled Mogwai on my lap, and put Patsy Cline on the stereo. Usually I go for more traditional blues, but there's a certain kind of ache that Patsy's voice always speaks to, her voice floating above the pain with deceptive ease, timeless and yearning and poignant.

The last time I'd listened to Patsy had been the day Sinclair and I met the Oak King. Not long ago at all, really, just a couple of months. It felt like longer. Cody was right—a lot could happen in a short time. Two months ago, I don't think I would have had the bravado to pull a Dirty Harry gambit on a vampire. Hell, I'd barely learned to create a mental shield two *days* ago. And two months ago, Sinclair and I barely knew each other.

Now he was my ex-boyfriend, and even though we'd only dated for three weeks and ending it was entirely my decision—and I was pretty sure it was the right one—I was home alone on a Saturday night, thinking Patsy Cline didn't sound at all crazy for feeling so lonely and blue.

I guess when it comes down to it, we all yearn for a sense of connection, humans and eldritch alike, hell-spawns and vampires and werewolves, fairies and hobgoblins, Outcast and moody teenaged high school students. Even Gus the ogre had a thing for my mom.

Lying on my chest where he'd inched his way up from my lap, Mogwai stretched out one deliberate paw, unsheathing his claws just enough to prick the hollow of my throat. Amping up his purr, he fixed me with one of those implacable cat stares that could mean almost anything. Behind those round green eyes, he could have been plotting my demise or preparing to impart the feline wisdom of the ages.

Or maybe he was just reminding me that I wasn't alone after all and shouldn't be throwing myself a pity party when I had such an awesome sort-of-familiar in my life, as well as a lot of people, human and otherwise, whom I cared about deeply.

"You know what, Mog?" I stroked his head. "You have a point. Thanks."

Retracting his claws, Mogwai closed his eyes in satisfaction and purred just a bit louder.

# Twenty-seven

For the next week or so, things were fairly quiet in Pemkowet. No rutting satyrs, no threatening obeah women, no suspicious hell-spawn lawyers, no abducted teenagers, not even a hobgoblin prank.

It was a relief. Tourist season doesn't actually end after Labor Day—the PVB does its damnedest to make Pemkowet a destination all year long, and with the exception of the frigid months of January, February, and March, it's gotten some results—but every local I know, myself included, counts on things ratcheting down a notch. This year, between Emmeline Palmer's ultimatum, an unexpected visit to Little Niflheim, and the melodrama out at the House of Shadows, I hadn't had the chance to properly appreciate the fact that I could find a parking place downtown on a weekday without circling the block or get a cinnamon roll at Mrs. Browne's bakery without waiting in line.

Now I did.

There wasn't more than a few hours' worth of filing to be done at the police station, but I had the entire backlog of the X-Files to comb through, and in a moment of expansive generosity, Chief Bryant had agreed that I should be paid for the time spent developing the database. On the one hand, it made sense—it would, after all, enable me to do my job better—but on the other hand, since I'd made it clear that I would be the only person to have access to it, he would have been within his rights to deny my request to log those hours on the department's budget.

To be honest, the chief hadn't been too thrilled with my stance. It had come up when I'd reluctantly refused to identify the membership of our local coven after their meet and greet with Sinclair. But we had a long talk about confidentiality, honor, respect, and the eldritch code, and although he didn't like it, he understood. A lot of the same principles apply in the police force, even in a tiny one like ours.

For example, Chief Bryant knew that Bart Mallick had been first on the scene at the satyr orgy and had failed to respond thereafter. Given what had gone down at Rainbow's End that evening, there could pretty much be only one reason for it, but Cody and I had covered for him—I think our report said something to the effect that Officer Mallick was engaged in conflict resolution, which was certainly one way of putting it—and the chief hadn't requested clarification. Like I said, he understood.

Anyway, I was grateful to get paid for the work.

I took a shot at tracking down the mysterious lawyer, whose full name was Daniel Dufreyne, in my spare time and hit a dead end. I got his name and contact info from a business card he'd left with Amanda Brooks at the PVB, but the weird thing was there was no business listed on it, nor a physical address—just a cell phone number and a Gmail address. Definitely sketchy. Amanda seemed surprised that she hadn't noticed, which I chalked up to the whole powers-of-persuasion thing. All I could do was leave a vague voice mail message and send an equally vague e-mail and hope Dufreyne responded. So far, he hadn't.

Most of the time, I concentrated on poring over the X-Files. While I didn't have an actual base in which to enter the data yet, the process helped me identify concrete working examples and additional criteria to provide to my genius programmer, Lee. For instance, I'd completely forgotten about the phooka that haunted the fields around Columbine Creek. One of the Donaghue kids came away with a broken arm a couple of years ago after the phooka took him for a wild ride. So, yeah, while I'd be responsible for entering all sensitive data such as the particulars of the incident, Lee needed to create a listing for phookas under the categories of eldritch beings, and a location listing for the creek.

I met with Lee a couple of times to give him my input and discuss the project, which was shaping up to be a lot fancier than anything I'd envisioned, insofar as I'd envisioned anything, which wasn't far. I'd figured he could create some kind of easy-to-use customized database software and load it onto my laptop, but oh, no. Lee was developing an online database that would be hosted on a dedicated server in an air-conditioned techno-vault in his basement, with backups and fail-safes and layers of encryption and a self-destruct sequence. Okay, I may be exaggerating and I probably have some of the terminology wrong, but basically he assured me it would be more secure than the Pentagon. At least I was pretty sure it would be safer there than loaded on my seven-year-old laptop, and it would be nice to have the luxury of accessing it anywhere.

Or anywhere in theory, I should say. On the downside, Lee informed me that it was too risky to use free Wi-Fi to access this or any password-protected site, which meant I'd have to start paying for Internet service instead of surfing on the bakery's. Good thing the project was generating a bit of extra income.

The one thing that did worry me was Lee's ability to access the database. He swore up and down that once I changed the password on the administrative panel, I would absolutely, positively be the only person in the world able to access it.

Did I believe him? Hell, no, not for an instant. I had no doubt that Lee would build some kind of back door into the program, and I'd never in a million years be able to find it or have the faintest idea of what to do about it if I did.

So I settled with threatening him with dire consequences if he went poking around in the database once I started entering confidential material. If it hadn't been for our trip to Little Niflheim, I don't think he would have taken me as seriously as he did, but the thought of being escorted to the underworld and facing down Hel in the full wrath of a goddess betrayed definitely gave him pause.

As it should. Although I also planned to use a private code for certain entries, just to be extra safe.

"You can trust me, Daisy," Lee promised, looking pale. "I swear, I won't do anything to jeopardize this."

"Good," I said. "Because if you do, I'm not taking the blame for your transgression this time."

He gave a nervous laugh. "Duly noted."

I spent time with Sinclair, too. In honor of his new commitment to a magical vocation, I rented one of my favorite guilty-pleasure movies from the library and spent an evening introducing Sinclair to *The Craft*.

To be honest, the video was just an excuse. It was good to spend time with him. There was a little lingering awkwardness, like figuring out how close together we should sit on the couch, but we found ourselves establishing new patterns of platonic friendship without a great deal of difficulty.

Ongoing home improvement projects aside, Sinclair had always kept a tidy house, but now it was immaculate. Apparently the ritual that Kim McKinney had overseen included not only a full-immersion bath performed in the Fabulous Casimir's backyard under moonlight—Sinclair glossed over the details on that part—but a thorough cleansing of the entire rental property. It had been scrubbed top to bottom with a wash that included essential oils of rosemary, juniper, and lavender, after which every nook and cranny was smudged with purifying sage smoke, all of which left his place smelling sweet and herbaceous. There was an altar set up on a sideboard in the living room. The thresholds of the front and back doors had been blessed with salt water, and there were crosses of rowan branches tied with red thread.

Theoretically, it meant that not only could no malevolent

spirit cross the threshold but no mortal could enter Sinclair's home with ill intent.

"Do you think it will work?" I asked him.

Frowning, he turned down the volume on the TV. "On a duppy? Yeah, I do. Magic here feels *strong*, Daisy, stronger than it does on the island. The roots go deeper. Everything's more powerful. Casimir says it's because of Hel and the underworld. All I know is that I can feel it working."

"But . . . ?"

"I don't know if it would work on Emmy," he admitted. "I can't ban her from my heart, which means the binding may not hold against her. And if she truly believes in *her* heart that she's doing the right thing, it wouldn't work anyway." He shrugged. "But safeguarding the house is only the first step. I need to learn to protect myself."

"You don't think Kim's magic bath did the trick?" I teased him. "How about the nice scarf Mrs. Meyers knitted for you?"

Sinclair gave me a look. "Hey, now! Are you making fun of my prayer shawl?"

"Not at all." What Mrs. Meyers had produced was a lightweight scarf striped in the pan-African colors of red, green, gold, and black. It actually looked rather dashing looped around Sinclair's neck. "I just didn't know knitting was a kind of magic."

"Neither did I." He stroked the scarf absentmindedly. "But it makes sense. Knots are a form of binding. It's the intention that it's done with that makes it effective, and I can feel hers in this."

"A blessing in every stitch?"

"Yeah." He nodded. "Believe me, that kind of focused intention is hard to maintain. I've been working on visualization techniques. It's tough."

"Like a shield?" I asked, hoping maybe we could compare pointers. Or maybe, truth be told, that I could show off a little. I'd held my own in the House of Shadows and I'd kept up my daily practice, including several more sparring sessions with Cooper out behind the Wheelhouse. I was proud of my progress.

But Sinclair shook his head. "Not exactly. More like an orb of white light. And chakras," he added. "I don't even know if I believe in them, but did you know Mrs. Sweddon can actually manipulate her entire aura? It's pretty amazing."

"Huh."

He stretched out his hands, regarding them. "So far, my favorite part is working in the nursery with Warren. I'd forgotten how much I liked working with plants."

"So no tattoo?"

Although I asked half as a joke, Sinclair took the question seriously. "I stopped by the shop and took a look at their portfolio. It's all beautiful work, but nothing felt quite right, you know? I think for that kind of commitment, it has to be right. Mark and Sheila told me it would be better to wait for my personal sigil to reveal itself than to choose something just for the sake of getting some protective ink."

I glanced involuntarily toward the altar. At this point it was pretty sparse, containing a pair of white candles, several seashells, including a conch with blue beads glued to it, and a small dried starfish. The conch shell was missing a few beads and one of the starfish's brittle arms was broken. I had a feeling those items had been in his possession for a long, long time.

Sinclair followed my gaze. "Yemaya's symbols. Could be an element of a sigil, but not a whole. Not anymore."

I'd done a little research since he'd mentioned being dedicated to her at the coven meet and greet, enough to know that Yemaya was one of the orishas, Yoruban deities whose worship was imported into the Caribbean via the slave trade. It appeared she was a benevolent goddess associated with the sea, a sort of oceanic mother-of-all. There was a wealth of information available about her role in what Mr. Leary called the syncretized religions like Santería. Obeah, not so much.

Some of the more fabulous depictions I'd found online reminded me of Lurine in her true form. It wouldn't surprise me to find out she'd served as the inspiration somewhere back at the dawn of time.

Anyway, I kept that thought to myself. "You'll figure it out," I said. "Don't worry. You don't need a tattoo to face down your sister, Sinclair. Not with the whole eldritch community of Pemkowet behind you."

He took my hand and squeezed it. "Thanks, Daisy."

I squeezed his hand back. "I mean it."

Both of us glanced down at our clasped hands, then let go and scootched a few more inches apart on the couch by mutual accord.

Sinclair turned the volume back up on the TV and reached for the popcorn, settling in to watch a coven of teenaged witches turn on one of their own. "You do know this movie is ridiculous, right?"

"Yeah." I smiled. "I know. But sometimes ridiculous is exactly what you need to make it through the day."

He laughed. "True dat."

# Twenty-eight

At the beginning of the following week, Lee finally unveiled his database to me. Not only that, but he actually suppressed his paranoia and made the bold move of divulging his address and inviting me to his house. I'd half expected to find that he was living in his mother's basement after all, but in fact he'd purchased a place of his own, a newish construction nestled in the woods across from the river on the west side of town.

There were a few items of geek-chic memorabilia on display, like a detailed replica of the *Enterprise* from *Star Trek* and a life-size copy of a British police box, which I knew just enough to identify as the TARDIS from *Doctor Who*, but not as many as I would have guessed, and he had a surprising number of pieces of Native American art from the Pacific Northwest, which fit well in the woodsy environs. I guess he'd become a bit of a collector in Seattle. Six years was a fair amount of time; Lee had probably developed facets I had yet to discover.

As for the database? It was *awesome*.

It didn't look like a database. It looked like the interface for a video game, with extensive, colorful graphics and a Norse rune–inspired font that managed to be at once decorative and easy to read.

At the top of the page, there was an ornate scroll bearing the words *The Pemkowet Ledger*. Beneath it were avatars for every category of eldritch being, with fields to enter proper names, dates, location, description, strengths, weaknesses, transgressions, favors. There was an interactive map with links to the pinpointed entries. There was a calendar that automatically logged documented incidents in the past by date, as well as providing the ability to enter projected incidents in the future—like, say, the next satyr rutting cycle—complete with alerts to be sent via pop-up, e-mail, and text.

Using the phooka incident as an example, Lee showed me how it all worked. "See here, if someone was missing in the Columbine Creek area"—he hovered over that section of the map with his cursor—"it pops up. Or if you thought maybe there was something significant about the date, and you wanted to refer to previous years . . ." He clicked on the calendar, flipping backward through the months. "You can search by date or you can check it out this way, which is more visual. I thought that might be useful when looking for patterns."

"Totally," I said. "Did you program full-moon cycles into it?"

Lee shot me an offended look. "Of course. Now, if you know what you're looking for, you can go directly to that entry." He brought up the phooka's listing. "Otherwise, you can search by keyword." He clicked on a search box. "Abduction, missing person, victim's name—anything you can think of. Everything's linked and cross-referenced."

"It's amazing," I said sincerely.

"Thank you." He appeared mollified. "Up here, see where it says *vault* and *penalty box*?" He clicked on PENALTY BOX, where a red X appeared next to a link to the phooka's entry. "Those aggregate entries from the favors and transgressions fields. So if you need to call in a favor in a hurry, maybe see at a glance who's on the black list or who you're in debt to, you can."

"I would never even have thought of that," I admitted. "Damn, Lee! You really are a genius."

"Yeah, I know." He smiled, getting up from his chair. "Go ahead, log in to the admin panel and take it for a test-drive."

I spent half an hour playing with the database. It felt more like ten minutes. It was just so easy—easy to navigate, easy to enter data, easy to search. And frankly, the graphic element made it fun.

"You've got it, Daisy," Lee said, returning from his kitchen to peer over my shoulder. "I did my best to make it idiot-proof."

"Gee, thanks."

"No offense." He proffered a bottle of what looked like iced tea, keeping another for himself. "Kombucha?"

"Sure." I accepted it, twisted off the cap, and took a sip. I wasn't about to tell him I had no idea what kombucha was. It must have been something else Lee got into in Seattle, since it hadn't made inroads into southwestern Michigan yet. In case you're wondering, it's basically tea, only it's fermented with a mass of yeast and bacteria. I looked it up later. For the record, it tastes like a lot like iced tea, only sort of fizzy and tart, and I'm glad I didn't know more at the time. "So, hey! How come other developers don't make software that looks this cool?"

Lee shrugged. "It's not cost-effective in terms of R and D, not to mention the amount of memory and bandwidth it takes to run. But since that wasn't really an issue, I approached this like I was designing a game. Database programmers usually don't think like artists or storytellers. That's the beauty of video games. They combine the best of all those elements."

"Did you design the graphics yourself?" I asked him.

"No." He took a swig of kombucha. "I used an illustrator I've worked with before. I didn't tell him anything about the project," he added. "I just sent him the specs. But if you need additional graphics, just let me know."

"I will." It occurred to me that between the designing and the outsourcing and the hosting, Lee really had in-

vested a lot in this project. "You really went above and beyond, Lee. I appreciate it."

"Yeah, well, I promised," he said. "And you delivered."

"Just don't ask again," I said. "That's not a favor I can
grant twice. Hel's tolerance only goes so far."

Lee nodded. "Oh, believe me, I won't. But . . ." Looking
down, he fiddled with his bottle of kombucha. "There might
be other ways I could help you, Daisy."

"Oh, yeah?" I was skeptical but curious. "Like what? No
offense."

Lifting his head, he gave me a wry smile. "Fair enough.
Can I show you something?"

"Sure."

"Back in a sec." Lee bounded out of the room on gangly
limbs, returning a few minutes later wrapped in his black
leather duster.

I did my best to raise one eyebrow at him, settled for
two. "I thought we talked about this, Lee."

"I know, I know. But there's a reason for it this time."
Undoing the buttons, he opened his duster like a flasher to
reveal a square white box strapped to his chest, then
thumbed a switch on his belt. "Check it out."

A blast of intensive white light blazed forth from the
box, bright enough that I shielded my eyes involuntarily.
"Gah!"

"It's full-spectrum lighting!" Lee shouted, as though he
needed to raise his voice to be heard over the sound of the
light. Which didn't make sense, but I totally got where he was
coming from. "The kind therapists recommend for people
with seasonal depression!" He switched it off. "Artificial sunlight, Daisy. Think about it! It's a great weapon to use against
vampires."

Damn, that really was kind of brilliant. I couldn't believe
no one had thought of it before. Or maybe they had, but if
so, I'd never heard about it. Or it didn't work, which was
also a distinct possibility.

"Have you field-tested it?" I asked Lee.

"Are you kidding?" He shot me an incredulous glance.
"By myself? Hell, no. I thought maybe you could use it."

I thought about it and shook my head. "I'm pretty sure that would be a violation of protocol."

Lee looked confused. "What protocol?"

"Yeah, exactly." I took a deep breath, exhaled. "See . . . it's hard to explain, but there's a set of understood rules that apply to the eldritch community. None of them are clear and some of them are arbitrary. It's . . . complicated. But honoring them is part of maintaining Hel's order, as is weighing them against what mundane law dictates. The House of Shadows is a sort of sovereign territory. Going in there armed with *dauda-dagr* means taking a firm stance in my role as Hel's liaison. But if I were to go in armed with artificial sunlight . . ." I shook my head again. "That's like a declaration of war. And there's no war, Lee. All of us here in Pemkowet are doing our best to maintain a peaceful co-existence. And I'm doing my best to facilitate it."

"Oh."

"It's still a great idea," I said.

"Well, what about me?" he asked. "What if I wore it out on patrol with you sometime? I could be your backup. Would that be a violation of protocol?"

I bit the inside of my cheek to suppress an involuntary smile. "Lee, I don't want to imply that you watch too much TV, because that would totally be a pot-kettle situation, but I don't patrol the town. That's what the active-duty police officers do. I only get involved if there's a reason for it."

"Okay, now I feel like an idiot." Lee slipped out of his duster, revealing the harness and battery pack that held the light box in place. "It's just . . . growing up in Pemkowet, surrounded by the eldritch community, it's like I've always been in it, but not entirely of it." He unsnapped the buckle on the harness. "It's always there, but you only ever catch sight of it in glimpses, out of the corner of your eye."

"Hello?" I turned my hands palm up. "You went to high school with me."

"Yeah, but you don't count." He backtracked. "I don't mean that, I mean . . . you only ever showed your human side. Ahh . . . mostly. At least I had the impression that's what you tried really hard to do."

I shrugged. "It's safer that way."

Lee nodded. "Okay. All I'm saying is that since the other night when you took me to Little Niflheim, since I saw Hel herself, I feel like I'm *of* that world. And I like it. I don't want to lose that feeling. Does that make sense?"

"Yeah, it does," I said. "I'm sorry. I didn't mean to rain on your parade."

"That's okay." He gave me another of those wry, genuine smiles. "I got a little carried away. So no patrolling the local graveyards, huh?"

"Nope." I smiled back at him. "Most of what I have to deal with is capricious, chaotic, and unpredictable, although I'm hoping the database will help. When it comes to vampires, Lady Eris actually keeps her brood on a pretty tight leash. There hasn't been a rogue vamp since years before I became Hel's liaison. There was, um, a little misunderstanding out at the House of Shadows last week, but it's been resolved. I don't expect to be going back out there for a good long time."

We talked for a while longer. Lee reminded me not to use free Wi-Fi to access the database, and I assured him that the guys from Comcast had gotten me hooked up with my very own Internet service two days ago. He offered to stop by and check it out just to make sure everything was secure, which I chalked up to his paranoid streak, but accepted anyway.

I thanked him again and left. Believe it or not, I was actually looking forward to doing database entry. I'd probably change my tune after the first few hours, but at least Lee had managed to make the prospect of it fun, and the idea of having my very own digital ledger was empowering.

Unfortunately, that part where I'd said I didn't expect to be going back to the House of Shadows for a good long time?

Turns out I was dead wrong.

# Twenty-nine

I got in a solid day's worth of data entry before Jen called me in hysterics the following morning. And Jennifer Cassopolis was *never* hysterical. Jen was tough. Not razor-blades-in-her-hair, she'll-cut-a-bitch tough, but she grew up in an abusive household, and it made her tough enough.

"Whoa, whoa, whoa!" I said when I could get a word in edgewise. "Slow down! Take a deep breath and tell me again. Who did what now?"

On the other end of the phone, Jen took several ragged gulps of air before swallowing convulsively. "Fucking *Geoffrey*!" she said, her voice thick with tears and rage. "He's fucking turning my sister!"

Oh, crap. I closed my eyes. "Shit! Okay, let me think. Maybe we can put together an extraction team. Stefan—"

"It's too late, Daise," Jen interrupted me. "It's already done. We got an invitation to the rising this morning. A fucking *engraved invitation*, like it's a fucking *wedding*, for Christ's sake! One of their minions hand-delivered it!"

I felt sick.

Turning a mortal into a vampire isn't a spontaneous decision. It's a process. Over the course of a month's time, the mortal ingests small amounts of his or her blood-bonded vampire mate's blood until it reaches the critical threshold necessary to keep the mortal's flesh from corrupting during the three-day period between dying and rising. And yes, in case you're wondering about the biblical echo, there are undead sects that claim Jesus was a vampire.

Anyway. It meant that Bethany Cassopolis was already lying dead in the House of Shadows, drained of mortal blood. And it meant that the process of turning her was already under way when I was there the week before.

That's why she didn't look as strung out as usual. And that's probably why Geoffrey gave her permission to recruit an acolyte, so they'd have their very own playmate and blood source on hand for her rising.

And like a good little half-breed clinging to my mundane human morals, I'd passed up the chance to plant *daudadagr* between Geoffrey the prat's shoulder blades and make an end to him.

"Daise?" Jen asked.

"I'm here." I was pacing the living room in a fury, my tail lashing, but I had no one to be furious at but myself, and it wouldn't do Jen any good to tell her about it. Not now. "Are you serious? They sent an invitation?"

"Oh, I'm serious!" A gasp veering back toward hysteria escaped her. "Apparently it's traditional. Nice heavy cream-colored stock, a deckled edge . . . you should see it!"

"Okay, girlfriend," I said in my best calm, take-charge tone. "I'm sorry. I'm *so* fucking sorry." Sorrier than she knew, that was for sure. "But we've talked about this. Bethany's an addict, Jen. She didn't want to be helped. You tried. We both did. We did our best, but we always knew this day might come."

"I know. It's just . . ." She sighed.

"I know."

It might not sound like much, but when you've been friends for as long as Jen and I have, you develop your own shorthand.

Jen took another deep breath. "Beth wrote a note on the invitation. They must have had it printed . . . before. She wants me there."

"For the rising?"

"Uh-huh."

I sat down on the edge of my futon. Mogwai wound around my ankles, not purring, just pressing his reassuring bulk against me. I reached down to pet him with my free hand. "What do you think?"

Jen was silent for a long moment. "You'd come with me?"

"Duh."

"Then I'll go." Her voice was grim. "And if anything goes wrong . . . I really, really hope there'll be hell to pay."

I shifted the phone to my other ear. "Oh, there will. I promise. And if it's okay with you, I'd like to ask Cody Fairfax to come with us. Because if anything *does* go wrong, we're talking about murder. And if that happens . . ." The words trailed away as it came home to me that I was talking about Jen's sister being irrevocably dead. I cleared my throat. "As Hel's liaison, I would say it becomes a matter for mundane authorities."

"Good," Jen said. "That's fine. I'd be glad to have him there. Daise . . . ?"

I waited. "Yeah?"

"I don't know which would be worse," she whispered. "Even though it's been awful, Bethany's still my sister. If she didn't rise, at least it would be over, you know? If she does . . . I don't know if I could ever consider her family again." She paused. "Am I a terrible person for thinking that way?"

My heart ached. "Not for an instant."

Bethany's rising was scheduled for midnight two days from now. Very clever of the House of Shadows to wait until someone was actually freaking *dead* to send out an invitation to the resurrection.

I spoke to Cody, who readily agreed to attend in his capacity as an officer of the law. He was still pissed off about what had happened with Heather Simkus.

I talked to Stefan, too.

Well, actually, it was Stefan who contacted me, calling to suggest that he evaluate my progress in the art of conjuring and raising a mental shield. "Cooper tells me you think I was holding back on you," he said to me.

"No," I said. "I *know* you were holding back. But I've been getting better."

He laughed. "Come to my apartment. We'll spar. This time I won't hold back . . . as much."

Frankly, I was grateful for the offer. I was in a foul mood and sparring with Stefan might help take the edge off it.

True to his word, he came at me harder this time. I'd become accustomed to the wild, surging attack of Cooper's beast. By contrast, Stefan's approach was deadly and disciplined. He wielded his hunger like a sword, battering straight at my mental shield, then sidestepping deftly to come at me from a different angle. We circled each other in his living room. I held *dauda-dagr* in my right hand, and the sunlight sparkling on the river beyond his window gleamed along the edges and runes of its blade. I let it fill me, pouring light and anger into my shield, letting it blaze. Stefan's pale blue eyes were like sun-shot ice, his pupils waxing and waning as his desire warred with his discipline.

There was a part of me that *wanted* him to lose control, that wanted to fall into him, to spill my anger into that cool, deep well of stillness within him. And another, darker part that wanted to explore what lay beyond that stillness, to unleash the full extent of the emotions I tried so hard to keep in check, to allow Stefan to unleash the full extent of the ravenous hunger he kept under ironclad control.

Since that was a dangerous, possibly cataclysmic idea, we kept sparring, rotating around each other like a pair of binary stars until Stefan called a halt.

This time, he closed his eyes and took a moment to collect himself. I was exhausted and there was sweat trickling down the back of my neck, but I felt good. Not only that, I realized that although I'd sheathed *dauda-dagr*, I hadn't dropped my shield altogether when Stefan stopped pressing me; it had already become instinctive to keep a faint spark kindled in my thoughts.

Stefan opened his eyes and smiled at me. "Well done. You *have* been practicing."

"Yep."

As before, he went into the kitchen to pour a couple of glasses of water. I wandered over to the display case with his father's ceremonial shield, gazing at the dark-haired knight kneeling before his queen, wondering about the story behind it. Stefan returned to hand me a glass of water without comment.

"Thanks," I said to him. "I really needed this today." I smiled wryly, remembering the bond between us. "But then you probably knew that, didn't you?"

He inclined his head in acknowledgment. "I sensed your unrest."

"My best friend, Jen—Jennifer Cassopolis, you met her the other day—her older sister's been out at the House of Shadows for eight years." I took a drink of water. "This morning, Jen got an invitation to her sister's rising."

"I see."

I shook my head. "No, see, here's the thing. I was out there last week. There was an, um, altercation. Under the terms of Lady Eris's decree, I had a legitimate chance to take down the vampire who's turning Jen's sister. And I didn't do it." My temper rose like the proverbial phoenix from the ashes of my temporary sense of calm, my anger again directed at my own hesitation. "I mean, I didn't know at the time that he was turning her. But I didn't fucking *do* it, Stefan."

Stefan pointed at the couch. "Sit."

I sat.

He sat in a chair opposite me. "Do you think it would have made a difference?"

"Well . . . yeah. Obviously."

Stefan gave me a look that was hard to describe—rueful, compassionate, maybe a little patronizing without meaning to be. The kind of look that spanned a six-hundred-year gap's worth of life experience. "Your friend's sister made her choice years ago, Daisy. Either she would have found another sponsor or wasted away trying."

"Maybe." I shrugged. "Okay, probably. But we'll never know for sure, will we?"

"No."

I have to say, I appreciated the fact that Stefan didn't mince words. He turned his head to gaze out the window, and we sat for a moment without speaking. I contemplated the clean, crisp, strongly drawn lines of his profile, his high, rugged cheekbones. I could see the resemblance to the kneeling knight on the shield.

He looked back at me, his pupils steady. "At least she had the luxury of making a choice, no matter how unwise or uninformed."

"You had no idea that you would become . . . Outcast?" I asked softly. I mean, I assumed it, but I didn't really know for sure.

"No one does." Tilting his head, Stefan Ludovic regarded the ceiling. "I loved my father," he said, apropos of nothing. "I revered and admired him above all men, and I do believe he was worthy of my regard. It was a golden age in the history of Bohemia—indeed, in the history of Europe—and my father was a nobleman in every sense of the word—a just and compassionate ruler, a highly educated and visionary thinker, a valiant knight. But he wed a weak-willed woman."

I didn't say anything.

"It was not his fault." Stefan glanced at me once, then looked away again. "In those days, the aristocracy did not wed for love. It was a union of political expedience. But while my father was away on one of King Charles's campaigns, she allowed my uncle to seduce her. And upon my father's return, my uncle, his own brother, poisoned him."

I swallowed. "Um, isn't that the plot of—"

"Yes," he said before I could finish. "It is very like it. But although I was my father's only son, I was no Hamlet. I was a man grown and a knight in my own right, a Knight of the Cross with the Red Star. I was a member of a branch of the order affiliated with a hospital in Prague that specialized in occult afflictions. When my father's spirit appeared to me in a dream, crying out for vengeance, I knew it was a true vision."

I set my glass of water down carefully on a marble coaster, trying not to let it clink. "I see."

"My uncle was everything my father was not," Stefan continued, still not looking at me. "Craven, ambitious, untruthful. But he could be charming, and he knew how to evoke pity. He was born with a twisted leg, which prohibited him from service in his majesty's army. When I returned to my ancestral home of Žatlovy, I stood in the great hall and accused him of my father's murder. He denied it. He denied it vehemently." He looked back at me, pupils surging to eclipse his irises as his voice turned savage. "And then he *laughed* and told me I could never prove it."

My shield flared from a spark to a buckler-size disk.

Stefan closed his eyes, regaining control. "Forgive me."

"No, it's all right," I said. "*I'm* sorry. I want to know, of course I want to know, but I didn't mean to pry."

He opened his eyes. "You didn't."

I cleared my throat. "So you killed your uncle?"

"Yes," Stefan said simply. "I struck him down then and there, with the very sword my father wielded at the Battle of Crécy. In a fit of pure rage and loathing, I killed my uncle, a defenseless cripple. Acting out of the depths of my profound and abiding love for my father, with the commandment to honor him blazing like a beacon in my thoughts, I exacted vengeance. I killed his treacherous, villainous, murderous brother in cold blood." He stretched out his hands, contemplating them. "I have sought to relive that moment a thousand times in my memories. To this day, I do not regret it. Although," he added, "I can still hear my mother's screams."

I swallowed again, wordless. I wanted to ask what had happened next, how Stefan had become Outcast, but my throat was too tight.

"My uncle's guards drew their poniards and fell upon me." Stefan answered my unasked question in a dry tone. "The very same guards sworn to my father's service not a month beforehand." He touched his chest and his back and sides—here and here and here. "There were many of them. Although I fought, they slew me."

I found my voice. "But you came back."

He gave a brief, brusque nod. "Yes. On my bier in the chapel. I returned to myself. Alive, awake . . . and Outcast."

There were a few thousand questions knocking around in my thoughts, but they were banging up against a pretty strong sense that Stefan Ludovic was gently but firmly closing the door on this conversation. He'd opened himself up to me as much as he was going to today, which, frankly, was a lot.

I mean, seriously . . . Stefan was basically freakin' Hamlet, only less indecisive? That was huge.

"Thank you," I said to him. "You didn't need to tell me that."

"I know." He held my gaze. "You've shared a great deal with me, Daisy, much of it not of your choosing. I wanted to do this."

"I'm grateful."

"I did not do it to earn your gratitude." Stefan's expression was unreadable, but I could sense the hunger behind it.

Damn. Maybe he really did have feelings for me.

If he did, it didn't appear that he was going to declare them today. I let the silence stretch between us. When it became obvious that he had nothing further to say, I returned to the original topic. "Okay, well, I'm going to Bethany Cassopolis's rising in two days," I said. "Any advice?"

Stefan frowned. "A newly turned vampire's rising is a volatile time," he said. "Physically and emotionally. While it may be a transformation of their own choosing, no one is ever truly prepared for it. Many panic upon rising. I would offer to accompany you if I thought it wise . . . but I fear I do not."

Good to know. "No problem," I said. "I've got backup."

"The lamia?"

I shook my head. "The cop."

"I see." Stefan steepled his fingers. "I would not anticipate difficulty. The newly risen possess considerable strength, but it takes many years to develop more dangerous skills, such as vampiric hypnosis, to their fullest potential. The others will be prepared to manage the situation, and it is my impression that Lady Eris is competent in ministering to her brood."

"So I should just . . . let it happen?" I asked.

He gave me another of those centuries-old, gap-spanning looks. "It has already happened, Daisy. You are merely there to observe the culmination as a courtesy."

"Right."

We gazed at each other.

"You should go," Stefan said presently, his pupils waxing, stabilizing with an effort. "My control is . . . strained."

I stood, hesitating. I couldn't resist asking. "Okay, look, I'm sorry, but . . . is it about you? Hamlet?"

He summoned a faint smile. "Are you asking if I knew William Shakespeare? No. By all accounts, the play is based on an old Scandinavian folktale. But if he had put words into my mouth, they would have been Laertes', not Hamlet's."

Since I couldn't remember which one was Laertes, I held my tongue.

Stefan looked into the distance. "To hell, allegiance!" he murmured. "Vows to the blackest devil! Conscience and grace to the profoundest pit! I dare damnation. To this point I stand." His voice dropped an octave, deep and menacing. "Let come what comes. Only I'll be revenged most thoroughly for my father."

I shivered.

Words, they were just words. But they were words that evoked a moment that defined the entirety of Stefan Ludovic's existence. I hadn't forgotten how Cooper had described it: that one terrible, horrible, glorious moment that could never be taken back, that could never be regained. The moment that he craved to re-create, forever and always.

And couldn't.

I wanted to say something profound and reassuring, but the truth was, I had no idea what that might be.

So instead I left.

# Thirty

Two days later—or to be more precise, two days and a night later—I returned to the House of Shadows.

In accordance with the instructions on the engraved invitation, Jen and I arrived at eleven thirty. The temperature had dropped and it was a chilly night, more like October than September. We stood shivering in the courtyard for a few minutes, waiting for Cody to pull up in a cruiser and join us. God knows what would happen if things did go wrong, but at least he looked reassuring and official in his cold-weather police duty jacket.

"Are you okay?" he asked Jen.

She gave him a wan smile. "Not really."

"Let's get this over with." I banged the door knocker.

Unsurprisingly, the undead doorman had a problem with Cody's presence. I suppose the only surprising thing was that he didn't have a problem with mine. Jen was prepared to claim me as family if necessary, but apparently being Hel's liaison included the privilege of attending vampire risings.

Lucky me.

In the end, Lady Eris was summoned, arriving in a cloud of irritation and impatience. "There is no justification for your presence here, wolf."

Cody planted his hands on his utility belt. "Are you kidding? There's a dead woman on the premises."

Lady Eris shot him a glare. "Unrisen, not dead."

He shrugged. "Until she rises, she's dead. And as long as she's dead, police presence is justified."

"He's right," I added, trying my best to sound authoritative. "He's here at my request. Just in case."

"There is no time to argue the matter." She pursed her carmine lips and turned her glare on me. "Fine. The wolf may remain on the premises, but he may not attend the ceremony. Once he has confirmed the initiate has risen, he will depart. Does that suffice to resolve the issue?"

Cody and I exchanged a quick glance. He gave me a faint nod. It was probably the best compromise we were going to get.

"Yeah," I said. "It does."

With that settled, the denizens of the House of Shadows assembled to file through the manor into the . . . crypt, I guess you'd call it. Back in the day, it was probably a cellar storage room, with stairs leading down from an aisle adjacent to an incongruous kitchen. As Jen and I were escorted past it, I wondered briefly why Lady Eris's vampire brood hadn't disassembled it, then remembered that their mortal acolytes still required human sustenance.

Anyway.

The walls of the crypt were covered with stucco, and dozens of candles burned in niches and on stands arrayed around the cellar. A fresco of the night sky adorned the ceiling, smudged with decades' worth of candle smoke. A big slab of marble like a sarcophagus sat hulking in the center of the space.

Jen let out a faint sound, reaching involuntarily for my hand. I grabbed hers, squeezing hard.

Bethany Cassopolis lay motionless on the marble slab, looking bloodless and pretty fucking dead. Her black hair was fanned out over the marble, her hands were folded on her chest, and her normally Mediterranean olive-toned skin was pale and ashen. The fact that she looked so much like her sister made it even more unnerving. Weirdly, a length of scarlet ribbon had been run beneath her chin and tied in a bow atop her head.

I took a deep breath. After the night's chill outside, the air in the crypt was close and stifling, but although I was beginning to sweat under the leather of my secondhand motorcycle jacket, the sweat turned cold on my skin.

"Brethren and sistren," Lady Eris said in a mellifluous voice. Okay, so apparently *sistren* is an actual word. "We gather here tonight to celebrate the initiation of a new member into our midst. Hail, sister!"

"Hail, sister!" a dozen-plus voices echoed.

Creepy, right?

She glanced around the crypt, her gaze settling on Jen. "Does the family of the initiate wish to bid her mortal sibling a farewell?"

"Are you *serious*?" Jen blurted. Lady Eris raised one perfect eyebrow. "Jesus!" Jen stared at her sister. Unheeded tears spilled down her cheeks. "Jesus, Beth! Did you *have* to?"

"You should be grateful," Geoffrey the prat informed her in a supercilious manner. "It is a tremendous honor that we accord her." Other vampires murmured in agreement. Jen fixed Geoffrey with a death stare filled with hatred. He actually looked slightly nonplussed.

"Very well." Lady Eris raised her voice. Not much, but it held an unmistakable ring of command. "Let the ritual commence."

She offered a series of invocations to the Goddess of Night in all her incarnations, of which there were many. I concentrated on taking mental notes for my database, counting the vampires in the crypt. Altogether, there were sixteen of them. Seventeen if I counted Bethany, which I wasn't ready to do yet.

Other than Jen and me, there was only one other mortal

present. I recognized him as the guy who'd played John the Baptist in the tableau vivant. He stood quiet and patient, gazing at Bethany with a look of glazed envy.

Bethany just continued to look dead.

I clutched Jen's hand in my left, my right resting on *dauda-dagr*'s hilt, its coolness caressing my palm. The candles burned, wicks crackling faintly here and there. I was hyper-aware of my heart thudding steadily in my chest, the soft whoosh of air entering and exiting my lungs.

Lady Eris beckoned. One of the other female vampires brought forth a silver chalice and set it on the edge of the sarcophagus. Another inclined her head to Geoffrey the prat, proffering a little silver knife with a curved blade.

Ceremoniously, Geoffrey unbuttoned his brocade waistcoat and removed it, handing it to the nearby doorman, who folded it neatly over one arm. Then Bethany's blood-bonded mate unbuttoned the ruffled cuff of his left shirt-sleeve and rolled it up to expose a pale, muscular forearm before accepting the knife.

Making a fist of his left hand, he held it over the chalice. With the knife in his right hand, he slashed the length of his inner forearm.

The other vampires sighed in approval, making the candle flames flicker and sway, sending dancing shadows around the crypt.

Okay, so it turns out that vampires *aren't* actually bloodless, which I guess I'd known on some level, since it's their blood that turns mortals. Exactly how it could work without a beating heart to circulate it, I'd never understood. It's just . . . it's not human blood that runs in their veins. What pulsed out of the gash in Geoffrey's arm was an opaque, pearlescent liquid that spidered over his skin and streamed into the chalice. The way it slithered and skittered reminded me of mercury from a high school science experiment.

I swallowed hard.

Jen squeezed my hand tighter.

The gash on Geoffrey's arm was already knitting, fading to a faint silvery line. He shook a few errant drops into the chalice before bowing to Lady Eris and offering the knife to her.

She pricked her forefinger and extended it. One, two, three perfect shimmering globules formed at the tip of her finger, falling into the bowl of the vessel.

There was a moment of silence, broken only by the faint sound of the candles and three mortals breathing.

Then Lady Eris bent over the sarcophagus. With one decisive slash, she severed the ribbon binding Bethany's jaw shut.

"Now," she said.

Bethany's jaw went slack and open, revealing nascent fangs. Two male vampires flanked her, raising her torso from the marble. Her limp spine sagged in their grip, and her slack jaw gaped wider.

Jen looked away, her nails biting into the palm of my hand.

I wanted to look away, too, but I didn't. I made myself watch as Geoffrey the prat raised the chalice to Bethany's lips with surprising tenderness, tipping its contents into her open mouth, carefully and judiciously.

For no particular reason, I counted the seconds that passed in my head.

One, two, three . . .

On *three*, Bethany's body convulsed. Her spine arched rigidly and her throat worked, swallowing. Her skin flushed in reverse, by which I mean that it turned even paler, taking on a faint luminosity. Her throat worked again as Geoffrey poured the last of the blood from the chalice into her mouth.

With the last gulp, her eyes flew open wide, dark and terrified. Her hands scrabbled frantically at her chest, her upper lip curled to reveal lengthening fangs, and she made a breathless choking sound.

"It's all right. You're all right," Lady Eris said in a soothing voice, laying one hand on Bethany's brow. Bethany's terrified gaze met hers. I could feel the weight of vampiric hypnosis emanating from the brood mistress. "It's the shock of rising, that's all. Do you remember we discussed this?"

Bethany gave the faintest hint of a nod, drawing in a gasp of air and gagging on it.

"There is no need to draw breath until you're ready to speak, sister," Lady Eris continued. "You're in your new body, your reborn body. Listen. Listen to its silence. Revel in the silence. Listen."

The panic in Bethany's eyes began to fade, replaced by something else. Something dark and needful.

"Yes." Lady Eris smiled. "You begin to understand, to truly understand. When all other needs are gone, only one remains."

"To feed," Bethany whispered.

"Yes." Lady Eris beckoned again. One of the female vampires led John the Baptist to the sarcophagus. "To feed."

I glanced over at Jen. She was watching now, a look of sick fascination on her face as her sister, still supported by a pair of vampires, reached for John the Baptist's outstretched arm, sank her brand-new fangs into his wrist, and began slurping down his blood.

Okay, ew. Earlier in the summer, I'd caught a glimpse of exactly how disturbingly erotic it could be to be fed on by a vampire, and let me tell you, that *so* does not apply to the newly risen. It was more like watching a starving person gorge herself in a particularly disgusting manner.

When John the Baptist sank to his knees with a guttural groan, the vampire attendants eased him away from Bethany. She sat upright and unsupported now, her eyes bright, twin rivulets of blood trickling from the corners of her mouth. She took a deep, experimental breath, licked all around her lips, and smiled broadly. "I feel good," she announced. "I feel *great*!"

A polite golf clap went around the crypt.

Geoffrey the prat spread his arms. "Welcome, my love," he said to her. "Welcome, my sister."

Bethany glanced at him. "Oh, fuck you!" His mouth fell open in shock. Lady Eris did the one-eyebrow raise. "You made me wait long enough for it." Bethany looked around the room. "Jen!"

Jen blinked. "Uh . . . yeah?"

Her sister grinned again, revealing bloodstained teeth. "C'mon, girl! We've got unfinished business at home. Let's go!"

"Huh?"

"Let's *go*!" Bethany hopped off the sarcophagus with startling speed, nearly falling over and catching herself in the blink of an eye. "Wow. That's gonna take some getting used to." She grabbed Jen's arm, yanking her away from me. "Car keys in your purse?"

"Hey!" I protested.

"You can call someone for a ride," Bethany said over her shoulder, already dragging Jen toward the stairs. "This is a family matter."

"Bethany!" Geoffrey said in a thunderous voice. "I do not grant permission for this!"

"I don't need your permission anymore," she retorted. "Unless her ladyship forbids it, I'll be back before dawn."

He shot Lady Eris a look of appeal.

She shrugged. "I'll allow it."

By the time he got his protest out, Bethany and Jen were halfway up the stairs, and by the time I pushed my way through the vampire throng in the crypt, they were out the door, leaving a puzzled-looking Cody in the foyer.

"I take it the rising worked," he said. "Should I have stopped them?"

"Probably," I said. "Maybe. I don't know."

He glanced toward the courtyard. "Should we go after them?"

"Definitely."

The taillights of Jen's old LeBaron were already vanishing in the distance when we set out after them in the cruiser, which didn't really matter since I was pretty sure that Bethany was headed for the Cassopolis home. Cody put on the siren and the lights and we took off at a good clip, which also didn't matter since apparently being turned into a vampire also meant driving like a . . . well, like a bat out of hell. I guess lightning-fast reflexes and a total lack of fear of dying will do that to a person. I hoped Jen was okay.

The Cassopolises' place was a dingy ranch house on the

outskirts of East Pemkowet. We arrived to find the front door standing wide open and lights on inside the house. Cody took the lead and I followed him, drawing *dauda-dagr* as a precaution.

Jen's kid brother, Brandon, was standing in the doorway of his bedroom, looking sleep-disheveled and shell-shocked. Without a word he pointed down the hallway toward his parents' bedroom, where we could hear shouting.

I didn't have a whole lot of love for Jen's father. Mr. Cassopolis was a mean drunk with a bad temper. He hit his wife, and the only reason Jen still lived at home was because she worried that he'd start in on Brandon.

Still, it was disconcerting to see someone I knew as a parent pinned up against his own bedroom wall inches above the floor, clad in a pair of light-blue pajamas, his bare feet kicking futilely.

Bethany held him effortlessly in place, one hand clamped around his throat. ". . . understand me, Dad?" she was saying. "If you ever, *ever* lay a hand on Mom, or Jen, or Brandon, or . . . fucking *anyone*, I will kill you." She bared her blood-crusted teeth and sharp fangs at him. "*I will drink you dry*. Understand?"

His eyes bulged. I'm pretty sure he couldn't have replied either way. I had a bad feeling that newly risen vampires weren't entirely aware of their own strength.

Bethany gave her father a little shake, using her free hand to bat away Jen's efforts to pull her off, ignoring her pleas. Their mother was pulling at her own hair and screaming; just screaming, over and over, like a police siren.

*"Understand?"*

"Bethany!" Cody shouted, drawing his gun. "Let him go!"

She laughed. "You gonna shoot me? Go ahead. I'm not finished here. Not until he agrees."

Cody and I exchanged a glance. Shooting Bethany with a service pistol wouldn't do much except slow her down and piss her off. Vampires don't die easily and they heal incredibly fast. Sunlight works, but that whole stake-in-the-heart thing is a myth. You pretty much have to cut off their heads to kill them.

Unless you have a magic dagger.

I planted the tip of *dauda-dagr* between her shoulder blades. "He can't *talk*, Bethany! You're fucking strangling him!"

She stiffened. "Don't. Just . . . don't."

"Let him down!"

"You're killing him, you fuckwit!" Jen shouted at her sister, helpless tears in her eyes. "Jesus! Is this your idea of *helping*?"

"I spent eight years waiting to get to this point!" Bethany shouted back at her. *"Eight fucking years!"*

Mr. Cassopolis's feet were kicking more feebly. I hesitated.

"Oh, for Christ's sake!" Cody growled at Bethany, green phosphorescence flaring behind his eyes. "Don't make me rip your throat out."

"I'd like to see you—"

"Daisy?" It was a new voice, a voice I recognized but couldn't place. "Shit!"

There was a click, and bright light flooded the Cassopolises' master bedroom. Artificial sunlight, full-spectrum lighting.

Bethany howled in agony, dropping her father. He crumpled, wheezing. She scrambled across the floor, eyes screwed shut and swollen, striking out blindly over and over.

"Ow!"

A sharp snap, like a stick breaking. Also, the very bright light went out.

I turned around.

Lee Hastings was huddled on the floor, his leather duster pooling around him, the light box strapped to his chest cracked and dented. He was cradling an obviously broken forearm and blinking owlishly. Bethany looked sort of scorched, her skin bubbly and flaky. Cody was wrestling his half-shifted features back under control, breathing hard, looking annoyed and disgruntled. Mrs. Cassopolis had stopped screaming, settling for clutching at the neckline of her nightgown. Twelve-year-old Brandon was peering around the door of his parents' bedroom, his expression uncertain.

I looked at Jen.

She looked back at me. "Well, *that* went well."

# Thirty-one

So I guess Lee really was kind of an all-purpose genius, since it turns out that artificial sunlight can do serious damage to a vampire, at least at close range. The downside is that being in close range to a vampire puts you at risk for sustaining some serious damage yourself. Lee was lucky it was just a broken arm.

"Where the hell did you come from?" I asked him while Cody checked on Mr. Cassopolis and Jen ushered her brother away from the scene. Mrs. Cassopolis was sitting, catatonic, on the side of her bed, staring blankly at her older daughter. Bethany, surprisingly calm, was leaning against a wall and squinting at herself through swollen eyes, picking off ashy bits of skin. The pale skin underneath looked whole and unharmed.

Lee grimaced. "You didn't see my car? It was pulled off by the side of the road just before the driveway to Twilight Manor."

Bethany gave him a sharp look—well, as sharp as possible with swollen eyelids—and bared her fangs.

"Sorry." He coughed. "The House of Shadows."

"How did you even *know* this was going down?" I asked. "I didn't say anything about it."

"Are you kidding?" Lee nodded toward Mrs. Cassopolis. "They got a freaking invitation. It was the talk of the town. Everyone knew."

"Tell your mother I said to thank her for the Bundt cake recipe," Mrs. Cassopolis said in a distant voice.

"Right," I said to Lee. "So you decided to . . . what, exactly?"

He sighed and rested his head against the wall. "I just thought I'd drive out and lurk around the outskirts. Just in case." He patted the busted light box with his good hand. "I wanted to know if it would work. When I saw the squad car hit the lights and fly out after Jen's old beater, I figured something was wrong, and I followed as fast as I could." He lowered his voice. "Cody Fairfax is in the database, isn't he?"

I glanced in Cody's direction. "Shh."

"Sorry."

"He's a werewolf, duh." Bethany dusted herself off. A flaky flurry of burned skin settled around her. "I should have figured that out in high school. Oh, but you're not allowed to gossip about any of this." She pointed at her mother. "Or I'll be back. And the next time, I'll be angry."

Lee gave a dry laugh. "This wasn't angry?"

"Everyone's still breathing, aren't they?" She jerked her chin at her father. "Including him. Is he gonna be okay?"

Cody straightened. "Yeah. No thanks to you." He ran one hand through his hair and looked soberly at her. "Listen, I'm not your enemy. And you've got to realize things are different now. For the rest of your existence, you're just one slipup away from villagers with pitchforks and torches. Okay?"

Bethany shrugged. "Whatever."

"I'm serious."

"I know. But this had to be done." Ignoring Cody, she pinned her father with a flat stare. "You *do* understand me, don't you, old man?"

He gritted his teeth. "Yes."

"Good."

At Cody's suggestion, I got Lee onto his feet and into the living room while Cody went to retrieve the first-aid kit from the cruiser. Jen was in the kitchen making coffee because that's the sort of thing you do when you're trying to reestablish a sense of normalcy and you have no idea what else to do, and Brandon was playing some kind of first-person shooter military video game with a twelve-year-old's determined intensity, blocking out the reality of the world around him in which his newly risen vampire sister had very nearly killed his father.

*"Korengal Valley Mission?"* Lee asked, settling onto the couch beside him with a wince, still cradling his arm.

Brandon glanced at him. "Yeah."

He smiled. "I might have a few tips for you."

Fifteen minutes later, Brandon had the mother lode of insider advice on how to advance in *Korengal Valley Mission*, Cody had Lee's broken forearm splinted and taped to his body, and Bethany was ready to go back to the House of Shadows.

"Give me a lift?" she asked her sister. "You don't have to come in, but I'd really rather not call Geoffrey. Or steal your car."

Hands wrapped around a mug of coffee, Jen gave her a slow, measuring look. "Beth, do you really expect me to believe you've been planning this for eight years?"

Her sister shrugged. "Well, not *exactly*."

Jen said nothing.

The television emitted staccato bursts of gunfire. Lee and Brandon bent their heads together, murmuring. Cody's portable police radio crackled and he stepped outside to handle the call.

"I was and I wasn't," Bethany said softly. "I mean . . . that's what I meant to happen at the beginning. That's how it started, that's what I went looking for. I got lost along the way. A *lot* lost. And I'm sorry. I never meant to abandon you. I didn't. I never meant to leave you alone to deal with all their shit and take care of Brandon. But I'm back now. I was weak for a while, okay? Maybe for a long while, but now I'm strong. You can move out, get a life. Quit worrying about Brandon. I'll make sure nothing bad ever happens to him."

Damn. If you'd told me that after eight years of being a sniveling, clingy blood-slut, Bethany Cassopolis would turn out to be one badass vampire, I wouldn't have believed it. Aside from a few flakes of charred skin clinging to her glossy black hair, she even looked good, already healed from the blast of artificial sunlight.

"What do you think, Bran?" Jen asked her brother.

"About Bethany?" He looked up from his video game console, his face stony. "Are you kidding? I think it's straight up *epic*."

Okay, so apparently I was wrong about the blocking-out thing, and Brandon was just fine with his new vampire sister. I couldn't blame him.

"Yeah?" Jen tousled his hair. "Okay, then. Are you going to be okay on your own while I run Bethany back out to the House of Shadows?" she asked him reluctantly. "Daisy and Officer Fairfax have to take Skelet—" She caught herself. "Lee, I mean Lee, to the emergency room."

"It's all right," Lee said ruefully. "I don't mind. People I work with in Seattle think it's cool. They call me Skel all the time."

"*I* mind," Jen said in a firm tone. "Lee, you're kind of the big hero of the night. I think that deserves a proper name."

He blushed. Hmm, interesting. "I can stay with Brandon until you get back," he offered. "It doesn't hurt that bad."

Jen eyed him. "Yeah, I don't think that's such a good idea. Your hand's starting to look kinda puffy."

"Brandon can ride with us," Bethany suggested, a little too languidly for her sister's liking. "I bet he'd love to visit the House of Shadows."

Jen shut that one down fast. "Um . . . no."

"I'm okay staying by myself," Brandon said, not sounding entirely convinced of it. "It's not like I need a *babysitter*."

Cody reentered the room. "Ready to go?" he asked Lee. "I've got the go-ahead to run you up to the ER in Appeldoorn. Daise, can you pick him up? I'll drop you off to get your car."

Gah! In the movies, no one ever has to deal with the logistics of transportation in the aftermath of a fight. They just cut away to the next good scene. "Why don't you go ahead?" I said. "It's going to take a while to get Lee patched up. Jen can give me a lift to pick up my car after she drops Bethany off, and Brandon can ride along with us."

Thankfully, that settled it. Everyone took off on their respective errands, and I plunked down on the couch next to Brandon to watch him play *Korengal Valley Mission*. I couldn't help but be uncomfortably aware of his parents in the bedroom nearby, his mother in a state of shock, his father with bruises darkening around his throat. I didn't have a whole lot of pity for them—I'd known the family for too long, and Mrs. Cassopolis had run into far too many doorways, if you know what I mean—but under the circumstances, it was hard not to feel *something* for them. After all, I was only human.

Well, half, anyway. I wondered if I'd feel differently if I invoked my birthright, if I'd undergo a complete personality transformation like Bethany.

The thought made me shiver a little. Since her original personality—at least since I'd known her—hadn't been all that great, it had worked out okay for her, but the thought of losing my human compassion and decency was pretty creepy.

So was the fact that I was even contemplating it, come to think of it. Maybe it had to do with the fact that I'd choked ... *again*. That made it twice that I'd failed to take out a vampire in mid-throttle. And I wasn't ready to make the argument that aside from Lee's broken arm, it had turned out for the best. I mean, sure, I was glad I hadn't had to kill my best friend's newly undead sister, but I wasn't entirely convinced that unleashing patricidal vampire Bethany on the world was a great outcome.

And always in the back of my mind was the awareness that the date of Emmeline Palmer's return was creeping closer and closer.

I hadn't lost too much face in our first encounter, but that was due to dumb luck and Jojo the joe-pye weed fairy's jealousy. The truth is that dear Emmy totally got the drop on me, and I'd panicked.

I couldn't let that happen again. This time, there would be witnesses. Casimir's coven was on standby, and I had every intention of calling in whatever additional backup I thought would be useful, whether it was taking the chief up on his offer of mundane assistance from the department, calling in a marker with Stefan to have an army of Outcast escort Emmeline out of town, or hell, even brand-new bad-ass vampire Bethany if it happened to go down after sunset. But ultimately, I was Hel's liaison. No one else. However I did it, whatever it took to get the job done, protecting Sinclair and upholding Hel's order was *my* responsibility. If I wanted to maintain any shred of authority in this town, I had to be tough, a hell of a lot tougher than I'd been so far.

I had to be strong. Ruthless.

Unhesitating.

# Thirty-two

W hen I was a kid, it was the days of summer that slipped
away too quickly, one lazy sunlit idyll blurring into
the next, punctuated by the occasional excitement of
a thunderstorm rolling across Lake Michigan.

September was the time when all of summer's indolence
ground to a screeching halt with the return to school, to
being trapped behind a desk on a hard seat that bruised my
tail no matter how much I tucked or squirmed, breathing in
the scent of chalk dust, listening to teachers drone, flies
buzzing against classroom windows, the minute hand on the
clock inching along with agonizing slowness.

Funny how different things are when you're an adult.
This year, the remaining days of September fled.

It's not like anything of note happened. I spent most of
my time going through the X-Files, inputting data into the
Pemkowet Ledger. It gave me a sense of satisfaction to see
the database growing from a vague inkling of an idea into a
useful, searchable tool. Plus, I was getting paid for doing the
work.

I'm happy to say that I also helped Jen move out of her

parents' house. After a lot of soul-searching, several long talks with her brother, and a visit to Sinclair's place to get a tour of his spare room and the battery of magical protections Casimir and his coven had implemented, she decided it was time. When I reminded her that dear Emmy's return was just around the bend, she shrugged.

"Yeah, I know," she said. "I plan on making myself scarce. But if that doesn't work, right now I figure when it comes to hostile sorceresses, Sinclair's is now officially the safest place in town."

She had a point.

I *would* have spent time helping Mrs. Hastings, Lee's mom. At the emergency room the night of Bethany's rising, it turned out that Lee had a broken ulna. It was a simple fracture and the orthopedist on call assured him that he'd be fine after six weeks in a cast, but it meant that it was difficult for him to assist his mom with some of her household chores, which was his whole purpose in moving back to Pemkowet.

Of course, I volunteered, thinking that an elderly widow—actually, she was only in her late fifties, but she was one of those women who'd seemed old and crabby her entire life—half-crippled by rheumatoid arthritis would be grateful for the offer. I mean, you'd think so, right?

Not a chance.

She informed Lee in no uncertain terms that no spawn of Satan would ever darken her door and that he should have nothing further to do with me, and hinted broadly that he should move back into her house while his arm healed, which would make it easier for him to wait on her.

Lee refused in equally uncertain terms. Maybe he'd been a bit of a mama's boy in high school, but no matter how strong a sense of filial duty she'd instilled in him, there was no way he was going to let himself slip back under her thumb.

No wonder he bought his own place. I found a solution by volunteering Jen in my stead, which turned out to be perfectly acceptable to Mrs. Hastings. Since Jen felt we all owed Lee for his successful artificial-sunlight intervention, she was amenable as long as I agreed to help her pack up her stuff.

Other than clothing, there wasn't that much of it. Granted, the LeBaron had a big trunk, but come moving day, it only took us two trips.

"Oh, my God." Jen stood with her hands on her hips, surveying the contents of her new room. "My life to date is pathetic."

I perched on the edge of the sagging mattress. "At least it's furnished."

"I don't have *sheets*."

"We'll get you sheets," I said. "You can buy them at the dollar store now, remember? And socks. And underwear."

It was an old joke in Pemkowet—you could buy a ten-thousand-dollar painting here, but there was no place to buy socks. Until the Dollar General opened on the outskirts of town a few years ago, it was true. Not a particularly funny joke if you grew up without a lot of money and had to worry about filling your tank with gas to drive to Appeldoorn to shop for sheets and underwear. There are downsides to living in a beautiful resort filled with boutiques and galleries.

Jen smiled reluctantly. "Probably pretty crappy sheets."

"Probably."

She sighed. "I should have done this years ago, shouldn't I?"

I shrugged. "Jen, if you hadn't been there when Brandon ran away to hide in the swamp earlier this summer, Meg Mucklebones might have eaten him. So who knows?" I paused. "He *has* promised not to do that again, right?"

"Uh-huh."

"And he's okay?"

"Yeah," she said. "As much as he can be. Playing a lot of video games." She smiled again, her expression softening. "He and some friends are working out some big pseudo-military strategy for the annual Easties vs. Townies Halloween battle. Something about an industrial-strength water-balloon launcher."

I raised a fist. "Go, Easties."

The front door opened and closed, and a few seconds later Sinclair poked his head into the spare bedroom, his dreads rattling faintly. A local glass artist who dabbled in talismans had made specially sized blue-and-white evil-eye beads for him. "Hey, roomie," he said to Jen, hoisting a six-pack of beer. "Would you two care for a welcoming libation?"

"Sounds great."

Okay, even though this was entirely my idea, I admit it, I felt a pang of jealousy. Sinclair looked good. He smelled good. Well, mostly he smelled like rosemary, which might just have been his weekly hair treatment but could have come from working in Warren Rogers's nursery, which specialized in herbs and perennials.

Oh, well. I didn't regret my decision, but I figured I was allowed to feel a little proprietary.

The weather had taken a turn for the warmer to usher out the month of September. The three of us sat on the back deck on rusty patio furniture, drinking our beers while Sinclair outlined the plans for the garden he intended to plant in the spring. It would be a combination of herbs for both magical and culinary purposes, a small but dense vegetable garden, a few perennials, and plenty of naturalized native species to beautify the place. He'd already gotten the go-ahead from his landlord.

We talked about improved home furnishings and the best places to salvage decent stuff at a good price—I had a lot of experience in that area. We talked about Lee's offer to hire Jen on a more permanent basis as a caregiver to his mother, and whether or not dealing with a cantankerous old biddy was worth getting out of the Cassopolis family business of housekeeping. We confessed to the worst guilty pleasures in our television-watching lives—Sinclair's was an outrageous Japanese game show neither of us had heard of, Jen's dated all the way back to *Dawson's Creek*, mine was Gordon Ramsay's *Kitchen Nightmares*. There's just something so cathartic about the furious way Gordon swears when he's worked up.

Eventually, it became obvious that there was one major topic we were deliberately avoiding.

It was Sinclair who broached it. "So I've been thinking about Emmy," he said in a casual tone. "And I wonder if maybe we aren't overreacting a bit."

"Oh?"

"I've been talking it over with my dad," he said. "It really reminded me that this is a family matter. And he wants to be involved," he said. "He'd like a chance to talk to her before we assume the worst." He took a drink of beer. "I'd like that, too."

"Your sister issued a pretty clear ultimatum," I said. "Does your dad think he can talk her out of it?"

Sinclair shrugged. "Like I said, he'd like the chance to try. It can't hurt. No matter when she shows, he can be here in within the hour."

I looked at Jen.

"Don't look at me," she said. "If I've learned anything this month, it's that I know fuck-all about sisters."

"See, here's the thing," I said slowly. "Your sister crossed a line when she went after me. I'm not just some girl, hell-spawn or not, you happened to be dating. I represent Hel's authority in Pemkowet."

Sinclair glanced at me. "You don't think Hel would appreciate a peaceful resolution to this?"

"It's not that." I shook my head. "When I told Emmy to leave town, I also told her she wasn't welcome back here. I can't back down on that at the eleventh hour. I can't totally abdicate *my* authority."

"No one's asking you to." He looked away, picking absently at the label on his beer bottle. Jen murmured something about getting another beer and made a discreet exit. "I'm just asking for a little time for my father and me to negotiate with her before we send in the cavalry. Is that so unreasonable?"

I sighed. "I guess not. But I do think I should at least be there as an official presence. And I want the, um, cavalry in shouting distance."

"Deal!" Sinclair said promptly.

"Why the change of heart?" I asked him. "Was it just talking to your dad?"

"Mostly." He took another pull on his beer. "With him on board, I really do think it might be our best chance of talking Emmy out of doing something foolish. But do you remember me saying that magic was more powerful here in Pemkowet?" I nodded. There was a rustling in the overgrown patch of wildflowers along the fence at the back of the yard. A chicory fairy's head poked over the top, her blue hair — if you could call it that — looking like a chicory-flower-shaped cap. "Hey!" Sinclair smiled. "Quit spying, you." Reaching down, he picked up an acorn that had fallen onto the deck from the big oak in his neighbor's yard and shied it at the fairy. She dodged it with a high-pitched trilling giggle, translucent wings blurring like a humming-bird's, then blew him a kiss and vanished in a puff of glittery dust.

I'm telling you, those fucking fairies really love Sinclair.

"So you're afraid Emmy's going to be too strong to handle here?" I asked him. "Even for the whole coven?"

"Not exactly." He frowned. "Island magic is unpredictable anyway. The coven asked me what would happen if Emmy tried to unleash a duppy here. Truth is, I don't know. And I don't want to take a chance on finding out. She might set loose more than she can handle."

"Like what?"

"I don't *know*," Sinclair repeated. "I just know there could be repercussions. On a primordial level, everything's connected."

Catching sight of Jen hovering behind the screen door, I beckoned to her. "It's okay. We're just talking about what would happen if Emmy succeeded in turning a duppy loose in Pemkowet."

Jen slid into her seat. "Well, that would *really* make Halloween more exciting this year."

I laughed. "No kidding."

The three of us sat in silence for a few minutes, sipping our beers.

"Hey, is that video rental place that no one ever goes to still open?" I asked Jen. "The one next to the dollar store?"

She shook her head. "It closed down. Why?"

"Because you still need sheets," I said. "And this conversation's given me a weird urge to watch *Ghostbusters*."

# Thirty-three

On the first day of October, the calendar on Lee's awesome database sent me a reminder via pop-up, e-mail, and text message that Emmeline Palmer might be returning tomorrow, which would have been four weeks to the day from her ultimatum. Not that I needed the reminder, but it was nice to know it worked.

Anyway, no Emmeline the following day, so I guess we were going by the date. Accordingly, I received a second reminder two days later. I'd entered both dates into the calendar just in case.

It's funny, but it never occurred to me that dear Emmy was being anything less than literal about her one-month deadline. An ordinary mundane mortal might say, "I'll be back in a month," meaning approximately a month's time depending on flight schedules and availability. But numbers and units of time have significance in the eldritch community. A month meant a month.

And on the fourth of October, the early-warning system I'd bartered for paid off.

It was Mogwai who sensed it first. I was at home in my

apartment working my way through the 2009 X-Files. I *should* have been practicing psychic shield drill, but it was already late afternoon and I was too jittery to concentrate. At a little after three thirty, Mogwai went from a sedate lump of cat dozing in my lap to a hissing, caterwauling wild thing flinging himself at the nearest window, claws splayed.

My heart skipped a beat. "What the hell, Mog?"

I went to the window to look. Across the park, the eldritch equivalent of a rugby scrum was headed our way—fairies, bogles, hobgoblins, and pixies, scrimmaging in a tangle of tattered wings and long, thorny limbs, all of them quarreling and shrieking at a decibel level barely within my range of hearing.

Leaving Mogwai behind, I clattered down the stairs just in time to see a trio of hobgoblins blocking like linebackers—okay, I'm mixing my sports metaphors, sue me—freeing a fourth to race free of the pack.

"Tuggle?" I peered at him as he gained the alley. Behind him, the scrum broke apart in disappointment. One lucky tourist snapped frantic photos before the disentangled fey winked out of visibility and the park abruptly sprouted a number of new shrubs and bushes, not to mention a pretty ring of poisonous mushrooms. "Is that you?"

The hobgoblin's beady eyes gleamed. "The sister is back!" he announced triumphantly. "That makes us even for the sunglasses, right? I get a clean slate in your ledger?"

"Right," I said. "So where is she now?"

Tuggle's hooked nose twitched. "What do you mean *now*? She drove into town in a car like before. You said the first to tell you when," he said in an accusatory tone. "You didn't say to tell you *where*."

"I thought it was—" I abandoned the thought in midsentence. "Never mind. Can you find out where she is now? Then I'll owe you."

"*Ha!*" a familiar voice shrilled. Jojo popped into view, hovering, green arms no bigger around than pipe cleaners folded over her slight bosom. "The sorceress has purchased residence in the same inn she frequented prior," she informed me. "*I* thought to keep watch there. And now thy debt to me is increased yet again."

Echoing her stance, I folded my arms. "My offer was to Tuggle, not you."

Her wings beat at an agitated pace and her luminous lavender eyes narrowed. "I assumed—"

I interrupted her. "You know what they say—"

Jojo hissed at me. In the window upstairs, Mogwai hissed back. Tuggle scowled and fingered his nose.

"Okay, okay!" I sighed. "Jojo, just keep an eye on her and stay out of sight. Let me know if she makes a move to go anywhere. For Sinclair's sake. Do that and I'll owe you. Deal?"

The fairy sniffed. "Thou hast a deal, scullion."

Great.

Upstairs, I petted Mogwai until he calmed down. First, I called the chief to let him know everything was under control, and then I called Sinclair to set the coven's phone tree in motion.

And then I changed my clothes and went to pay a call on dear Emmy herself.

Strolling over to Idlewild Inn, I felt surprisingly calm. To be honest, a good wardrobe helped. One of the other things I'd done in the intervening weeks was turn my mom loose on mine. She'd designed a simple jersey knit dress for me that had just the right amount of motion, drape, and cling, and actually worked with the broad belt from which *daudadagr* hung. In charcoal-gray with a pair of knee-high black patent leather boots—sophisticated, but practical, with just a one-inch heel—it made for a reasonably elegant working outfit. I felt grown-up and competent wearing it. Plus, it left my tail free.

The boots had been a splurge. Although I had to wait another two months for it, I was kind of counting on collecting that two hundred and forty dollars I'd turned in after I busted Tuggle & Company's shell game.

I had to show my police ID to the desk clerk at the Idlewild before she agreed to ring Emmeline Palmer's room and announce me as a visitor. Then I had to wait, idling in the

Idlewild's quasi-Victorian lobby until dear Emmy deigned to emerge.

Maybe it was all the training in psychic self-defense that I'd been doing, or maybe it was just that Emmeline wasn't bothering to hide her light under the proverbial bushel, but this time I sensed her power as she glided into the lobby.

Her dark gaze swept over me, possibly taking in the up-graded wardrobe—Emmeline herself was wearing a beautifully cut pantsuit of taupe silk with a cream-colored blouse underneath—and then skated past me to look out the window at the street beyond. She seemed mildly surprised to see nothing out of the ordinary there.

"Have you come to escort me out of town?" she inquired. "I would have expected a posse. Isn't that how you Americans do things?"

"Sinclair wants a chance for the two of you to talk things out reasonably," I said. "And I've agreed to it."

Her eyelids flickered. "He does? I wouldn't have—" She stopped.

"Wouldn't have what?" I asked suspiciously.

"I wouldn't have thought he'd bother," Emmeline said flatly. "My brother knows when my mind's made up."

"Yeah, well." I shrugged. "Maybe he's got a few things to say that you haven't considered." I wasn't about to give her any hint that her father was going to be part of the parley.

She eyed me dubiously. "And you would have me believe you simply agreed to this?"

"I don't care what you believe." I eyed her in return. "What was *your* plan if I had come in with a posse?"

Emmeline didn't answer, her face taking on a shuttered look.

"Right." I handed her a slip of paper. "In case you don't have it, here's Sinclair's number. Give him a call and work out a time and place to meet on neutral territory."

"No posse?" she asked.

"I'll be there to observe," I said. "And the posse will be close at hand. But you'll have a chance to talk. It's more than I would have given you."

It was a good exit line, so I took it, leaving Emmeline standing in the lobby without a response.

I'm not going to lie—that part felt satisfying. There was a stirring in the hydrangea bushes alongside the inn's front door as I passed, and Jojo peeked out to give me a grim-faced thumbs-up.

Half an hour later, I was feeling a lot less complacent.

"You agreed to *what*?" I shouted into my phone at Sinclair. "To meet *where*? Are you serious? The *graveyard*? At freakin' *sundown*?"

"Emmy called on her right to have the dead bear witness on her behalf," he said, as though it were the most logical thing in the world. "It was either that or agree to meet her with no witnesses of my own."

"Uh, no!" I could feel the air around me tightening, and I tamped down my temper. "She doesn't get to dictate the terms, Sinclair. We do."

"Look, you agreed to let me set this up, Daisy." There was a faint note of impatience in his voice. "She invoked a protocol. I accepted a compromise. Would you rather I'd agreed to meet her alone?"

"No," I said. "I'd rather you hadn't agreed to meet her at duppy ground zero. I mean, that's what a cemetery is, right?"

There was a clicking sound on the other end of the phone as Sinclair shook his head, beaded dreads clattering. "Only if you want to catch 'em newly dead," he said. "I checked the obituaries; no one's died in Pemkowet in the past week. No wandering souls around. Anyway, I'm not worried about her catching duppies, just unleashing one. And if she decides to unleash a duppy she's already caught, it won't matter where we are. Trust me—Emmy's just grand-standing. She probably thinks it will scare you," he added.

Beneath my charcoal-gray knit jersey dress, my tail swished back and forth. "Don't goad me."

Sinclair gave a brief chuckle. "Sorry."

"You're *sure*?" I pressed him. "What does Casimir say? What about your dad? Is he on his way?"

"Casimir said the coven will only gain strength from

making a stand on hallowed ground," he said. "And my father should be arriving in about ten minutes. Okay?"

I sighed. "Okay."

After I got off the phone with Sinclair, I called Stefan to inform him that I needed a posse. I mean, we'd talked about it before, so he was expecting my call. He just wasn't expecting me to call it a posse.

"We will be there," he assured me. "Cooper, Rafe, myself, and two others. I trust that will suffice?"

"Do you think I'm overdoing it?" I asked him.

"No," Stefan said after a moment's pause. "She challenged you on your own turf. I think a show of strength is wise."

"Good," I said. "And . . . thank you."

"I owe you my life," he said. "I remain in your debt. And it is your right as Hel's agent to call upon your allies to defend her demesne."

With that, he hung up.

If you like cemeteries, Pemkowet's was charming. It dated back to the 1800s, when the town was founded, and featured lots of weathered headstones turning green with moss and lichen under somber pine trees and a few scattered maples. I arrived around seven o'clock, a good twenty minutes before the sun was due to set, steering my Honda along the narrow two-track that wound through the grounds, pulling off near the designated meeting place, which was in front of the elaborate Italianate mausoleum where the remains of axe murderer Talman "Tall Man" Brannigan were said to be interred. If you were to guess that it was a popular place for high school boys to bring girls to ply them with cheap beer and scare them with ghost stories, you would be correct.

But tonight it was Sinclair and his father who stood waiting before the sealed door of the mausoleum. The other members of the coven were arrayed on either side of them in a semicircle some twenty yards away. We nodded at one another.

"Daisy," Sinclair greeted me. "Dad, this is Daisy Johanssen. Daisy, my father, Thomas Palmer."

I held out my hand. "A pleasure."

Mr. Palmer studied me, his eyes wary. He didn't take my hand. He was a good-looking man, and I remembered Sinclair had said he was also a hardworking, God-fearing man. "So you're . . ."

My tail flicked. "Yeah," I said. "I'm the hell-spawn."

"Huh."

Apparently, he was also a man of few words. I hoped they would be enough to persuade his daughter.

Stefan's posse arrived in a rumble of motorcycle engines. He directed Cooper and the others to array themselves around the cemetery in a loose circle, straddling their bikes and guarding the egresses, then parked his own gleaming Vincent Black Shadow behind my Honda and came to acknowledge me with one of his courtly half bows. He had a sword strapped to his back, and his pupils glinted in the fading light. "Hel's liaison. I ask the honor of serving as your personal guard tonight."

"Thanks," I said. "That would be great."

His mouth twitched ever so slightly, then he inclined his head and took a stance about ten paces away.

On the whole, I was feeling pretty good about our show of strength.

The sun hadn't set yet, but it had sunk beneath the tree line in the west and dusk was deepening in the cemetery. Things stirred in the shadows—members of the fey, creeping closer to observe the coming showdown.

Sinclair's father shuddered.

"It's okay, Dad." Sinclair laid a hand on his father's shoulder. "They don't mean any harm. They just want to see."

Everyone waited. Cooper and the ghouls waited on their motorcycles. Casimir and the coven waited in their semicircle. I waited with Sinclair and his father, and Stefan not far away. Curious fairies, hobgoblins, bogles, and whatnot whispered and lurked in the shadows, also waiting.

In the distance, headlights.

There was a faint popping sound, and Jojo blinked into existence, her wings buzzing like a tiny helicopter. "They're coming!" she shrilled, her narrow chest heaving. "They're on their way!"

Wait a minute.

"Um . . . Jojo?" I said. "What do you mean, *they*?"

She shot me a disdainful look. "The sister and the other one, lackwit."

"Other one?" My temper flared. "*Other one? What fuck-ing other one, Jojo? Why didn't you tell me there was an other one?*"

Backing away, Jojo bared her sharp, pointed teeth at me. "Because, you lumpish, hedge-born harpy, you didn't *ask*!"

I gritted my own teeth. "I would have assumed—"

In midair, she folded her skinny arms and looked smug. "You know what they say."

I did.

The rented convertible approached slowly along the winding cemetery drive. The top was down. I was guessing the car probably had heated seats. It stopped before us, headlights blazing. Two figures emerged, silhouettes in the glare of the headlights—one tall and slender and elegant, one stalwart and blocky.

"It's Letitia," Thomas Palmer said in a low voice. "It's her."

Sinclair swallowed audibly and shot me a single stricken glance before returning his gaze to the car. "Mom?"

It seemed the Right Honorable Judge Palmer had ar-rived.

# Thirty-four

Note to self: When striking a bargain with fairies, be very, *very* specific.

I'd like to say a cloud passed over the moon and thunder rumbled as Letitia Palmer and her daughter approached our group. It didn't happen, but it felt like it should have. Sinclair's mother wore a lavender suit that looked like one of Hillary Clinton's more ill-advised fashion choices. She carried a matching clutch purse in one hand and an empty glass jar in the other, and an aura of power surrounded her like a storm cloud.

Still, she wasn't expecting to see her ex-husband. The sight of him brought her and Emmeline up short.

"Thomas."

"Letitia."

There was a whole lot of history in that exchange of names. Sinclair's father gathered himself, standing taller.

"You've got no business doing this," he said sternly. "The boy's made his choice. You need to learn to respect it."

"I did." Her gaze swept around the cemetery, taking in the lurking fey, the waiting coven, Stefan, and the hovering fairy before coming to rest on me with an expression of profound distaste. "Until I found out what it brought him to."

"Hey, don't use me as an excuse," I said, raising my hands. "We're not actually dating anymore."

Mrs. Palmer ignored me. "I've been patient with you, boy," she said to Sinclair. "But enough is enough. Are you ready to come home where you belong?"

"I'm not going anywhere." Sinclair's voice was strained. He cleared his throat. "This *is* my home."

She let out a snort. "This? You've got no roots here, son. Home is where the bones of the past are buried. Home is where the soil is soaked with the blood of your ancestors. This place?" She shook her head. "This isn't home. These aren't your dead. And these most assuredly aren't your people."

"Just come home, Sinny," Emmeline added in a pleading tone. Apparently she was playing good cop to her mother's bad cop. "I *miss* you!"

"No." Sinclair's voice grew stronger. "I'm sorry, Emmy. I miss you, too. But you're wrong. This is my place. And these are my people. Not because I was born here, not because they're my blood kin. But because *I chose this*. And I'm not leaving."

Casimir and the coven had drawn close, ranging themselves behind us. In the headlights, their faces looked stern and different. Even Kim McKinney's, and I usually thought of sliced cheese and cold cuts from the deli counter when I saw her.

"Your son is under our protection, ma'am," Casimir said, polite but firm. "And he's given you his answer."

Letitia Palmer gave him a stony look, but the Fabulous Casimir didn't quail before it. She took in his height, his false eyelashes, and the crimson satin turban he was wearing. She took the coven's measure, took in the hand-knitted scarf knotted around Sinclair's throat, the evil-eye beads sewn into his hair. She took in the sight of Stefan leaning casually on his sword, his face almost vampire-pale in the headlights. She took in me.

"Letitia, go home," Thomas Palmer murmured. "Sinclair's a grown man. Let him live his life."

"No." She handed her clutch purse to Emmeline and grasped the glass jar in both hands. "Not like this. Not surrounded by imps and goblins and ghouls, she-males and demon-spawn."

I had a bad feeling about that jar. Like maybe it only looked empty.

"Don't!" Sinclair's voice rose. "There's no point in threatening me, Mom. I'm protected!"

She looked at him. "Oh, I'm not threatening *you*, son. This is for everyone else in town."

He held out one hand. "Give it to me. You don't know what you're doing. Magic's stronger here. You don't know what you might unleash."

"On the contrary, I know exactly what I'm doing." Letitia Palmer stroked the empty jar. "This is my father's spirit in here, your grandfather Morgan's. I put the jar to his lips and caught it myself on his deathbed."

Okay, this would be the time to get authoritative. "I don't care who's in the jar, Mrs. Palmer," I said in a firm tone. "You're not setting it loose in Pemkowet. Give it to Sinclair, or set it down and walk away."

She gave me a scathing glance. "Or what?"

"Or I'll take it from you myself," I said, suiting actions to words without waiting for her response.

In a perfect world, I'd be rewarded for acting without hesitation, right? I took two swift steps toward Letitia Palmer, reaching for the jar to wrest it out of her grasp. Her eyes widened in surprise. She wasn't accustomed to being defied, and she hadn't expected me to act so quickly and decisively. And if Jojo hadn't had the exact same idea at the exact same time, I'm pretty sure it would have worked.

A green blur streaked past me on translucent wings, then recoiled violently, colliding with my face in an explosion of sparkling dust.

Sinclair's mother wore a cowry shell like her daughter's around her neck on a gold chain. Apparently, the ward worked on fairies.

All around us there was shouting, chanting, and commotion, a sense of power thrumming in the night air. I scrubbed at the fairy dust in my eyes and swore at Jojo, who swore back at me. How the hell she'd ever thought she was going to get those pipe cleaner arms around the jar, I couldn't say.

"Here." Stefan's voice, calm and steady. He handed me a clean bandanna to wipe my face.

When I could see again, whatever magical throwdown I'd missed witnessing had turned into a standoff. Letitia Palmer had positioned herself behind a headstone, and her daughter was guarding her back. Sinclair's mother had the jar raised above the headstone, and her face was grim.

"Tell them!" she shouted at her son. "If I smash the jar, there'll be *no* putting him back!"

"She's right," Sinclair said in a low tone. "Stand down. Don't provoke her."

Stefan gave me an inquiring look, his sword held lightly in one hand.

And I hesitated.

I don't know if he would have killed her. I don't know if he *could* have killed her, not with the ward she was wearing. Not without breaking the jar. Maybe. Or maybe Stefan was just testing me, testing the bounds of my humanity. It doesn't matter. I couldn't give the order. Obeah woman or not, Letitia Palmer was human and mortal. Killing her in cold blood would have violated Hel's rule of order. And even if that weren't the case, hell-spawn or not, I wasn't a murderer.

I shook my head.

Letitia Palmer permitted herself a small, victorious smile. "I have spoken at length to your grandfather's spirit," she said to Sinclair. "The country needs you. Your sister needs you. *I* need you. I'm running for Parliament, you know. There's a great deal at stake. Blood calls to blood, spirit to spirit. Your grandfather knows. He understands. When you're ready, truly ready, to come home for good, you'll be able to recapture his spirit and return it to Jamaica where it belongs. When you do, I'll lay it to rest. Until then—"

"Mother, I am begging you," Sinclair said. "Don't—"

She did.

With a simple, deft twist, the Right Honorable Judge Palmer opened the jar. In case you were wondering, there wasn't anything special about the jar. I don't know what it held before it held her father's spirit. Pickles, maybe.

An eddy of ice-cold air spilled forth from it, circling all of us. My skin prickled at its touch, rising into goose bumps, and I tucked my tail involuntarily between my legs. It smelled acrid and foul, like gunmetal and burning hair, with a powerful underlying note of death and decay, like meat left to rot. The stench of it triggered my gag reflex, and I came seriously close to throwing up. A handful of maple leaves rose in a flurry.

And then the wind died down as abruptly as it had sprung up. The maple leaves settled back onto the grass with a soft rustling sound. We all stood around waiting for something to happen.

"That's it?" I said to Mrs. Palmer. "That's your big, scary Grandpa Morgan duppy? A stinky breeze?"

She gave me a flat stare, but behind the bravado there was a hint of uncertainty in it. "Wait."

"For what, exactly?" I returned her stare. "You don't know, do you? Sinclair's right. You've turned this thing loose on us with Little Niflheim underfoot, a functioning underworld, and you don't have the faintest idea what's going to happen." My tail untucked and began lashing. "Right. Well, you're not going to stick around to find out. As Hel's liaison, I'm ordering you out of town. Now."

"Or what?" It was the same response she'd give me before, this time dripping with contempt. Any trace of uncertainty in her eyes had vanished. They were hard, hard as the granite headstones around us. Her voice dropped to a lower register, laden with power as she uttered a word. Don't ask me what word, but it was in a language that sounded like it dated back to the dawn of time, and every syllable of it tolled like a bell. "You don't dare lay a hand on me, child."

I opened my mouth to reply, but the word she'd spoken seemed to have lodged itself in my throat like a stone. I couldn't talk. In fact, beyond opening my mouth, I couldn't move. I wasn't entirely sure I could breathe. Letitia Palmer's eyes glittered in the headlights. Maybe I was human enough that her ward didn't protect her from me, but I was also human enough to be vulnerable to her magic. The Seal of Solomon charm that Casimir had given me felt hot against my breastbone. Apparently it wasn't doing shit.

I got angry. I mean, *really* angry. It was the kind of rich, molten fury I almost never let myself indulge in. I let it fill me until the pressure hurt my ears and the sap began to crackle in the nearest pine trees.

It felt like something physically breaking when her hold on me cracked, like the stone stuck in my throat had shattered.

I tried an experimental cough. Yep, that worked. I went back to Plan A and closed the distance between us, but this time, instead of grabbing for the jar, I reached across the headstone and grabbed the cowry shell strung around her neck, yanking the chain taut. I could feel a vibration of power against my palm, but the ward didn't repel me.

"Here's *or what*," I said to Letitia Palmer, our faces inches apart above the headstone that separated us. "You will swear on the bones of your ancestors to leave immediately and never return, or I'll jerk this thing clean off your neck and turn the tall ghoul with the large sword loose on you. And that goes for your daughter, too."

There was a sheen of sweat on her brow, but she didn't back down an inch. "You don't have it in you."

"Oh, it's not about what I have in me." I smiled grimly. "It's about what *you* have in you, Mrs. Palmer. Pride. Ambition. Hope. Patriotism. Dignity. Your daughter didn't seem familiar with the Outcast, so maybe you're not, either. That's what they do. They subsist on human emotion. And I *will* feed you to the ghouls. Everything that defines you? I'll let them take it all, every last ounce. I'll let them suck you dry until they're ravening, until there's nothing of you left but an empty husk. And when they're done with you, I'll let them drain your daughter. Stefan?"

He appeared at my side. "Hel's liaison." There was a

dark, dangerous note of hunger in his voice. "I await your bidding."

There was some scuffling behind her as the coven moved to surround dear Emmy, and I heard Sinclair speaking to his father in a low, urgent voice, but I kept my gaze locked on Letitia Palmer's. She hadn't been afraid before, but she was now. I could see it in her eyes, in the sweat beading on her forehead. "You did what you came to do, lady," I said to her. "You've fulfilled your threat. Take your victory and go, before the taste of it turns to bile in your mouth."

Fancy wording, right? That's what comes from hanging out with a six-hundred-year-old Eastern European nobleman. But I have to give the Right Honorable Judge Palmer credit—she was one tough lady. Curling her lips with distaste, she gave me the briefest of nods.

"Swear it," I said without relinquishing an ounce of pressure on her necklace.

"I swear it on the bones of my ancestors," she said in a bitter voice. By the sound of it, I was a little late with the whole taste-of-bile thing. "Emmeline and I will leave Pemkowet immediately, never to return."

"Good." I let go of the cowry shell. "Stefan and his men will give you an escort. As soon as you retrieve your luggage at the Idlewild, I want you out of town."

Letitia Palmer straightened the chain on her necklace and dusted off her lavender suit as though to brush away any lingering hell-spawn taint. She presented Sinclair with the empty glass jar.

"You know what to do, son," she said to him. "When you're ready, you and your grandfather come on home."

He took the jar in one hand, rubbing at his eyes with the heel of his other in a quick, fierce gesture. "Do you know the one thing that might have made a difference, Mom? You could have told me you loved me. You could have said you wanted me back because you loved me, not because you're running for Parliament."

"Of course I love you!" She looked surprised. "You're my son."

Sinclair laughed, but there was no humor in it. "You might want to lead with that next time. By the time you've passed the point of supernatural extortion, it's a little too late."

"Sinny—" Emmeline began.

He looked at her. "Don't. Just don't."

She fell silent.

There were a few more fraught exchanges and awkward logistics to be sorted out, but ten minutes later, Letitia and Emmeline Palmer were on their way out of town with a four-motorcycle escort of hungry, glittering-eyed ghouls. Sinclair and his father had departed, as had most of the coven, with promises to confer tomorrow. Casimir and nice Mrs. Meyers from the historical society were the only ones still lingering in the cemetery with me.

It was quiet. Too quiet. I mean, I know that's the nature of a cemetery, but after all that dramatic buildup, I felt like there should be a ghost wailing and shrieking among the headstones, or maybe taking on some of the bizarre and terrifying appearances that duppies were said to manifest.

I kicked at the dry grass scattered with brown pine needles and maple leaves. "Grandpa Morgan?" I called. "Are you there?"

Nothing.

"Daisy, I want to apologize to you," Casimir said to me. "We concentrated our efforts on protecting Sinclair. That was a mistake."

I shrugged. "We all agreed it was the right approach. The question is, what happens next?"

Mrs. Meyers was sitting primly on the stoop of Talman Brannigan's mausoleum. She'd taken her knitting out of her handbag and her needles were clicking away. "No one knows, dear. That's the problem."

"Maybe it just ... fizzled," I suggested. No one was buying it. Another thought struck me. "Or maybe ... maybe Hel claimed Grandpa Morgan's spirit herself! She is a goddess of the dead, after all."

It was a nice idea, and it cheered me up while it lasted, which was as long as it took for Mikill the frost giant to pull into the cemetery in his dune buggy and summon me to an audience with Hel.

Oh, crap.

# Thirty-five

Hel did not have the spirit of Grandpa Morgan in custody. Hel's sway over the dead was limited to those of the Old Norse faith, of which there were actually more than you might guess these days, but still few enough that it probably wasn't a good idea to comment on it to a goddess.

Especially a pissed-off goddess.

To make a long story short, I was an idiot for having agreed to a parley without dictating the terms of the meeting. I was an idiot for allowing it to be held in the cemetery. I was an idiot for not knowing in advance that a second, more powerful sorceress would be in attendance. I was an idiot for not ensuring that they were disarmed of any and all magical weaponry, including what appeared to be an empty pickle jar.

Hel didn't actually say "idiot." She said I was foolish and that I was remiss in my duty, her voice as cold and implacable as ice, her ember eye glaring at me.

The worst part of it was that I agreed with her. I'd known better. I just hadn't trusted my instincts.

So I didn't defend myself. I didn't blame anyone else. I

didn't point out that if Jojo hadn't intervened at exactly the wrong moment, everything might have been fine. I just stood there, miserable and shivering, until Hel was finished.

Then I said I was sorry.

Hel closed her ember eye and opened her compassionate one. To be perfectly honest, I'd preferred the baleful stare. You know that look parents get when you've disappointed them by screwing up really, really badly? The one that makes you feel sick and squirmy inside? Well, magnify that by the power of divinity. I'd almost rather Hel punish me with her heart-squeezing trick than look at me that way.

"Is there aught else you wish to say, Daisy Johanssen?" she inquired in her sepulchral voice.

I took a deep breath, and envisioned *dauda-dagr* cleaving a line between me and my guilt and discomfort. At this moment they were useless emotions, and I set them aside. "Yes, my lady." I was glad to hear the words come out firmly. "I beg your counsel. What's going to happen because of the mistakes I made? And how can I set it right?"

Her disappointed look didn't vanish, but it softened. "A powerful spirit has been unleashed and the dead of Pemkowet are restless. If the spirit is not contained, I fear some of them will rise."

I swallowed. "Are we talking zombies?"

Hel hesitated. "Necromancy is an uncertain magic, and not even I can say what will manifest. I do not believe the dead of Pemkowet will rise in corporeal form. As for this . . . duppy . . . it should not be possible, since his body lies many leagues across the sea."

"But you're not sure."

She inclined her head. "It would be for the best if the young sorcerer fulfilled the terms of the burden his mother has laid upon him."

There hadn't been a lot of time for Sinclair and me to discuss the issue, not with his father present, but there had been enough for me to sense his fury and frustration at the catch-22 situation in which his mother had placed him.

"I don't know if he *can*, my lady," I said. "It's an unwanted burden, and I don't know if he can accept it in good faith. But even if he can . . ." The icy mists of Little Niflheim were creeping into my bones. I balled my hands into fists and pushed them into the pockets of my motorcycle jacket, hunching my shoulders into its collar against the cold. "He's claimed your demesne as his home. And as your agent, I've declared him under my protection."

"I see." Hel's ember eye blazed open. Behind her, the attendant frost giants murmured and then fell silent.

Hel gazed at . . . I don't know what. Although I stood in her line of vision, I was pretty sure she was looking through me, her lucent, long-lashed blue eye and the smoldering red one in its charred socket gazing at whatever goddesses contemplate in the unfathomable distances of time.

I stood and shivered, alternating between blowing on my ice-cold fingers and shoving them back into my pockets.

Hel's gaze came back from the distance. "Then it is a matter of honor, Daisy Johanssen," she said somberly to me. "And we must fight."

"How?" I asked her.

She beckoned to Mikill. He strode forward, bowing and leaning toward the saw-blade throne to hear her bidding, then striding out of the old sawmill.

We waited.

It's hard to calculate the passage of time in the underworld, at least for this half-human mortal. Hel and her attendants simply went motionless, suspended in a kind of divinely patient stasis. I had the feeling that whether minutes or days or years passed, it was all the same to them.

Me, not so much. I shifted my weight from foot to foot, trying to stay warm without looking utterly uncomfortable.

When Mikill returned, he was followed by a retinue of *duegars*, the taciturn dwarves whose magic had carved out the realm of Little Niflheim beneath the shifting sands. All of them knelt before Hel's throne, and the foremost among them raised something bright and shiny in his gnarled hands. Returning once more from the distance, Hel accepted it with both hands, the fair and shapely right hand, the hand of life, and the blackened claw of her left, the hand of death.

She held it aloft. It was an old-fashioned lantern wrought of silver metal, the kind with shutters that block out the light, the kind you could imagine smugglers using to signal ships at sea. But either it wasn't lit or the infamous dwarfish workmanship was so exacting that not a single ray of light escaped it.

Hel opened the shutter with her right hand.

Light spilled forth: white light, gloriously radiant, tinged with the faintest ethereal hint of blue. It emanated from a crystal that hung suspended in the center of the lantern, and in the dark, misty confines of the abandoned sawmill, it threw everything into stark relief. I raised one hand without thinking to shield my eyes, my shadow stretching behind me.

Hel closed the shutter.

The light winked out as though it had never been, plunging us back into an underworld of murky darkness lit only by the lichen glowing faintly on the walls. Yep, definitely dwarfish craftsmanship.

"Come." Hel beckoned to me with the withered forefinger of her left hand, the crabbed claw of the hand of death.

I approached the throne. "It's very beautiful, my lady," I said respectfully. "May I ask what it is?"

She placed it into my hands. "It's a spirit lantern."

"Um . . ."

Hel sighed. Okay, she didn't really sigh. She regarded me with an expression like a sigh, or like the immensely patient and divine equivalent of an expression like a sigh, if you know what I mean. Maybe not. Maybe you had to be there. "To return the incorporeal dead to rest, you must fix their shadows with a hammer and an iron nail. To cast an incorporeal shadow, a spirit lantern is required."

The frost giant Mikill chuckled faintly into his icy beard. I resisted the urge to shoot him a dirty look. Maybe that was common knowledge in days of yore, but I was a child of the twenty-first century, and it's not like this job came with an instruction manual. Maybe that should be my next project after I finished entering the backlog of files into the database. A handbook for agents of the underworld.

Anyway.

"Ah . . . do I need a special hammer and nails?" I asked. "Can I buy them at the local hardware store? Because if the nails have to be pure iron, I'm pretty sure I'd have to order them from, like, Restoration Hardware or something."

Hel looked at the dwarves, who huddled to confer among themselves.

"An ordinary hammer and nails will be fine, liaison," one of them assured me. "The iron content suffices."

"Great." I tucked the spirit lantern under my left arm. "So all I need to do is find Grandpa Morgan's duppy and fix his shadow?"

"Perhaps." The slightest hint of a frown creased Hel's brow. Well, the fair-skinned and luminous right side, anyway. The blackened-skull side was pretty immobile. "This spirit that has never been laid to rest has no rest to which to return, save the vessel which contained it. Your young sorcerer must be prepared to recapture it." Her ember eye flared in its socket. "That responsibility lies on his head."

"Yes, my lady." I hesitated. "Um . . . just in case, what if there *are* zombies?"

"You bear a weapon capable of killing the immortal undead, Daisy Johanssen," Hel said to me in a dry tone. "If the dead rise from their graves, I suggest you use it."

"Oh. Right."

"Is there aught else?"

I shook my head. "No, my lady."

"Have you aught to report on the other matter?" she asked. "The person of interest?"

"The . . . oh. The hell-spawn lawyer. No, I haven't. There hasn't been any sign of him, and I've had no luck trying to contact him." It occurred to me that tracking down an elusive lawyer might be a good job for a computer genius like Lee. "Do you, um, want me to make it a priority?"

"No." It was a definitive "no," accompanied by a blazing left eye. "The Winter Nights will be upon us soon, Daisy Johanssen," Hel said grimly. "The unleashing of this spirit has opened a gate between the world of the living and the dead in my demesne. If the dead are not laid to rest by the time your All Hallows Eve has passed, I fear the gate may never be closed."

"I see." Okay, so this was a more serious business than I'd realized. I cleared my throat. "I'll make sure it's done."

Hel inclined her head. "That is well."

With that, I was dismissed. Mikill began escorting me back to the dune buggy. But as we reached the big doors of the sawmill, Hel addressed me once more.

"Daisy Johanssen."

I turned back. She had her blue eye open, and although her gaze was stern, it wasn't disappointed. "You did well to gain the sorceress's oath."

That was all she said, but it was enough. I took a sharp breath, my eyes stinging a little. "Thank you, my lady. I'm sorry about the rest."

Hel inclined her head. A mortal in this situation would have said, "Just see that it doesn't happen again," or something like that. Hel didn't need to. She was a goddess. And she didn't say I'd be stripped of my authority and dismissed as her liaison if I screwed this up a second time. Again, she didn't need to.

That, I'd figured out myself.

# Thirty-six

Although it felt like it should be the wee hours of the night when Mikill dropped me off at the cemetery to retrieve my car, it was only eleven o'clock. I drove in a slow circuit around the winding two-track, the spirit lantern nestled carefully in the front passenger seat. I was prepared to jump out of my skin if a zombie came shambling into the headlights, but everything was quiet.

I should have called the chief from the cemetery—well, I *should* have called him before I left it the first time, but a summons from Hel takes precedence—but being alone out there under a full moon, knowing there were ghosts and/or zombies in the offing, creeped me out.

So I drove home to my apartment. I could really have used some feline comfort while I made the call, but apparently Mogwai was out hunting.

Chief Bryant was none too pleased to hear from me—I had a feeling he'd already gone to bed or fallen asleep on the couch watching the evening news—and even less pleased when I reported that Letitia Palmer had succeeded in unleashing a duppy and that Hel had informed me that there was a good likelihood that Pemkowet was going to be haunted in the near future, if it didn't turn into something out of *The Walking Dead*.

"Goddammit, Daisy!" he said. "I thought you had this under control."

I winced. "I'm sorry, sir. So did I."

"You should have let the department pick them up." He sounded disgruntled. "They're under mundane authorities. We could have held them on something, at least long enough to confiscate any dangerous materials."

I wanted to say, "Like an empty pickle jar?" but I didn't. "We're talking about a judge and an Oxford-educated lawyer, sir," I said humbly. "Two women of color, a mother and daughter. I didn't think it would be good for Pemkowet's public image if they were picked up on trumped-up charges."

Well, that was half true. I hadn't known Letitia would show up, but it was why I'd decided not to involve the department in confronting Emmeline.

Chief Bryant offered a noncommittal grunt that suggested he agreed, but he wasn't prepared to give me credit at the moment. "All right. I'll get the word out. So this spirit lantern . . . you're ready to tackle the restless undead?"

"Absolutely," I said. "Well, as soon as I stop at the hardware store for a hammer and nails."

"Do it first thing in the morning," the chief said before hanging up.

Feeling hollow, I poured myself a few inches of scotch and put Big Mama Thornton on the stereo to tell me everything was gonna be all right. It didn't work. Big Mama may have felt it in her bones, but not even the blues made me feel any better tonight. Not even with Muddy Waters on guitar.

I'd screwed up.

God, and it had been *so close*. If Jojo hadn't chosen that exact moment to intervene, my plan would have worked. Mrs. Palmer hadn't expected anyone to just try to snatch her precious pickle jar. Hell, it *had* worked when I tried it the second time with the cowry shell charm. Take one foulmouthed, love-struck fairy out of the equation, and I'd be getting praise instead of a dressing-down.

Just . . . gah!

Flopping onto my futon, I allowed myself a good long seethe laced with equal parts self-pity and castigation, finishing with a firm resolution to trust my own instincts in the future. Then I set my alarm, so I could get to the hardware store as soon as it opened, and went to bed. I probably ought to own a hammer and nails anyway.

As it happened, I didn't need the alarm.

My phone rang at six thirty in the morning. It was still pitch-dark out and I had to fumble around on my nightstand to find the phone.

"Daisy." The chief's voice was grim. "Get out to the cemetery. Now."

Shit.

I sat bolt upright. "Is it ghosts? Or zombies?"

"Neither." He hung up.

I threw on yesterday's clothes, buckled *dauda-dagr* around my waist, grabbed the spirit lantern just in case, and hustled out to the cemetery in the predawn darkness through a light rain.

The chief hadn't told me where to meet him, but it was a small cemetery. Even if it hadn't been, I could have guessed. As soon as I turned onto the two-track, I saw a pair of cruisers parked under the pines in front of Talman Brannigan's mausoleum. The door to the mausoleum was ajar, and there were lights moving inside it. I got out of the car, my stomach sinking.

Chief Bryant and Ken Levitt, one of the younger officers with whom I was on good terms, emerged from the mausoleum, flashlights in hand.

"What is it?" I asked apprehensively.

"Grave's been robbed." The chief beckoned to me. "Come have a look."

I fingered *dauda-dagr*'s hilt. "You're sure it's not zombies?"

He pointed at a rusty padlock hanging from the door of the mausoleum. One side of the U-shaped shackle had been sheared clean through. "Not unless they were using bolt-cutters."

Inside, there were more signs of human vandalism. Some-one had used a crowbar or something like it to pry the lid off the huge sarcophagus, leaving clean scratches in the dis-colored old marble. The dusty floor of the mausoleum had been swept to obliterate footprints, and there were smears of something dark.

"Blood?" I asked.

The chief shook his head. "More like grease."

"Huh." I made myself peer into the sarcophagus. It held a wooden coffin, which had also been pried open. A scent of decay rose from it, but other than a bit of debris, which I chose to believe was decomposing clothing, it was empty. There was only the impression of a body having lain there, staining the rotting satin fabric that lined it. A *big* body. The Tall Man's nickname was no joke. He must have stood seven feet tall. "What the hell?"

"The chief asked me to make sure I took a turn around the cemetery before my shift ended," Ken Levitt said. "I spotted the open door and got out to take a look."

"You didn't see anything?" I asked him.

He shook his head. "Just this."

"Did you test the crime scene?" I asked Chief Bryant.

"Mm-hmm." He pulled out the silver pocket watch I'd given him a couple of years ago and let it dangle over the violated sarcophagus. It had been made with the same ex-acting dwarfish craftsmanship as the spirit lantern, only it was responsive to the residue of eldritch presence. If this grave robbery had been the work of a member of the el-dritch community, living nonhuman or undead human, the watch would have swung like a pendulum, its hands spin-ning frantically backward. Instead, it hung motionless on its chain, its second hand clicking clockwise with ordinary mortal precision. "Whoever did this was human."

I stared into the coffin. "Why the hell would anyone steal a hundred-and-thirty-year-old corpse?"

"It was probably kids." Ken shrugged. "Teenagers. Hell,

there are a couple of troublemakers in town crazy enough to do anything on a dare. You went to Pemkowet High, Daisy— you remember how it was. And Halloween's coming."

"True." I glanced at the chief. His eyes were gleaming under their deceptively sleepy lids. "But you don't think it's a coincidence, do you?"

"Do you?" he countered.

"No."

Chief Bryant gave a decisive nod. "Something's hinky. Levitt, if it's all right with you, I'd like to turn this one over to Fairfax. He and Daisy worked together well on the Vanderhei case."

Ken Levitt shrugged again. "It's your call, sir."

The chief looked at his pocket watch. "Fairfax is off duty, and he's not answering his phone. Daisy, you mind stopping out there? Make sure he's on board?"

I glanced involuntarily at the sky; I couldn't see through the cloud cover, but I knew the full moon had already set. Cody might be a little edgy for another twenty-four hours, but he should be okay to work, at least during daylight. Probably, anyway. "Sure."

"Good."

Before I drove out to Cody's place, I stopped at Drummond's Hardware and bought a sturdy hammer and a box of heavyweight framing nails from the yawning salesclerk who was just opening the store for business.

What can I say? I felt better for being prepared.

The sky was only just beginning to turn an ominous gray in the east as I drove north of Pemkowet along the river. The maple trees were yellow and gold, glowing unnaturally bright underneath the lowering clouds, and the narrow, serrated leaves of the staghorn sumac were turning a brilliant crimson, complementing the conical clusters of their unlikely fuzzy-looking scarlet fruits. I passed the entrance to Sedgewick Estate, making a mental note to call my mother later, and drove deeper into the countryside until I reached Cody's house.

It was quiet, but the front door was standing open. That

didn't seem right, not at seven-something on a rainy autumn morning.

"Cody?" I called softly. There was no answer. Trying the screen door, I found it unlatched and let myself into the house, closing the front door behind me.

Traces of pine needles and dirt led from the tidy little bachelor kitchen into the living room beyond. I followed them and found Cody Fairfax curled in a pile of blankets on the floor of his living room. The blankets were a hunter green plaid wool and Cody was stark naked beneath them, grime under his fingernails and pine twigs caught in his disheveled bronze-colored hair. Well, he wasn't exactly lying beneath the blankets. It was more like he'd nestled into them the way a dog would. Or, apparently, a wolf.

I drew a short, sharp breath. I'd never seen Cody like this—implicitly dangerous, yet at his most vulnerable. It stirred a complicated mix of emotions in me. I wanted to ease the twigs from his tangled hair. I wanted to stand guard over his sleep. I wanted to curl up behind him and bite his earlobe to wake him. He was lying on his side, and beneath his skin I could see the oblique muscles of his rib cage expand and contract with his slow, steady breathing. While I watched, a muscle in the hollow of his bare flank jumped and twitched in a restless dream.

A sound escaped me. It may have been, "Eep!"

The next part happened fast. Cody's eyes snapped open, phosphorescent green behind the amber. Baring his teeth, too many teeth, he lunged from his nest of woolen blankets and took me down, all naked skin, lean muscle, and werewolf speed.

I hit the floor hard, the impact driving the breath from my lungs. Thank God for shag carpeting. Cody pinned me, then snarled in pain and raised his torso as *dauda-dagr*'s hilt seared his bare skin. His face hovered above mine, his nostrils flaring as he inhaled my scent. I saw recognition dawn in his eyes.

"Daisy," he growled, his fingers digging into my biceps. "You shouldn't be here. Not now."

"Why not?" I whispered.

It's funny how desire can hit you out of nowhere like a ton of bricks at the most inappropriate times. Maybe it was the glimpse of Cody's true innermost self in an unguarded moment. Maybe it was born of my long-standing crush, maybe it came from the loneliness I'd felt after breaking up with Sinclair. Maybe it was a combination of guilt and anger and frustration, or maybe this had been coming ever since the night of the satyr-funk orgy.

All I knew was that I wanted this. Here and now. Cody's eyes were gleaming above mine, his naked skin was hot, hotter than a human's. And I knew, beyond a doubt, that he wanted this, too.

"It's not safe." His breath was warm against my skin.

To hell with the Seven Deadlies, to hell with duppies and zombies and grave robbers, to hell with *safe*. Cody wasn't human and neither was I. I wanted this moment. I wanted his wildness. I wanted his fierceness. Wrenching one arm free, I reached between us and plucked *dauda-dagr* from its sheath, tossing it several feet away on the carpet.

"I don't care," I informed him, twining my free hand in his twig-tangled hair and yanking.

He kissed me.

It wasn't sweet and it wasn't nice. It was hungry and primal, and there may still have been a few too many teeth involved. If I'd been thinking in words, words like *ravaging* and *plundering* would have come to mind, but I wasn't. Lowering his head, Cody nuzzled my neck, the bronze stubble of his chin rasping against my skin, nipping at it with strong white teeth. I bit his bare shoulder in response, laughing when he snarled at me.

He pushed my thighs apart, hands fumbling at my underpants, human hands turned rough and clumsy with need and the full moon's lingering imperative.

I helped. I held him off long enough to shrug out of my leather jacket and unbuckle my belt, to peel off my panties, strip off my dress, and unfasten my bra, until I was as naked as he was in his nest of blankets.

I felt molten inside, my heat rising in answer to his. I raised my hips as Cody settled between my thighs.

With a wordless, guttural sound, he pushed himself inside me.

It felt good.

Again and again and again, mindless and primordial. Somewhere in the back of my mind, my father, Belphegor, was laughing.

Somewhere, maybe, God in his heaven frowned in disapproval, and ranks upon ranks of angels, thrones and powers and dominions, nodded their heads in sorrowful agreement.

I don't know. The only entity beyond the Inviolate Wall ever to speak to me was my father.

Somewhere beneath us on her throne of antique saw blades, Hel gazed into the mists of time. A goddess diminished, but a goddess nonetheless.

Cody arched his back and howled.

Shuddering, I came.

# Thirty-seven

It should have been awkward, right? The aftermath, I mean. It wasn't.

I lay on my belly in a tangle of woolen blankets, my head pillowed on my arms as I told Cody what had happened and why I was there. Outside, the rain had turned into a downpour, complete with thunder and lightning. Inside felt safe and warm. He listened silently, stroking the length of my spine from the nape of my neck to the tip of my tail.

Yeah.

Okay, I know you've been wondering. For the record, my tail is approximately nine inches in length, tapering to a point from a diameter of about two inches wide, although it's broader and flatter at the very base, where the big muscles attach to the coccyx. There's a fine ridge of pale blond hair that flares out from the base and runs atop it, and it stands on edge and prickles when I'm alarmed, just like the hair on the back of your neck does.

I know, I've omitted that point until now. Sue me. Anyway, otherwise it's hairless. I'm not sure if it qualifies as prehensile. I mean, I don't *use* it like monkeys do to grasp objects . . . but I could. Like now, curling it around Cody's fingers.

And the best part was, he thought nothing of it. He just tweaked it in response, then scratched the base idly. Now I knew why dogs wiggle their butts when you scratch them in just the right spot. It feels ridiculously good. I guess a were-wolf ought to know.

"All right," Cody said when I'd finished my explanation. "Let's go take a look at the scene."

Sitting upright, I gestured at the two of us. "Are we going to talk about this?"

"Eventually," he said. "At the moment, I don't have the first idea what to say about it, and we've got a grave robbery to investigate. So I figured maybe we'd just get to work. You okay with that?"

I thought about it. "I wouldn't mind something to eat first. And maybe a shower."

"Well, I suppose another hour's not going to matter to the Tall Man." Cody got to his feet, shedding a few pine needles. "I'll get you a towel and go look in the fridge."

The only other time I'd eaten at Cody's, it had involved very, very rare steaks and nothing else. "How about I look in the fridge, and you shower first?"

His mouth quirked. "Fine."

Less than an hour later, we were on our way, clean and scrubbed, with full bellies. Venison sausage and scrambled eggs, for the record. Cody's refrigerator didn't contain anything remotely resembling a vegetable.

Now it started to feel awkward. Pemkowet didn't have the budget for take-home cars for its officers and since Cody wasn't scheduled to work that day, there wasn't a spare cruiser available. It was strange seeing him in uniform behind the wheel of his pickup truck, and it felt strange as hell sitting beside him, my nether regions still pleasantly swollen and tingling. I didn't know where to look or what to do with my hands. Plus, I'd discovered in the bathroom mirror that I had a couple of serious love bites on my neck. There wasn't anything I could do about it except turn up the collar on my jacket.

The storm had passed and the rain was easing by the time we reached the mausoleum. Ken Levitt had cordoned off the scene with police tape. Normally, there would have been gawkers alerted by the grapevine, but between the heavy downpour and the early hour, the looky-loos weren't out yet.

Cody's nostrils flared as he surveyed the scene, sniffing the air. "Not much left of a scent trail after the rain. Even if there was, there were too many other people's scents muddling the scene here."

"What about inside?" I suggested.

"Good idea."

Unfortunately, the door of the mausoleum had been left open, and wind-driven rain had sluiced into it, dispersing the trail there, too. The scent of decay emanating from the coffin made Cody gag. "Sorry." He pressed the back of his hand against his lips and gave me an apologetic look. "My sense of smell isn't as keen as a scent hound's, and the scent of the Tall Man's remains is masking anything else. I'm pretty sure the perp wore gloves."

I shuddered. "Wouldn't you?"

"Good point." He shone his flashlight at the floor. "I'm thinking maybe those grease stains are from a jack. It would have taken a lot of leverage to lift that marble slab."

"So we're looking for a physics student?" I said.

Cody shrugged. "Could be. Could be someone who works on cars."

After Cody had determined there was nothing more to be learned inside the mausoleum, we went back outside and did an informal grid search of the surrounding crime scene. If there had been an identifiable set of tire tracks, which wasn't likely given the amount of traffic there in the past twelve hours, the rain had obliterated them. The groundskeepers were pretty diligent, so despite the popularity of the Tall Man's resting place among high school students on the make, there wasn't a lot of trash. A few cigarette butts and a gum wrapper, all of which looked at least several weeks old, and a more recent coffee cozy from Mrs. Browne's Olde World Bakery.

I winced when Cody held it up on the end of a stick, remembering that I'd seen a member of the coven with a to-go cup of coffee last night. "Yeah . . . I think that might belong to Sheila Reston."

"From the tattoo parlor?" he asked.

Busted. I'd been careful not to name anyone until now. "Uh-huh."

Cody smiled wryly. "It's okay, Daise. You know I'm the last person in Pemkowet about to call anyone out against their will."

"I know."

We had a little moment then, gazing at each other through the lingering rainfall, which was more like a heavy mist at this point. It occurred to me for the first time that I didn't know how I felt about being with someone who felt the need to conceal his membership in the eldritch community. Not that we *were* together—I wasn't foolish or desperate enough to attach any significance to this morning's unexpected and impulsive hookup—but it was something I definitely hadn't thought through. I know Cody felt he had the Fairfax clan to protect, but I had an ideal to uphold, too.

After all, I was Hel's liaison. I was proud of it, and I damn well meant to do everything in my power to keep that title.

I cleared my throat. "Canvass the area for witnesses?"

He nodded. "Police work at its most exciting."

No kidding.

A couple of hours and some twenty houses later, we had confirmed that no one in the vicinity had seen anything. Well, that's not strictly true. There were a number of people who'd noticed a bunch of cars and motorcycles congregating in the cemetery around nightfall when our showdown with the Palmer ladies had occurred, but since the gathering dispersed without incident, no one had bothered to report it.

After that, nothing.

I let Cody handle the last few inquiries and took the time to check in with Sinclair.

"I heard," he said without preamble when he answered his phone. Of course he'd heard the news. The whole town had probably heard it by now. "So what's up? What's going on? Do you think it's related?"

"Other than the fact that someone stole the decayed corpse of Pemkowet's most infamous murderer, I don't know what's going on." I shifted on the passenger seat of Cody's truck. Yep, still tingling. "Do *you*?"

"It was definitely . . . stolen?" Sinclair asked.

"Looks that way," I said. "Although Hel summoned me last night to warn me that Pemkowet's dead are restless and may rise, hopefully but not definitely in incorporeal form, and that if we don't get your grandfather's duppy contained by Halloween, the gate between the living and the dead may never be closed. Any thoughts?"

He drew in a sharp breath. "Daisy, I am so, *so* sorry."

"Yeah, me, too," I said. "It's not your fault. We all made mistakes, and ultimately, it was my responsibility. So what about Grandpa Morgan?"

"Hell, I'll try." Sinclair gave a harsh, broken laugh. "Do you think I can fake sincerity well enough to fool a duppy?"

"I don't think you have to," I said. "You're under my protection and Hel is willing to fight this. She gave me a spirit lantern."

"A what?"

*Thank you!* So this wasn't common knowledge. "It makes ghosts cast a shadow," I said. "If you fix their shadows to the ground with an iron nail, it lays their spirits to rest. But since your grandfather's spirit never was at rest, you're still going to have to, um, recapture it and return it to the vessel in which it was contained. The pickle jar, I mean," I added in case it was unclear.

"That makes sense. How do you know it was a pickle jar?" Sinclair sounded bemused.

I rolled my eyes. "I don't! It looked like a pickle jar, okay? Anyway, tell me you can do this, Sinclair."

"I have to, don't I?"

"Yeah, you do," I said. "And the sooner the better. How do we find him?"

"You don't find a duppy," Sinclair said. "A duppy finds *you*. He'll find us when he's ready. But thanks to my mother, it could be anywhere. She set him loose on the whole town."

Crap. That wasn't exactly what I wanted to hear, but there wasn't a whole lot I could do about it. "You'll be ready when he does?" I asked him.

"Damn right I will." His voice was stronger and more certain this time. "And, Daisy . . . I appreciate it."

Glancing through the windshield, I saw Cody approaching, shrugging his shoulders to indicate he'd had no success. "Thanks. Sinclair . . . about this grave robbery. I mean, it's got to be related, right? But how?"

"I don't know," he said. "But we're not talking about some ordinary spirit. My grandfather was an obeah man. A powerful one. He could make people do things. Things they wouldn't normally do."

"Like steal a corpse?"

"Yeah. Maybe."

"Why?"

There was a rattling sound as he shook his beaded dreadlocks. "Death magic? I don't know. But maybe if you find the corpse, you'll find my grandfather's duppy."

"Okay. Stay tuned. Let the coven know what's going on. I'll talk to you later." I ended the call as Cody opened the driver's-side door of the pickup and slid behind the wheel, mist dampening his bronze hair.

We regarded each other.

"No luck?" I hazarded.

"No." Cody stuck the key in the ignition and turned it. "You?"

"Grandpa Morgan was an obeah man," I informed him. "It's possible his spirit could have convinced someone to steal the Tall Man's remains for unknown nefarious purposes, and it's possible that if we locate said remains, we may find Grandpa Morgan. Otherwise, no."

Cody raised his eyebrows. "Nefarious?"

"Uh-huh. What next?"

He put the truck in gear. "Well, I guess we'd better inform the Tall Man's nearest living kin."

# Thirty-eight

The flagstone walk leading to Clancy Brannigan's, aka Boo Radley's, rambling old Tudor house showed years of neglect. The moss-covered stones were cracked and crumbling, weeds growing between them. Warped shutters covered the windows of the gazebo where he got his groceries delivered and the breezeway that connected it to the house was boarded over with gray plywood. Behind a film of dirt on the garage window there was the vague silhouette of an antique truck that looked like it dated back to the 1960s and probably hadn't been driven since. On the old Tudor house itself, a tide of green mold was creeping up the white stucco walls.

All of which made it rather surprising that the place had a state-of-the-art two-way video monitor for a doorbell.

There was a long wait after Cody rang the buzzer, and I was starting to think maybe Boo Radley was an urban myth after all when a voice came over the intercom. "Yes?" It was a man's voice, wary, but not as old and feeble as I would have imagined. "What is it, Officer?"

"Clancy Brannigan?" Cody inquired.

"Yes."

"Can we come inside and have a word with you?"

A screen on the monitor blinked to life to reveal one owlish eye, magnified behind a thick lens. "Do you need to come inside?"

"Um . . . no, I suppose not. Would you prefer to step outside?"

"I'd prefer neither."

Cody glanced at me. I shrugged. I had no idea what the departmental protocol was for notifying crazy shut-ins that their ancestor's corpse had been stolen. "That's fine, sir. I'm afraid I have some bad news for you. It seems that Talman Brannigan's tomb has been vandalized."

"Again?" He had a point. If you were talking about a little graffiti, that was something that happened on a regular basis.

"This time it's serious, sir," Cody said politely. "I'm afraid the mausoleum was broken into and the remains are missing. I want you to know that we're making every effort to find the perpetrators and restore the remains."

The screen went dark, although we could hear faint scuffling sounds inside.

"Sir?" Cody called. "Mr. Brannigan?"

The screen lit up again, the magnified eye looming. I wondered why he bothered with a two-way monitor. Maybe just to demonstrate to the outside world that he was alive and capable in case someone called Social Services on him. Or maybe he just thought it was nifty. If the stories were true, he'd been some sort of inventor before he became acutely agoraphobic. While I was pondering, he spat out a name. "Cavannaughs!"

"Excuse me?" Cody said.

"Cavannaughs!" Clancy Brannigan repeated with disgust. "You want to find your grave robber, look for a Cavannaugh. You won't find the body, though. Bet they've chopped it to bits and thrown it in the river. They're afraid of the curse."

"What curse?"

"Ask the Cavannaughs. I don't believe in curses. I'm a

man of science." The screen went dark again. "Good day, Officer," his disembodied voice said over the intercom.

Ohhh-kay, then.

Cody made a few more attempts at communicating with him, then gave up. "I guess we've done our duty," he said dubiously.

"I guess." If you ask me, some of the freakiest people in town are the ordinary human beings. "So what now?"

"I guess we talk to one of the Cavannaughs," he said. Oh, great. The nearest descendants of the Cavannaugh family I knew of were Pemkowet Visitors Bureau ballbuster Amanda Brooks and her daughter, Stacey. And by the amused look on Cody's face, that's exactly who he had in mind. "You'll live. It's probably for the best that we give Amanda a heads-up anyway."

Once we were back in the truck, the awkwardness returned in the form of silence. Apparently, violently intense sexual encounters aren't entirely conducive to a professional working relationship. Who knew? The silence made me fidgety, and fidgeting rekindled that pleasant tingling. Talk about your vicious circle.

"So . . . Clancy Brannigan was supposed to be some kind of inventor, right?" It seemed like a safe topic. "What did he invent?"

Cody answered without taking his eyes off the road. "I think it was the Flowbee."

"*What?* The vacuum-cleaner haircut thing? Seriously?" I asked. Cody shot me a sidelong glance, the corner of his mouth twitching. I laughed and cuffed him on the shoulder. "Jerk!"

"I don't know for sure," he admitted. "I don't think he invented something that's a household name. More like he's the guy who figured out how to make a better widget."

I was suspicious. "Is there really such a thing as a widget?"

He smiled again. "No. It's just shorthand for a mechanical I-don't-know-what. Sounds better than thingamabob."

I contemplated his profile. "You know, we're pretty good together, you and I." I hadn't meant to say it; it was one of those things that just slips out. Like after a violently intense sexual encounter with someone you've had a crush on for ages.

Cody pulled into the PVB parking lot and cut the engine. "Daisy—"

"I know, I know! Sorry. Later, when we're not on the verge of a zombie apocalypse, okay?"

His expression was serious. "It's just . . . we've talked about this. And you know the bottom line."

I did. "I'm not a suitable mate. And you care about me too much to mislead me."

"Right."

I sighed. "All I'm saying is that we're good together. I don't even know if that's what I want, Cody. I'm just saying we are. Or at least we could be, if you weren't on the down-low, and I wasn't . . . not a werewolf."

Cody took a moment to parse the double negative in my last sentence, then broke into an unexpected grin, rakish and charming. "Well, I'll say one thing, Daise. For a demon's daughter, you sure as hell fuck like a werewolf."

"I can't believe you just said that." I paused. "That was a compliment, right?"

His grin widened, getting toothier, and green shimmered behind his topaz eyes. "What do you think?"

"I think it was a compliment." I opened the passenger door. "Come on, let's go talk to Amanda Brooks."

Inside, we had to wait a few minutes while Amanda finished up some important business on the phone. Thanks to Cody's presence, Stacey was on good behavior at first, but as soon as he wasn't looking, she pointed at me and then at her own neck, mouthing the word "Classy!" in an exaggerated fashion, upon which I realized that the collar of my jacket had fallen down to reveal those spectacular love bites.

Great.

I flipped my collar back up and returned her gaze with what I hoped was perfect equanimity. I figured if I was going to take "fuck like a werewolf" as a compliment, I might as well own it.

It wasn't long before Amanda ushered us into her office and got right down to business. She didn't even bother asking why we were there. "Officer Fairfax. Daisy. Do you have any leads?"

Cody took a seat opposite her desk. "What can you tell us about the Cavannaugh curse, Mrs. Brooks?"

She stared at him for a few seconds, her perfectly lip-sticked lips parted. "You can't be serious."

"Why not?" he asked reasonably.

Unaccountably, she shivered. "It used to give me nightmares as a little girl. But it's just a ghost story. You can't possibly think it had anything to do with Talman Brannigan's remains being stolen."

"Clancy Brannigan does," Cody said.

She blinked. "You actually spoke to him?"

"Yes."

"Then you know he's out of his mind," Amanda said dismissively. "You can't give any credence to a word he says."

"Actually, he seemed pretty lucid," I offered. "Agoraphobic, but lucid. So what's the curse?"

Her lips compressed. "My great-great-grandfather, Andrew Cavannaugh, was Talman Brannigan's partner in the lumber business. According to what I've always been told, he was the one who discovered the massacre in progress and shot Talman in the back. Before Talman died, he accused my great-great-grandfather of betraying him and vowed to take vengeance on his family even if he had to rise from the grave to do it."

Yeah, I could see where that would give you nightmares.

"Huh." Cody rubbed his chin. "I've heard about Andrew Cavannaugh shooting the Tall Man. But I never heard about the curse."

"No." Amanda removed her stylish glasses and polished them with a cloth she removed from a desk drawer. "That's been kept within the family."

He gave her an apologetic look. "Which, when you think about it, does give the Cavannaughs a plausible motive for wanting to ensure that the Tall Man's remains were destroyed."

She put her glasses back on and regarded him coolly.
"After a hundred and thirty years?"

Cody shrugged. "You did say the curse gave you nightmares. And 'betrayed' is an interesting choice of word for a
man in the middle of slaughtering his own family."

Amanda Brooks fiddled with a letter opener. "My great-
great-grandfather saw the writing on the wall, Officer.
When it was obvious to him that the lumber industry in
Singapore was doomed in the long run, he sold his interest
in the company to Talman Brannigan, who subsequently
lost everything, including his mind. So, yes, in that sense, he
betrayed him."

"Interesting."

She put down the letter opener. "I do believe that he felt
a measure of guilt. It was my great-great-grandfather who
arranged for Talman Brannigan's remains to be interred in
the Pemkowet cemetery."

"If that's true, he spent a lot of money on that mausoleum," I murmured. "How come the Tall Man's the only one
in it?"

"Talman's wife had family in Chicago," Amanda said.
"They didn't want her and the children buried with him."

"But there was a survivor, right?"

She nodded. "Clancy Brannigan's grandfather, I believe.
He was the youngest, only seven years old. If I remember
correctly, he was raised by his aunt, Talman's sister. You
can't blame them for not wanting to share his final resting
place, either."

"True," I said.

"Just to rule out the possibility, can you tell us where you
were between the hours of eleven o'clock last night and six
a.m. this morning?" Cody asked her.

"Home in bed," Amanda replied flatly.

"Alone?"

Her lips thinned again. At this rate, she was going to
smudge her lipstick. "Yes. But I assure you, I had nothing to
do with this. No one in the Cavannaugh family did. You're
welcome to talk to anyone you like."

"Oh, we will." Cody glanced at me. "On a related note,

there's another matter that you should be aware of, Mrs. Brooks."

Taking his cue, I politely notified her that a spirit had been unleashed, Pemkowet's dead were restless, and the entire town was very likely going to be haunted in the near future. She took the news better than I expected. In fact, we left her in the process of brainstorming ways to tie our forthcoming haunted status in with the annual Halloween promotion.

I'll admit, I was looking forward to Cody asking Stacey about her alibi—after all, she was a Cavannaugh descendant, too—just for the malicious pleasure of having to hear her admit that she, too, spent the night alone, because I knew for a fact that she wasn't dating anyone at the moment, but Cody headed for the door without questioning her.

"What's up?" I asked him in the truck.

"I had an idea." He turned on the ignition. "There are a lot of Cavannaughs to question, and they stick together. I wouldn't put it past Amanda to warn them to get their stories straight just in case. Back in the summer, your favorite ghoul said he could tell when people are lying as long as they're not sociopaths."

"You want to recruit Stefan?" The notion gave me an unsettled feeling in the pit of my belly. Or maybe it was just the venison sausage.

"He owes me." That was true. Stefan credited me with saving his life, but it was Cody who'd done the actual saving. I'd just created the opportunity. "What's the matter?" There was an edge to his tone. "I thought you'd gotten pretty cozy with him."

I wagged my finger at him. "Ah-ah! You're not allowed to get jealous over an unsuitable mate."

He shrugged. "I just think you're playing with fire when it comes to ghouls in general, and Ludovic in particular."

"As opposed to whatever we're doing here?" I said.

Cody smiled wryly. "You have a point."

# Thirty-nine

It was an uncomfortable meeting.

In a lot of ways, I was far more at ease in the Wheelhouse than I had been only a few short months ago. It was still a biker bar, still a hangout for ghouls and the skanks they fed on, but I'd learned to think of the ghouls as Outcast, the Outcast had learned to regard me with a measure of respect, and even the skanks were looking healthier. According to Cooper, Stefan's prohibition against chemically induced emotions had sent a few of them to rehab. Now their only addiction was the ghouls themselves.

Unfortunately, I still hadn't gotten used to the fact that Stefan had a direct pipeline to my emotions, distance no object. The second I saw his polite, guarded expression, I realized that he'd gotten a major hit of raw, unbridled lust this morning. And I promptly blushed like a teenaged girl, my blood scalding beneath my skin as I dropped the mental shield I'd automatically raised upon entering the place. My mortification sent a ripple through the Outcast. All around the bar, pupils dilated in a sudden rush.

So much for equanimity.

Stefan hustled us into his office in the back. "I take it you haven't contained the spirit that was unleashed."

"Why?" I asked him. "Because the Tall Man's corpse was stolen?" He gave a brief nod in response. "What do you know about obeah and death magic?"

"Nothing of use, I fear," Stefan said with regret. "Only that I have heard rumors throughout my life of sorcerers in the West Indies capable of raising the dead."

Great. That sounded a lot like zombies to me.

"We're trying to locate the remains," Cody said. "Sinclair Palmer says that if we do, we might find his grandfather's, um, duppy. We could use your help questioning suspects. As long as they're not sociopaths, you can tell if they're lying, right?"

"Of course," Stefan said. "Do you require my presence, Officer, or will one of my lieutenants suffice?"

"You trust your lieutenants?" Cody asked. It was a fair question—it was a betrayal by one of Stefan's lieutenants that had led to the turf war that had nearly gotten all of us killed or worse—but that edge was back in his voice.

Stefan didn't rise to the bait, but his pupils did a quick, irritated wax-and-wane. "I trust Cooper."

"I trust Cooper, too," I added quickly.

Stefan inclined his head. "I will place him at your disposal. Is there any other means by which I may assist?"

"Not at the moment, but stay tuned," I said. "You're sure the Palmer ladies are safely out of town?"

"Yes." He didn't elaborate and I didn't ask him to. I did tell him about my meeting with Hel and her warning. "Call upon me at need," he said when I finished. "If there is widespread panic, we can assist in alleviating it."

"Without ravening?" Cody asked bluntly.

Stefan turned his ice-blue gaze on him. "Did the Outcast not serve you well in the matter of the rutting satyr?"

My tail twitched at the memory of that night. "They were great," I assured him. "I can totally tell that they're more disciplined. So, um . . . can we borrow Cooper now?"

Stefan looked back at me, pupils dilating a bit and then steadying. Whether I liked it or not—and the jury was still out on that one—we had a bond, and the silence that stretched between us was filled with unsaid things. "Yes."

For the remainder of the day, Cody and I drove around Pemkowet with Cooper on his vintage motorcycle as our wingman, interviewing Cavannaughs and the descendants of Cavannaughs.

Although it would have delighted me to no end if Stacey Brooks had turned out to be a grave robber, alas, it wasn't so. Cooper confirmed that her mother wasn't, either. And in fact, neither were any of the other seven members of the community who were direct descendants of Andrew Cavannaugh.

"Sorry to waste your time," I said to Cooper, while Cody was on the phone reporting to the chief.

Cooper shrugged, hands deep in the pockets of his jeans. "It was a lead worth following. And I'll tell you what, none of them may have been lying when they said they didn't do it, but they were nervous."

I remembered how jittery Amanda had been in her office, fidgeting with stuff on her desk. "About what?"

"Can't say. I can't read thoughts, just emotions. But at a guess, I'd suspect none of them were sure that one of the others hadn't done it."

"But none of them did," I said.

"Right."

"Do you think they know more than they're saying?" I asked.

Pulling one hand from his pockets, Cooper cocked a thumb at himself. "Again, not a mind reader, me. But . . . no. More like fear and uncertainty."

"Huh." I wondered if we should cast a wider net, maybe interview husbands and wives instead of just blood relatives. I glanced over at Cody, who was listening and nodding into the phone. It was getting late and the fading sunlight glinted on his stubble; he needed to shave again. I shivered a little at the memory of his chin rasping against my shoulder.

Cooper followed my gaze. "There's no future for the likes of you with a wolf, missy."

I eyed him. "You could tell me what he's feeling, couldn't you?"

"I could, but I won't," he said with another eloquent shrug. "Myself, I'm Team Stefan all the way."

"Ha-ha," I said. "That might actually be funny if your boss had indicated he was interested in me that way."

Cooper's pupils contracted. "You think he hasn't?"

"I don't know. Has he?" Now I was uncertain. Sure, there was the hunger I sensed in Stefan, but that had more to do with *what* I was than who I was, didn't it? And yes, he'd made a comment or two that could have been construed as flirting, but I hadn't taken them seriously for reasons that seemed pretty damn obvious to me. "Cooper, we come from different worlds. Different centuries. He's a freakin' medieval knight, for God's sake!"

"Aye," he agreed. "And some days, he feels the weight of six hundred years' worth of immortality, six hundred years of being Outcast, six hundred years of hunger. He feels the cut of every betrayal, everyone who turned against him, called him a ghoul, called him a monster, called him unnatural. He feels the loss of every loved one who succumbed to age and death, while he went on and on; sometimes dying, only to be thrown back into the feckin' mortal coil in no more time than it takes your heart to beat once."

I had a feeling Cooper wasn't just talking about Stefan.

"But you know what?" he continued, gazing steadily at me. "Some days he feels just like the regular old boyo he used to be before heaven and hell slammed the door in his face. Some days, all he wants to do is have a laugh with his mates, drink poteen, and steal kisses from a pretty lass without creeping into her soul along the way. And those days? Those are the loneliest days of all."

I doubted that was the sort of regular old boyo Stefan Ludovic had been, but I got the point. "I'm sorry," I said softly.

Cooper looked away. "You're suited, is all I'm saying. You being a bit of a tempest and all. You'd have a good run. And he'd take care of you when it was over."

"Excuse me?"

"When it was over," Cooper said patiently. "You're . . . what? Mid-twenties? You'd have at least ten years." Looking back at me, he grinned. "Maybe longer these days, eh? You'll be what they're callin' a cougar in your forties."

My mouth had fallen open. I closed it. Well, duh. Of course it would end that way. How else could it end? Even Ashton Kutcher and Demi Moore couldn't make it work, and an immortality gap was a hell of a lot bigger than an age difference. And I didn't doubt that Stefan would take good care of me in my dotage. More and more, I was realizing he had a highly developed sense of honor.

"Thanks," I said to Cooper. "But I think I'd rather spend my life with someone I can grow old with."

"Or of course," he said in a casual tone, "you could always invoke your birthright and bargain for immortality."

"And risk unleashing Armageddon?" I stared at him. "Are you out of your fucking mind?"

"Don't think so, no." Cooper rocked back and forth on his heels. "But some days? Some days, I'd welcome Armageddon."

Cody finished his call and rejoined us. "Okay, Daise. I told the chief that the Cavannaugh curse was a dead end so far. Levitt's pulled files on a handful of kids with priors for vandalism in the cemetery, and that's what the chief wants us to follow up on tomorrow. Sound good to you?"

"Sure."

He glanced at Cooper. "You willing to lend a hand again?"

Cooper sketched a bow. "The big man's placed me at your disposal. Just tell me when and where."

"The big . . ." Cody frowned. "Oh."

"I'll call you," I said to Cooper. With a nod, he straddled his bike, brought it to life, and chugged away.

Cody watched him go. "He looks so young."

"I know. But he's over two hundred years old." It occurred to me that Cooper might be the perfect candidate to tell Heather Simkus, the underage vampire acolyte wannabe, a few things about the burden of immortality. That was either a great idea or a recipe for catastrophe. I'd have to think about it more. I didn't have a lot of faith in my judgment right now.

Cody had to drive me back to his place to pick up my car, which of course resulted in an awkward parting with the two of us standing in his driveway, both of us feeling that something needed to be said, neither of us knowing what it was.

"This has been a very, very disconcerting day," I said finally.

He looked relieved that I'd broken the silence. "No kidding."

"I should go." Something howled in the distance, long and mournful. Cody's head turned. "Kinfolk?"

"No. Bob Conklin's dog. He keeps her tied up around the full moon." He glanced up at the darkening sky, then at the shadows falling around the woods, then at me, and there was regret in his gaze. I didn't need to read minds to read his at that moment. If I were a suitable mate, we'd hunt beneath the just-past-full moon tonight, running with the pack and calling to one another, the autumn air ruffling our pelts. We'd hunt and kill and feast, and then we'd go home and fuck like werewolves, and one day we'd teach our own little wolf cubs to do the same thing. Well, just the hunting part with each other, obviously.

I sighed. "Just make sure you get some sleep. God only knows what tomorrow will bring."

"I will." Cody hesitated, then grabbed my shoulders and kissed me. It was quick, but firm and decisive.

"You confuse me," I informed him when he released me, feeling slightly breathless.

"Sorry." He took a deep breath, possibly feeling the same way. "I'll talk to you tomorrow."

I got in my car, settled the spirit lantern I'd been toting around all day in the passenger seat, and did what any sensible hell-spawn in my situation would do: I called my mom.

Less than ten minutes later, I was sitting at the old Formica dinette table she'd found at a thrift store when I was still a kid, shuffling the deck of *lotería* cards she used to tell fortunes, which was the ostensible reason for my visit. It

wasn't a total lie—Mom had done a reading on the Vanderhei kid's death last July, and it had been uncannily accurate.
And as close as we were, I wasn't ready to tell her that I'd
hooked up with Cody this morning. Not yet. I'd found the
bandanna that Stefan had lent me in the cemetery in my car
and tied it around my throat in what I hoped was a jaunty
manner to conceal the evidence.

I plucked out El Diablito, my significator, and laid it
faceup on the table, then shuffled the cards a few more
times, doing my best to hold the image of Talman Brannigan's mausoleum in my mind before cutting the deck
three times and handing it to Mom.

She turned over the first card. La Luna, the moon. Cody's
significator.

"Wait." I held out my hand. "Something doesn't feel
right. Let me try again."

Mom waited while I shuffled and reshuffled, cut and re-
cut the deck. Once again, she turned over the first card, indicating the crux of the matter.

La Luna.

I sighed. "This isn't going to work tonight."

Mom returned La Luna and El Diablito to the deck and
set it aside. "Did something happen with Cody, honey?"

"I don't want to talk about it." I laid my forehead against
the Formica table with a thunk. "Mom, I screwed up big-
time."

She paused. "With Cody?"

"No," I said without lifting my head. "Yesterday. Everything went wrong. And it's my fault."

"Oh, sweetheart!" The chair legs scraped as she got up
and came around the table to stroke my hair. "It didn't
sound like it from what I heard."

"Well, if Jojo hadn't—" I lifted my head. "Wait a minute.
What did you hear?"

"Sandra said that the coven made a mistake focusing on
protecting Sinclair Palmer," she said.

I stared at her. "You knew Mrs. Sweddon was in the coven?"

"It wasn't my place to tell you, sweetheart." Mom sounded apologetic. "But it's all right to talk about it now that you know."

"Well, there's not a lot to say." I shrugged. "Whatever mistakes were made, the responsibility is mine."

Mom went to the sink to fill the teakettle. "I understand the coven is thinking of trying a summoning spell to capture this ... duppy, is it?"

"Uh-huh. Sounds like you know more about it than I do," I said. "I hope they were planning to inform me."

"Of course." Mom set the kettle on the stove and turned on the burner. "We were just talking. Sandra's been after me to join the coven for years." She gave me a faint smile. "She thinks I have a gift."

"Why didn't you?" I asked her.

Her smile faded. "I've had enough of summoning for one lifetime, honey," she said quietly. "I'm happy with my cards."

I didn't say anything. I knew the details of my conception. The whole town knew. Mom had been vacationing in Pemkowet with college roommates when it happened. They'd awakened in the middle of the night and witnessed the, um, results of my mother's inadvertent summoning. Mom had never hidden anything about my heritage from me. From my earliest memory, everything was on the table for discussion, including the difficulty of raising a half-demon baby as a single mother and her decision to move permanently to Pemkowet, where at least there was a community that understood eldritch issues.

But the one thing she never talked about was the ... act ... itself. And God knows, I never asked. I mean, duh. It's not something parents discuss with their children under the best of circumstances.

Now I felt a sharp stab of anger at my absent father, sharp enough that cans of fruit on a shelf in the tiny kitchen jumped and rattled.

"Daisy!" Mom said in alarm.

"Sorry." I wrestled my anger under control. "Sorry, sorry.

It's just . . ." I asked the question I never thought I would. "Was it awful?"

My mom drew a quick, short breath as though I'd struck her, then met my gaze with her clear blue eyes. "No," she said simply. "Not at first, not while I still thought I was dreaming. Not until I awoke to my friends' screams and understood that what was happening to me was real. Then . . . yes."

Getting up from the table, I put my arms around her and leaned my brow against hers. She hugged me back hard. We stood that way until the teakettle shrilled, making both of us jump.

"Oh, for goodness' sake." Turning away, Mom shut off the burner and poured water for two mugs of tea, letting it steep until it was good and strong before adding sugar and lots of milk. "Sweetheart, you know I love you, and I'm proud of you no matter what." She handed me one of the mugs. "Don't be so hard on yourself. That coven's got years of experience on you, and they didn't know any better."

"I did." I blew on my tea. "I didn't trust myself."

"Next time will be different," she said in a firm tone. "You'll find a way to fix this, Daisy baby. I have faith in you."

Apparently, that was exactly what I needed to hear. I smiled at her. "Thanks."

"Anytime." My mom sipped her tea and cast a speculative glance at the bandanna knotted around my throat. "Do you want to talk about Cody Fairfax now?"

So much for jaunty. Jaunty was no match for mom-radar and the *lotería* cards. "No."

"Are you okay?"

"Yeah," I said, my eyes stinging a little. "I'm just not a suitable mate for a werewolf, that's all."

"Oh, honey." There was sympathy and concern in her voice. Mom knew all about my breaking up with Sinclair and my long-standing crush on Cody. But she also knew when to push me for my own good and when to leave me be. I imagine anyone who's ever parented a hell-spawn child learns that pretty quickly, what with the random damage we wreak on our surroundings when our emotions are out of control. "How about I make popcorn and we watch a few episodes of *Gilmore Girls*?"

I wiped away a surreptitious tear. "That sounds great."

# Forty

Every police force should have a ghoul on it. That was the conclusion I came to after a second day of having Cooper ride shotgun on this assignment.

I mean one of the Outcast, of course, but the thing is, *ghoul* is the word people know. And when it comes to sullen teenagers—I'm not saying all teenagers are sullen, but the five we tracked down and questioned that day were—it was particularly effective to have Cooper slouching beside us, angelic blue eyes glittering feverishly in his too-pale face as he let his beast slip the leash enough to filter their emotions for the particular taste of fear that telling a lie engendered.

That was the good news.

The bad news was that none of them knew anything about the theft and none of them were lying. If the Tall Man's remains had been stolen by one of Pemkowet's disaffected youth, it wasn't someone with a prior for cemetery vandalism. We were out of leads.

After we struck out with the last possible suspect, I called Sinclair to report our lack of progress and ask him about the summoning attempt my mom had mentioned.

"The coven's working on a ritual, Daise," he assured me. "We're just being really, really careful, because we got it wrong with our last plan."

"Well, tell them to step it up," I said. "Because we're not making any progress finding the Tall Man's remains, which means we're no closer to finding Grandpa Morgan's duppy. As long as he's on the loose, the gateway between the living and the dead is ajar, and that's not a good thing."

Sinclair's voice took on a worried tone. "Has something else happened?"

"Not yet," I said. "But time's a-wasting."

No kidding.

No sooner had I ended our conversation than Cody and I got a call from dispatch reporting a disturbance in progress at a wedding reception aboard the SS *Osikayas*. A distinctly supernatural disturbance.

"Ten-four," Cody said into his radio handset. "We're on our way." He leaned out the window of the cruiser—we were parked in the driveway of the Kendrick house, where the last sullen teenager we'd interviewed lived—and called out to Cooper. "Hey, tell your boss we've got our first haunting! There's a wedding party in full-blown panic down at the *Osikayas*."

Astride his bike, Cooper saluted, touching two fingers to his temple. "Meet you there, chief."

Cody turned to me. "Ready?"

I fumbled for the spirit lantern, which was wedged between my feet along with the hammer and nails I'd bought at Drummond's. "Do I have a choice?"

He grinned and hit the siren. "Nope."

Arriving at the scene, we found pandemonium. A handful of guests had fled the ship and were clustered on the dock, staring up at the tall steamship with disbelief and horror in their eyes. Everyone was still in their wedding finery, women shivering against the autumn chill in their gowns, some lucky enough to have a solicitous male companion to lend them a jacket, others with bare arms prickled with gooseflesh. A few guests were still clutching glasses of champagne. I didn't see anyone I knew, which wasn't a surprise. I figured the wedding party had to be summer people or out-of-towners, since the only person I knew with enough money to rent the *Osikayas* for a wedding reception was Lurine, and I didn't imagine she planned on remarrying anytime soon. Or under the same identity, for that matter.

Anyway.

Seeing a policeman in uniform, the guests surrounded Cody, gabbling things like "Horrible!" "Hideous!" "Macabre!" and "Dead bride!" Ignored, I stood juggling the spirit lantern, hammer, and nails while he did his best to calm them down and figure out what was happening.

Someone sidled up next to me. "So is there a ghost or not?"

I turned to see Stacey Brooks looking scared but determined, a compact, expensive video camera in hand. "What the hell are you doing here?"

"Documenting," she said in a defensive tone. "I mean . . . maybe. As long as it's not the Tall Man. It isn't, is it?"

"It's not the Tall Man." Cody ordered the wedding guests to proceed down the dock, where Cooper was waiting. I hoped their collective panic wouldn't send him ravening. "It's a woman, and yes, it appears she's a ghost. And you shouldn't be here, Miss Brooks. How did you find out about this anyway?"

"The PVB has every right to know what's going on in town," Stacey retorted. "Which is why my mother monitors the police scanner."

Of course she did.

"Just keep your distance and don't get in our way." There was a hint of growl in Cody's voice. "Daise?"

"Hammer or lantern?" I asked him in response, gesturing with my full arms. "I can't do both."

He extended one hand. "Hammer. The last time I touched something Hel gave you, I got frostbite."

Stacey raised the video camera. "What exactly are you doing?"

"Ghostbusting," I said shortly. "And will you *please* get the fuck out of our way, Stacey!"

She did, but she trailed after us. Our footsteps boomed

on the metal ramp that provided access to the *Osikayas* from the dock. Inside the ship, we could hear shrieks and more gabbling voices coming from the ballroom on the upper deck.

In case I haven't made it clear, the SS *Osikayas* is a seriously big ship. Think *Titanic* on a slightly smaller scale and without the tragic ending. Back in her heyday, she was a passenger steamship on the Great Lakes. She had more than a hundred staterooms, some of them with private baths, which was pretty impressive for the time. Some of the original furnishings are long gone, but structural elements like the gleaming mahogany grand staircase with its gilded balustrade remain.

I followed Cody up the staircase and along the state deck toward the ballroom—or at least I did until Cody froze.

"What?" Stacey said behind me. "What is it?"

I ignored her.

The ghost was blocking the entrance to the dining hall and ballroom, trapping the remainder of the wedding party inside—and make no mistake, it *was* a ghost. A ghost bride, straight out of a Tim Burton movie. She wasn't entirely transparent, but she wasn't opaque, either. Her misty figure hovered a few inches above the floor, her head canted to one side at an unnatural angle, her feet dangling in ivory-colored satin pumps.

Cody and I exchanged a glance. "Right," I said, and took the lead, hoisting the spirit lantern.

The ghost in the doorway turned, creating an eddy of cold air that smelled like rotting lilies.

I sucked in my breath and promptly gagged on the scent. There was a long tulle bridal veil knotted around the apparition's neck. Her face was dark and mottled. Her eyes bulged in their sockets, the whites laced with a patchwork of broken blood vessels, and her tongue protruded from her lips, swollen and blue.

"'Ere'th my huthband?" the ghost bride asked me, forcing out the words with difficulty. She held out her arms in a pleading gesture. "'Ave oo theen my huthband?"

Ew. And yet I couldn't help but feel sorry for her. Something very, very bad must have happened on her wedding night.

"No," I said softly. "I'm sorry, I haven't seen him. But you don't belong here, ma'am. This isn't your place anymore. And I'm here to help you find your way back to where you can rest in peace."

I opened the shutter on the spirit lantern, and radiant white light tinged with an ethereal hint of blue spilled forth. The ghost flew backward, arms windmilling, her unlikely shadow manifesting behind her on the worn green carpeting. In the ballroom beyond her with its hand-carved mahogany wall panels and etched-glass skylights, wedding guests cried out in alarm at the sudden change of events.

Cody darted past me, hammer in one hand and a nail in the other. "Hold it steady, Daise!"

I did.

Unfortunately, we hadn't counted on the fact that beneath the carpeting, the floors of the *Osikayas* were steel. Cody's hammer rang out with a resounding metallic clang, but his nail simply fell over.

He grimaced at me. "Sorry."

The ghost drifted, toes trailing over the carpeting. "'Ere'th my huthband?" she asked a pair of bridesmaids in lavender satin huddled in a corner, clutching each other. "'Ave oo theen my huthband?"

Eyes screwed shut tight, they shook their heads.

"Oh, my God!" Stacey Brooks was in the middle of the ballroom, camera raised. "This is fantastic!"

I flashed her with the spirit lantern.

"Ow!" She glared at me.

"Daisy!" Cody pointed toward the far end of the ballroom, where there was an inlaid parquet dance floor. "We've got to get her over there."

"Right." Now that the ghost was no longer blocking the exit, wedding guests were making a break for it, including the tear-streaked living bride and her new husband. As the groom shouldered past me, I grabbed his arm, thinking one guy in a tuxedo looked a lot like any other. "You. I need you to go stand over there in the far corner."

He gaped. "Are you out of your mind?"

My temper flared, and I channeled my anger into my voice, letting it crack like a whip. "Goddammit, just do it! Do it for your bride!"

It worked. The groom stumbled across the room to stand trembling in the corner of the dance floor.

I shuttered the spirit lantern and approached the ghost. "Hey," I said to her, pointing. "Isn't that your husband over there?"

Her bulging eyes blinked, or at least they almost blinked. Her eyelids couldn't quite close. "'Oo!" she moaned, drifting toward the dance floor, toes dangling, head canted. "'Ow could oo do thith do me?"

In the corner, the groom shuddered and covered his face with his hands, peering between his fingers in terror. I waited until the apparition had reached the edge of the parquet before opening the shutter on the spirit lantern again, letting the brilliant light cast the ghost's shadow on the squares of polished wood.

From the right side of the dance floor, Cody flung himself onto the parquet, pulling off a knee slide worthy of Kevin Bacon in *Footloose*. He planted a nail smack-dab in the center of the ghost bride's shadow, raised the hammer, and pounded the nail into place in one solid, satisfying blow.

The ghost vanished.

My knees gave way beneath me and I sat down abruptly on the floor.

"Daisy," Stefan's voice said behind me. He came around to crouch in front of me, pupils like pinpoints in the lantern's crystalline blaze. "Are you all right?"

"Yeah." I closed the shutter on the spirit lantern. "Delayed reaction. Give me a hand up?"

"Of course." He took my free hand and rose, pulling me effortlessly to my feet. We stood there for a moment, hands joined. I could feel my residual fear and anger draining away into his deep, still center.

I cleared my throat and pulled my hand away. "I'm fine. You should see to the wedding guests."

Stefan inclined his head. "As you say, Hel's liaison."

I couldn't help glancing toward Cody. A flare of green shimmered behind his eyes, but his expression was studiously neutral.

With the aid of Stefan and his Outcast crew, we got matters under control in short order, alleviating the worst of the terror among the wedding party and the catering staff. Actually, that's not fair to the catering staff, who were all Pemkowet locals. Although they were shaken, none of them had panicked.

In fact, it was one of the caterers who identified the ghost for us. "Marjorie Tucker," she said in a steady voice. She was one of those salt-of-the-earth types with a thick braid of hair that hadn't been cut for decades, and only her trembling hands betrayed her nerves. "Her family had a summer cottage down the street from me. I was a kid when it happened, but I remember it was 1976, the year of the bicentennial."

"What happened?" I asked, partly out of morbid curiosity, partly because I planned to enter it in the ledger.

"She caught the groom boinking a bridesmaid in one of the staterooms at her wedding reception," she said soberly. "Went home and hanged herself with her bridal veil. Funny, we always thought it was the Tucker cottage that was haunted afterward."

"Poor thing." I felt a surge of indignation on behalf of Marjorie Tucker's ghost. "Her fiancé must have been a real piece of work."

The caterer shrugged. "Men."

Somewhat to my surprise, the wedding party elected to carry on with the reception. Stefan and his crew had siphoned off their shock and fear, leaving them in a state of hectic bravado.

"Thank you," I said to Stefan. "I appreciate it."

He gave me one of his courtly bows, his pupils dilated

and glittering. The pull I felt from him now wasn't his inner core of stillness, but the vast hunger that lay beneath it. "You are welcome."

Without thinking, I raised my mental shield between us. "Um . . . it's probably best you were going now, right?"

"Yes." Stefan paused, and I had the impression he was struggling unsuccessfully to regain his usual self-control. "If there is another such incident within the next few hours, it would not be wise to call upon us."

"Duly noted," I said. "Sorry—I wasn't expecting an entire wedding party on the first outing."

Although his pupils were still huge, Stefan smiled, his unexpected dimples appearing. "You did well."

"Thanks."

All in all, I felt pretty good about the incident. I hadn't screwed up. I hadn't lost my cool. When an unexpected problem arose, I'd found a solution. Hell, I could already hear the bridegroom in the background, bragging about his role in the whole affair. Even the presence of Stacey Brooks—

I looked around. "Hey, Cody! Where did Stacey go?"

"Huh?" Cody glanced up from a table containing an abandoned serving tray filled with skewers of chicken satay, his mouth full. He chewed, then swallowed. "Sorry, couldn't resist. She took off a while ago. Why?"

"Just wondering." Wondering what she meant to do with that footage she shot was more like it.

"She's fine." Cody wiped his hands on a napkin, tossing it on the table. "When you get right down to it, she's pretty ballsy."

I scowled at him.

He grinned. "Lighten up, Pixy Stix. We did a good job here, didn't we?"

"Yeah, but you know this is probably just the beginning, right?" I said. "And I'm really not loving the nickname. Especially now."

Cody's grin widened. "Consider it an endearment."

And consider me still confused, I thought. The thick-braided caterer bustled past us to reclaim the tray of chicken satay, shooting me a sympathetic look in passing. I wasn't always down with the whole solidarity-in-sisterhood thing, because it can get bitter and acrimonious—and yes, *acrimonious* is one of the vocabulary words Mr. Leary drilled into me in high school—but sometimes, it's exactly what you need.

*Men.* Gah!

# Forty-one

Stacey Brooks uploaded footage of the haunted wedding reception to YouTube at five forty-three p.m. on Saturday afternoon.

By Sunday, it had gone viral. It turns out that Stacey had a knack for this whole social networking thing. I found out about it because Lee Hastings turned up on my doorstep to tell me.

"There's something you should see," he said without preamble, whipping out his computer tablet to show me.

"Holy crap." I watched the footage with dismay. "Can she do that? Post it without our permission?"

"Pretty much, yeah," Lee said. "You can file a complaint for violation of privacy, but it takes a few days to resolve it. Which they might not even do, since you're not actually identified by name or anything."

On the screen, a series of wedding guests babbled about the experience in a state of giddy excitement. I got a sinking feeling watching it. "This is a bad idea," I said. "A very bad idea."

Lee halted the playback. "Yeah, I thought you might think so."

"Can you make it go away?" I asked him.

He shook his head ruefully. "If you're asking if I can hack the PVB's YouTube account, probably. But this thing's already been mirrored a dozen times. It's out there, Daisy. Even if it wasn't, Stacey still has the original footage. All she has to do is upload it again, and if other hackers think someone's trying to scrub it, they'll do their best to spread it further. Your best bet's to ask her to take it down and hope people decide it was just another hoax."

"I'm calling her mother," I said, fishing out my phone.

Not only was Amanda Brooks unsympathetic to my concerns, but she had no intention of telling Stacey to remove the footage. "Do you have any idea what kind of publicity this could generate?" she asked me grimly. "Or any idea how long I've been trying to find the perfect off-season marketing angle for this town? Daisy, you do your job and let me do mine. I'll go over your head if you don't drop the matter. As long as this lasts, we're going to exploit it for all it's worth."

"I just think you're asking for troub—"

She cut me off before ending the call abruptly. "Something's come up. Just do your job and stay out of our way."

I let out a low hiss of frustration. "Goddammit!"

"No luck?" Lee said.

"No."

Lee fidgeted with his tablet. "I guess you can't blame her for wanting to find the silver lining," he offered. "And you can't blame people for wanting a glimpse of real magic."

"I just hope the coven gets their shit together soon," I muttered. "Because—"

My phone rang.

It was Cody. "We've got another one," he said tersely. "Grab your gear and meet me at Riverside Grove."

I gave Lee's good arm a squeeze. "Thanks for the heads-up. I've got to run."

Riverside Grove's School of the Arts was a charming

establishment out in the woods overlooking a lagoon. Back in the lumber days, the site boasted a hotel situated on a bend of the Kalamazoo River that catered to passengers traveling on Lake Michigan, but it was left stranded when the course of the river was altered around the turn of the century, cutting off the hotel from its patrons. Thanks to a handful of visionary artists and architects, the hotel and its surroundings got a second life as a haven for the arts, and it remained a thriving program to this day.

Which is also one of the reasons that until the dollar store opened, you could buy a painting for ten grand in Pemkowet, but not a pair of socks.

Anyway, the majority of Riverside Grove's programming takes place in the summer and it should have been fairly empty at this time of year, but as luck would have it, the Pemkowet Historical Society was hosting an open house on this particular Sunday and had arranged hourly tours of the rustic campus with commentary by local historians.

It was a nice idea, and I understand it was a rousing success before the caretaker's ghost showed up.

"Hello, dear." Mrs. Meyers greeted me placidly when I emerged from my Honda onto the grassy parking area, where would-be tour-goers and other members of the historical society were hiding behind their cars. She nodded toward the insubstantial figure of a stocky man who was patrolling the verge and scowling, a double-barreled shotgun over his shoulder. Unlike the ghost bride's, his feet appeared to make contact with the earth, presumably because he hadn't died dangling above it. "I was just telling Officer Fairfax, I'm afraid Leonard's risen."

I raised my eyebrows. "Leonard?"

"Leonard Quincy," Cody informed me. "Off-season caretaker of the facility until he was found dead of a gunshot wound to the head in the winter of 1968."

"Suicide?" I asked.

Cody shook his head. "According to Mrs. Meyers, it was an unsolved homicide."

"It was probably an accident. Hunters, you know. Poaching. I always suspected one of the Thornberrys, myself." Mrs. Meyers lowered her voice. "I tried a banishing spell, but Leonard only flickered."

A shiny black SUV came barreling out of the woods and pulled into the parking area, disgorging Stacey Brooks, camera in hand. "Did I miss it?" she asked eagerly. "Tell me I didn't miss it!"

I rolled my eyes. That was probably the something that had come up while I was on the phone with her mother—an alert on the police scanner.

"You didn't miss it," Cody assured her. "And it's not the Tall Man. Ready, Daise?"

"Yeah." I hoisted the spirit lantern and shot a scathing look at Stacey. "Just make sure you stay out of *our* way."

From the front, Leonard Quincy's ghost didn't look that bad. His scowl deepened as Cody and I approached. "Hey! This is private property. Didn't you see the signs?" He raised his shotgun, resting the butt of the stock against his shoulder and sighting down its length. "Trespassers *will* be shot."

Okay, I know he was a ghost, but staring into the twin barrels of that shotgun was really freakin' scary.

"Mr. Quincy?" I called. "It's all right. We're here to return you to rest."

Leonard's head turned as Cody veered to the left, angling to get behind him. Now I could see that the back of his skull contained a ragged hole of blood and splintered bone where he'd been shot from behind by a hunting rifle. Yep, definitely not suicide. "Hey! What are you doing, boy?" Pointing his shotgun skyward, he pulled the trigger and fired a shot.

I flinched. It might not have been real, but it sure as hell sounded real. I could feel my eardrums reverberating.

"Daisy!" Cody shouted, an edge of panic in his voice. It must have sounded real to him, too. "Now!"

As Leonard Quincy's ghost lowered his shotgun to take aim at Cody, I unshuttered the spirit lantern, throwing his shadow long and stark across the grounds of the Riverside Grove School of the Arts. A second blast sounded as Cody dropped to one knee and hammered a nail into the sandy soil.

Like the ghost bride's yesterday, the caretaker's apparition vanished.

Some yards away, Stacey Brooks lowered her camera. "Well, that was almost too easy, wasn't it?" She sounded disappointed.

"Speak for yourself." I closed the shutter on the spirit lantern and went over to Cody, who was still kneeling, his head hanging low. "Are you okay?"

"Yeah." He got to his feet with an effort, pressing one hand to his chest. "Jesus! I swear I could feel the buckshot hit me."

Moving his hand away, I examined the front of his dark blue uniform shirt. "It's okay. There's nothing there."

He shuddered. "That could give a person a heart attack."

I glanced toward the parking area. "Let's hope it didn't."

The fact that it hadn't could probably be attributed to Mrs. Meyers's calm presence as much as anything else, but if this kept up, sooner or later our luck was going to run out. While Cody talked to the reassembled members of the historical society and Stacey dashed off to upload her latest, I steered Mrs. Meyers to one side.

"What's going on with the coven?" I asked her. "Aren't you supposed to be working on a summoning ritual?"

She patted my hand. "Oh, I promise, the others are hard at work on it, dear. I'm afraid I've been busy with the open house."

I stared at her. "No offense, ma'am, but don't you think maybe the open house would have been better served by de-haunting the town?"

"Well, I see your point, but you and young Officer Fairfax did a fine job. Poor Leonard," she added. "He always was a terrible grump."

I wasn't sure if nice Mrs. Meyers was a little batty or just particularly sanguine about the dead. Either way, I guess it didn't really matter.

As it happened, although I wish I could say otherwise, the whole summoning thing didn't really matter either.

It wasn't the coven's fault, or at least I'm pretty sure it wasn't. Jolted into a sense of urgency by my pestering and two back-to-back manifestations, they made the attempt at midnight on the following day in the Fabulous Casimir's backyard.

To be honest, I was starting to have my doubts about the coven's effectiveness, but even I could feel that this spell *should* have worked. Since it didn't, I won't belabor the details, but I was watching from the sidelines as they encircled Sinclair, who stood in the center with the empty pickle jar, a look of determination on his face.

According to Casimir, if the coven could bind Grandpa Morgan's spirit in the circle, it wouldn't matter that Sinclair wasn't willing to fulfill the terms of the burden his mother had laid on him. Once the duppy was bound, their collective will would overpower it, and Sinclair could recapture it on his own terms.

It sounded good, anyway. And when the coven finished their incantation with a resounding, "So mote it be!" a flicker of white light raced along their joined hands before rising into the night sky with a sense of purpose that's hard to describe.

Well, actually, it's not all that hard—it felt like the supernatural equivalent of casting a net or a fishing line. For a few tenuous moments, my hopes soared. And then it felt like the supernatural equivalent of that net or fishing line coming back empty, or at least what I would imagine it would feel like, since the closest I've ever gotten to fishing was accidentally getting sucked into an episode of *Deadliest Catch* on the Discovery Channel.

A bitter sense of loss suffused me. Until the coven's effort failed, I hadn't realized exactly how much hope I'd pinned on their success. I let the disappointed members confer among themselves for a few minutes before asking what their failure meant.

"It means his spirit is already bound," Casimir said soberly.

"To what?" I asked. "Or who? By who? Or . . . whom?"

Despite Mr. Leary's best efforts, I still had a hard time with that one.

Casimir shook his head. "I don't know. I would have said there wasn't anyone outside this circle capable of it."

"What about Liz Cropper?" Mark Reston from the tattoo parlor suggested, which triggered a five-minute discussion about the coven's history of infighting and bitter quarrels with former members.

I pulled out my notepad and jotted down "Liz Cropper" and a couple of other names they mentioned, watching Sinclair out of the corner of my eye. He was quiet, not taking part in the conversation.

"You don't think it's a disgruntled ex-coven member, do you?" I asked him.

Sinclair shrugged. "I can't say for sure, Daisy. Whatever they're talking about was before my time. But . . . if my grandfather's duppy is bound to someone, I'm guessing it was him that did the binding."

"To . . . whom?" I asked. "Like, whoever . . . whomever . . . stole the Tall Man's remains?"

"Whoever," he said. "Yeah, maybe. Do you have any new leads?"

"No," I murmured. "I was really, really hoping this summoning ritual would work. Any further thoughts on what kind of death magic we might be talking about?"

"No." Sinclair was silent a moment. "I've tried, you know. Tried to will myself to consent to do what my mother wants."

"You don't—"

He shot me a look. "Yeah, I do. I brought this on Pemkowet. If it's within my power to stop it, I have to try. But it's not working. Either I just can't, or my mother was wrong and my grandfather's spirit isn't bound to the terms of their agreement."

"Or both," I said.

"Or both." He summoned a wry smile. "Hey, at least those videos are going to be good for the paranormal tour business. And you look pretty badass in them."

"Yeah, that's an unexpected bonus." I tucked my note-pad back into my messenger bag. "Do you think it's worth it?"

"No." Sinclair's smile vanished, his expression turning grave. "I think that if we don't catch my grandfather's duppy before Halloween, something very, very bad is going to happen."

I sighed. "Me, too."

# Forty-two

Over the course of the next couple of weeks, after Stacey Brooks's ghostbusting footage went viral, Pemkowet experienced an unprecedented boom in tourism for the month of October. A skeptical reporter from the *Chicago Tribune* got wind of the story and came out to investigate. Under pressure from Amanda Brooks and the PBV board, who were over the moon about the publicity, Chief Bryant strong-armed Cody and me into letting him ride along on a call to a site where we laid to rest the particularly gruesome ghost of an old lumberman who was crushed to death by a skid of falling logs in 1857.

After that, the reporter was convinced; and after *his* story was published, tourism doubled again and other news crews followed, hoping to get a scoop as good. I drew the line at cooperating with any more of them, though. So far we'd been lucky, but the bad feeling I had about this whole thing persisted. Maybe Letitia Palmer's unleashing her dead obeah man father's spirit had proved a boon instead of a bane for Pemkowet, but I didn't think that was going to be the case in the long run.

Grandpa Morgan's duppy was still out there somewhere, and the longer he went without showing himself, the more my nerves were on edge.

And Pemkowet's dead continued to manifest in a variety of grisly manners.

Cody and I did our best. I hadn't given up hope of finding the grave robber and the Tall Man's corpse. We tracked down a few disgruntled ex-coven members, all of whom Cooper confirmed were false leads.

We even paid a second visit to Clancy Brannigan, or at least to his doorstep. One of his neighbors, poor crazy Marcia Hardwick, provided a handy excuse by phoning in a complaint about seeing strange lights through gaps in the plywood covering the clerestory basement windows in the rear of his house.

Okay, she thought he was building a spacecraft in his basement, but it was still a good excuse.

There was a long wait after Cody pressed the buzzer, but eventually the video screen lit up to reveal the distorted, close-up image of Clancy Brannigan's face, a slick of sweat on his skin, the visor of a welding mask propped above his brow.

"What is it now, Officer?" he asked testily. "Has one of the Cavannaughs confessed?"

"Ah . . . no," Cody admitted. "We had a report of strange lights, sir. Is everything all right?"

Clancy Brannigan snorted. "Right as rain, boy. I'm working on an important project. Come back when you get the truth out of the Cavannaughs. Until then, don't bother me." His hand rose, blurring the screen.

"Wait!" I said quickly. "Mr. Brannigan, can you think of anyone other than the Cavannaughs who'd want to steal your great-grandfather's remains? *Anyone?*"

He hesitated, then nodded slowly. "Yes. Yes, I can." A crafty look crossed his face. "Anyone who married into that cursed family."

I sighed. "Okay. Thanks for your time, sir. Sorry to disturb you."

"You ought to be." The screen went dark.

"Damn," Cody said as we headed back toward the cruiser. "That old coot's really got a hard-on for the Cavannaughs."

"No kidding. I'm starting to rethink that whole lucidity thing. Although he's right—we probably should interview spouses and significant others. I was going to suggest it earlier." I glanced over my shoulder. "So he must have some kind of lab down in his basement, huh? What do you suppose he's working on? A new and improved widget?"

"A spaceship," Cody said drily. "To take him to a planet without any Cavannaughs."

I laughed.

Unfortunately, that was pretty much the only thing I had to laugh about. Clancy Brannigan's obsession notwithstanding, interviewing associates of the Cavannaugh family was a dead end.

And as for the dead, they just kept rising.

And Cody and I continued to work as a team, spending a succession of glorious autumn days laying the dead to rest with the spirit lantern and a hammer and nails, while tourists continued to flock to town in the hope of witnessing an actual haunting before we could get to it, buying out the historical society's stock of a slender volume titled *Bloody Pemkowet*, taking Sinclair's tour, and staking out sites that they thought were likely to reward their patience.

Oh, and the other thing that didn't happen? Yeah, that would be a serious and candid conversation between Cody and me about our relationship, or nonrelationship, or whatever it was. Or wasn't.

Which is not to say we didn't hook up again, because in fact we did after a particularly difficult and grueling ghost-busting assignment that left us both emotionally wrung out and desperate for life-affirming connection. And okay, yes, horny. It's weird how death's presence can have that effect.

In a totally different way, it was as intense as it had been the first time. Less primal, but no less urgent and with more manual dexterity.

Afterward, I gathered my scattered clothing from his bedroom floor. "Hey, Cody? Are we ever going to talk about this?"

A faint snore escaped him in answer.

At that particular moment, I couldn't blame him. It had been a really, really hard day. Still, we couldn't go on like this forever.

I should probably have talked to my mom about it; or at least Jen or maybe Lurine. I didn't know why I hadn't already, except that I didn't know what to say about it. It was hard to explain how and why it had happened the first time. The storm, post-wolf Cody curled naked in his blanket, that unexpected surge of raw desire . . .

This time was different, but it wasn't something I could explain to anyone who hadn't lived through what Cody and I had experienced that day. I'm not saying it compared to the sort of PTSD-inducing trauma that soldiers in combat and some police officers experience in the line of duty, but it was rough enough that I got why they don't want to talk about it with someone who hadn't been there.

And, too, there was a *Casablanca* factor that kept me from feeling inclined to discuss it. Between the relentless manifestations of the dead and the fact that Halloween was approaching and we were no closer to finding Grandpa Morgan's duppy than we had been weeks ago, it was fair to say that the problems of one little hell-spawn and a were-wolf on the down-low didn't amount to a hill of beans.

Well, not the romantic problems, anyway. The actual problems—those were my responsibility.

Damn, I was tired. Smoothing my dress in place, I caught a glimpse of my reflection in the birch-bark-framed mirror on Cody's bedroom wall. I looked a bit like a stranger to myself—bone-weary, yet sexually satiated. Determined, yet uncertain. Things that didn't add up to a coherent whole.

Which was pretty much how I felt. *Well, here's looking at you, kid,* I thought to myself. If I'd had a fedora, I would have tipped the brim in salute.

On the bed, Cody lay sprawled, loose-limbed in the abandon of sleep, dark circles of exhaustion under his eyes. There was no trace of the wolf in him tonight except for the light of the lamp on his bedside table glinting on the bronze stubble that grew faster than a mortal man's. I ought to know—I had the beard rash to prove it.

"Sleep tight, partner," I murmured, leaning over the bed to kiss his rough-bristled cheek. "But when this is over, assuming we all survive whatever the hell is coming, we *are* going to talk."

There was no answer, not even a snore.

Turning off the lamp, I let myself out.

# Forty-three

Altogether, Cody and I laid thirty-seven spirits to rest during the days and nights leading up to Halloween, and as far as I was concerned, that was reason enough to ensure that the gate between the realm of the living and the dead was closed.

It was exhausting, draining, and downright soul-wearying.

Some were easier than others. God help me, but I actually got inured to the ones who had died quickly or unexpectedly without much suffering—the bar patron shot in a lovers' quarrel, the drunk settler who froze to death in a blizzard, the victims of a head-on collision who died instantaneously, the elderly cat lady who died of carbon monoxide poisoning in her sleep.

Others were harder.

Children were harder, just because. Any cop who's ever worked homicide will tell you. Children just are.

Sometimes it was the ones I couldn't have anticipated, like the ghost of a Potawatomi Indian woman who manifested in the middle of a Pemkowet city council meeting, clad in a buckskin dress adorned with elaborate quillwork.

She carried the fur-wrapped bundle of a stillborn baby in her arms and pleaded softly with the horrified council members in a tongue none of them spoke, her eyes dark and sorrowful in her gaunt face.

I don't know her story. I'm guessing she died in childbirth, but it wasn't recorded in *Bloody Pemkowet*. Somehow it felt unfair to silence her voice forever.

In terms of sheer volume, the worst day was the one when the dead of the old hospital rose, haunting its empty corridors. Cody and I laid the spirits of almost a dozen men, women, and children to rest that day, me confronting the wandering dead with the blaze of the spirit lantern, throwing their shadows behind them down hallway after hallway, while Cody grimly pounded nail after nail into those same shadows in the worn linoleum.

And in case you're wondering, yes, it was after that incident that we hooked up for a second time.

In between manifestations, I logged every encounter in my database and looked for correspondences, trying to find a pattern. Other than the fact that the dead appeared to like an audience, I couldn't find one. And they certainly did seem to like an audience. Thank God for Stefan and his ghoul squad. I was judicious about calling on him for assistance, but without them, I don't doubt there would have been a lot more panic and a lot less voyeuristic giddiness.

Three days before Halloween, it stopped. Just . . . nothing. An ominous nothing. A calm-before-the-storm nothing.

And in three days, Pemkowet would see its biggest crowds of the season.

Just the thought of it made my skin itch. Halloween fell on a Saturday this year, and between that and our new notoriety, the PVB was making the most of it. Corn-shocks and stacks of pumpkins donated by a local farm decorated every street corner. An all-day celebration was planned for downtown Pemkowet, with face painting, bobbing for apples, and a pie-eating contest in the park for the kids, and live music and a beer tent for the adults, followed by a children's costume parade throughout the town, at the end of which a reading of "The Legend of Sleepy Hollow" would be staged, including an unannounced appearance by the Headless Horseman.

Which, by the way, is a badass costume.

And that was just during the daylight hours. By dusk, the younger kids would be all over the place trick-or-treating. Older kids like Jen's brother, Brandon, and his friends would be lying in wait in alleys and on rooftops to ambush one another with eggs and paint guns and water balloons in the annual battle of Easties vs. Townies. Come nightfall, it was the adults' turn. Every bar in town—and I don't know the actual total, but for a small town, trust me, we have a *lot* of bars—was hosting a costume contest. At ten o'clock, the adult costume parade would take place on the main street of East Pemkowet.

It was going to be mayhem.

Which is why on the second day of ominous supernatural silence, Cody and I called for a joint meeting with Chief Bryant and Amanda Brooks to ask them to cancel the festivities.

It didn't go over well.

Amanda Brooks was apoplectic—another of Mr. Leary's vocabulary words and a fitting one—and ranted for a solid ten minutes about tourism being the lifeblood of Pemkowet, and how we were the only small town in Michigan to have weathered the economic downturn with our property values intact, which generated revenues that allowed us to have an excellent school district that sent a high percentage of its students to college, which in turn made more people eager to move here and raise families, generating more revenues that paid for things like, for example, the Pemkowet Police Department.

All of which was true, but beside the point. "None of that will matter if it turns into a fiasco," I murmured.

She turned her acid gaze on the chief. "Tell me you're not considering this, Chief Bryant."

The chief sighed as though the weight of the world was on his shoulders. "Do you have any proof?" he asked Cody and me.

We shook our heads.

He steepled his thick fingers. "These ... ghosts. They haven't actually harmed anyone, have they?"

"No, sir," Cody said. "But—"

The chief cut him off. "In fact, has there been any indication that their presence in Pemkowet is malevolent?"

"No," I said. "But the duppy—"

"I don't want to hear about the goddamn duppy, Daisy!" He'd raised his voice. "That's a situation *you* assured me you had under control. Well, you didn't, and now we've got ghosts. I'm not happy about it, but if there's an upside to this whole business, we need to take advantage of it."

Amanda Brooks sniffed in pointed agreement. "And *I* don't understand why you've been wasting your time pestering my family."

"Because I think the duppy was responsible for whoever took the Tall Man's body," I said stubbornly. "And they're both still out there."

"That magic watch you gave me says otherwise," Chief Bryant reminded me. "Whoever took the Tall Man was human."

"That's what I'm saying!" I said in frustration. "According to Sinclair, there's a good chance that human is possessed by Grandpa Morgan's spirit. That's not something the, um, magic watch would register."

Cody cleared his throat. "The dead aren't considered part of the eldritch community, sir. Only the living and the undead. Even magicians and sorcerers are only tangentially related. And the dead are just ... dead."

"Well, I wish the goddamn dead would stay put," the chief said sourly.

"Chief Bryant, if you cancel the festivities, I *will* call for your resignation," Amanda Brooks said in a stiff tone.

He ignored her. "We're not canceling," he said to Cody and me. "I'll put everyone on duty. Twelve-, thirteen-hour shifts, whatever it takes. Time and a half for overtime. We'll make a round of the bars, make sure no one stays open after closing time. By two a.m., I want everyone off the streets. But we're not canceling."

Failure felt like a leaden lump in my belly. "Two o'clock's

too late, sir," I said quietly. "If we don't catch this duppy by midnight, the gate between the living and the dead may never be closed."

The chief's world-weary gaze slewed my way. "Well, I'm afraid that's *your* job, Daisy."

I bit my tongue, then said what I was thinking anyway. "With all due respect, sir, you're not making it easier."

He continued to regard me. "Neither are you. Meeting dismissed."

I won't lie, the chief's failure to trust me hurt. He'd been a father figure to me for a lot of my life.

But he was right. I'd screwed up and I hadn't found a way to fix it yet. When it came down to it, I couldn't blame him.

"What now?" Cody asked me in a low voice on the sidewalk outside the station, standing a little closer than professional courtesy dictated. "Plan B?"

"What's Plan B?" I asked him.

He smiled ruefully. "I was hoping you'd tell me."

I smiled back at him, wishing we had a real relationship, wishing I could ask him to hold me just long enough to bury my face in the curve of his throat and inhale his scent of pine needles, musk, and a lingering trace of Ralph Lauren's Polo. Which, come to think of it, would also be pretty damn unprofessional. "I think we need to assume the worst and call for whatever backup we can."

A reserved look settled over his face. "You mean Ludovic."

"I mean *everyone*," I said sharply. "I want anyone we can trust not to lose their head carrying a hammer and nails, Cody, because we don't know what's coming down the pike! Sinclair said the Tall Man's body could be used for death magic. For all we know, his grandfather's planning to raise a host of Pemkowet's dead going back to the Paleolithic era, and if that happens, all those tourists clamoring for a glimpse of a ghost are going to freak the fuck out, so yes, I want Stefan and the Outcast on hand. And I want Sinclair and the coven on hand to catch this damn duppy, assuming he finally makes an appearance, and I want anyone who can't help keep the peace to stay the hell home and out of the way, because I'm *scared*!"

"I know." Cody reached out and gave my shoulders a squeeze. "I know, Daise. So am I."

"Sorry." I took a deep breath. "I didn't mean to shout at you."

"It's okay," he said. "Believe me, I'm frustrated, too. And, Daisy . . . you know this *isn't* your fault, right? You didn't set some damn Jamaican witch doctor's ghost loose on the town."

"No, but it was my job to prevent it from happening," I said. "I didn't. And now it's my responsibility."

"Right," Cody said. "Plan B it is. Let's start by heading over to Drummond's to buy out their stock of hammers."

It wasn't much of a plan, but like he said, it was a start.

# Forty-four

While everyone else was carving jack-o'-lanterns, I spent the day before Halloween handing out hammers.

"The, um, particular talent of the Outcast will probably be more useful," I said to Stefan. "But just in case."

"Of course." He inclined his head, a shadow of regret behind his ice-blue eyes. "Some of us may find peace in laying the spirits of the dead to rest." He paused. "Are you well, Daisy?"

"Not exactly," I said honestly. "But I'm doing my best."

Stefan's pupils were steady. "I could alleviate your fear."

I raised my mental shield without thinking. "No. Thanks, but no."

Unexpectedly, he smiled. "Better. In battle, fear is a warrior's friend. You are wise to keep yours honed to a fine edge."

"Um . . . thanks." Keeping my shield in place between us, I eyed him. I couldn't help but think about what Cooper had said about us, not to mention Cody's occasional flares of jealousy. "Stefan, exactly what am I to you?"

He frowned slightly. "How do you mean the question?"

"I don't know." I really wasn't sure what I was asking, but I also wanted to see how he would answer without any guidelines.

Stefan was silent for a minute. "A rarity."

Okay, that wasn't what I'd expected. "Excuse me?"

"A rarity," he repeated. "A demon's seed conceived in innocence, born in faith, raised in love. That makes you a rarity, Daisy Johanssen." Leaning forward, Stefan raised one hand to cup the back of my head and kissed me on the lips.

Whoa.

It was a gentle kiss, but authoritative; a kiss that staked a definite claim. A jolt of electricity, or whatever the thing that feels like electricity is, shot through me. I'm not sure, but I may actually have gasped out loud.

Stefan released me and straightened, his pupils waxing into dark moons. "Does that answer your question?"

"Not exactly, no." My heart was beating fast and hard, and my knees felt wobbly. "But it raises plenty of others. Only—"

He finished my thought for me. "Only now is not the time."

"Right."

Stefan smiled again, this time faintly, but with genuine affection. "You should know that there are those of us who appreciate you for what you are and do not dismiss you for what you are not, Daisy. The Outcast will support you as best we can in whatever manner necessity dictates. I have conceived a fondness for this ridiculous town, and I do not wish to see it forevermore haunted. When All Hallows Eve has passed, I will answer any question your heart desires. But for now, it is best that you go."

I went, the impress of his kiss lingering on my lips. Life can be incredibly inconvenient at times.

Although I debated it, in the end I asked Lurine to be on hand to provide backup. I figured that if she was in costume, the odds that anyone would recognize her would be reduced.

Lurine agreed readily to help out after dark. "No worries, cupcake," she said, idly tossing the hammer I gave her. "Some of the prettiest boys from Rainbow's End are planning to march in the adult parade as an entire squadron of Lurine Hollisters. No one will recognize the real deal."

"What about . . ." I struggled to remember the name of the satyr, who was nowhere in evidence. "Nico?"

"Nico?" She looked blank for a second. "Oh, right. He got a little tiresome. I sent him off to pick apples at Pomona Orchards. Perfect place for a rustic deity. Do you want him there?"

"No, that's okay. I'd rather have people I know well enough to trust," I said. "I just thought maybe you were an item."

"An item." Lurine looked amused. "That's not really a term that applies to satyrs, cupcake. Satyrs are for . . ." She gave a little wriggle that managed to suggest serpentine undulations even though she was in human form. "Oh, let's just call it a down-and-dirty celebration of the urge to merge, shall we?"

Kind of like Cody and me, I thought. Well, except for the part where I wanted an actual relationship, which wasn't an option for a werewolf and a hell-spawn, because we were unsuitable mates incapable of producing little half-breed werecubs. Not that it was anything I was contemplating, but . . . God, I wondered if members of the Outcast could have children. I'd never heard of it happening, but I didn't know if there was a physiological reason for it, like maybe the plane of mortal existence between salvation and damnation was a sterile one, or—

"Daisy?"

I blinked at Lurine. "Huh?"

"I lost you for a minute there, baby girl." There was concern in her blue eyes. "Everything okay?"

"Are you kidding?"

"No." It was a good, solid "no," a bracing, cut-through-the-bullshit "no." Lurine sat on the couch opposite me, arms spread casually along its back, legs crossed at the knee, one dangling foot flashing the trademarked crimson sole of a spike-heeled Christian Louboutin pump. The wisdom in her patient gaze dated back to the Bronze Age, rendering Stefan Ludovic a mere child in her experience.

I sighed. "Didn't you tell me heartbreak was a rite of passage?"

"I did."

"Well, I might be stumbling toward a new phase of maturity."

"Oh, baby girl." Lurine came off the couch in a graceful slithering motion to embrace me. "It's all right."

I closed my eyes. "It's not, though. It's really not, Lurine. All this crap that's going on in my personal life doesn't matter. I screwed up. And I'm scared. Hel's disappointed in me. So is the chief."

Lurine shrugged. "Oh, fuck them."

I inhaled sharply. "Lurine!"

"Oh, you know what I mean, cupcake." Letting me go, she ruffled my hair. "I'm on your side. And you can do this."

My eyes stung with tears. "Thanks."

"What can I say, baby girl?" Holding me at arm's length, Lurine regarded me. "*I* believe in you. Go out there and make your mama proud."

It heartened me.

It's surprising what an affirmation from a millennia-old monster can do for your self-esteem; and I don't use the word *monster* lightly. The truth is, Lurine was a monster by her own admission. In a way, so was I. And it was good to be reminded of it.

Feeling a little better about tomorrow's prospects, I stopped by Sinclair's after his last tour was done for the day.

Jojo the joe-pye weed fairy was lurking outside his place, huddled under the juniper bush, clutching her slingshot. She looked weary and bedraggled, a brownish cast to her green skin, the purple clumps of her hair going to seed. It was late in the season for a wildflower fairy like her to be out and about. Usually, they vanished by this time, hibernating or taking to the hollow hills or whatever it was that nature elementals did during the winter.

"I come in peace, Jojo," I said, eyeing the slingshot. "This is business."

"Yes, I know." Although she didn't insult me, she summoned the energy to cast a disdainful look in my direction. "Someone must needs keep a vigil."

"Are you expecting the duppy to show up here?" I asked her. "Do you know something I don't know?"

"Like as not." Jojo bared her teeth in a pointed grimace. "But not about the spirits of the mortal dead, no." Her grip on the slingshot tightened. "I would fain keep him from harm, 'tis all."

"Okay, then," I said. "Be careful."

Inside, Sinclair promised to distribute hammers and nails to all the members of the coven and assured me that they had a phone tree in place and were prepared to convene on a moment's notice at the first sighting of his grandfather's duppy.

"They won't be able to help with the hammering thing if that happens, though," he warned me. "They'll need to form a spirit circle around him."

"That's okay," I said. "I'm just trying to get as many people armed and ready as possible. God knows, we could be overrun by ghosts before Grandpa Morgan decides to make his grand entrance. We might need all the help we can get."

Sinclair nodded at the silver acorn whistle hanging around my neck. "Have you thought about . . . ?"

"Summoning the Oak King?" I touched the gleaming metal. "I don't think this is something even he can help with, Sinclair. The fey don't wield influence over the dead. Although Jojo's determined to try," I added. "She's out there with her slingshot. Says she would fain keep you from harm."

He smiled tiredly. "Poor thing. She's been dogging my footsteps ever since it happened."

"She's been dogging your footsteps ever since *before* it happened," I pointed out.

"True."

The front door opened to admit Jen and a tall, lanky,

good-looking guy in corduroy pants, a cable-knit fisherman's sweater, and a chestnut-colored suede jacket. Even given the fact that the jacket was draped over his shoulder to accommodate the cast on his left forearm, it took me a couple of takes to recognize him.

*"Lee?"*

"Oh, hi, Daisy!" He grinned. The Velcro landing strip of beard was gone from his chin and he had a new haircut. He still had the steel hoops in his earlobes, but now they contributed a mild hint of subversiveness. He looked surprisingly good, in a heroin-chic-meets-Abercrombie-&-Fitch sort of way. "So what's up? Are we on the verge of a zombie apocalypse?"

Clearly, I'd been distracted. I shot Jen a *WTF, girlfriend?* look. She shot me a *We'll talk later* look in return.

"Um, yeah," I said belatedly. "I mean . . . I don't know. I hope not, but we're on the verge of something, that's for sure."

"You're recruiting ghostbusters?" Jen set down a shopping bag and picked up one of the hammers, hefting it. "Cool. I'm in."

"Those are for the coven," I said without thinking. "Not you."

"Why not?" Her voice turned cool, but the hurt registered in her brown eyes. "I'm not good enough to help?"

I could have kicked myself. "No, I didn't mean that! But they've got spells and magic and stuff to protect them."

*"You* don't."

"No, but—" I sighed. "Jen, if you really want to help, the biggest thing you could do is convince Brandon and his friends to call off the Easties vs. Townies fight. That would be huge. The fewer kids out there I have to worry about, the better."

"Fine," she said promptly. "Actually, I've already talked to him about it. Now can I be a ghostbuster?"

"You did say we might need all the help we could get," Sinclair reminded me. Lee didn't say anything, glancing back and forth between us. Lee was a pretty smart guy.

"I just don't want to put you at risk," I said to Jen.

She smiled wryly. "Look, Daise, I know I'm the Xander in your Scooby Gang. But at least Xander could hammer a nail. So can I. And I promise, whatever happens, I won't freak out. Let me help?"

I hesitated, then nodded. "Deal."

# Forty-five

A s if to mock my sense of impending doom, Halloween day dawned bright and clear and unseasonably warm. By noon, the festivities in the park were in full swing. The sky overhead was that deep, vivid blue that you sometimes get in October in Michigan. A light breeze ruffled the river, but the thermometer registered seventy-four degrees. A band played in the gazebo. Grown-ups danced and drank beer. Kids with jack-o'-lanterns and black cats with arched backs painted on their cheeks laughed and shrieked, chasing one another over the grass, bobbing for apples, burying their faces in pies donated by Pomona Orchards, rolling pumpkins for prizes.

"I feel kind of silly now," Jen muttered to me. She was wearing an old carpenter's apron she'd appropriated from her father at some point in time, nails in the front pocket, hammer slung through a loop.

"I can live with silly." I was sporting *dauda-dagr* on my hip and I had the spirit lantern tucked under my arm. As far as I was concerned, "silly" was a luxury that meant everything was quiet and calm. Ken Levitt was present in uniform representing the Pemkowet PD—Cody was on road patrol until later that evening—and he had a hammer and nails, too. Stefan's second lieutenant, Rafe, was perched solitary on a motorcycle on the rise at the far end of the park, observing from a distance, his inhuman pallor hidden behind riding leathers and a helmet with a dark visor.

Sinclair was off on his tour bus route, but he was only a phone call and ten minutes away, tops. Sandra Sweddon, Mrs. Meyers, and Sheila Reston were all volunteering to help staff the festival.

So was my mom, which was a bit of a sticking point. Once it was clear that the event was going forward, she'd refused to back out of her commitment when I asked her. At least she'd promised to go home when the shindig in the park ended.

And right now, it looked like I was being an alarmist. If it meant we got through the next twelve hours without a catastrophe, that was okay with me, too.

I nudged Jen with my shoulder. "So tell me about you and Lee."

She shrugged. "Nothing to tell." I gave her a look. "Okay, okay! I talked him into letting me give him a makeover."

"Good job."

"I know, right?" Jen couldn't resist a quick satisfied smirk. "He's got a good frame for clothes."

"So . . . would you ever?" I asked her.

"Date him?" She started to grimace, then caught herself. "Seriously, I don't know, Daise. I mean, there's a part of me that thinks, hey, why not? He cleans up sort of cute, he's really smart, and a fairly nice guy once you get to know him. Then I think . . . ew, but it's *Skeletor*." She glanced guiltily in my direction. "I'm not proud of that, but I can't help the way I feel."

"I get it," I said. "But it's probably way past time to let that old high school shit go, you know?"

"I know, I know!" Jen sighed. "But if it were that easy, they wouldn't make movies about it."

"True words, Romy. Or were you Michele?" It's not like I was one to talk, although I was pretty sure Stacey Brooks had earned a lifetime exception to the "grow up and get over it" clause.

She smiled. "Can you imagine the two of us turning up at our ten-year class reunion on Lee's arms?"

"I can imagine worse things."

"Yeah, me, too." Jen's smile faded. "Listen, if Lee ever does ask me out, I'll think about it, I really will. But it's not just the Skeletor thing. He's got this weird paranoid, secretive streak, you know?"

"It's not paranoia if they're out to get you." I dodged the halfhearted smack Jen aimed at my arm. "Okay, seriously! I don't know about that whole corporate espionage thing—maybe it's true, maybe it's not. But remember, Lee's got his own high school damage. I think he's been burned a lot of times and it's hard for him to trust people. He was so sure I was trying to trick him when we visited Little Niflheim, and I was *nice* to him back in the day."

"Point taken." Jen cocked her head at me. "Um, speaking of *secretive*, Miss Johanssen . . . ?"

"What?" I flushed. Jen folded her arms. "Okay, look . . ." I glanced around, half hoping for a timely manifestation. Unfortunately, the scene in the park was the very picture of a charming small-town harvest festival. If it weren't for Sheila Reston's neck tattoo, it could have been a Norman Rockwell painting. Since everything was quiet on the Western Front, maybe it was finally time for me to spill the beans. "It's complicated."

She raised her eyebrows. "Oh?"

"Remember the day the Tall Man's remains went missing?" I said in a low voice. "Well, Cody and I sort of hooked up that morning."

"Sort of?"

"Sort of as in totally," I admitted. "And one other time. After the ghost uprising at the old hospital."

"Wow." Jen let out a long breath. "How was it?"

"Intense." I shivered, my tail twitching involuntarily. "Especially the first time. He was still a little . . . wolfy." There was a look on Jen's face I couldn't quite decipher, a look that said she was suddenly seeing me as someone unfamiliar. "Look, don't say anything to anyone about it, okay?"

The look turned to indignation. "Duh. So?"

"So . . . nothing," I said ruefully. "I mean, we're still not the same freakin' species. Like I said—"

"It's complicated," Jen finished. "So that's it?"

"Not exactly." I looked around again to confirm that no one was in earshot. "Yesterday, Stefan kissed me."

Her eyes widened. "No shit! The hot ghoul?"

"Uh-huh."

She glanced toward Rafe, sitting motionless on his motorcycle. "Is that him up there now?"

"No," I said. "That's one of his lieutenants."

"Okay." Her gaze returned to me. "So?"

"I don't know, Jen," I said honestly. "Any of it. I don't know what to think about or even *how* to think about it, let alone talk about it. Any of it. All of it. Either of them." My tail began lashing with the pent-up agitation I'd been suppressing for days. "And I feel like with Halloween barreling down on us and Grandpa Morgan's duppy out there, I've barely had time to breathe—"

Across the park, a beer keg blew a gasket and my mom sent an inquiring look in my direction. "Whoa, whoa!" Jen grabbed my arms. "Daise, chill."

With an effort, I chilled. "Sorry."

"No, my bad." She let go of me. "I shouldn't have pushed you."

"It's okay." I gave my mother an apologetic wave. She nodded and returned to duct-taping down plastic sheeting on the table for the pie-eating contest. Up on the rise at the other end, Rafe was pointing at me, his helmeted head cocked in a questioning manner. Great, so he'd felt it, too. When I waved him off, he settled back into a watchful pose astride his bike.

Jen glanced toward him again. "It's funny, isn't it? Stefan's lieutenant keeping his distance. You'd think he'd want to get his ghoul on in a place where everyone's happy and having fun. I mean, I know they're not supposed to feed on the unwilling unless it's an emergency," she added quickly. "But as long as he's here doing panic control, you'd think he'd want to skim a little of the good stuff off the top. *I* would."

"Cooper says it's painful," I murmured. "Happiness, that is."

"Who's Cooper?"

I gave Jen a sharp look, but the question was genuine. In the weeks that I'd gotten to know Cooper, I hadn't mentioned him to her. It made me realize how much distance my role as Hel's liaison was creating between me and my best friend. "He's Stefan's other lieutenant."

"Oh." Judging from that one syllable, she was realizing it, too.

"Hey." I shifted the spirit lantern in my left arm, grabbed Jen's hand, and squeezed it. "I'm sorry if I've been secretive. I don't mean to be, it's just that I've had a lot going on. And I'm sorry I didn't ask you to help out with this from the get-go, but I'm really glad you're here now. Okay?"

"Okay." Jen squeezed my hand back.

On the street alongside the park, Sinclair's red, yellow, and green bus pulled up to let passengers disembark, PEM-KOWET SUPERNATURAL TOURS painted on its side. I couldn't help but gaze wistfully at it. I'd liked Sinclair. Well, I still did, of course, but life would have been a lot different if things had worked out between us. "Does he ever talk about me?" I asked Jen. "Now that you're housemates?"

She followed my gaze. "A little, sure. I mean, he knows we're friends, obviously. I think Sinclair feels bad about what happened. Aside from his familial baggage, which is a fairly huge deal breaker at the moment, he's a sweetheart." She paused. "Do you think you made a mistake breaking up with him?"

"No," I said. "But I wish I did."

Jen nodded. "I don't blame you."

A little before three o'clock, the harvest festival began winding down and young kids and their parents began to assemble across the street for the children's parade. Not a single ghost had manifested and not a single hammer had been drawn. I was glad, but it didn't do anything to alleviate the uneasiness I felt in the marrow of my bones.

"You be careful out there tonight, Daisy baby," my mom said to me, hugging me in farewell. "And you, too, honey," she added to Jen.

"We will, Mom Jo," Jen assured her.

Jen and I followed the parade on foot down the main street of downtown Pemkowet, which was easy enough to do since the array of pint-size lions, witches, skeletons, zombies, and princesses moved at a snail's pace. Ken Levitt brought up the rear in a squad car, creeping behind the procession.

At the end of the parade route, parents and children gathered on the municipal basketball court, where folding chairs on loan from the Women's Club had been set up, and Mrs. Brophy from the library read an abridged version of "The Legend of Sleepy Hollow" in a loud, theatrical voice.

Even though I knew what was coming, it was effective. There was a paved footpath that led up the hill alongside the basketball court, and when Mrs. Brophy got to the story's climax, the Headless Horseman himself came clattering down the footpath astride a coal-black horse, looking about seven feet tall in the saddle thanks to the long, dramatic cape obscuring his entire head and torso. Children shrieked, local parents cheered—it was an annual event, and the guy who played the Horseman had a riding stable a few miles outside of town—and adult tourists shouted in excitement and reached for their cameras and phones, many of them believing it was a real apparition. Like I said, it was a badass costume.

The Headless Horseman drew rein long enough to hurl a jack-o'-lantern onto the court, smashing it against the cement, before whirling and trotting briskly back up the footpath.

Once he'd vanished, the mood broke and the crowd began to scatter, sheepish tourists putting away their cameras, realizing it had all been part of the act. Rafe, who'd circled around town to position himself across the street during the parade, roared away on his motorcycle. Stefan and I had agreed to limit the utilization of the Outcast to large public gatherings where widespread panic could prove dangerous.

At least we'd gotten through the first one without incident. I let out a sigh of relief. "Well, that's phase one over with, anyway."

Jen tapped the hammer hanging from her carpenter's apron. "On to phase two?"

"Yep."

We retrieved Jen's convertible and drove up the hill—it's not much of a hill, but it's the only one we've got—to the main residential area of Pemkowet, parking on the street in front of the high school, where we'd have a good view of the neighborhood.

Ken Levitt pulled up alongside us. "Are the two of you going to be all right here on your own, Daisy?"

"Yeah," I said. "We've got additional backup coming in a few."

"Good." He nodded. "I'll be cruising the neighborhood up here on the hill. Cody's doing the same over in East Pemkowet, and Bart Mallick's making a circuit of those new developments on the outskirts. Anything happens, call dispatch."

"Will do," I said. "And if you see anything . . . call *me*."

Jen watched him drive away. "Call me a wuss, but I'm hoping that additional backup comes quickly."

"You're a wuss," I said obligingly.

"Thanks."

As it happened, we didn't have to wait long. Mark and Sheila Reston arrived within a few minutes, parking behind us. We milled around in the street, making the sort of awkward conversation that arises when a handful of people who don't know one another well gather to prepare for a possible massive ghost uprising or zombie apocalypse. Things went more smoothly when Sinclair arrived after his final tour of the day, sputtering up the hill to join us in the battered Chevy Lumina he'd purchased a few weeks ago.

That made four people on backup. To be honest, I'd rather have had Cody there, but it made sense to spread our resources around, coven members and police presence alike. If anything did happen, we'd have to converge, fast. But I'd chosen the hill since I figured it would get the most traffic from trick-or-treaters, and as I'd observed, the dead seemed to like an audience.

Perched on our cars and swinging our heels, we waited while a soft pre-dusk dimness settled over the hill and kids in costume flitted from house to house.

Despite the hour, the unnaturally balmy conditions persisted, a warm breeze springing up to rustle the piles of fallen leaves along the streets. Halloween in Pemkowet is old-school—none of that sterile contemporary business of determining a preordained time and place for trick-or-treating. People take the holiday seriously. Houses on the hill were decorated for the occasion, candlelit jack-o'-lanterns flashing flickering grins on every doorstep, fake gravestones in the front yards, fake cobwebs in the windows, plastic cauldrons from the dollar store spewing swirls of fake fog. Roving bands of trick-or-treaters went on foot from door to door, mostly accompanied by parents, but not always.

At around half past five, Jen's phone rang. She took the call and hung up after a brief exchange. "Oh, crap."

"What?"

"That was my mom," she said in a grim tone. "Brandon's missing. So's his bike. That little shit! He promised me."

"Damn." I called in to dispatch. "Sue, it looks like the Easties vs. Townies battle is on after all. Can you notify the officers on patrol?" When I ended the call, Jen was on her phone again, leaving a voice mail.

"Just left a message for Bethany at the House of Shadows," she said when she finished, her voice still grim. "She did promise to make sure nothing bad ever happened to him."

"She probably hasn't, um, risen for the night yet." I glanced toward the west. The horizon was obscured by trees, but amber luminosity lingered in the sky. "Looks like another hour until the sun sets."

"Great."

"He's a kid," Sinclair said quietly. "He just wants to have fun with his friends. I would have done the same thing at his age."

"On the verge of a zombie apocalypse?" I asked him.

He smiled wryly. "Probably."

Over on the hood of her car, Sheila Reston shuddered. "Can we not call this a zombie apocalypse?"

"I don't care what you call it," her husband, Mark, grumbled beside her. "I just wish something would happen. I'm bored and I'm *starving*."

I eyed a Harry Potter lugging a brimming bag of candy down the sidewalk. "You could always mug a trick-or-treater."

"Don't tempt me."

I wasn't about to complain about being bored any more than about feeling silly, but he had a point about being hungry. We should have gotten hot dogs at the harvest festival, or at least appropriated the leftover pies from the contest.

Just as I was thinking that very thing, another car pulled up to park behind us. I assumed it would be another member of the coven, but instead Lee emerged. "Hey," he said uncertainly. "Mind if I join you? I brought pizza."

"Oh, my God, Lee!" I scooted over and patted the Le-Baron's hood. "You really are a genius."

I was on my second slice of sausage-and-mushroom when the Easties bicycle posse rounded the curve at the end of the street and came pelting past us, seven kids around Brandon's age wearing hoodies and laden backpacks. One of them hurled a water balloon in our direction. It broke against the side of the LeBaron in an explosion of water and red food dye, most of it splattering Jen.

"Goddammit!" she shouted, hopping down. "Brandon Cassopolis, *get back here*!"

They didn't even look back, let alone stop, instead pedaling hell for leather like kids in a Spielberg movie.

"We're going after them." I shoved the pizza box into the backseat. "Guys, hold the fort."

Jen got behind the wheel and gunned the LeBaron. We nearly caught up with the Easties at the corner of Prospect, but a group of trick-or-treaters walked blithely across the street and she had to slam on the brakes while the bicyclists veered around the pedestrians. By the time we got through the intersection, the figures of the Easties were vanishing in the gathering dusk.

"That way." I pointed, catching a glint as the last one turned onto Elm.

They ditched us in the labyrinth of short roads leading down the hill. "Left or right?" Jen asked at the next stop sign.

"Turn left," I said. "They're probably doubling back into town." The victorious team in the Easties vs. Townies battle wasn't exactly determined by scientific method. It was based on a rough estimate of who inflicted the most damage in the other's neighborhood, or at least who bragged about it the loudest afterward. In the rearview mirror, I saw a second bicycle posse zooming around the corner of Elm in the opposite direction. That would be the Townies in hot pursuit. Apparently, the battle was shifting to East Pemkowet. "Uh-oh. My bad. They're headed for the bridge."

"Shit." Jen tried to do a U-turn and had to wait for another group of costume-clad pedestrians.

I called Cody. He picked up immediately, his voice tense. "Daisy. What is it?"

"No ghosts yet," I said. "Easties on bikes are on the move for home turf, Townies behind them. Can you head them off at the bridge? Brandon Cassopolis is with them."

"On it." He hung up.

At a bend in the road, over the river we caught one last glimpse of the Easties posse silhouetted in the lowering twilight as they pedaled furiously across the bridge, bent low over their handlebars, legs pumping. The Easties made it across and scattered into their own territory seconds before Cody arrived to pull the cruiser sideways across the street, strobe lights flashing red and blue.

Jen swore again, pounding the steering wheel with both hands. I winced. "I'm so sorry! I really thought they were headed back into town."

She glanced at me, water and red dye still dripping from her hair in an unnerving Carrie-at-the-prom manner. "It's not your fault, Daise. He shouldn't be out here in the first place."

The convertible top was down and the backwash of evening air over my skin made the fine hairs on my arms prickle, which in turn made me shiver. Everything felt wrong. It shouldn't be this warm in October. It should be cool and crisp, the scent of wood smoke and autumn leaves hanging in the air. Not this. And I couldn't shake the feeling that something very, very bad was coming.

"No one should," I said to Jen. "Not tonight."

# Forty-six

Cody had succeeded in rounding up four Townies. Two had gotten away, as well as all of the Easties. The only information the Townies could give us was their next rendezvous point in East Pemkowet.

"Sorry about your brother," Cody said to Jen. "I came as quickly as I could."

"I know."

While Cody dealt with the Townies, we cruised around East Pemkowet looking for Brandon and the other tween-aged bike hooligans. No dice. Even the Townies' rendezvous point behind the storage shed at Tanner's Landing was deserted, abandoned after their friends were caught. No one knows hiding places like twelve-year-old boys do. After half an hour, we gave up and drove back across the bridge to rejoin the others, eating cold pizza and watching the number of trick-or-treaters dwindle.

Ten minutes or so after full nightfall, Bethany called her sister back and promised to look out for Brandon. That was considerably more reassuring than I ever would have imagined just a few short weeks ago.

Otherwise, nothing continued to happen.

By nine o'clock, it was quiet on the hill. If the dead were waiting for an audience to make an appearance, it was obvious that it was going to happen elsewhere. Technically, that could mean any bar in town, but my money was on the adult parade in East Pemkowet, and everyone else agreed. Like I said, this community goes all-in for the holiday. It makes sense in a way. As far as tourism goes, for three hundred and sixty-four days of the year, ordinary mundane mortals play second fiddle to the eldritch. On Halloween, they set out to join them, which is why the adult parade has become such a massive spectacle. And this year, it seemed the parade participants were determined to pit themselves against whatever spectacle the dead might offer.

Back in East Pemkowet, we staked out a position on the front stoop of the State Farm Insurance building, which gave us a good vantage point to see over the crowds already beginning to throng the sidewalk. The other members of the coven joined us, and, to my considerable relief, Cody and Lurine also showed up: the former in uniform, the latter wearing a fabulous mask of feathers and an embroidered velvet robe that made her look like something out of a Venetian masquerade.

"I thought you weren't worried about being recognized," I whispered to Lurine.

She ruffled my hair. "Just a precaution, cupcake. I trust your little coven here, but if I should have to shift for any reason . . . well, better to be safe."

"Good thinking."

Stefan came to take up a post at the foot of the stoop, pale and somber, his broadsword strapped to his back. Jen elbowed me in the ribs when he and Cody exchanged curt greetings. "Hel's liaison." Stefan inclined his head to me. "One of the Outcast is in place on every corner. In the event of trouble, I've bidden them do what they may and hold their positions as long as discipline allows."

"Thank you." It was hard not to think about the fact that he'd kissed me. Yes, even now. I pushed the thought away. "I appreciate it."

He inclined his head again, then turned to survey the crowd.

I'm not good at estimating numbers and the tally probably wouldn't sound that impressive if I was. After all, the entire length of the parade route is a few short blocks. But if you cram, say, several thousand people into that space, it's a lot. And I'm guessing there were at least three thousand spectators lined five- or six-deep along the route on both sides of the streets, some in costume, many in ordinary clothes. Police tape cordoned off the street, Ken Levitt and Bart Mallick were stationed next to their squad cars at either end of the route, Chief Bryant was observing on foot, and there were a dozen volunteers in SECURITY T-shirts doing their best to keep visitors in line, but it was still a recipe for mayhem. A lot of spectators were already drunk and raucous, getting amped up further by the Halloween spooktacular sound track blasting from the speakers that the owners of one of the boutiques had set up across the street.

A block and a half from our post, the parade participants were amassing in front of Boo Radley's house. Stacey Brooks was flitting around filming or taking photos. She wasn't exactly in costume, but it looked as though she had on a headband with a set of plush cat ears. Gah, it figures.

At a quarter after ten, the parade still hadn't started and I was getting jittery. In less than two hours, Pemkowet gained permanently haunted status, and I officially failed utterly and completely in my duties as an agent of Hel. "C'mon, Grandpa Morgan," I muttered. "Where are you? You're never going to have a bigger audience than this one."

Sinclair, holding the empty pickle jar, shot me a miserable look. Cody laid a hand on my shoulder and gave it a surreptitious squeeze. "Hang in there, Pixy Stix."

"You should take up knitting, dear," Mrs. Meyers said calmly, needles clicking away. "It calms the nerves."

"I'm considering it myself," Sandra Sweddon murmured, fingering a set of crystal worry beads.

"Dahling, I think we should *all* take up knitting when this is over," Casimir said, his voice strained.

"I just wish I knew where my goddamn brother was," Jen said. "Or my goddamn sister, for that matter."

"You don't have to stay," I said to her. "We've got enough backup."

She gritted her teeth. "Oh, I'm staying."

"Well, I think it's quite exciting," Lurine said idly. "But I do wish they'd get the damned thing under way."

At approximately ten thirty, half an hour late, the parade finally began.

Unlike the children's parade, there was nothing quaint about the adult parade. There were mad scientists in goggles and blood-splattered lab coats, rotting zombies with latex eyeballs falling down their cheeks. There were ugly witches and sexy witches. There was a guy in a skeleton suit walking expertly on stilts and brandishing a plastic axe who was clearly meant to be Talman Brannigan back from beyond the grave.

That got a big round of applause.

There was a middle-aged heavyset guy in a corset, fishnet stockings, and pumps, with a placard around his neck and a whip-wielding dominatrix beside him, representing some political scandal I'd missed out on. Actually, there were several of those. I really needed to pay more attention to the national news. There was a twelve-foot-tall Pumpkinhead puppet operated by a local theater troupe. Like the Headless Horseman, it was a regular feature. Even though you could see the puppeteers working the poles that supported it, the effect as it bobbed and swayed above the crowd, an evil grin fixed on its ginormous orange head as it turned this way and that, skeletal hands outstretched, was pretty uncanny.

There were nuns and priests and pirates and mummies, and there was a group dressed as the cast of *The Wizard of Oz*. There was always a *Wizard of Oz* group. It wasn't a regularly planned appearance, it just happened that way.

And of course, there was the squadron of Lurine Hollisters from Rainbow's End. Drag versions of Lurine paraded down the street in a bloodstained lace slip and stiletto heels from her B-movie horror classic *Revulsion Asylum* and the bloodstained wedding dress and deranged streaks of mascara from the sequel, *Return to Revulsion Asylum.* There was the famous scarlet suit, pillbox hat, and veil that she'd worn during the trial regarding the challenge to her late husband's will. There was the figure-hugging, sparkling Dolce & Gabbana gold gown—well, a decent approximation of it, anyway—that Lurine had worn after the verdict was announced in her favor.

Okay, I admit it, I got caught up in the moment enough to cheer.

There was even a Drag Lurine in the dowdy gingham dress she'd worn in one of the few serious movies she'd done, an indie film called *Lindy's Crossing.*

The real Lurine smiled beneath the edge of her feathered mask. "Well done, boys. I wasn't expecting to see that one."

"You know, that was actually a really good—" I stopped when Cody grabbed my shoulder again. "What is it?"

"He's here." Cody's fingers tightened on my shoulder. His head was up, nostrils twitching, and there was a feral sheen in his eyes. "The Tall Man, or at least his remains. Come on!"

Without waiting for a response, Cody vaulted off the stoop and began pushing his way through the crowd, ignoring complaints. I followed in his wake, stepping awkwardly over the police tape.

"Daisy!" Sinclair shouted after me. "Should we ... ?"

"I don't know!" I called over my shoulder as I hurried to catch up with Cody.

My first thought when I saw the apparition shambling toward the rear of the parade was that it was one hell of a costume, or maybe a larger-than-life puppet like the Pumpkinhead. What else would you think if you saw a seven-foot-tall skeleton clad in steel-plate armor, wreathed in crackling blue lightning, holding a wicked-looking axe in one hand? As it drew near, spectators were craning to get a better look at it and already beginning to cheer.

But then Cody stopped dead in the intersection, so quickly I nearly ran into him from behind.

It wasn't a costume, and there were no clever puppeteers controlling it with poles. Those discolored bones were real, and a foul, acrid scent mingled with the odor of rot and decay hung in the air around the figure. That axe wasn't plastic; it was a serious and deadly sharp-looking tool for splitting wood. Whatever was causing the lightning, it wasn't some clever use of LED lights. And the armor . . . I don't know what the hell the armor was about, but it definitely wasn't decorative.

The Tall Man's grinning jaw gaped and blue flames flickered in his hollow eye sockets as he released a booming laugh that seemed to come from everywhere and nowhere, reverberating against the walls of the buildings.

The pit of my stomach dropped and my blood felt like it was turning to ice water in my veins.

"What the hell?" It was Chief Bryant, sounding angry and bewildered. "What the hell *is* it?"

"Talman Brannigan, sir," Cody said flatly.

Sinclair arrived at a run, breathing hard. "And my grandfather's duppy."

Chief Bryant stared at all three of us, at the members of the coven, the Scooby Gang, and the ghoul squad converging behind us. The Tall Man stood motionless, axe raised. Several yards away, Stacey Brooks stood frozen in terror, the camera forgotten in her hands.

The noisy crowd had fallen silent and uncertain, and the parade participants were retreating into an uncertain cluster.

Behind the figure of the Tall Man, an elderly man in a leisure suit capered and cackled. There was something familiar about the tenor of that voice. I'd heard it over an intercom, although it hadn't been cackling at the time. The Tall Man's jaw gaped again, one bony hand rising to point at Stacey Brooks as he uttered a single word.

"CAVANNAUGH!"

Stacey let out an earsplitting scream.

Oh, shit.

It had been right in front of us the whole time. It wasn't a descendant of the Cavannaughs that had stolen the Tall

Man's remains. That capering man in the leisure suit was
Clancy Brannigan. It was the Tall Man's sole living descendant that Grandpa Morgan's duppy had possessed in order
to work death magic. Unless I was mistaken, it looked very
much as though Clancy Brannigan, former inventor and
self-proclaimed man of science, hadn't been building a
spaceship or a new and improved widget in his basement.
He'd been welding armor onto the stolen bones of his dead
ancestor, now inhabited by the duppy and hell-bent on carrying out the Tall Man's dying curse.

And not only had we conveniently assembled the parade
outside the decrepit old Tudor house, but we'd provided a
scion of the Cavannaugh bloodline as a handy target.

"Do something!" the chief shouted at us, then turned
toward the crowds and the huddled parade participants,
waving his arms. "Clear the street! *Get off the street!*"

After that, things got chaotic.

The Tall Man lunged toward Stacey Brooks, swinging his
axe, and I reacted without thinking, summoning my mental
energies the way I'd been drilling for hours. Stefan had
made me promise not to attempt using them as a weapon,
but I didn't know what else to do. I didn't even know if I
*could* do it, but as much as I disliked Stacey, I couldn't just
stand there while the resurrected corpse of Pemkowet's infamous axe murder hacked her to bits. And so instead of
kindling a shield as I'd been taught, I visualized a bullwhip
of blinding light and cracked it in my mind, wrapping it
around the Tall Man's right arm and yanking on it.

It worked. The axe didn't fall.

For a split second, I was suffused with a sense of power
and triumph. Sinclair, who was closest to Stacey, sprinted
forward to haul her behind him with one arm, breaking her
paralysis and backing her out of danger.

And then the Tall Man turned his skull in my direction,
gas-lamp blue flames flickering in his eye sockets, the end
of my mental bullwhip wrapped around his bony fingers,
and I realized I couldn't retract my energy, realized he was
drawing on it, the flames leaping higher, and I could see the
malevolent joy of the obeah man's spirit in those fiery hol-

lows, riding the madness of Talman Brannigan's ghost like some supernatural jockey, working death magic and sowing destruction, draining my very life essence to gain even more strength.

All the power and triumph I'd felt leached out of me, pouring into the apparition along the invisible tether that joined us, the tether *I'd* created. The sounds of shouting in the background grew faint and muffled. It felt like I was falling into a deep well of sleep, and I wondered if this was what dying was like. My knees hit the concrete, the spirit lantern falling from my nerveless fingers.

If I'd had the strength to cry, I would have.

A voice raised in bronze-edged fury rent the night, penetrating the cotton wool that seemed to be stuffed into my ears.

Lurine had shifted, her basilisk stare fixed on the Tall Man behind the feathered mask as her powerful coils lashed out to encircle the skeleton's armor-clad waist. The invisible tether broke as he turned his attention to chopping at her with his axe, and I fell to my hands and knees in the street.

"God's blood, Daisy!" Stefan's hand jerked me partially upright, his eyes searching mine, pupils as dark as night. "I *told* you not to use it as a weapon!"

"I know," I whispered. "But—"

Somewhere beyond us, Lurine snarled in ancient Greek, a note of pain mixed with the fury.

"Tend to her," Stefan said to Cody, stepping back to draw his sword. *"Kyria!"* he called to Lurine. "Guard the innocents, leave the creature to me!"

"Daisy." Cody crouched in front of me. "Are you with us?"

I managed to shift one hand to point at the spirit lantern, lying on the street a foot away. "Take it."

Cody hesitated, then gave a grim nod, picking it up and opening the shutter. Nothing happened. He swore, gave it a shake, and tried again, to no avail. "Either it's broken, or it has to be you, Daise." He wrapped my limp fingers around the lantern. "Try."

I promptly dropped the lantern, then fumbled for it on the ground. Sitting on my heels, I struggled to pry open the shutter. It seemed to take forever, the sound of steel clashing against steel ringing in my unstoppered ears as Stefan engaged the Tall Man, but at last I succeeded. Blue-white light spilled forth, illuminating the combatants' lower legs and feet, shinbones behind steel greaves, blue jeans and motorcycle boots. Somewhere something was buzzing, a shrill voice spitting out curses.

"Daisy." Cody's voice was strained and urgent. I found the strength, barely, to lift my chin and look up. "Daisy, we need you."

I looked past him. It was Jojo I'd heard, the joe-pye weed fairy darting around Stefan's head, slingshot in hand, hurling pebbles at the Tall Man's eye sockets. With no shield or armor, Stefan had his leather jacket wrapped around his left arm, and he was fighting for his life against an immensely tall armor-clad opponent who couldn't be killed. Off to the side, Lurine had drawn herself to her full height, coils stirring as she stood guard over Sinclair and Stacey.

"Daisy!"

I placed my free hand on the concrete, pushing and trying to rise. My arms trembled with the effort. "Sorry," I whispered.

"Beslubbering, addlepated apparition!" Jojo shrilled, amethyst eyes ablaze, tattered wings gone dry and brown, beating the air as she fitted another pebble into her slingshot of woven grass. "Vile, grave-ridden—"

In the heat of her furious passion, she darted too close to the Tall Man. It happened so fast, the axe rising and falling in a swift flash. One second, Jojo was there in midair, a look of terrible agony on her tiny face.

Then, gone. A flurry of glittering pollen drifted away, and a limp, ragged stalk of joe-pye weed fell to the street.

A wave of rage filled me, lifting me to my feet with an incoherent shout. I held up the spirit lantern, sending the Tall Man's bony shadow stretching the length of the street. The concrete street, unfortunately.

"Over there!" Cody pointed toward a patch of landscaping on the corner, tall plumes of grass nodding. "Either corner, Daise!"

"Go!" I shouted, moving sideways to angle the Tall Man's shadow toward the far corner. My arm was still trembling with the effort, but the anger burning inside me gave me strength. "Anyone who can! *Go!*"

Cody was already dodging past the Tall Man, but the Tall Man was pressing Stefan backward toward me, and I had to retreat. All along the sidewalks, the remaining spectators were shouting and shoving in a frantic effort to flee the scene, terrified parade participants crowding them from behind.

"Daise!" On the near corner, Jen signaled me with raised arms, waving wildly, light glinting off the hammer. Amid the chaos, she'd managed to slip down the street unseen. "Here!"

"Bingo," I whispered, sidling to the left to send the Tall Man's shadow in her direction. She hammered the nail into the soil with one solid *thwack*.

And nothing happened.

The Tall Man loosed another booming laugh, making the windows rattle all along the street. The capering figure in the leisure suit echoed it with a demented cackle.

Shit.

Hel had warned me that the spirit lantern and an iron nail might not work on Grandpa Morgan's duppy because his spirit had never been laid to rest in the first place. And it didn't work on the Tall Man because he *wasn't* a spirit; he was flesh and bone, or at least bone and metal-plate, thanks to former inventor and insane agoraphobic Clancy Brannigan. Although I guess he wasn't agoraphobic anymore, since he'd emerged from his lair for the first time in decades. Maybe being possessed by a duppy before it ditches you to animate your great-grandfather's corpse has that effect.

"Man of science, my ass!" I shouted across the intersection at him.

He cackled in reply. Maybe he wasn't agoraphobic, but whatever shreds of sanity he'd been clinging to were gone.

"Hel's liaison," Stefan said in a formal tone, parrying another mighty swipe of the Tall Man's axe. "I fear my strength is not without limits. The same does not appear true of the creature."

I winced. "Sorry!"

I knew what I had to do. I just didn't know how the hell I was going to do it. I set down the spirit lantern. *Daudadagr* sang as I drew it, the hilt cool and reassuring against my palm. The ridge of hair along my tail prickled as I assessed the embattled Tall Man for a weakness in his armor at a vital point.

There was one—there, when he turned his skull, his spine was exposed beneath his helmet at the nape of his neck.

Only I hadn't the faintest idea how to reach it.

There was a thrumming sound from the rooftop of one of the buildings on the intersection, one that had sat empty and for sale since the Birchwood Grill it once housed had closed. A thrumming sound followed by a *splat*.

The Tall Man staggered backward as a water balloon filled with red dye burst against his breastplate.

Atop the roof, there were cheers and whoops, heads peering over the edge. I felt a fierce grin stretch my cheeks. "Go, Easties!"

"Oh, I don't think so. No, I'm afraid that won't do at all." In the middle of the intersection, Clancy Brannigan calmly withdrew a pistol from the waistband of his polyester leisure suit. Considering that he'd gone entirely around the bend, he sounded surprisingly coherent. He raised his arm to take aim at the figures on the rooftop and cocked the safety. "Let's let this play out, shall we?"

I froze in shock. A gun, or an insane mortal with a gun, was the last thing I'd expected. But Cody spun around and drew his service pistol, his expression grim and determined. "Drop it!"

Talman Brannigan's last living descendant moved with startling dexterity, grabbing Jen around the neck with his left arm and positioning her between them, his gun to her temple. "I'd say it's a standoff, Officer. Why don't you drop yours?"

Jen let out a faint squeak, her dark eyes wide with terror and helpless fury, showing the whites. Cody hesitated.

"Oh, God," I whispered, the blood running cold in my veins. "Jen, no!"

There was another sound, a whooshing sound, as one of the figures atop the roof vaulted over the edge, the panels of a long coat flaring like dark wings, briefly blotting out the streetlights overhead. Someone let out a shriek as the figure dropped like a stone. A highly cinematic stone. Clancy Brannigan swung his pistol and fired at it, the gunshot echoing loudly along the street.

"Missed me." Bethany Cassopolis landed in a three-point stance, straightening to adjust the folds of her long Victorian frock coat. She showed her fangs. "No one fucks with my brother and sister, creep. Not anymore." Brannigan lowered his pistol and fired on her at point-blank range, but a bullet to the chest barely even slowed Bethany down as she fell upon him with inhuman speed, wrenching the gun from his hand as she jerked him away from Jen and sent him stumbling in Cody's direction. "Count yourself lucky I don't drink you dry, asshole!"

Cody slapped a pair of handcuffs on Clancy Brannigan. One psychotic mortal down, one possessed zombie skeleton to go.

Okay.

"Wait!" I shouted. "Stefan, everyone, just hold on!" I addressed the Tall Man's figure. "Mr. Morgan, I want to parley!"

The helmeted skull turned toward me, eye sockets filled with blue fire, blue fire crackling along its bones. Grandpa Morgan was listening. Opposite him, Stefan braced his hands on his knees, keeping his grip on his sword, taking deep breaths. Blood was running down his left arm, dripping from his wrist.

"Let Talman Brannigan's spirit go," I said. "He committed a terrible crime. Don't let it happen again. That can't be what you want."

Blue flames surged in the hollow sockets. "Let my *grandson* go, she-devil!" It was a different voice, not as booming, but creaking with sharp, rusty edges. Well, that and a Jamaican accent. "That's all I ask. Give me my grandson, and you and your cursed bloodclot of a town can have your murderer's bones!"

"No one *has* me, Grandfather!" Emerging from behind the protective barrier of Lurine's coils, Sinclair confronted the apparition. There were tears on his cheeks. "This is my town and these are my friends. I chose this path, and you have no right to choose a different for me; not you, not my mother, not my sister! No one! You can force me to change my mind, but you can't change my heart." He opened one hand to reveal the withered remnants of a joe-pye weed. "You can only break it."

On the outskirts of what had been a crowd of spectators, there was still shouting and pushing, but the street surrounding us had gone quiet. Everyone who wasn't already fleeing was transfixed with a combination of horror and fascination. I caught Lurine's eye and pointed toward the Tall Man's ankles, then held up one finger to indicate she should wait for my signal. Lurine nodded, slithering forward a few feet. Behind her, Stacey Brooks stood with her arms wrapped around herself, teeth chattering in the warm night air.

In silence, we waited for the Tall Man's—for Grandpa Morgan's—response.

"Sorry, bwai." There might even have been a hint of regret in the rusty voice. "But your mother bound me to her will."

And then, "CAVANNAUGH!"

Grandpa Morgan had loosed the reins on the Tall Man and given him his head. The axe rose, the skull turning in search of Stacey Brooks. Stefan straightened, hoisting his sword, his irises like pale rims of frost around his pupils.

"Easties, fire!" I shouted, praying that Brandon and his friends were still up there manning the ramparts.

My prayers were answered. Atop the roof of the old Birchwood Grill building, the industrial-strength water-balloon launcher twanged over and over, launching a barrage. The Tall Man flailed, batting at the onslaught. It wasn't

anything more than an annoyance to him, but all I needed
was a moment's distraction.

"Now!" I shouted to Lurine.

Her iridescent tail shot forward, snaking around the
skeleton's bony ankles, upending him with a single yank.
The Tall Man clattered to the ground, bones and armor rattling. Stefan was on him in a flash, both booted feet stomping down hard on the skeleton's axe-wielding arm, the point
of his sword jamming into the exposed vertebrae at the
back of the Tall Man's neck through the same gap under the
helmet that I'd spotted.

Of course, there was no magic in his blade, only skill, and
it seemed the skeleton was held together with death magic,
not sinew. Blue lightning crackled as the Tall Man flung him
off with supernatural strength, rising to one knee.

One knee was good enough for me. It put the nape of the
Tall Man's neck at right about eye level.

Stealing up behind him, I drove *dauda-dagr* home.

It cut through the brittle old bones like butter. The blue
lightning vanished. The Tall Man's figure collapsed.

I breathed a sigh of relief.

Too soon, of course. The air around the fallen heap of
bones and metal roiled, smelling of scorched hair and rot.
Without a host to contain it, Grandpa Morgan's duppy was
manifesting at long last.

"Gentlefolk of the coven!" Casimir called in a fierce, determined voice. "My darlings, our time has come!"

Sinclair turned to me. He held the empty pickle jar in
one hand and the sad, trampled reminder of Jojo in the
other, and the determination in Casimir's voice was echoed
in his level gaze. "Stand back, Daisy. We've got this."

I nodded. "Do it."

I admit it—I'd had my doubts about the coven. But they
converged in a circle around the Tall Man's armored bones
and held hands, with Sinclair in the center, facing his grandfather's spirit. Sandra Sweddon, Warren Rogers, Mark and
Sheila Reston, Kim Crandall, Mrs. Meyers, whose first name
I really ought to learn . . . their ordinary, mortal faces were
strong and beautiful as they chanted an invocation.

Grandpa Morgan's duppy fought them. It manifested in a shifting array of forms: a bull-calf with fiery eyes, chains jangling around its neck; a black dog with its hackles raised; a giant fish leaping and twisting in midair.

Members of the coven held fast to one another's hands and chanted louder, their voices strong.

In the center of the circle, Sinclair opened the empty jar, the sprig of joe-pye weed tucked into the breast pocket of his polo shirt. He uttered a word—a word like the word his mother had uttered in the cemetery, all stern, tolling syllables that sounded as if it came from before the dawn of recorded time.

The duppy's appearance dwindled into that of a stooped, elderly man with tired, bloodshot eyes, gazing at his grandson with a pleading expression.

Sinclair said the word again.

A cool, crisp autumn breeze sprang up, banishing the scent of decay and blowing the manifestation of the duppy into tatters. There was a . . . a sucking sensation, like what happens when contestants on *Iron Chef America* use the vacuum sealer.

With a deft, deliberate twist, Sinclair screwed the lid onto the pickle jar, capturing his grandfather's spirit.

It was done.

# Forty-seven

In the aftermath, I burst into hysterical laughter. I couldn't help it.

"Daisy." Stefan's calm voice anchored me. "Are you harmed?"

"No." I wasn't entirely steady on my feet, but the sense of debilitating weakness was beginning to fade. "I'm okay. Is everyone else okay?"

Unfortunately, the answer was no. At least the Tall Man hadn't succeeded in doing a lot of damage. His axe had nicked Lurine's coils, and Stefan had a gash in his forearm. He assured me it was nothing, although blood was soaking through the bandanna he wrapped around it. Jen was shaken by her encounter with Clancy Brannigan but otherwise unharmed. Her sister, Bethany, was displaying the bullet she'd expelled from her chest—don't ask me how, since I'm not up on the intricacies of vampiric healing abilities—with all the pride of a first grader with the coolest item at show-and-tell. While Stacey Brooks was either in a state of shock or pretending to be in order to justify clinging to Sinclair's arm, she didn't have a scratch on her.

But despite the best efforts of the ghoul squad, there were injuries among the spectators. No fatalities, thank God, but there were a lot of scrapes, bruises, and sprains, two nonfatal cardiac incidents, and one probable case of broken ribs.

And Cooper was ravening.

It was the panicked cries for help somewhere in the crowd that alerted us. I kindled a feeble shield and followed Stefan as he strode down the street, leaving the police and the arriving EMTs to deal with the injured.

Aside from Stefan, all the other Outcast had beat a prudent retreat when they'd reached the limits of their discipline. Not Cooper. He'd overestimated his abilities, and now he was confronting a trio of tourists: Mom, Dad, and a teenaged daughter who was standing slumped and vacant-eyed in the circle of her mother's arms while her mother shouted for help and her father, looking terrified, took a protective stand in front of them.

". . . scared, are ya, boyo?" Cooper was taunting the father. "That's all right, then. I *like* scared, me." He made a rude, deliberate slurping noise, his features contorting in ecstasy. "Yum, yum!" The tourist dad's face turned slack and blank. "That's right, let good old Cooper take care of you, make all your fears go away. Though there's nothing quite as tasty as the terror of a sweet little bird like your daughter, innit?"

"For the love of God, *leave us alone*!" the mother cried in a shrill voice, wrapping her arms tighter around her daughter.

"Don't you worry yourself, Ma," Cooper replied jauntily. "God's got nothing in the world to do with it. But I promise, it won't hurt a bit."

"Cooper!" Stefan said sharply. "Stand down!"

"Big man." Cooper turned. There was a note of scorn in his voice. His pupils were fully dilated, swallowing all traces of his blue irises, and his eyes shone like dark moons in his narrow face. "Always trying to make us into summat we're not. When are you going to learn? We're not heroes, not the likes of us. We're *Outcast*."

Stefan locked gazes with him. "Nonetheless."

"The lass was out of her head with terror, boss," Cooper said, looking away with an effort. Reaching past the unresisting father, he chucked the teenaged girl under her chin. "Look at her now! Meek as a lamb."

The mother screwed her eyes shut tight, shutting out the world. "Will somebody please *do* something?"

Cooper turned the black pits of his gaze back toward Stefan. "You heard her, big man. Do something. Why don't you do the lady a kindness and take away her fear?"

Stefan hesitated.

He wanted it. I could sense that void of yearning opening, the emptiness longing to be filled, the beast straining to slip its leash. He glanced sideways at me, pupils zooming to leave an icy blue rim around the edges.

Cooper followed his gaze. "Oh, but it's *her* you want, innit, boss?" He leered at me and licked his lips. "Can't say as I blame you."

"Goddammit, Cooper!" For the second time that night, a wave of fury rose in me—fury mixed with helplessness. This time it made my shield blaze, and I found I'd drawn *dauda-dagr* without thinking. Light danced along the runes etched on its length, along its razor-sharp edges. My eyes stung with tears, my hand trembling. "I thought we were friends. Don't make me threaten you!"

"The angel of feckin' death." Something stark and bleak surfaced behind Cooper's black, black eyes. "You know there's a part of me that wants you to do it, don't you, sweet Daisy?"

"I don't—"

Stefan threw a punch, a solid roundhouse that connected with Cooper's jaw just below his ear and sent him sagging to the pavement.

I let out a sigh of relief.

"Do you need a hand here, Daisy?" Cody said behind me. His tone was terse, and although he'd addressed me, I had a feeling it was meant for Stefan.

So did Stefan, since he replied for both of us. "The situation is under control, Officer Fairfax," he said, pulling a cell phone from the pocket of his black leather vest and sending a quick text. "I kept a number of my men in reserve in case it should be necessary to perform an extraction."

Cody's nostrils flared, a muscle in his jaw twitching. "Such foresight."

Stefan's tone remained courteous, but his pupils glittered. "I do my best."

The alpha male standoff might have gone on a while longer if the poor terrified tourist mom hadn't interrupted it.

"Officer, please, help us!" she said frantically to Cody. "Look at them! Look at my daughter and my husband! What did that creature *do* to them?"

"He fed on their emotions, ma'am. Too deeply." Cody examined the father and daughter, making sure there were no head injuries to account for their condition. They endured it without complaint, standing like slack-jawed mannequins. He glanced at Stefan, his lip curling. "Tell me they're going to be all right, Ludovic."

"They will recover," Stefan said quietly. "It will take some days. A week, perhaps. But they will recover."

"They'd better," Cody said.

"They will."

A trio of Outcast arrived on motorcycles, wending their way past the police barricades. Two of them grabbed the still-unconscious Cooper under the arms and slung him into a sidecar. Cooper stirred and murmured a little, eyelids fluttering, looking almost as young and harmless as the teenaged girl he'd drained. It was hard to reconcile the sight of him with the ravening ghoul he'd been just minutes ago.

"Hel's liaison." Stefan inclined his head to me. I could see the strain on his self-control reflected in his widening pupils. "It is best that I go with them."

"Right." I nodded. "Thank you. I couldn't have done this without you. And Stacey Brooks owes you her life."

"You did well." He straddled one of the bikes, two of his henchmen doubling up on another without a word spoken. A faint smile touched his lips. "We will speak later of the folly of using the pneuma as a weapon before you were ready."

I winced a little. "I know, I know."

The motorcycles roared away into the night, taking the Outcast with them.

"I don't understand how you can just let this happen!" the tourist mom burst out. "Let creatures like that walk the streets! We came here to be entertained, we came here to see ghosts, not, not . . ." She gestured at her daughter and husband. "Not this! God! Oh, God! What's *wrong* with you people?"

My tail twitched. I wanted to tell the woman that she was an idiot for assuming that the eldritch community, a haunted eldritch community, for Christ's sake, was safe, that it was the paranormal equivalent of Dollywood, everything sanitized for their protection. But it wasn't her fault, not really. She'd done exactly what the PVB had encouraged tourists from all across the country to do.

Cody shot me a quick glance. He might not have been able to read my emotions like one of the Outcast, but he knew my temper. "One of those creatures saved a young woman's life tonight, ma'am," he said gently. "Are you staying in the area? Miss Johanssen and I would be happy to accompany you and your family to your car, or I can have an officer take you to your hotel if you're not feeling up to driving."

The tourist mom blinked away tears, sniffling. "We're staying at the Ridgeway Motor Lodge. I can drive. I just want this all to be over."

Cody and I escorted the three of them to their car, which was parked in the little lot behind the coffee shop. It was disconcerting to see how empty and lifeless the father and daughter were after having been drained of their emotions. I'd had a run-in with a ravening ghoul of my own, but it hadn't been anywhere near this severe. I'd been lucky; or maybe my super-size emotions had saved me. God knows, I'd spent enough time wrestling with them, but I'd never thought before about how much of what animates us as human beings—or semi-human beings—depends on our feelings.

Without them, we were dead inside.

The tourist dad sat placidly in the front passenger seat, gazing at nothing, his hands resting idly on a camera with a big, fancy lens that dangled from a strap around his neck. Behind him, his daughter slumped in the backseat.

"You're sure they'll recover?" the tourist mom whispered. "You're *sure*?"

"Positive." I put all the conviction I could muster into the word, which was a fair amount. I didn't think Stefan would mislead her, not with his well-developed sense of honor. "And if you'd like to stay here in Pemkowet while they recover, the PVB will be happy to cover the cost of lodging."

Okay, I was going out on a limb with that one, but as far as I was concerned, Amanda fucking Brooks owed me. If she'd canceled the Halloween festivities like Cody and I had asked her to do, none of this would have happened.

Of course, there was no telling what would have happened instead.

At any rate, the tourist mom was having none of it. A look of horror crossed her face. "No," she said hastily, getting behind the wheel of her Audi. "No, thank you. I think we've seen quite enough of this town."

I nodded. "I understand."

Cody and I watched them drive away. "Too bad," he murmured.

"It could have been a lot worse without the Outcast." I was feeling a little defensive of the ghoul squad. "It was a mob scene, Cody. We're lucky none of the spectators was killed."

"I know." He stroked my hair. "I'm not arguing, Daise. I'm sure they'll be fine, eventually. They shouldn't have been here in the first place. It's just . . ." He shrugged. "I should have known."

I was confused. "Known what?"

"The Tall Man's remains." Cody bared his teeth in a half snarl. "That lunatic Clancy Brannigan had to haul them into his house somehow. He must have used that old pickup truck in his garage. But there should have been a scent trail. I should have smelled it the first time we visited the place."

"How did he hide it?" I asked.

Cody gave me a look, green flaring behind his eyes. "He didn't. The rain did. The thunderstorm. Remember?"

Oh, I remembered. "You couldn't have known. Cody, we didn't even suspect Boo Radley! We just went there to notify him."

"Right," he said brusquely. "And if we'd done it *before* the storm, I would have picked up the Tall Man's scent."

There wasn't a lot I could say to that. "I'm sorry."

"It's not your fault," Cody said. "You didn't know any better. I did. But . . ."

The word trailed away, dangling a host of unsaid things. We hadn't gone out to investigate immediately because I'd found Cody in a feral state, still moonstruck from the night before. I'd startled him. He'd yanked me down, and I'd liked it. I'd kissed him. I'd initiated a bout of savagely intense lovemaking. Afterward we'd lain together in a nest of woolen blankets and Cody had listened to me explain what had happened in the cemetery, stroking my back from the nape of my neck to the tip of my tail while lightning cracked the sky, thunder rumbled in the marrow of our bones, and the rain poured down, washing away the scent trail.

It had been one of the nicest moments I'd ever known.

"I don't want to regret it, Cody." There was a tremor in my voice. "I really don't."

"I know." He slung an arm around my shoulders and kissed my temple. "Come on, Daise. Time to go back."

By the time we returned to Main Street, things had quieted. Most of the crowd had dispersed. Somewhere in the aftermath, Lurine had shifted back into human form and vanished discreetly along with them. The EMTs were tending to the injured.

Clancy Brannigan was in custody in the back of a police cruiser. The Easties had clambered down the fire escape from atop the Birchwood Grill and were getting a stern lecture from the chief. They were doing their best to look abashed, but I was pretty sure they were delighted with themselves, and I couldn't blame them.

The Tall Man's bones still lay in a heap in the middle of the street, moldering under gleaming steel plate.

"Daisy!" Jen was standing in a small cluster that included her sister, Lee, Casimir, Sinclair, and, unfortunately, Stacey Brooks. Jen waved me over, and I saw that Lee had retrieved the spirit lantern and had it tucked into the crook of one arm. "We kept it safe for you."

"Thanks." A belated wave of guilt swept over me. In the heat of the moment, I'd forgotten I'd set it down. "You guys were amazing tonight."

"You totally saved my life," Stacey said to Sinclair. She shuddered at the memory, the plush cat ears on her headband trembling. *"Totally."*

He glanced at me. "Actually—"

"It's okay," I said. There was no way in hell I was going to try to explain to Stacey that I'd nearly gotten myself killed saving her stupid life with an invisible bullwhip of mental energy. Other than the members of the coven, no mundane human could have guessed what had happened there. "I'm just glad no one but Jojo . . ." A lump rose to my throat, and I couldn't finish the thought.

"I know," Sinclair said softly, touching the sprig of joe-pye weed drooping over his breast pocket. "She was a brave little thing."

"She was a foulmouthed, obnoxious little shit, and I'll miss her." I rubbed my eyes and nodded at the seemingly empty pickle jar that Sinclair held tight in his other hand. "So what happens now?"

"I'll take my grandfather's spirit home and lay it to rest where his bones are buried," Sinclair said in a grim voice. "And I'll tell my mother and my sister that if they want me to have any part of their lives, they'll never, ever threaten me or the people I care about again."

"Amen, brother," Casimir murmured.

"Is it safe?" I asked. "I mean . . . isn't going back to Jamaica exactly what they wanted you to do?"

"Oh, I'm not staying." Sinclair hoisted the pickle jar, contemplating it. "And after tonight, there's no way they can make me."

"Young Mr. Palmer here showed a considerable amount

of strength tonight, Miss Daisy," Casimir said to me. "And gained a considerable amount of power in the process."

Interesting.

But speaking of strength and power, now that everything was under control, I was feeling the acute drain on my own reserves. Also, Bethany Cassopolis was staring at my throat, a spark of vampiric hypnosis in her gaze. Feeling my pulse quicken under her gaze, I kindled my shield with an effort. "What?"

"Nothing," Bethany said unapologetically. "It's just that I'm hungry. And you smell . . . interesting." She smiled, showing the tips of her fangs. "Funny, I never noticed how cute you were."

Gah! And yet . . . goddamn eldritch Kinsey scale. My shield flickered as I stared at my best friend's sister's gleaming fangs, trying not to imagine them piercing my skin.

"Okay, ew!" Jen said in a firm tone. "Beth, cut it out. If Chief Bryant's done yelling at the Easties, I'm taking Brandon home and you're riding with me."

"You're my ride," I reminded her.

"I'll drive you," Lee offered.

"Will you give me a ride?" Stacey Brooks asked Sinclair in a pleading voice. "I'm too shaky to drive."

I laughed again; and again, I couldn't help it. At least it was only a little hysterical this time. Sinclair gave me an uncertain look. "It's okay," I said to him. "It's fine. Go. Take her home."

Before taking Lee up on his offer, I touched base with Chief Bryant. He looked as tired as I felt, the streetlights above the intersection throwing the dark pouches under his eyes into stark relief. "Daisy."

"Sir."

"I should have listened to you and Cody." He smiled wryly. "I'm sorry I didn't."

"You had your reasons, sir," I said. "I made mistakes. Big ones."

"Not tonight. And I appreciate your enlisting the help of the eldritch." The chief paused a moment to rub his chin. "I, um, don't suppose you want to tell me exactly who or what that half-woman, half-giant snake creature was?"

"She's, um, a lamia. Or the lamia." I wasn't entirely sure if Lurine had peers, and it had always seemed impolite to ask. "Otherwise . . . I'm sorry, but no."

"Never mind." He clapped one meaty hand on my shoulder. "You did a good job, Daisy. Go home and get some rest."

"Thanks."

It didn't feel like well-earned praise, but I didn't tell him about the one big mistake I'd made tonight, or about the mistake Cody and I had made the morning after the Tall Man's remains vanished. Maybe that was a cop-out, or maybe there were some things the chief didn't need to know. Either way, I was just too tired.

In the intersection, Cody and Ken Levitt had donned latex gloves and were carefully shifting the Tall Man's bones onto a tarp.

Cody glanced up as I passed, his expression a complex mixture of regret and affection. He lifted one latex-covered hand to give me the little two-fingered salute we'd developed during our ghostbusting forays. "Later, partner."

I returned the salute, pretty sure my expression echoed his. "Later."

On the drive home, I gave my mother a quick courtesy call to let her know everything was more or less all right, which she'd already heard from Lurine. I promised more details in the morning. Lee insisted on escorting me up the stairs to my apartment. I'd left the door to the screened porch ajar so Mogwai could come and go, and the place was as cold as a meat locker now that an autumn chill had replaced the unnatural balminess. On the plus side, Mogwai was there, winding around my ankles as I closed the door and turned up the thermostat.

"Are you all right, Daisy?" Lee hovered uncertainly. "No offense, but you look like shit."

"Thanks," I said. "I'll be okay."

He frowned. "What happened to you out there?"

"I'll explain later." I yawned, the kind of huge, gaping

yawn that feels like your jaws might crack. Attractive, right? "Now that this is over, I need to talk to you anyway."

"About what?"

"Using the Internet to find a guy," I said wearily. "A mysterious lawyer."

Lee's eyes lit up. "On a Venn diagram, the intersection of 'Internet' and 'mysterious' is where I live."

I blinked at him. "What?"

"Nothing," he said gently. "We'll talk about it later. You're sure you're okay?"

"I'm sure." I wasn't sure, but I didn't think there was anything Lee or anyone else could do about it. I'd acted without thinking and I'd learned the hard way that it was dangerous to trifle with death magic. I'd used up all my reserves and now I felt drained to the dregs, as surely as Cooper's victims. Except at least I was still myself . . . just a very, very tired version of myself. "Go home."

"Okay," he said. "Call me if you need anything."

"I will. Oh, and, Lee?" I added as he turned to go. "You should ask Jen out on a date. I'm pretty sure she's willing to consider it."

"Gee, thanks." His tone went flat. "I'm honored."

"Oh, don't be like that." I yawned again. "You know you like her. Now get out of here."

After Lee left, I stowed the spirit lantern atop my nightstand, unbuckled *dauda-dagr* from around my waist, and collapsed onto my bed without bothering to undress further, assuming I'd fall into a dead sleep. But letting unconsciousness claim me felt too much like what I'd felt when I was linked to the old obeah man's duppy by an invisible tether, feeling my life force ebb away from me. Every time I came close to falling asleep, I awoke with a jerk, my entire body tensed at the memory.

Exhausted as I was, it seemed I couldn't let sleep claim me. Not yet.

So after a futile hour I staggered out of bed and drew a hot bath, stripping off my clothes and sinking into the soothing warmth. Mogwai perched on the side of the tub, reaching out one cautious paw to bat at drops of water dripping from my leaky faucet. It was an old building with old plumbing.

I mulled over the mistakes I'd made, evaluating them without dwelling on them, hugging my knees and swishing my tail back and forth in the warm water. Bit by bit, my tense muscles relaxed.

I let myself grieve for Jojo in all her ridiculous, foul-mouthed valor. If I hadn't screwed up, Jojo would still be alive. Hell, I hadn't even known fairies could be killed. Not like that.

But Jojo had made her choice, too. I hadn't asked for her help, I hadn't promised her credit in my ledger this time. If she'd offered, I would have told her to stay far, far away from Sinclair tonight.

Her choice, her sacrifice.

"I'm sorry," I murmured, brushing my fingertips over the Oak King's talisman, the silver acorn strung around my neck. "She died bravely."

Somehow, I thought he would understand.

The water was tepid by the time I finally hauled myself out of the bath, dried off with a towel, pulled on a clean tank top, and crawled under the covers.

According to the glowing red numbers on my clock radio, it was almost three in the morning. Midnight had long since come and gone. Halloween was over and I'd beaten its deadline with time to spare. Downstairs, I could hear the sounds of Mrs. Browne bustling about efficiently in her kitchen. From the warm, yeasty smells of bread rising through the vents, I could tell she'd already fired up her ovens for the first batch of the day. I was one of the few people who'd ever been privileged to witness Mrs. Browne at work in her bakery.

Oh, in case I haven't mentioned the obvious, Mrs. Browne isn't human. Mrs. Browne is a brownie.

Eyes closed, I inhaled deeply. It smelled like warm bread baking, it smelled like comfort, it smelled like normalcy; at least in Pemkowet, where Mrs. Browne bakes her supernaturally delicious crusty bread, meltingly flaky pastries, and cinnamon rolls like spicy clouds with cool drizzles of icing.

Curled against my side, Mogwai purred loudly in approval.

All was well with the world.

The gate between the realm of the living and the dead was closed. I was Hel's liaison, and I had kept my town safe.

At last, I slept.

# Forty-eight

For about a week afterward, Pemkowet was crawling with reporters.

To no one's surprise, Amanda Brooks managed to spin the Tall Man's return from beyond the grave to carry out the curse of the Cavannaughs into an enthralling, multigenerational ghost story, glossing over the finer points of how and why it had occurred.

At my insistence, she also made it clear that the episode was over and that Pemkowet's days as a destination for ghost hunters had come to an end.

Okay, she may have hinted that the cycle could repeat itself in another generation, but I could live with that.

Although my image was out there, thanks to Stacey Brooks's earlier ghostbusting footage, not to mention a handful of spectators who'd had the presence of mind to document the battle with the Tall Man, I kept a low profile. So did Cody, my partner in ghostbusting, and Stefan, whose skill with a broadsword was drawing a fair amount of attention in historical reenactment circles. In fact, everyone in the eldritch community kept a low profile. Whatever else may be true of us, none of us are media whores.

Well, in another day and age, Lurine may have been an exception, but times change. There's a big difference between being immortalized in prose by John Keats and being outed by Gawker.

Anyway.

Once it was apparent that Pemkowet's dead were staying put, interest waned and the town was left in peace again.

The coven took up a collection to buy Sinclair a ticket to Kingston to lay his grandfather's spirit to rest. He was gone for four days and quiet upon his return, saying only that it was done and there would be no more trouble from his family, living or dead.

I'll admit it, there was a part of me that felt a little cheated by the lack of resolution in my own confrontation with Letitia and Emmeline Palmer. Obviously, there wouldn't have been any point in my going all the way to Jamaica with Sinclair, even if I could have afforded a ticket, which I couldn't, but it would have been nice to know that they were smarting at their defeat.

But that was just pride talking, and pride was one of the Seven Deadlies. I had to tread carefully there. I reminded myself that it was enough to have kept Pemkowet safe, that I'd made mistakes, that a member of the eldritch community had paid the ultimate price for them.

Speaking of Jojo, after Sinclair returned from laying his grandfather's spirit to rest, we went together to do the same for the fairy's remains.

On an overcast November day, we took the limp sprig of joe-pye weed to the meadow where I'd first summoned a gaggle of fairies with cowslip dew last summer. It had been lush and green then, filled with indigenous plants and wildflowers. Now the meadow was brown and desiccated, dry grass and the thin stalks of weeds crunching underfoot. I stood shivering in my leather jacket while Sinclair cleared a patch of earth. He dug a hole in the dirt with his bare hands, laying the ragged bit of joe-pye weed in it and covering it tenderly. Side by side, we gazed at his handiwork.

"Maybe she's not gone for good," Sinclair said. "Maybe she'll return in the spring. Do you think?"

"I don't know," I murmured.

He shook his head, beaded dreadlocks rattling. "I don't know what I did to deserve that kind of loyalty."

"She loved you," I said simply. "Why not? You're a pretty awesome guy."

Sinclair smiled, but there was sorrow in it. "Thanks. You, too, Daisy. An awesome girl, I mean."

Hands in my pockets, I nudged him with one elbow. "You should say something."

He took a deep breath. "Jojo . . . thank you. Wherever you are, I hope you're at peace. I promise, I'll never forget you."

Inside my jacket, the silver acorn strung around my neck on a chain tingled against my skin. Overhead, the gray clouds parted to let a single shaft of sunlight angle across the meadow, illuminating the shadows beneath the dense pine trees, pinning a gilded mantle on the tall figure that stood there, crowned with antlers.

It was the Oak King.

Although he didn't move, the meadow seemed to contract around him, growing smaller. From where we stood, I could see the bottomless wells of grief and knowledge in his deep, deep brown eyes, and I understood that although he was older than history, older than the written word, he still mourned for the least of his subjects.

Across the meadow, the Oak King raised one hand in salute, sunlight streaming between his spread fingers.

I raised mine in acknowledgment.

And then the clouds closed, obscuring the sun. The bright shaft of golden autumn light vanished, and the Oak King vanished with it, fading back into the pine shadows without a single motion.

I let out a long, shuddering breath I hadn't realized I was holding. Beside me, Sinclair did the same.

"I don't think Jojo's coming back, Daisy," he whispered. "Not ever."

I reached out to slide my hand into his, entwining our fingers, and squeezed. "Yeah. I know."

Some things come to an end.

And some things begin, too.

You may have noticed that I haven't mentioned Hel. Well, that's deliberate, because I'm still trying to figure out how I feel about what happened the night that she summoned me to Little Niflheim in the aftermath of the Halloween affair.

It's . . . complicated. As usual.

I don't mean the visit to Little Niflheim. Although I was a bit apprehensive, far from satisfied with how I'd handled the whole crisis, that part went fine. I should have known it would. It may have come down to the wire, but I'd upheld Hel's rule of order, which was all that mattered. Whatever mistakes I'd made along the way were forgiven and forgotten in light of the fact that I'd produced the desired results. If Hel were a CEO rather than the Norse goddess of the dead, I'd say she was outcome-oriented. She even let me keep the spirit lantern as a bonus. Well, more of a precaution, but still.

It was on the way out of Little Niflheim that the first disconcerting thing happened. As Mikill and I approached the sacred well beneath the canopy of Yggdrasil II's massive root system, one of the Norns stepped forward and held up a hand to halt the dune buggy.

I clambered out of the buggy for a little soothsaying. At a distance, the Norns don't look terribly intimidating. At close range, it's another matter. It was the youngest of them who beckoned to me now, fingernails like long silver talons, her eyes as colorless as mist.

"Young Daisy," she said to me, her voice echoing as though it came from the depths of the well that lay beneath the roots of the world tree. "Embrace your mistakes. Learn from them. When the time comes, the fate of the world may hinge on the choices you make."

Oh, great.

"Do you have any counsel for me, my lady?" I asked her. The Norn maiden reached out with her long, long silver talons to caress my cheek, razor-sharp edges rasping against my skin and drawing a shudder from me. She gave me a faint smile, the pale mist that filled the hollows of her eyes swirling. "Trust your heart."

I waited to see if any more sooth was forthcoming, but she withdrew her hand and returned to rejoin the other two Norns in the endless process of tending Yggdrasil II's roots, drawing buckets from the well.

"Any idea what that was all about?" I asked Mikill, climbing back into the dune buggy.

The frost giant shook his head, the ice in his beard crackling. "The Norns see many possible futures."

"Are they ever more specific about them?" I asked.

"No." Mikill revved the engine. "They reveal as much as they may without breaking the skein of time."

"Okay," I said. "It's just . . . um, the fate of the world? I mean, no pressure or anything."

Mikill gave me a long, grave look and for a moment I thought he was going to say something profound about how no one chooses their destiny no matter how humble or terrifying, or something reassuring about the many possible futures, or maybe a pep talk about how I was only just coming into my own, and I possessed reserves of strength and courage I hadn't yet begun to tap. After all, we'd spent a fair amount of time together on our excursions to and from Little Niflheim by now.

But no.

"Keep your limbs well within the vehicle during the ascent, Daisy Johanssen," he said quietly to me before gunning for the rampway that spiraled up the inside of Yggdrasil II's mammoth trunk.

So, yeah, that was the first disconcerting thing that happened the night Hel summoned me. I didn't know what to think about it or even *how* to think about it. On an intellectual level, of course, I'd always known about the danger my existence posed to the Inviolate Wall. It's why I tried to tread lightly when it came to the Seven Deadlies and why I resisted even considering my father's temptation scenarios. But as long as I maintained my hard-fought self-control — or at least enough of it not to breach the Inviolate Wall itself—those were only hypotheticals.

This . . . this was different. This was an immortal sooth-sayer, one of the Norns, telling me that a moment of choice was coming for me and the fate of the world would hang in the balance. Or *may* hang in the balance, what with the many possible futures and all.

I sighed, a distinctly unsettled feeling in the pit of my belly.

It didn't help when Mikill pulled into the alley beside my apartment and the dune buggy's headlights tagged the sleek, matte-black form of a Vincent Black Shadow motorcycle parked there.

"It appears you have company, Daisy Johanssen," Mikill announced in a formal tone.

"So it does." I got out of the vehicle. "Thank you, Mikill."

He raised one hand in farewell, put the dune buggy in reverse, and backed out of the alley, chugging away into the night, his frosty beard wagging in the breeze.

"Daisy." Stefan, leaning against the wall, peeled himself upright. The lamp above the door cast his eyes in shadows. "I wanted—"

"I'm fine," I interrupted him. "You don't need to check up on me at every turn."

He frowned. "Is it—"

I talked over him. "I mean, it's just the fate of the world, right?"

"—so difficult to believe that . . ." Stefan paused. "What?"

We stared at each other. "Nothing." I swallowed. "Just something one of the Norns said to me. I'm sorry. What?"

"Is it so difficult to believe that I'm here because I wished to see you, Daisy?" Stefan said gently to me.

"A little, yeah," I said honestly.

He smiled. "I wanted to tell you that Cooper is lucid enough to express his apologies to you."

"That was fast." Based on what I knew, it took at least a week for a ghoul to stop ravening.

Stefan shrugged. "Cooper has considerable strength of will. Still, I will see that he is kept in seclusion. It will be some days yet before the ravening has fully passed."

"Okay."

Oh, in case you're wondering, this was definitely the other disconcerting thing to happen that night.

"The Norn?" Stefan prompted me.

"It's nothing," I said. "I mean, it's nothing *yet*. And it's nothing specific. Just that the fate of the world may hinge upon the choices I make."

Stefan took a step closer to me. I was acutely aware of his presence; of his height, of the breadth of his shoulders, of the impossibility of his immortal existence. "That has always been the case, Daisy."

"I know," I whispered. Part of me felt crowded by Stefan's presence. Part of me felt elated by it. "Is that why you came? To tell me about Cooper?"

"No."

The air between us hummed with possibilities. I forgot about the Norn's soothsaying. "Um . . . Stefan, wouldn't it be dangerous? You and me, together?"

"Are you afraid of losing yourself in me?" His pupils dilated in a rush. "You could. Or I could let my control slip and you could send me ravening. But that's part of the allure, isn't it?" He was close enough that I could feel the warmth of his skin. "You've been with one of the eldritch, Daisy. There may be no future for you and the wolf, but do you really think you could go back to ordinary mortals?"

"No, but . . ." My mind was reeling. "There's no future for us in the long run, is there? And Cooper said it's human companionship you crave. In case you've forgotten, I don't entirely qualify."

Stefan cupped my face in his hands. "Your heart is human, Daisy. Human and more."

He kissed me.

It was one hell of a kiss. I'd been impressed by the last one, but Stefan had definitely been holding back. If that first kiss had staked a claim on me, this one made good on it; and there was nothing gentle about it. That man did masterful things with his tongue, things that turned my knees to water and made my head spin, igniting a blaze of lust between my thighs. I guess six hundred years of practice will have that effect. I heard myself moan into his mouth and realized that my hands were fisted in his dark hair, pulling him closer until I could feel his erection pressed against me. It felt good. I could feel my yearning spilling into him, feeding him, and that felt good, too. I wanted more.

Damn.

A rill of terror mixed with desire ran through me, and I kindled a shield without thinking, pushing Stefan away.

Somewhere on the far side of the Inviolate Wall, my father, Belphegor, chuckled.

Stefan's pupils waxed and waned, steadying in his ice-blue eyes. "We are well matched, you and I. I cannot offer you eternity, Daisy, but I can offer you the here and now." He inclined his head to me. "Think about it."

"Um . . . okay," I said in a dazed tone. "I will."

Stefan had the courtesy to make his exit on that note, straddling his black motorcycle and roaring away.

So, yeah.

That was more than a week ago. Since that time, Stefan hadn't pressed me and I hadn't sought him out. He was giving me time and space, and I was grateful for it.

I wanted what he offered. I wanted it a lot.

But it scared me, too.

And then there were my feelings for Cody, which hadn't gone away. And we *still* hadn't had a real conversation about it. Now that we weren't working an eldritch case together, he was back on night shifts and I hadn't seen him for days. He might have been avoiding me on purpose. I know he felt guilty about the fact that if our tryst that morning hadn't happened, if we'd gotten to Clancy Brannigan's house before the storm, he would have found the scent trail and the Tall Man's remains. It's not like I could blame him. I felt guilty about it, too. But it didn't seem fair that it should completely invalidate what had happened between us, because let's face it, what happened was shockingly intense and pretty damn amazing.

Of course, even if it hadn't been for the element of guilt, there was the fact that I was an unsuitable mate. Nothing in the world was ever going to change that. It's not like in the movies where a werewolf's bite infects a human with lycanthropy—not that I would consider that, but still. Werewolves can only reproduce with their own kind. That's why they're so stringent about it. The survival of their species depends on it.

So maybe it was time I acknowledged it, gave up, and quit pining for Cody Fairfax for good. Maybe it was time I explored my attraction to Stefan, a prospect that filled me with equal parts of exhilaration and terror.

Or maybe that was the very choice the Norn warned me about. On the one hand, it seemed pretty freaking arrogant to imagine that the fate of the world might hang in the balance because Daisy Johanssen of Pemkowet, Michigan, decided to try dating the hot ghoul.

On the other hand, Stefan was one of the Outcast, banned from heaven and hell, and I was a demon's daughter. As my old teacher Mr. Leary might say, that made for a heck of a potent eschatological cocktail. Eschatology—look it up. I did.

And of course there was the fact that Stefan Ludovic was the medieval Bohemian version of Hamlet, for Christ's sake, a six-hundred-year-old immortal knight with a tragic backstory, and I was a twenty-four-year-old file clerk with a high school diploma.

That's the sort of thing that looks ridiculous on paper, right? And yet it didn't feel ridiculous.

After all, I wasn't just a file clerk. I was Hel's liaison. And despite everything, Stefan was a man—a man who had once been mortal, who had been Outcast in the prime of his life. He had the same longings and desires as any other mortal man. Well, plus one major addition, what with the subsisting on emotion and all.

Anyway.

Whether or not it was in reference to this particular choice, the Norn had told me to trust my heart. The problem was, Stefan was right. My heart was human. More, maybe; human, definitely, with all the confusion, messiness, and uncertainty that being human entailed. They say the heart wants what it wants. Well, mine wanted a lot of things.

I wanted what Stefan offered me.

I wanted what Cody couldn't offer me, too.

Hell, there was a big part of me that wished Emmeline Palmer had never come to town and I was still dating her brother, Sinclair, still riding on the handlebars of his bicycle and enjoying a harmless romance that wasn't overshadowed by insurmountable complications or inherent peril.

But you can't turn back the hands of time, at least not that I'm aware of. What was done was done.

Sooner or later, I was going to have to make a choice. When all was said and done, I doubted that the fate of the world hung on this one. The Norn was probably talking about something else, something I couldn't yet begin to envision.

At least I hoped so.

I'd have to think about it some more.

Read on for an exciting excerpt from the next
Agent of Hel novel by Jacqueline Carey,

## *Poison Fruit*

Available now from Roc.

On Monday morning, I arrived at the police station to catch up on filing, only to walk into a situation. I'd call it a domestic disturbance, except the wild-eyed guy and the skinny bleached blond chick screaming at each other weren't in their own domicile.

"—want to file a report, goddammit!" he yelled at her. "Some crazy old bitch breaks into our apartment in the middle of the night—"

"—need to go back on yer meds!"

"—fucking sits on my chest—"

"Yuh need to go back on yer meds, Scott!"

Behind the reception desk, Patty Rogan looked more annoyed than frightened, probably because Chief Bryant was in the process of lumbering out of his office like a bear disturbed from its hibernation.

"What seems to be the problem here?" he rumbled, hitching up his duty belt. "Oh, morning, Daisy."

"Morning, Chief." I kept my distance. I'd rather face down an ogre than get in the middle of a domestic dispute, especially since the only ogre I know is a friend of the family.

The feuding couple began shouting at the same time again. The chief winced and held up one big hand for silence. It worked. For an ordinary human being, the chief has a lot of presence. He looked at Patty Rogan, who cleared her throat.

"Mr. Evans here would like to file a report regarding an intruder," Patty said in a neutral tone. "Mrs. Evans is of the opinion that there was no intrusion."

Chief Bryant pointed at the wild-eyed guy. "Scott Evans, right? Braden's boy?" The guy nodded, looking marginally less agitated. "You first."

"That ain't—" his wife began indignantly.

The chief silenced her with a look. "You'll get your turn, ma'am."

The upshot of Scott Evans's story was that he'd awakened in the middle of the night to find an elderly woman sitting on his chest—an elderly woman with skeletal features, glowing red eyes and long, lank hair, that is. He'd been terrified and unable to move as she'd reached down and begun to throttle him, leaning over to inhale his breath. He was sure he was going to die, but then his wife, Dawn, rolled over in her sleep, and the scary old lady fled.

Somewhere in the course of Scott's less than coherent recitation, the chief gave me an inquiring look, which I answered with a slight shrug and head shake. I wasn't sure if a succubus was anything like an incubus, but it didn't sound at all similar to my mother's experience. Other than that, I couldn't think of anything in Pemkowet's eldritch population that would fit the profile.

"All right, ma'am," the chief said to Dawn Evans when her husband had finished, "what's your version?"

She sighed, her shoulders slumping. "There weren't no old lady, sir." There were dark circles under her eyes. "Scott's got the PTSD. Sometimes he sees thangs. And he ain't bin takin' his meds."

"It's got nothing to do with the meds!" he shouted. "She was there, dammit!"

"Oh, honey! Ah know yuh think so." Sorrow, a whole world of it, had replaced the anger in her tone. "But she weren't."

It was enough to convince Chief Bryant. "All right, here's what we're going to do. Scott, Mrs. Rogan here's going to take your statement, and I'll send Officer Mallick over to examine the apartment for any sign of forced entry. Meanwhile, I want you to go home and take your medication. Can you do that for me?"

"I guess."

"Is that an affirmative, soldier?" The chief pressed him.

Scott Evans stood a bit taller. "Yes, sir!"

"Good man." The chief nodded in approval. "All right, then. Carry on."

Feeling bad for Dawn, I sat with her while her husband repeated his story and Patty took down the details. "I take it you're not from here?" I said to her.

"No'm." She gave me a tired smile. "Is it that obvious?"

"Kind of, yeah," I admitted. "Where are you from originally?"

"Alabama," Dawn murmured, tears filling her eyes. She sniffled and knuckled her eyes. "Ah'm sorry. It's just that this is so hard. Ah love Scott—ah do—but this is so goddamn hard. His family tries to help as best they can, but . . ." A stifled sob escaped her, and she clenched her teeth on another.

"Hey, hey!" I put my arm around her shoulders. "It's okay. I mean, it's not, but . . . just breathe, okay?"

Dawn swallowed and nodded. "Thank yuh."

I found a tissue in my messenger bag and handed it to her. "So how did you end up here in Pemkowet?"

She blew her nose. "We met in Iraq," she said, pronouncing it "eye-rack." "Same ole story. Girl meets boy, falls in love and gits married, moves to his hometown."

"You served in Iraq?"

Dawn gave me a sidelong look. "Yes, ma'am. U.S. Army, maintenance and repair personnel. Ah drive a mean Humvee."

"I'm impressed," I said.

"Yuh mean surprised?" she asked wearily.

I was beginning to regret my initial assessment of Dawn Evans as "skinny bleached blond chick." Okay, I stand by the hair—it was pretty bad—but there was a lot more going on here. God knows, I knew what it was like to be underestimated because of my looks and age, and the thick Southern accent probably wasn't doing her any favors in these parts. "Look." I lowered my voice. "You're probably right about this whole thing. I mean, you know Scott. You know what he's been through. I don't. I can't even begin to imagine what you guys have seen and done and how you're coping with it. But just to be on the safe side, it wouldn't hurt to sprinkle your bed with holy water. And, um, hang some cold iron over your front door. An old horseshoe or something. It keeps away the fey."

She knit her brows. "Yuh think—"

"I just think it's worth taking the precaution," I said. "I'm going to look into it. And if it happens again . . . call me. Oh, I'm Daisy, by the way. Daisy Johanssen."

"Ah know who yuh are," Dawn said, fishing for her phone so we could trade numbers. "Yer the ghostbuster. Ah seen yuh on YouTube."

I winced. "Right."

"Ah 'preciate it," she said to me, direct and forthright. "And ah'd 'preciate if you didn't say nothin' to Scott 'lessen yer sure. He's got enough bad thoughts in his head. He don't need no one else puttin' none there."

I nodded. "Understood."

Dawn reached out to grasp my hand and squeeze it. "Thank yuh."

"Anytime." I returned her squeeze. "Seriously. Even if you just need to talk . . . call me."

Seeing Scott approaching, she stood. "Ah will."

Call me crazy, but I just don't get the whole concept of a war of choice. I mean, war's awful, right? I guess at some point there's a choice involved in everything, but when it comes to war, it seems to me it should be the absolute last resort. And it's a choice that should only be made for majorly compelling reasons, like defending your loved ones, or at least a grand humanitarian cause, not some trumped-up excuse to carry out a political agenda that turns out to be totally ill-conceived.

But hey, that's just the opinion of one lone hell-spawn. Humanity's been waging war against itself since the dawn of recorded history, so maybe I'm missing something. All I know is, I'm glad it's a choice I'd never had to make.

Anyway.

I put in a couple of hours filing, then used the department's laptop and secure connection to covertly check the Pemkowet Ledger, which is the name of the top secret online database that Lee created for me. Covertly, because Chief Bryant was a little touchy on the subject of my refusal to allow anyone else in the department access to the ledger.

I felt a little guilty about that, but not enough to change my mind. For one thing, the eldritch code requires that I respect the privacy of members of the community, and as Hel's liaison, I had to honor it. For another, it turns out that the ledger was a valuable tool in terms of negotiating with the community. The eldritch have a healthy regard for the notion of favors and debts owed, and I'd realized that I could use my ledger to influence individual members who were eager to rack up favor points or have past transgressions erased.

The Pemkowet Ledger was a work in progress—I was still inputting data from the past few years—but I did several keyword searches to see if they turned up any cases I'd forgotten that involved a scary old lady sitting on someone's chest or attempting to throttle them in their sleep.

No dice.

I checked the Vault and the Penalty Box, which aggregated favors and transgressions. Nothing useful there, either, but one entry in the Vault gave me a pang.

Jojo (nickname) the joe-pye weed fairy: One large favor owed for identifying a hex-charm created by Emmeline Palmer.

Jojo the joe-pye weed fairy never got to claim that favor. Talman Brannigan—or at least his reanimated remains—had cut her down in midflight while she was attempting to defend my ex-boyfriend Sinclair Palmer, whose secret twin sister had hexed me some weeks earlier.

Have I mentioned that my life is complicated?

I let the cursor hover over Jojo's entry, thinking I should probably delete it, then decided against it. Maybe someday I could repay the favor to one of her clan, assuming joe-pye weed fairies had a clan.

Since there was nothing of use to be found in the ledger, I elected to pay a visit to one of my favorite resources: Mr. Leary, my old high school Myth and Literature teacher, who knew more eldritch folklore than most members of the community themselves.

Mr. Leary lived in a charming old cottage in East Pemkowet, which is a separate governmental entity from the city of Pemkowet proper and Pemkowet Township—a distinction that often confuses tourists since the three are joined at the hip for all intents and purposes.

"Daisy Johanssen!" He greeted me effusively at the door, waving a mug. "Welcome, my favorite ontological anomaly. I hope you've brought me an interesting conundrum to ponder. Can I entice you to join me for a hot rum toddy on this dreary day?"

I considered the offer. After all, it was a dreary day, and technically speaking, I wasn't on the job. "You know what? That sounds delightful."

"Wonderful!" Mr. Leary beamed at me. Well, maybe "beamed" wasn't the right word. With his long, saturnine features and majestic mane of white hair, Mr. Leary wasn't a beamy kind of guy, but he definitely looked pleased. I guess when you're that passionate about your libations, it's nice to have someone to share them with.

He ushered me into his tidy bachelor's kitchen, where I perched on a stool and watched him set about making a rum toddy with all the ceremony of a priest preparing to offer communion. The teakettle was filled with fresh water. Once that reached a boil, Mr. Leary used a pair of silver tongs to place one sugar cube in the bottom of a mug. After dissolving the sugar in boiling water, he added two precisely measured ounces of rum, topped the mug with more water and garnished it with a slice of lemon.

"Le pièce de résistance," he announced, retrieving a whole

nutmeg and a microplane grater from the counter. With judicious care, he passed the nutmeg over the grater three times, studied the results, then took a final swipe. "One simply must use fresh whole nutmeg." He handed me the mug with a grave nod. "I consider that one of life's great truths, Daisy. Heed it well."

I hid my smile behind the mug. "I will."

In the living room, we followed our familiar ritual and took our seats on the overstuffed furniture draped with old-fashioned crocheted antimacassars. For the record, I had no idea what Mr. Leary's sexual orientation was. Although he always seemed pleased to see me, he also seemed perfectly content without companionship. I thought for a while, when he was spending time with poor old Emma Sudbury, that that might turn into something, but it appeared their friendship was purely platonic.

"So!" Mr. Leary set his mug on a coaster and rubbed his hands together in anticipation. "What do you have for me?"